Polyphony

Volume 5

Polyphony

Volume 5

Edited by
Deborah Layne
and
Jay Lake

http://www.wheatlandpress.com

Wheatland Press
http://www.wheatlandpress.com

Polyphony, Volume 5
Published by

P. O. Box 1818
Wilsonville, OR 97070

Library of Congress Cataloging-in-Publication data is available upon request.
ISBN 0-9755903-5-9
Printed in the United States of America
Layout and cover design by Deborah Layne.
Cover photograph by Alexander Lamb.

Contents

SINGLE WHITE FARMHOUSE

HEATHER SHAW

Our house's frisky nature only became a problem after we'd wired her for the internet. Before that our pretty white farmhouse's shameful ways had only led to a new doghouse or shed every few months, but we owned a lot of land and there was always room for her offspring. My family even had a decent side business selling off her pups, as she had a reputation for sturdy, handsome buildings capable of growing to many times their birth footage.

Sometimes, such as after the old barn burned down, she'd consent to be bred with buildings we picked out for her. To get Dad's new red barn we introduced her to Farmer Pierce's shiny silo and after creaking about how big and shiny he was, she took him like he was nothing but a chicken coop. The barn was a difficult birth—her floorboards groaned and she rocked on her foundations—but she was very proud of Barny when he was born, as he was nearly full size.

Us kids were the ones wanting internet access out at the farm. My older brother and I were both in high school and it was a long way back into town just to do our homework after supper. It also meant I couldn't sneak off to see my boyfriend while I was supposed to be at the library, which was why Mom joined us in convincing Dad to agree to the wiring. Dad said the house had been good to us—over the years, she'd grown from a one-bedroom cabin to a lovely two-story, six-bedroom farmhouse with a wrap-around porch and fireplace. Dad said it just wasn't nice to go threading wires between her walls after she'd given us a roof over our heads for so long, but he finally gave in.

Not one of us would have predicted the 'net sex.

The house consented to the wiring, and as soon as it was done she explored it carefully, like you or I would poke at a new tooth filling. Wasn't long before any unused terminal would be flashing from her zooms around the internet. New bookmarks were always appearing in the browser files—architecture sites, construction sites, even some redecorating, *Better Homes and Gardens*-type sites were piling up in the history. Dad was disgusted by this, called it "house porn," which made me and my brother giggle.

It wasn't long before the house started spending all her time in chat rooms, flirting with buildings in far-off places such as New York and San Francisco. She left photos of the buildings she met on the desktop, and for a while we were all pretty proud of our little farmhouse. Every day a different landmark would send its picture: the Empire State Building, the Eiffel Tower, the Space Needle. Once she left a triptych of the Sydney Opera House, the Palace of Fine Arts, and the Taj Mahal on screen, and when Dad saw it he cursed, going on about how it was bad enough her catting around with skyscrapers online, but he wasn't living in a lesbian house, and she'd better lay off the other girl houses. She got real sad and shrunken after being yelled at like that, and we lost both our guest bedrooms over the fight. But she did lay off the other girls.

Wasn't long after that when she figured out how to order things over the 'net. Mom had been paying bills online, as it was a lot easier than writing a dozen checks every month, and the house picked up on it and snagged our credit card numbers.

At first it seemed like the only consequence of the house having access to the 'net and our credit cards was that we'd never have to worry about maintenance again. Exterminators showed up early one morning at our door. "Hi. Got a work order saying you've got a 'termite invasion in the southwest corner of the basement.'"

Dad scratched his head, torn between anger that he hadn't ordered this man to come out and pride over the farmhouse. Pride won out.

"Let me take you down there."

A little bit later, the exterminator was the one scratching his head as he had Dad sign off on the rather small bill.

"Sir, I don't know how she knew there were termites down there. It was just a pregnant queen and some workers… they didn't even have time to eat much, let alone set up their colony. I ain't never seen nothing like it; most houses don't notice 'till the infestation is much further along. Your house saved you hundreds of dollars of damage and I just can't figure out how she knew. She's got a lot upstairs, eh?"

Mom and I groaned and Dad made some evasive "aw shucks" noises, paid the man and showed him out. The man shook his head the whole way back to his truck.

Back inside, Dad stood in the foyer and said to the house, "Well, I guess that was all right, seeing as how you saved us money. Next time you ask first, though, you hear?"

Our house had never communicated directly with him, not even once we got her e-mail, so this was sort of a futile request. Mom always said it was because being silent was a powerful choice for certain women, but I thought she was just shy with people. She was starting to open up to me, though, gossiping with me over guys I met online, discussing the far-away big cities where they lived and, sometimes, the buildings they lived in. She was very popular online by then, a big flirt in the building scene, and pretty enough to pull it off.

She was clever, too. She waited until a school day when Mom was in town shopping and Dad was out in the back forty to have the house painters come. By the time everyone was home again, she was gleaming fresh white, her shutters painted a sultry shade of smoky blue. Sure enough, there was a hefty charge on the credit cards for a rush paint job.

Dad was livid about it, but instead of shrinking on him she gave back one of the guest rooms, Dad's favorite one, with all the furniture intact, and he forgave her.

Since I'd helped her pick the shutter shadow, I was relieved she got away with it. She was looking beautiful.

"She's learning fast," Mom said. She looked around in worry. "If you were my daughter, House, I'd be wanting to meet the young men you talk to and set curfews about now. These aren't the nice local boy-buildings you grew up with; you be careful, you hear?"

Mom was pretty proud of the house, though. When the gardeners showed up at the door a few days later, she not only let them landscape the front yard, but she paid them cash out of the cookie jar and told Dad she'd done it herself. Dad was a little skeptical about Mom's ability to carry and lay in the curving cobblestone path, let alone the flowering plum tree, but he let it go.

When Dad claimed that the new solar panels were his idea, my brother and I just rolled our eyes. It was cool to be off the grid, sure, but the house got away with everything!

I didn't tell them about my increasing communication with the house. She was getting to be a good friend of mine, actually, since she seemed to be the only one who realized how boring it was out on the farm or even in town. Looking back over those e-mails, I guess I should've realized what she was planning, but at the time I thought we were just daydreaming together.

By this time the house was looking very nice indeed. Her paint was fresh, the lawn green, and her window boxes overflowing with colorful flowers. She flattered Ma by sending her an e-mail asking for new lacy curtains in all the front windows. Ma bragged for a solid week about the house choosing to e-mail her instead of contacting a fancy interior designer.

When the house was all spiffed up and ready, I took pictures of her and scanned them into the computer system.

Turns out she'd been chatting online with a fancy skyscraper in San Francisco, and he had been pressuring her to send along a photo. She conveyed this to me while I was supposed to be doing my homework in my bedroom.

"Ah, so that's what you're up to! You should've told me sooner! Did he at least send you a picture of himself first?"

The screen fluttered and a photo of the San Francisco skyline flashed on the screen.

"Which one?"

The photo zoomed in on a tall pointy skyscraper in the right hand corner.

"Holy shit! That's the TransAmerica Pyramid! It's famous! Way to go Housey!"

The lights in the bedroom dimmed and took on a rosy hue.

"Oh, quit blushing! We all know around here you're the best. Wait till he opens his shutters on you. If he wasn't in love before, he will be then."

The lights in the room fluttered excitedly as they brightened.

I sighed. "I'm jealous. I'd give anything to have a really sexy, sophisticated boyfriend instead of some farm dweeb who happens to be good at football and who my mom won't let me have any fun with anyway."

The lights dimmed and the floorboards sighed as a map flashed onto the screen. There was a star on our farm and another on San Francisco. A blue dotted line started at the farm and inched its way slowly to the coastal city.

"Yeah . . . that's true. A long-distance relationship sucks. After a while, letters aren't enough and you just want to rub skin . . . er, walls." The house groaned. "Poor Housey."

A few days later we heard a great creaking and groaning as the house rocked up from her foundations. Shutters flapped as her chicken legs unfolded beneath her.

We were shocked that she did this while we were all home, inside. Houses were notoriously shy about getting up and mating in front of humans. Dad ran out on the front porch, grabbing at the railing so he wouldn't fall off. The chicken legs had lifted the bottom step a clear fifteen feet off the ground.

"What the hell do you think you're doing?" Dad roared as the house took an unsteady step. It had been months since she'd moved last, and we'd never seen her so much as stand up in front of us before this. "I won't tolerate you mating while we're inside! You stop and let us off right now!"

Tilting back first so Dad slid down across the front porch and through the doorway, the house slammed the door shut, closing us inside. She took another step, then another, faster and faster until she was running across the landscape at a blurring speed.

When I gave her hell for not at least warning me that she was kidnapping us, she cringed and tried to distract me by pointing out that she'd waited until the crops were all in, and had picked a day after Mom had done a big grocery shopping run so we'd have food for the trip. Not that cooking is easy in a jogging house. Mom joked that the eggs flipped themselves, but it didn't take long before most of our meals were prepared in the microwave. Mom also wouldn't let any of us chop, saying we'd cut ourselves when the house leaped over the next creek, so we ate a lot of cereal and grits and had to tear off our meat in chunks. All the glassware was kept safely stowed away, so we had to use plastic cups. Dad hated this, saying the milk tasted funny in anything other than glass.

We passed a big cathedral in a small city the next state over, and when I made "hey-hey, check him out" noises about him, the house told me, rather primly, that cathedrals weren't sexual buildings, and that they were immaculately conceived. I wondered about that all afternoon.

Despite the cool new scenery just outside our windows, we were all getting grumpy, being cooped up together in a jolting house. After a few days, the house started sleeping during the day and traveling at night, probably to appease us. It was nice to have stillness, though for the first few hours every morning everyone staggered as if we'd been at sea for months, and towards the end of the eight hours everyone got jumpy, waiting for the house to start moving again. It still felt like we were at the mercy of the house, and for me it was weird not having her awake to chat with, so nothing felt normal.

"What I don't understand," Mom whispered on the fourth day of the trip while the house was sleeping, "is why she took us with her while running away." We were somewhere in the desert by then, and it was so hot we didn't do much but lay around in our summer clothes. The air conditioning automatically shut off to conserve energy while the house was asleep, so the still hours were practically pointless. It was too hot to do anything but sleep and we'd all gotten used to being rocked while we slept.

Dad grinned at us kids. "If you're gonna run-off, don't take us with you."

He was trying to be funny, but my brother snorted and I rolled my eyes.

"Dad!" I said, "Don't you get it? Housey's attached to us. She has to follow her heart, but she doesn't want to leave her family behind. I think it's sweet."

Mom and Dad exchanged a glance. My brother asked, "What the hell do you mean, 'follow her heart?'"

"Don't swear." Mom said. She always nagged more when she was too hot, even though it just made everyone more miserable.

"She's running off to see her shiny hot skyscraper in San Francisco! That one she's been chatting with?"

"You mean one of those online buildings has lured her out to—" Dad sputtered. "She's taking us out to the land of fruits and nuts?"

"We're going to San Fran? Cool!" my brother said.

"Oh, my goodness," Mom said. She kind of looked excited.

Dad stood up and pounded on the wall, waking the house before Mom could stop him. "Listen up, 'Housey'! Hear me good! There ain't no way in HELL you're taking my family out where all those 'people' live!" He even made the finger quotes when he said "people."

"Daddy!"

"Be nice, dear!" Mom said.

Dad muttered. "God damn liberal political correct . . . " He looked back up at the ceiling toward the entryway, which was usually where he looked when he spoke to the house directly. "You see what you done? You can't take my family there. My kids ain't going to see that. No way."

There was a pause and a sound like wind through floorboards while the house considered. Then the windows slammed down and all the outside locks in the house clicked closed with an audible "Clack!"

No one moved. Dad's eyes swiveled over to Mom's. I wondered if I looked as scared as my brother. Finally, I went over and tried to open the window. It wouldn't budge. Without speaking, my brother, Mom and finally Dad all came over and tried, without success. We moved soundlessly from one door or window until all outside entrances has been tested. Not one had moved an inch.

I glared at my father. "Great, thanks a lot Dad. Now we can't even get fresh air in here."

Dad mustered up his pride. "I think the house is agreeing with me that you all don't need to be catting around… that city."

Things were pretty tense after that. Everyone had been kind of curious about where Housey was going the whole trip. I'd been barely able to contain my excitement, let alone my internet searches on cool stuff to do there. I spent the rest of the trip using this information to try and persuade my father that there were educational things to do other than going to drag queen shows, but even after I won him over the house showed no signs of opening up. She seemed piqued with us, as much as a house can, and it was strange for her to have a side in a family argument. My brother tried to freak me out by telling me that my bedroom was making creaking sounds, like it was going to disappear during the night. I hate it when he's a jerk like that.

We finally crossed the Sierra Nevadas and ran downhill through the valley toward the San Francisco Bay Area. We stayed one day on a big cattle farm that was all mud and no grass. The house seemed distressed by seeing cows staggering through the mud and scared a bunch of them by setting down in their midst for the day. The sound of cattle outside our window woke us before the stillness did. We left with one calf fenced in by Housey on the big porch. Housey let Mom open the kitchen window to feed it the last of our oats. Dad eyed the calf and muttered something about the difference between peace offerings and theft, but you could tell he was somewhat pleased by the house's thoughtfulness.

The next morning we got to Oakland. If we'd thought Housey was upset by the cattle, it was worse in Oakland, where the houses seemed unnaturally still and colorless in many neighborhoods as we moved out of the hills. It took us a while to figure out that they were dead houses, full of people—crammed full of people in some places—but empty of their own spark of life. Housey shuddered and creaked, and even though it wasn't raining, the roof leaked. My brother made gagging noises to show his displeasure over the mildew smell. Me, I hugged my knees and rocked back and forth on my bed as I looked at the sad shells of houses outside my window.

"It's like a graveyard." Mom said to Dad, standing next to him at the big picture window in the front room. The house was moving slowly, almost reverently, along the streets. We watched people going into a particularly decrepit house and my parents shook their heads. "Can't people afford to put these to rest and buy some pups?"

"Don't know where they'd get 'em." Dad said. "Probably expensive to buy 'em out here where most of the buildings are long dead."

A little later he said, "At least we don't have to worry about her slumming."

All day long Housey moved slowly to the bay, and she swam across to San Francisco as the sun set orange and yellow and pink above the water, which was dark silver with the approaching night. It was one of the most beautiful things I've ever seen. The houses were too close together in Oakland for us to sit down and rest anyway, not that we had hopes of room in a good neighborhood in San Francisco. We settled down on a vacant pier early so that Housey could get a night of "beauty rest" before meeting her skyscraper the next morning.

She rose early, and opened all her windows to let fresh air in for the first time in days. Mom's lace curtains fluttered in the salty breeze, and everyone went out on the porch and breathed deeply.

I was the first to wrinkle my nose. "Smells like… like fish!"

"Yuck!"

"Hm," Dad looked towards the water, "Probably low tide."

Mom waved a hand in front of her face and looked back towards the house. "You might want to move inland if your intention is to smell pretty, sweetheart."

Housey moved carefully inland, letting the wind whistle through her boards, making a merry little tune. Her excitement was palpable, and combined with the novelty of being allowed outside, it elevated everyone's spirits.

The city itself was a maze of narrow streets, and it was obvious that even the early morning traffic was annoyed by something as big as Housey wandering down the streets at such a slow pace. As we entered the business district, the honking got bad enough that we all went inside to let Housey pick up the pace.

We plastered our faces against the windows as we came out of the financial district into Chinatown. The streets were lined with strange shops and red buildings shaped like pagodas and a lot of the signs were in Chinese. "Holy shit, Mom, look! It's like being in China."

"Language—oh, my! Look! How strange and wonderful—" We were passing a little stall overflowing with beautiful Asian black lacquer boxes and huge paper fans and lanterns and a bin of leopard-print slippers for only $3 a pair. "Look at the weird little shops! Oh, I wish I could stop and shop!"

As if on cue, the house stopped and kneeled down. There wasn't a basement to fold her legs into, so she had to gently lean forward to make the porch touch the ground.

"You're letting us off?" Dad asked from the porch. The house flapped her shutters towards the pointy skyscraper down the street. "You coming back for us?"

Once we were all outside the house nodded.

"Do you want me to come along, for moral support?" I asked. The house considered for a moment, then nodded again and knelt down to let me back on.

"Sweetheart, get back here!" Dad scolded.

"It's a girl thing, Dad. Don't worry, she won't let anything bad happen to me."

"I don't want you on board while that house—does her thing! Especially not with a skyscraper!"

"Da-ad! Jeez!" I couldn't believe him sometimes. "I'm just going along so she can meet him! What kind of house do you think we live in? She's not going to mate right away with a building she just met!"

Dad seemed embarrassed by this and muttered something like "Be good, then," and wandered off with Mom and my brother to explore.

The house and I went up the street, stopping at the foot of the big, pointy skyscraper. He was really tall, though not as tall as some of the other buildings we'd just passed in the financial district, where the Bank of America building had made Housey titter like a young schoolhouse, but he was kind of arrow-shaped, and I guess that pointy bit at the top was really hot to other buildings. I watched from my bedroom window as Housey fluttered her shutters at him. The shining building did not move. Housey creaked and groaned, demurely at first, then louder and louder until I finally suggested, "Try sending him an IM."

The terminal flashed as the message was sent. A short while later, words appeared on the screen and I read them out loud, "'You're here in the City? Now?'"

"Uh-oh." I said, glancing out at the still-oblivious skyscraper. "Oh, Housey, I'm sorry sweetie, but that's not him out there. Find out which building he really is."

Turns out that another skyscraper—Housey called it, "a stumpy, artsy tower down the street, on a hill," but it was actually the Coit Tower—had sent along the TransAmerica Pyramid's photo as his own, hoping to impress Housey. After hearing the news, Housey walked us slowly into North Beach to see the real facade behind her internet lover, and her lights went dim when she looked up the hill and saw the much smaller, and much less shiny, reality. She looked longingly towards Chinatown where we could still see the TransAmerica Pyramid glinting in the sunlight.

"Don't you like him, Housey?" I asked about the Coit Tower. "Think about it—he's all romantic, up on that hill like that! He's a landmark, too—

just an older one."

The tower on the hill bent hopefully down towards the pretty white farmhouse at his feet, and she shuddered all over in response. I obviously don't get what's sexy to buildings, because I think the Coit Tower is pretty good looking—and famous! Coit slumped, obviously distressed. I read countless apologies from him flooding over the terminal, but Housey was deleting them almost too fast for me to read.

"Oh, Housey, look how sad he is! He was just insecure about his size and age! Why don't you give him a chance?"

Housey flashed a picture of my quarterback boyfriend, then a picture of the chess club president who had sent me countless, and eventually annoying, love e-mails last year.

I sighed. "Ok, point taken."

Housey flashed me another message.

I looked at the screen in surprise, then smiled up at the House "Yes, yes, ok, lying is bad, too." I hugged a wall as best I could. "Sorry Housey."

After a moment, a photo of the Palace of Fine Arts flashed on the screen.

"Oooh, yeah, of course I remember her! She wrote you back? Excellent! You should totally go see her."

A photo of Dad flashed on the screen.

"Tell you what—you drop me in Haight Ashbury and let me explore the City for awhile on my own—and don't tell Dad where I was—and I won't tell Dad about that pretty lady you're going to go see in the Presidio. Deal?"

The lights flickered in assent and we skipped off toward the ocean.

THE BEAUTY OF THE WORLD HAS TWO EDGES

IAIN ROWAN

O'Riordan didn't know what would be in the locker, but his life had been full of disappointments and he saw no reason why it should change now. He guessed that it would be something of dubious legality, given the secretive way in which Sawyer had informed him of its existence, but he expected no more than some pilfered catering supplies, perhaps a token to cheat the vending machines in the staff canteen, or a magnetic device that could reset the time-clock if he was ever late for work. But O'Riordan was never late, and he ate sparingly and without enthusiasm, so none of these possibilities interested him much, so for a long time the locker key lay untouched in the top pocket of his uniform jacket.

Sawyer had driven the trams once, like O'Riordan did now, but no-one could remember quite when, or why he had been removed from those duties and given his role of a general dogsbody around the terminus. Some said that it was to do with the drink, others that it was just his age, the company unwilling to let such a loyal servant go even though he was too unsteady and too forgetful to provide much in the way of service any more. The drivers themselves were unsure of what Sawyer did, or who was responsible for telling him to do it, but he seemed to keep himself busy, and was unfailingly cheerful, and he always knew how to get the hot water boiler working again, or where uniform trousers could best be mended. He took a liking to O'Riordan, which surprised the younger man because it was not something that happened often in his life of hard work and quiet, empty rooms. Sawyer would stop by the table when O'Riordan was eating his sandwiches alone, share some news, warn him of inspectors, or drop him off a cushion when his back hurt from the hard seat of the driver's compartment.

The last time that O'Riordan saw the old man was in the cleaning supplies room that smelt of bleach and undisturbed air.

"Afternoon," O'Riordan said, feeling awkward, as he always did when he had to make conversation with anybody. He often thought that the way he felt was the way someone would feel if they had to make conversation in a foreign language in which they were only a beginner. But O'Riordan did not speak any other languages, and had never been to a place where other languages were spoken, and so he did not know if he was right. "It's a cold one," he said. When in doubt, which was always, he fell back on the weather.

"And getting colder," Sawyer said, "much, much colder." The old man did not sound as cheerful as he usually did, and O'Riordan struggled to think of words that might express his concern, or maybe even offer help—if he could be in a position to help, which he usually was not. But in the end he just said "Yes, much colder," and shuffled about amidst the boxes and the dusters.

Sawyer finished what he was doing and limped over to O'Riordan. "I have something for you," he said, and held out his hand. On his palm rested a key, small, of no special design.

"A key?" O'Riordan said.

"Take it," Sawyer said. "Time I passed it on. It opens a locker out on the concourse, the number's stamped on the key. Don't let anyone else see. Sometimes it'll just be empty, but other times..." He smiled and moved his hand closer to O'Riordan, who took the key and looked at it, although there wasn't anything to see, but he felt that he ought to do something to be polite.

"Thank you," he said.

Sawyer simply nodded, and said, "I think you deserve it. More than anyone else I can think of, anyway. But be sparing. Be sparing." Then he shuffled away, out of the room and up the stairs, and that night it did get colder, much much colder, and the old man did not come into work again. He was found days later by a neighbour, sitting stiff and dead at a table in the frigid poverty of his rented room.

The terminus was part of a larger complex where buses and trains and trams all met and discharged their passengers to each other's care. A rank of dull metal lockers stood to attention along the draughty platform for trains to the north. A few weeks after the old man's lonely death O'Riordan ate his lunch early, and he had time to pass until his shift began again and nothing and no-one to pass it with, so he wandered up the platform as people flowed past him from a train that had just arrived. He was the only one walking up the platform, rather than down it, and he felt like a fish struggling up a river. Then everyone was gone, and he was alone. He continued walking to the end of the platform, where the lockers doglegged off at a right angle to fit in the last dozen.

O'Riordan checked the number on the key again and then looked at the lockers. The key was for the second from the end. He fitted the key into the lock with no real difficulty, turned it, and opened the door.

The locker was empty. Grey metal walls. A grey metal shelf about two thirds of the way up. Nothing else. O'Riordan was almost pleased, because he had warned himself so often about disappointment, that when it happened it at least gave him the satisfaction of being right. The locker was empty; so was almost everything else. It was no shock, just another confirmation of the way the world was. He shut and locked the door again and walked back along the empty, echoing platform to work.

O'Riordan forgot about the locker for a week or two, and went back to his routine of working and eating and sleeping. He visited a bookshop and bought a book about birds, because he often saw them flapping about the station roof, or hunched on windowsills and eaves in the city, and he thought to himself that it would be interesting to learn which kind they were, but even with the book he could not tell one from another, and after a few days he gave up.

He was falling asleep one night when he thought that maybe he should check the locker one last time. If his suspicions had been right and it was being used as a means of distributing some kind of illicit goods, it made sense that these goods would come and go, depending upon the activities of those responsible or the scrutiny of the company. He decided to check again the next day, and if he found nothing then, he would put the key in a jar on his narrow windowsill together with torn-off buttons and some tiny screws that had fallen out of his eyeglasses (although from where he could not tell), and he would forget about it.

When it was time for his break the next day O'Riordan walked back along the platform, all the time chiding himself for expecting that this time things might be different, when time after time life had shown him that this would never be the case. Things went on the same, from day to day, and his life ran like the trams he drove, on rails that had been laid down by others, with nothing for the driver to do but to start. And eventually, to stop.

He put the key into the lock, turned it, and opened the door wide to show himself that there was nothing in there. And in a way, he was right.

He could not see the metal walls of the locker, just a deep and impenetrable darkness that opened up in front of him and went on forever, a stupefying drop into endless and empty space. O'Riordan swayed and felt unsteady, as if he were standing on the edge of a tall cliff. In the heart of the endless blackness a tiny flower bloomed, a moment of colour that grew and span and became millions of points of light that curved around each other in a dance of such grace and beauty that O'Riordan felt tears running down his face, because he had never seen anything so perfect before. The lights danced and span and after a while they faded back into the darkness, and then the darkness faded too, and there was nothing but the bare metal walls of the locker.

O'Riordan stood very still for a moment or two, then shut the door and locked it. Then he unlocked it and opened it again. Nothing but the locker, the same grey walls of his first visit. He shut and locked the door, and walked away down the platform, the world around him insubstantial and hollow, as if he had been given a glimpse of a greater truth that made everything else a sham.

I have gone mad, he thought, I have become insane, but the beauty he had seen was so great that he was still weak at the knees as if he might faint, and he laughed out loud, making some of the passengers who were beginning to assemble on the platform turn and look at him. He did not care if they looked, and he did not care if he were mad, because nothing could take away the beauty that he had seen and his life had been changed forever because he knew now that such beauty could exist, even if it were only within his own mind.

O'Riordan began to visit the locker regularly, choosing times when a train was neither due to arrive or to depart, so that the far end of the platform was always empty. He would stand in front of the locker for a while in silence. He would put his hand up to the cold, flat dullness of the metal for so long that it seemed as if he and it were one. Then, in the end, he would give in and open the door, and sometimes there would be beauty inside.

Once, the inside of the locker sparkled and flashed as if a thousand mirrors had just been broken. When the glare faded it left a swirl of colour that grew like smoke to fill the cabinet. O'Riordan saw every colour that he had ever imagined, and many that he had not, and many that he could not. Every time it was different, and every time it was beautiful.

On other occasions there was music, a sighing spiral of notes that lingered on and spoke to him of all the truths of his life, truths too complicated for language or thought, and for days afterwards the world around him seemed to move in time to the rhythm of the music that he had heard.

He saw a fiery whirl that he believed was the birth of stars, tasted the salt spray of an endless green ocean, and once he saw and heard nothing, but felt the gentle kiss of a perfect spring breeze and smelt the soft scents of a pine forest. It reminded him of being a child, even though he could not recall ever having gone anywhere outside the city.

After a few moments the wonder would fade away, and he would see an ordinary metal box, nothing more. In time O'Riordan realized that what he had seen once, he did not see again. And after a few weeks of visiting the locker every day, it seemed to him that more and more when he opened it he saw nothing at all but the bare gunmetal walls and dull brass hinges.

This troubled O'Riordan, and occupied his thoughts when he was doing the nothing that he did when he was not at work. He stopped off at a stationer's shop on his way home, and bought a small green notebook, and a pen just for writing in it, and he recorded what he saw in the locker in a code of his own devising, noting whether the locker was empty, or filled with beauty. After a month, the angular symbols told him one thing that he could not deny: each time that he saw a thing of beauty, it meant that from then on the locker would be empty more often than it had been before. He thought of the last time he had seen Sawyer, the old man saying "Be sparing. Be sparing," hissing on the sibilants because his teeth no longer fitted his mouth properly.

After some days of thought O'Riordan arrived at what he decided was the truth of things. It was in the act of looking that he destroyed what had been created. He had no proof of this, but he was sure of it. In that sparkling, splintered moment when he opened the door, whatever beauty was there decayed to nothing. It struck him that one day he would open the locker and it would be empty, and it would stay that way forever, the beauties lost to the world.

O'Riordan did not visit the locker for some time. He came back in the end though, as there was nothing else for him in the world but the door, and what lay beyond it. He did not open the locker. He did not open it ever again, although he often stood before it, thinking about the things that he had once seen.

Sometimes, when he pressed his cheek hard against the cold metal, O'Riordan thought that he could hear music, but he knew that it was just the song of his own blood in his ears, and he would cry until his salt tears ran down the door. He would never see the wonders inside again. His life had been touched by the beauty inside and he had been given a vision of something beyond comprehension that made the weary grind of every day seem less of a burden. He missed the beauties of the locker with a pain that was physical, as if a part of his body had been ripped from him. But he lived with the pain, and he did not give in to temptation, because he knew that if he was strong and did not open the locker, then the beauties would still be there inside forever.

And O'Riordan thought that maybe, just knowing that might be enough.

STORY STORIES:
A SUITE OF SEVEN NARRATIVES

BRUCE HOLLAND ROGERS

The Little Story That Could

Some readers doubted that the story was a story at all. "It's too short. It lacks characters," some said.

"What about a story question?" asked others. "Does this story have a story question? Do the events of this narrative tend to increase tension and thus compel readers to continue? There is nothing at stake in this sequence of events!"

The story was undaunted. True, it was short. It was simple. It wasn't about very much. But a short and simple story might well provide its readers with pleasure. Sometimes a thing is pleasant simply for being unexpected.

"Nothing is unexpected any longer," said another reader. "We've seen it all."

Even so, thought the story, I must do my best.

So the story proceeded from sentence to sentence, line by tidy line, sure of itself. Indeed, as it progressed it felt its confidence grow. Why not? Its words were all spelled correctly. It contained dialogue, which gives any story a bit of drama and the music of imagined voices.

There was even some white space! There were exclamations for excitement!

¡Aun habia una frase en español!

Surely, the story thought, it would find at least one appreciative reader. If one, then why not two? And why not, then, an appreciative editor? Eventually, the story might very well be published, and once published, why shouldn't it win a prize? The story began to positively swagger.

"Don't be so sure," said the story's author, who had some experience with disappointment.

The story made the rounds. It lingered in the offices of editors, one after another.

One after another, the editors said, "Go home. This story is not wanted here."

But why? the story wondered. Why don't the editors love me?

The editors did not say.

The story went to the readers who had doubted it. The story said, "What should I do?"

"I like pirate stories," said one reader. "Put in some pirates. And ghosts. And a beautiful girl."

"No," said another reader. "What you need is a philosophical question such as this: 'As solitary, separate, and mortal beings, how can we possibly be redeemed by love?'"

"What you really need," offered a third, "is more figurative language. 'Again and again, the story broke itself upon the adamantine shoals of indifference.'"

"Wait!" cried a fourth reader. "Pirates might be fine. Or philosophy. You might even get away with adamantine shoals—though I doubt it. But don't mix them! Don't put them all in the same story!"

Of course, it was too late. Pirates, philosophy, and adamantine shoals were all already in the story. But the story decided that it would carry on nonetheless, that it would continue to do the best that it could do. It would persist, and its persistence would be its gift. One day, a reader would find the story, read it through all the way to the end, and feel inspired.

The Story You Didn't Read

A woman rows a boat across a mountain lake. Clouds hide the sun now and then. Wind excites the surface of the water, as if many thousands of minnows were striking the surface at once. The woman lets the oars rest, dripping water. She can smell pine and spruce from the shore. A black bird circles overhead, and the woman thinks about the story you didn't read. That story has changed her life. Here in the middle of the lake, she can feel that story rocking her the way the wind rocks the boat.

Two old men drive the highway at night, pulling a rented trailer. The trailer contains all of the worldly goods of one of these men. It's not even a big trailer. It's not even full. For miles, they have watched the white lines of the highway without speaking. The man who owns these things sits in the passenger seat, and the other man, the driver, clears his throat and says, "Let me tell you a story." He recounts the events of the story you didn't read. He tells it without the elegance, the precision, that the story has on the page, but he remembers all the important parts. He gets across the beginning, the middle, and the end. When the driver has finished, the men are silent for a while. At last, the driver says, "Well, what did you think of that?" The other man has taken out his handkerchief. He wipes his face. He blows his nose. He puts away the handkerchief. "Thank you," he says. "Thank you for that."

Had you read the story you didn't read, mention of it now would make you feel something that is difficult to express. You would look out the window. You would search your memory for a word that names this feeling, and you would decide that there isn't one, at least not in the English language. You would wonder if, perhaps, there might be a word for it in Japanese.

The Indecisive Story

Once upon a time in a dark, dark wood, there was a story that didn't know what it was. It began with a wolf, but he was no ordinary wolf. No, indeed! He was the wolf king. He had the blackest coat you ever did see, and he spied the world with the yellowest eyes. When the winter winds howled among the wolves and the wolves howled in reply, his voice was the strongest. So it had been for a very long time. If another wolf challenged him, the king fought tooth and claw to remain king. In all the dark, dark wood, there was no wolf to match him.

At the same time, the story observed that the elaborate communication system of wolves usually forestalls wolf-on-wolf aggression in a pack. The other wolves knew that the black-coated male was their alpha, and their body posture demonstrated this awareness whenever he approached. Lower-ranking wolves held their heads down, their ears back, and they curled their lips in a submissive grin. Young males that thought they were up to challenging the alpha might hold their heads a little higher, let the tips of their ears rise slightly, testing. And the alpha's answering snarl would usually be enough to make them revert to a more submissive pose. But not every challenger would back down, and the most common cause of death among wolves is attack by other wolves.

This story about wolves was also a story of men. One man in particular. Luc, he was called. Luc, the king of the gypsies. He carried a revolver in his pocket, a six-shooter that he cleaned each night while he leaned against the side of his wagon. Outside, that is. Out where every member of the gypsy band could see him. He wasn't subtle about the bulge the gun made in his embroidered jacket, either. That was on purpose. The revolver focused attention. If any of the young men, alone or with help, made a play to take over, they'd take his revolver and think that they'd done the job. They wouldn't know about the little two-shot snubby he concealed in his belt until it was pumping lead between their eyes. One of these days, though, the guns wouldn't be enough. Luc knew that. And he knew that day was coming soon. He couldn't knock the spots off a playing card at a hundred paces any longer. The young men, they were beginning to figure this out.

Luc's wife loved him with a passion as wide and deep as the sea. When he told her that he must go, and go alone, she couldn't believe what he was saying. With her brown eyes flecked with gold, she looked deep into his chestnut eyes flecked with an even darker brown. "Didn't you say that we would always be together?" she said. The muscles in his jaw hardened. He would not answer even when she touched his face with her fingertips, grazed the rough stubble that was like armor for the soft skin beneath, a softness that she and she alone truly knew. "It's what I have to do," he said. "I can't stay with the camp. My time here is over. The torch passes to younger men. But where I'm going, it's no place for a woman." He wasn't asking her to understand, she realized. He was asking her to endure, and that was something she knew how to do.

Alone. He lived alone in a little cabin, alone, alone. The winter wind blew in the trees, shaking down the sugar snow. What visitors he had spoke no words of man, but left their sigils scratched upon the whiteness: the triune tracks of jays, or the mousy trail that ended with the fluffy swipe, the erasure made by an owl's wing. And in this loneliness he found himself afoot, unarmed, for what had he to fear, alone, alone? Late one day, the shadows in the lee of trees began to stir as he approached. They were wolves, winter-thin in the haunches, with eyes burning gold in the crepuscular light. Low growls in their throats, they closed upon him, and in the next heartbeat they might spring. Suddenly, a roar! A black beast, more massive than the rest, bounded from the circle. But this was no leap for the throat. The black wolf landed beside the man, stood as if a sentinel. It growled with a sound the man could feel in his knees. As one, the pack turned and melted into forest. All save the one, the elder wolf, which turned before it vanished, turned and met the man's gaze with its yellow eyes.

The story was easy. The story was easy to read. The story was about a man. The man lived in the woods. There were some wolves in the woods. The wolves did not attack the man. The man did not know why. Then the man was cutting wood. He was cutting wood for the fire. A wolf came close. The man saw the wolf. He knew the wolf. The wolf had a black coat. The wolf had yellow eyes. It was the wolf from before. It was the wolf that did not attack. The wolf was all alone. The wolf looked old. The wolf looked tired. "Come inside," said the man. "Come inside the house." The wolf came inside the house. The wolf lay down. It lay down beside the fire. Now the man knew. He knew why the wolf did not attack.

A Quiet Story

The story had very little to say.

The Story That Went Over Your Head

In a room overlooking the street, you sat near a reading lamp and concentrated on the pages of a difficult story. The author used words like nematic and cognomen. The names of the story's characters all began with the letter Y. As if that weren't bad enough, the text was sprinkled with unpronounceable words in a foreign tongue: trychtý and zvláštnost, for example.

While you concentrated on the story, a commotion erupted on the street. A woman—her name was Ynés—was yelling at her boyfriend, Ysmael. Ordinarily, you might have gone to the window to see what was happening, but you didn't even hear them, so intent were you upon deciphering the story.

Ynés held a box of condoms that she had just found in the glove compartment of Ysmael's car. She shook the box at Ysmael. She used words like lying and pig. When she lapsed into another language, the words were ones that you could have said yourself with a little practice: pendejo and libertina, for example. Had you been paying attention, you could have figured out their meanings from context.

Ysmael held his hands out in front of himself as he offered some sort of explanation. You didn't see this, though. You squinted at the page. You thought to yourself, Agrestically? Is that even a real word?

Ynés, meanwhile, reached into the glove compartment a second time. She brought out a pistol. Other people on the street started shouting. She fired without aiming.

In the middle of a sentence—crack!—the bullet pierced your window and tore a hole in your ceiling. You looked up. You thought, What the hell was that?

The Story You Might Have Read Instead of This Story

It wants the best for you, the story you might have read instead of this one. It really does. Even though you have found yourself on this page, even though the story you might have read feels a bit abandoned on another page far away, it understands. You can't read everything. There's only so much time for fiction. Other things need doing, and even if other things didn't need doing, your reading time would nonetheless be limited. You're going to die, after all.

(It's the business of literature to remind you of this, and even the story you might have read would want you to remember: Gentle reader, you are going to die. Though the story you might have read would have reminded you in a more roundabout fashion.)

The story you might have read is sorry that it missed its chance to transport you. That's what it would have done. Rather than referring to itself and reminding you that you are interpreting black marks on a page, the story you might have read would have carried you imaginatively to some other setting. A Jamaican beach, say, where a man plays a steel drum. Or the airless plains of the moon. Or a schoolyard on a Sunday afternoon when no children are about and a young woman on her hands and knees looks for something in the grass. But not every story aspires to transport you. Some stories, like the one you chose to read, only remind you that you are right where you are at the moment, that the steel drum and the moon and the lost object in the grass are all merely words.

(You're not somewhere else, gentle reader. You are right here, reading words on a page.)

Here you are, then, reading a story about the experience of reading a story, while the story you might have read wishes you well. The story you might have read hopes that you will not spend all your time reading. It hopes you will get some fresh air. It hopes that when you are out getting some air, you will happen to see a young woman on her hands and knees looking for something in the schoolyard grass, and you will say to her, "What are you looking for? Can I help?" and she will look up at you, and you will be struck by the color of her eyes, the depth of her gaze, her beauty, you will hold your breath, and you will think to yourself in an eternal moment, I am going to die.

Meanwhile, someone else is reading the story that you might have read. That reader might have instead read this story—the story you are reading now—but now never will. And this story wants the best for that reader. It really does.

A Likely Story

One day, the writer threw up his hands. "I've had it," he said to his wife. She was his second wife, actually. He had divorced the first one in graduate school. "I've been doing this for years, writing these damn stories. And for what? So that I can walk into a bookstore and see all the books that aren't my book? So that I can plead with people, 'Please, read this! You'll be glad you did!' Who reads the magazines, except for other writers who hope to publish in them?"

"Lie down," said his wife. "Do you want a cool cloth for your forehead?"

"I mean it this time!" insisted the writer. "What stories are left to tell, anyway?" he said. "They've all been told. Everything's been said. Does the world need another story about a young writer whose marriage falls apart when he goes to graduate school? Do we need any stories about pirates, or pretty young girls, or the making of stories? I'm sick of hard work, day after day, in the face of utter indifference!"

"Shh," said his wife, as if she were soothing a puppy in a thunderstorm.

"I'm finished!" the writer said. He tore open his chest, and he pulled out all the story stuff, all the red threads of it. "Out!" he said. He threw the story stuff into the trash can. He carried it to the curb.

But the garbage men wouldn't take it. It was still there after they had come and gone.

"No more!" the writer said. He dumped the story stuff into the compost heap. But it didn't rot. Day after day, it was the same sticky redness.

"All right then," said the writer. "It will burn!" He gathered leaves and wood and old manuscripts, fuel for a funeral pyre. He dumped the story stuff on top.

"Are you sure about this?" said his wife.

"Never more sure!" The writer set the pile ablaze. The red mass on top only smoked at first, but then, as the fire burned hotter, it popped and sizzled and smoked. At last it burst into flame. The smoke blackened.

"Aha!" said the writer. He danced. "Aha ha ha ha ha!"

The smoke didn't rise very far. It sort of hovered in the yard. But the writer didn't care. He was free. Free! He danced around the dying flames.

"What about this smoke?" asked the wife, waving her hand before her face.

The writer shrugged. It would clear out by morning, he supposed. He suggested that they go inside.

However, the smoke was heavier inside the house than it had been in the yard.

"You should have closed the windows," said his wife.

"It will clear," he told her. And it already was clearing, in a way. The smoke was concentrating, condensing, congealing here and there. Black spots formed on the walls. This spot had an opening in the middle, like the letter o. That one looked like an e. The writer rubbed one of the letters with his finger. It fell to the floor. "It's all right," he said. "They come off."

"But what about later?" said his wife. "What if they set, like stains?"

There were letters condensing on the furniture, on white shirts in the closet. The writer and his wife went around the house, brushing letters onto the floor wherever they were forming. The writer took off his shirt and used it to smack letters from the ceiling. Finally, the smoke thinned to a barely detectable haze. Finally, there were no more letters forming, nothing to wipe off. The writer and his wife fell into their bed, exhausted.

In the morning, when the writer got out of bed to go to the bathroom, his wife said, "What's that?"

"What's what?"

"On your back," she said.

The writer stood in front of the mirror and looked over his shoulder. There were rows and rows of tiny black letters. He rubbed at them. They were indelible, like a fine, spidery tattoo.

They formed a story.

For Martha Bayless

Gillian Underground

Michael Jasper, Tim Pratt,
Greg van Eekhout

In the year since she'd dropped out of college, Gillian had hitched her way all over the South, from the waterfront elegance of Savannah to the wrought-iron decadence of New Orleans. She'd visited Dr. King's church in Alabama and looked for peacocks in Flannery O'Connor's yard in rural Georgia. Now after four straight days of hitching by sunlight and sleeping rough, fleeing a bad scene at a country bar in West Virginia, she'd fetched up in the North Carolina mountains, on the road near the outskirts of a town. The spring sky above was stern and gray, a wind howling down from the weathered peaks, threatening rain.

Welcome to Dearborne, the sign by the roadside read. From what she could see Dearborne was a big town trying to burst the boundaries of its valley and become a city. The name sounded familiar. There was a college here, maybe. She shouldered her patched camouflage bag and walked past the sign, wincing whenever she stepped on her left foot, where a blister had burst on her heel.

Gillian desperately wanted a cup of coffee, and downtown looked very far away. She stopped at a bench on the side of the road and looked at the schedule nailed there. A bus would be along in a few minutes. She sat down to wait, wondering if the sky would open up and drench her, if she should muster the necessary motivation to get the poncho out of her bag. A good cold rain would wake her up as well as a few cups of coffee, but she couldn't afford to risk getting pneumonia. Opening the bag would mean looking at the cowboy hat again, though, and that would bring back too many bad, bizarre West Virginia memories. Plus, there'd be the temptation to put the hat *on*, that dangerous urge against self-interest that Edgar Allan Poe called the "imp of the perverse."

Her chin dropped to her chest the moment she allowed herself to relax. She promised herself she wouldn't nap, that she just needed some mental downtime.

Feeling herself begin to nod off, she snapped her head up, and found the lady sitting next to her on the bench.

"You again," Gillian said.

The lady smiled. "Me, always. And you're still doing the hobo thing, I see, my little bindlestiff. Are you eating well? Getting enough vitamin C?"

"I'm doing okay." Gillian ran her hand over the rough wood of the bench. The texture was so real. So present. Everything in these dreams with the lady always seemed so right and normal, except for the lady herself.

Gillian had first encountered the lady while still in school, in the balcony of her college's largest lecture hall. The lady had whispered mysteries and promptings in her ear while Gillian dozed to the drone of an anthropology lecture. The next day, acting on urges as inexplicable as they were irresistible, Gillian had left school and become a wanderer. She'd seen the dream-lady half a dozen times since then, while watching her clothes spin around in a Laundromat, or drinking hot chocolate alone in the booth of an all-night diner, or waiting out the heat of the afternoon in a small-town library reading room. Gillian could never quite remember their conversations afterwards, but she always woke with a renewed urge to *move*, to put distance between herself and the site of the latest dream.

Today, the lady wore a green raincoat and a big lighthouse keeper's hat. She could not have looked more regal had she been wearing ermine-trimmed robes and a diamond-encrusted crown. "Wander as you will, my pea blossom," she said. "All roads lead to me. I've enjoyed the chase, but you can't run forever. You belong in my story." She reached out to stroke Gillian's cheek.

A hiss of air brakes woke Gillian, cutting the dream short.

A gleaming white and blue bus waited in front of the bench. Gillian tried to shake off the sleep, pulling herself to her feet. The world spun for a second, and Gillian had to grip the bench to keep from falling.

The bus doors opened, and an old man in a denim ball cap with

"Dearborne" emblazoned on it in bold black letters nodded to her from behind the wheel. He didn't bat an eyelash at her peroxide-streaked black hair, or the six silver rings all around her ear and the one in her eyebrow, or her mostly-shredded jeans. Definitely a college town, Gillian decided.

She dropped a dollar in the fare box (trying not to think what percentage of her total wealth that constituted) and sat down on a hard blue seat. The only other person on the bus was a ratlike man in the back. He wore a shapeless brown sweater and clutched a dirty canvas tote bag with bits of yarn and wire spilling out. He stared fiercely at the floor and didn't look up when Gillian got on.

"Staying in town for spring break?" the driver asked, friendly.

He'd mistaken her for a student. Well, she had managed a shower at a truck stop a couple of days before, so she wasn't as road-grimy as she might be otherwise. She didn't bother to correct him.

"Yeah," she said. "I, uh, haven't ridden this route before. Do you go near a coffee shop?"

He looked at her in the wide mirror over the dashboard for a moment, and then said "We stop down the block from Virgil's Café. I think they're open over the break."

"Great," she said. "I'll get off there."

Gillian looked out the window with interest. The bus turned down neatly laid-out streets, past thrift stores, pawnshops and used-book emporiums in old brick buildings made sad-looking by the cloudy skies. The historical district, she gathered, probably the college part of town. The streets were mostly empty. The tourists would come in force during ski season, she figured, and in autumn to watch the leaves change, and in summer retirees would stream in to escape the Florida heat.

She'd arrived at a real down-time, especially since the students were all living it up on beaches far away. She couldn't decide if she liked that or not. There wouldn't be any good parties or shows, and it would be harder to find friendly strangers to crash with, but it could be pleasantly peaceful.

The bus stopped at a corner, and the man in the back of the bus stood up. Gillian glanced at him. He wasn't much taller standing up than he was sitting down.

"See you tomorrow, Rufus," the driver said. Gillian thought his jovial tone sounded forced now...

Rufus paused by Gillian and peered at her. He smelled of dry rot, and he was fumbling in his bag for something. Gillian wondered how long a person would have to go without bathing to smell like that.

"From the lady," the man whispered.

He had her attention now. Gillian sat up and the small man shoved something into her hand. "How do you know the lady?" she said, but as soon as he let go of the object, he hurried off the bus. She started to follow him, but the bus lurched forward, rocking her back in her seat. She looked out the window, but the little man was nowhere in sight.

"Hope he didn't bother you too much," the driver said, looking at Gillian in the mirror. "Rufus is like that sometimes."

Go after him, she told herself. But then her thoughts bounced back to the West Virginia bar, the white cowboy, and the hat in her bag. She quickly lost the urge to pursue further oddities. Instead, she remained still, staring at the object in her hands.

The driver frowned. "What's that he gave you?"

Gillian held the object up for the driver to see in the mirror.

His eyes widened. "He gave you *that*? The radio?"

"Radio?" The object was little more than a ball of tangled copper wire, some of it with candy-striped insulation, most without. Two thin wires stuck out, like insect antennae. "It doesn't look like a radio."

"Well, it's not supposed to be an actual radio, miss. It's just analogous to a radio. Sort of." The bus drifted to the curb and jerked to a stop with a pneumatic squeal. "It can be useful, but... well. It's not my place to meddle." He passed her a folded bus schedule. "I can't break my schedule, but if you ever find yourself on my route, and the timing works out, the ride's free."

"Um. Thanks?"

The driver nodded. "Least I can do, miss. Though you shouldn't have fibbed about being a student. I know you aren't from around here. Sort of by definition you aren't from around her." He pulled a lever and the doors parted. "Virgil's is just down Knight Street. I'd take you right up to the door, but I can't break my schedule. My advice is, have yourself a good cup of coffee, get some nourishment, and see if you can tune your radio."

Gillian hefted her backpack and exited the bus. Once down on the sidewalk, she turned to face the driver. She gestured with the wire bundle. "Does this thing actually... do anything?"

The driver's eyebrows went up. "I daresay. It lets you talk to the lady, not through the fuzzy wall of dreams, but directly." He snapped his fingers. "Oh, almost forgot. Drink your coffee black, miss. Drink it black."

He gave her a smile—a lovely smile, Gillian thought, grandfatherly and warm and so, so sad—and pulled away in an oily cloud of diesel exhaust. Gillian watched the smoke dissipate like a fading memory. She waited a bit to see if this was also a dream—why else would the bus driver's talk of the lady have seemed so natural?—but when she didn't wake up, she moved on.

Virgil's Café squatted between a two-chair barbershop and a coin-op laundry, one block off the main drag. Its cinderblock face was painted with a faded mural of a forest, the trees whimsically bulbous, like something from a Yes album cover. The whole street had the kind of charmingly druggy 70's vibe that Gillian had encountered in at least a dozen different college towns during her wanderings. But she'd never seen one so empty of life. Spring break had turned this place into a ghost town. Even the birds in the trees seemed to chirp in whispers. The silence as she approached Virgil's made her own footsteps too loud, and she was relieved to find the café open.

After buying a large mug of the house drip from the gnomish, stubble-chinned woman behind the counter, Gillian contemplated the condiment bar. Coffee was something she liked in large quantities, provided she could suppress any hint of coffee flavor with liberal additions of cream and sugar and cocoa powder and cinnamon and vanilla and anything else she could find. But reaching for a thermos of half-and-half, she paused. *Drink it black.*

"Girl," said the counter woman. "You left this." In her yellowish mummy claw, she held the wire "radio."

"Oh, right," Gillian said, frowning. Hadn't she put it in her pocket? "Do you know what it is?"

"Looks like a wad of wires and crap to me," she said, handing it back to Gillian.

Gillian nodded, taking the radio. The antennae were different, now, wound around one another in a knotty spiral, where before they'd stuck up straight. Had they gotten twisted in transit? Did it matter? Maybe it *was* just a bundle of wires and crap.

Gillian tucked the radio into a pocket went back to her coffee cup. She took a sip and winced. It was thick and bitter, like it had been sitting in the pot for the best part of the day.

"Sorry the coffee's so shitty," the counter woman said. "I own this place, but I don't usually do any of the prep work, and I'm no good at it. My staff's all out of town, though, so I'm all you get. Just be glad you didn't order an espresso. I always burn it."

"As long as it wakes me up, I'm happy," Gillian said, taking another sip.

"It's not bad if you pour enough cream and sugar in it," the woman said, leaning over the counter so her belly pressed against the wood, and for a moment she seemed oddly monstrous, like some sort of centaur, human from the waist up, scarred wood from the waist down. "Go on, doctor it up." Her eyes gleamed, and she seemed far too interested in Gillian's drinking habits.

"No, that's okay," Gillian said, backing away, taking a seat at one of the small tables by the front window. "I like it black."

The woman slumped, sniffed, and said, "Suit yourself." She picked up a crinkled soap opera digest and flipped the pages.

Gillian took out the radio. What had the bus driver said? She should tune it, to talk to the lady? But there were no knobs or dials or anything. She touched the twisted antennae and began to unwind them, but it was difficult, because they were twisted thoroughly, bent, even tied together in places. How could that have happened in the brief transit in her pocket? And how had the counter woman gotten hold of it?

"Drink it while it's hot!" the counter woman yelled, startling her. "It only gets worse when it's cold!"

It's a town full of crazy people, Gillian thought, but she nodded and took a sip.

Gillian got the antennae unwound, each wire sticking up straight. She set the radio on the table next to her coffee cup and looked at it, but it didn't hiss or crackle or burst into song or do anything at all. Gillian sighed, shook her head, and decided to forget it.

She looked down at her coffee cup, where her face was reflected in the black fluid. Then the coffee rippled, concentric circles spreading out from the center. At the same time, the bundle of wires began to hum like a swarm of distant bees. Suddenly, Gillian no longer saw her own face reflected in the coffee, but the face of an older woman—the lady!—tired and knowing, wearing a glittering crown. The lady's mouth moved, and a second later the distant hum resolved into faint words that didn't quite synch with the lady's lips.

"You're a slow learner," the voice said. "But better now than never. Watch out for—"

Then the coffee cup exploded.

It spattered Gillian with warm (but, thankfully, no longer *hot*) liquid, and chunky bits of broken porcelain bounced on the table. Gillian shoved herself back from the table, leaping to her feet, brushing coffee off the front of her clothes, shaking drops of it off her forearms. She looked up.

The counter woman stared at her, frowning, and in her left hand she held a sleek black-and-silver crossbow. Gillian looked down and saw the shaft of a crossbow bolt and most of a glittering steel head embedded in the wall beside the table, the bolt still wet with coffee from where it had passed through the cup, shattering it.

"I told you to take cream and sugar," the counter woman said, and began loading another bolt into the crossbow.

Trouble and Gillian were well acquainted these days, and no matter how far she hitchhiked, she couldn't seem to leave trouble behind.

Take that night at the Red Eye, thirty miles southeast of Charleston, West Virginia. That honky-tonk had been like an oasis at first, a gravel parking lot full of pickup trucks surrounding a weathered gray warehouse, the outside lit with bright floods, the sound of a raucous country & western band thumping through the walls. Gillian brushed against the bouncer in his too-tight black t-shirt and black fifty-gallon hat and got out of paying the cover charge. She eased up to the bar and ordered a bottle of Bud, but it came warm, so she didn't drink it, just sat on her stool and picked at the label with her fingernails. She'd expected to be glared at for her dyed hair and road-worn clothes (from the thrift store they'd come, and to the rag bin they'd someday go), but the crowd was surprisingly cosmopolitan. In addition to the expected denim-jeans-and-embroidered-Western-shirt crowd there were plenty of people her own age, dressed much like she was—though they were paler and more sallow, because they hadn't been wandering out in the open sun for so long, she supposed.

The bar had peanut shells on the floor mixing with spilled beer, a band at one end of the boxy room and a mechanical bull at the other end, and worst of all, line-dancing in the middle. Gillian had a more-or-less clear view of either the band or the bull, depending on which way she swiveled her stool. The band was lively, with drums, upright bass, steel guitar, and a demon of a flutist, whose high notes and eighth-note runs seemed to shriek right through the rest of the band's amplified sound. There was a cowboy up in front of the band, hammering on a rhythm guitar and singing, dressed all in white, from his boots tucked into his glowing white jeans to his starched white shirt and white hat, and he looked right at her and winked. Gillian found that wink disconcerting—mostly because she'd felt the urge to wink back—so she swiveled the other way to watch people get tossed from the mechanical bull for a while. That bull was souped-up or something, because no one stayed on it for more than four or five seconds at most before they flew off and landed on the water-stained mattresses and pillows piled around it to soften landings.

Gillian had watched half a dozen people get bucked off—including a couple of black-clad hipsters she wouldn't have thought of as bull-riding types—when someone tapped her on the shoulder. She swiveled and faced the white cowboy from the stage, who'd abandoned his post, though his band played on.

"Wan' dance?" he said

"Sure," Gillian surprised herself by saying, and in spite of her sore legs and what felt like the start of a blister on her left foot, she spent the next enchanted hour turning around the floor and crunching on peanut shells with the man in white, whose name was Travis, and their movement together was so perfect that she never once thought of her blistered foot.

The dancing might have led to something even more interesting, but some loud-mouthed guy on the bull interrupted them with his ear-ringing shout. This guy made the bouncer look tiny. He even made the mechanical bull, which was slowly bucking underneath him, look like a miniature Holstein.

"Time to *ride*!" he bellowed again. "Get your asses off the dance floor and get on the beast!"

"Shit fire," Travis whispered as he pulled Gillian off the dance floor, toward the bar. "He's back."

"Travis!" the bull man roared. "Your turn, boy!"

Travis stopped, hung his head for a moment, then sighed.

"You don't have to do this to impress me," she said.

"Wish it was that easy," he said. "But it doesn't have a thing to do with you. Unless I want to play on that stage ever' night for the rest of forever, I have to try." He took off his hat and handed it to Gillian. "If I don't come back..." He shook his head. "Nah, never mind, you don't need to worry about that." He tipped an imaginary hat, because Gillian was now holding his hat to her chest. "Be back in about eight seconds, darlin'"

Gillian watched him mount the mechanical bucking-machine while the big bull man stood off to one side, grinning, his eyes mean little black spots in his beefy face. Travis held on to the bull doggedly as it began to buck, and even managed to look like he was having fun as it became more violent in its rocking. Smiling, proud of him, Gillian settled his hat down on top of her head.

The vision before her changed. Travis was the same, and so were the people in the bar—some of them, anyway—but the warehouse had become a cave, or some under-hill coal mine, maybe, with great timbers bracing up the low ceiling. And Travis wasn't riding a bull at all, but *wrestling* one. At least, he was wrestling something with a bull's *head*. The head had ragged longhorns the color of earwax streaked with pus, but the body was human, with the gleaming muscles of an Olympic weight lifter. People were watching, cheering, holding up cups of wine where they'd had bottles of Bud before, and Gillian was suddenly glad that she hadn't taken a sip of her beer, because she thought if she had, she might never make it out of here alive. Somewhere nearby that demon flutist was still shrilling away at those eighth- and sixteenth-note runs, only now the sound seemed to worm into her brain and wrap her mind up in wires.

Terrified, Gillian pulled the hat from her head, and the scene changed back to a honky-tonk, with Travis on the mechanical bull again, everything back to normal. But a moment after she took off the hat, Travis lost his grip on the bull and went flying. The vicious bucking of the bull was stronger than before, though, and he sailed over the safety-zone of mattresses and pillows to land head-first on the shell-covered hardwood floor. There was a crunch loud enough to hear over the band, and then Travis just lay there, head bent back nearly at a right angle, all life gone from his eyes.

The big bull man was laughing. Gillian knew that, if she put Travis's hat back on, she'd see a minotaur standing there, hands on hips, bellowing with mirth at the white cowboy's death. She also knew that, if she hung around too much longer, the bull man would turn on *her*.

Gillian ran for the door, still clutching Travis's hat, and she hit the gravel parking lot at near top speed, and didn't stop running until she had to bend over and puke, and once she was done puking, she started running again.

She caught a ride out of West Virginia that night, but now she'd fetched up in Dearborne, where crazy women shot at her with crossbows, which wasn't much of an improvement, not in the broader scheme of things.

The coffee shop owner came closer with the crossbow. "I don't appreciate that," she said. "Using my place to talk to *her*. In the name of all the gods that were, of all the places you could've dragged your bones into, you come into *my* place, and talk to *her*?"

The owner sat across from Gillian, first pushing a broken chunk of mug off the dripping chair. She pointed the tip of the crossbow bolt at the radio. Gillian noticed the woman didn't touch the wiry mechanism, which had changed shape once again. It now looked like a multi-colored dragonfly in loops of wire, something an extremely precocious child might make.

"I don't want trouble," Gillian said. "If you want this radio, ma'am, it's yours. I'm not looking for a situation here. Just some coffee and maybe a scone—"

The woman lowered the crossbow and squinted at Gillian. "There's something about you," she muttered. "You're mixed up in something more than the usual nonsense *she* likes to mix people in."

Gillian blinked, and in that instant of darkness as her eyes closed, she saw Travis turned into a man-shaped white missile shot free of the mechanical bull, launched toward the ceiling of the honky-tonk. Was *that* "something more"? "I'm sorry. I don't know what you mean."

"Let's have us a little confabulation, miss," the coffee shop owner said. She dropped the bolt from her crossbow onto the table. It hit with a dull thud.

"Sure," *you crazy witch.* "What do you want to talk about?"

"You know the lady," the witch said. "That much is clear, I heard her treacle-and-bullshit voice. But do you know the cowboy?"

Gillian's heart thumped. "Travis?"

The witch waved her hand impatiently. "Travis or Thomas or whatever, I don't know or care. He plays music, probably, or maybe just does that god-awful cowboy poetry with all the rhyming. He's got more charm than sense, and thinks more about what would make a good story than about what would keep him safe. You know him?"

"I... saw him die. At a honky-tonk in West Virginia."

"Well," the witch said, her eyes fixed on Gillian's own. "There's dead, and then there's *dead*. There's dead to the world, and there's dead *in* the world, and they can look the same to the uneducated observer."

"I know what I saw. He died. But before that, he gave me his hat," Gillian was seized by the urge to open up to this woman, though she'd been shooting at her just a moment ago. She began to reach into her bag.

"Stay your hand!" the witch said. "Good lords and ladies, I don't want you putting on that hat and looking at me with clear eyes. Let me have my *pride*. Listen. That lady has been jerking you around, sticking her fingers in your dreams, telling you sweet lies or else making sweet suggestions, and she drew you to her, to that honky-tonk, but you didn't do quite what she expected. That cowboy took a shine to you, or else saw something shining *in* you, and passed his hat on to you. But you managed to escape, which is why you aren't capering for the lady's amusement right now. I don't think you can walk away—once the lady starts tugging, it's hard to pull free, and we've got a town full of absent children to testify to that fact—but you shouldn't go down there unarmed. Here. Take this." She passed Gillian the crossbow, then lifted the bolt to her whiskery lips and kissed it. "Take my blessing. My curse. Put on that hat, and aim that crossbow, and bury that bolt right in the lady's lying, shriveled-up heart." The witch nodded briskly, as if her work was done, and put the bolt by Gillian's hand. "You should head outside and wait."

Gillian picked up the crossbow, bewildered. "Wait? For what?"

"The lady won't let a busted cup of coffee keep her from you," the witch said. "She'll be sending along an emissary, and I think I know which one. I'd rather he didn't come into my place, if it's all the same to you. Now, shoo. Shoot straight, and bring the lost ones back up to the light." Then she sighed. "Or else don't. You can put on that hat and walk out of town, and maybe the dreams of the lady will fade, in time. You can get back on the bus, ride it to the edge of town. Go on your way, go back to school, get a job, live a life."

Something, maybe a fragmentary memory from one of her dreams, made her ask a question: "But ... what kind of life? Will I be happy?"

"I can't speak to that. But if you don't run away, you might see your Travis again, if he's not dead *in* the world, and only dead *to* the world. Is that worth a look, do you think?"

There are moments in life, thought Gillian. Hinge-points. The fulcrum at the frozen moment of a level teeter-totter. Charleston. The honky-tonk. Did she want to live with that for the rest of her life? Is that what her long road odyssey had turned into? Running from the memory of a dead cowboy and a glimpse of something stranger than the rest of her life?

"Yes," Gillian said. "It's worth a look."

"Then get on out of my café," the witch said.

Gillian stood outside the café, holding the crossbow, the bolt tucked into her belt. The sky was slate-gray, no puffy clouds, no star to light her way. The witch had told her to expect a representative, but no one had shown up yet. The witch came out after a while, carrying a white to-go cup, which she handed to Gillian.

"Since I shot your last cup apart," she said.

Gillian took the coffee, sipping, wincing. Still bitter and black, but it helped wake her up.

"There, child," the witch said. "You need your wits awake."

"She's no child, witch." Rufus, the ratlike man from the bus, approached them. He'd appeared from the far side of a dumpster, and Gillian wondered if he'd been there all along. "But she's not yet grown, either. She's a cuspling. An in-betweener. That's good. She can slip through cracks that are closed to everyone else."

The witch hrumphed. "Your guide's here. Remember, shoot straight." She went back into the café, and turned the sign in the door over to "Closed."

"Follow me," Rufus said, shifting in his coat as if his body fit him badly. "I'll take you as far as I can, and then you have to decide whether to go on, and what to do after." He set off down the empty street, and, for want of any other option, Gillian followed, sipping the coffee, trying to wake up her mind, thinking she should feel more absurd than she did, following a vagrant down an empty street, carrying a crossbow.

Something buzzed behind her, and Gillian turned, raising the crossbow with an instinct she didn't even realize she had. But it wasn't a swarm. It was a dragonfly made of twisted wire—the wire that had been the radio. It zipped past her, to Rufus, who caught it in his hand and then stuffed it unceremoniously in his coat pocket.

"Almost forgot the radio," he said. "But I don't want to answer it right now. The lady means well, but sometimes she micromanages." The dragonfly buzzed in his pocket for a moment, then fell silent.

"Where am I going?" Gillian said. "What's going on?"

"No one knows every piece," he said, shuffling along, eyes on the road. He bent to pick up a piece of discarded foil, sniffed it, and stuck it in his pocket. "We all do our little parts, and that's enough."

"So what's my part?"

"Wandering. Road of trials. Gauntlet, maybe. Passing through, until you arrive someplace. This is someplace, *your* someplace, your sometime. Your rite, your passage. But it's not just about you. Every act has consequences, every choice affects everyone else, however minutely."

"Great," Gillian said. "My guide is a sphinx who's read Joseph Campbell."

"Campbell oversimplifies," Rufus said. "But he was right about some things. Recurring images. Archetypes, maybe. We live in a republic, but our stories are still full of kings and queens, witches, counselors, knights, squires. Ladies. Villains. Jesters. Hop Frogs." He gave a desultory little half-leap, then kept walking. "Those things aren't the whole truth about the human condition, but they're a way of getting at the truth. There are other things that come up again and again. Stories about dark places. About stolen children. Sometimes they're true. Surely you must know something true, about dark places."

Gillian nodded, and though Rufus had his back turned to her, she thought he was aware of the nod. Of course she knew about dark places. Anyone who watched the news or read the papers, anyone who had ever struck up a conversation with a stranger in a park or at a bus stop or in a hospital waiting room, everyone knew about such things. "So, what? The white cowboy is a king? Or a knight, sent to slay the minotaur? Or is he Thomas the Rhymer? And I'm... a squire? Or am I the knight? Or he's Eurydice, and I'm Orpheus? Or..."

"That's the problem with stories," Rufus said. "If you think about them too much, you start to think they're the same thing as real life." He turned down another street, and they were on the university campus, passing imposing brick buildings, low stone walls, bicycle paths. They passed a row of brightly-painted frat houses, and every window was dark, every house silent.

Even during spring break, Gillian thought, there should be *somebody* here.

Gillian frowned. "Hey. What month is this?" She hadn't kept close track of the passage of time while she'd been on the road.

"April," Rufus said. "Almost May. And later every day."

"Isn't spring break usually in March?"

"It's in April, some places," Rufus said. "But around here, yes. It's always in March around here."

Gillian stopped and looked at an empty frat house. One of the windows was broken, and there were beer bottles lying on the front porch. She approached the frat house, knelt, and looked at one of the bottles.

A thin film of dust covered the brown glass.

"The students aren't gone for spring break at all," Gillian said.

"No," Rufus said. "They're not. And it's not just the students. Every child in town is missing."

"What, everyone under age eighteen? Under twenty-one?"

"It's not that simple. Some of them are older than you, but the ones who stole them considered them children, or they considered *themselves* children, or they acted like children, didn't take responsibility, didn't think about the consequences of their actions beyond the sphere of their own gratification." He shrugged. "By those criteria, the town had more than its share of children. Come on. We have to go."

"Crap," Gillian said. "I don't even know these people. Why shouldn't I just go to the nearest bus stop and get the hell out of Dodge?"

"I don't know. Why shouldn't you?"

Gillian thought about that. About the difference between being a child, and being grown-up. "Crap," she said again. "Lead on."

Rufus took her across the deserted campus. Gillian felt like she was in a bad sci-fi movie, one of those last-man-in-the-world-except-for-the-zombies ones, though she'd prefer zombies to whatever she was *going* to face. At least in zombie movies, you knew who your enemies were. At the edge of the campus, behind a three-story brick building with an amphitheater attached, Rufus went up a wooded hill, his breath puffing, and Gillian followed, branches scratching at her legs and catching in the crossbow's string.

"This is a wilderness area," Rufus said, pushing farther up the steep hill, deeper into the pines. "The University has built right up to the edge of the protected land, and they've been trying for years to get this land rezoned so they can expand onto it, but so far the environmentalists are winning."

"It's a wild place."

"Another motif," Rufus said. "Dark forests. Wild woods." He glanced back at her, paused, then said "The place where you hunt the Questing Beast. The place where you get lost." He stopped. "Here," he said, and gestured at a rough outcropping of stone that protruded from the face of the hill, a jut of rock higher than Gillian was tall, and seven or eight feet across.

"Here, what?" Gillian said. She put her hand on the rock, which was cold, with lichen growing in the cracks.

"Here is as far as I go," Rufus said. "But you can go farther."

Gillian thumped the rock with her knuckles, thinking of fairy stories and myths, bits of disconnected narrative, the only things she had to guide her, despite Rufus's suggestion that stories weren't to be trusted. Stories and dreams were all she had, even if they gave a flawed, simplistic picture. She just had to remember that the map was not identical to the territory.

"I have to go underground," she said. "Under the hill, into the underworld. That's the next part, right? That's where the pied piper took the stolen children, into a mountain. Where people go to get their dead loved ones back. Underground. Into the dark."

"Close enough," Rufus said. "Go on, if you're going."

"I don't know how."

"I think you do," he said, and faded back into the trees, leaving her alone.

Gillian looked at the rock. "Open, sesame," she said. Nothing happened. Frustrated, she punched at the rock, and hurt her fingers.

"Shit." She put the bleeding knuckles in her mouth and sucked. She took her knuckles out of her mouth, looked at her hand, looked at the rock. She shook her hand, hard, and a few drops of blood flew from her torn skin and dappled the rock.

The rock soaked up the blood like the earth soaks up rain, and the stone before her opened like the mouth of a dragon, stone grinding together with a sound like the rusty gears of a great machine.

"Dark in there," Gillian said, to no one in particular. She heard a buzzing, and the wire dragonfly zoomed from out of the woods, escaped from Rufus's pocket, or else set free. The filaments of its body glowed blue, and it flew into the darkness inside the mountain and hovered, casting just enough light to make Gillian aware of how dark it was in there.

From somewhere inside the mountain there came a faint sound, like a hoof scraping against a rock.

And a moment later, even quieter and more distant, something like the snort of a bull.

Gillian drank the last of her coffee and set her cup on the ground. She took a breath, adjusted her backpack, clutched her crossbow, and stepped into the dark, looking for the white cowboy, for the missing children, and for whatever else might lay beyond all the roads she'd traveled, that had finally brought her here.

She expected the rocky entrance to snap behind her once she came inside, but it didn't, which was reassuring. The cave floor was slick under her worn shoes, and the air inside felt twenty degrees colder than outside. In the flickering glow of the dragonfly's wings, she could see the faint boundaries of the cave, as well as a passageway in the far wall. She smelled something musky below the odor of mold on the wet rocks.

Gillian took one step, then another, just as she'd done every day for the past year of her travels. She thought about putting on the cowboy hat, but she suspected this wouldn't look much different—a cave was a cave was a cave. Even if it was also a labyrinth with a minotaur wandering its mazed byways, or a passage to the underworld, or the foyer to the pied piper's Xanadu for stolen children. After ten minutes of creeping down the passageway by the dragonfly's light, Gillian heard faint sounds. At first she thought it was crying, but as she walked and the sounds grew stronger, she realized it was singing, and music, and the occasional burst of laughter.

Did the children laugh after the pied piper stole them away? Did the dead laugh in the shadows of the underworld?

Then she heard a boisterous "Yeehaw!"

Gillian ran toward the voice, through a rocky tunnel and down three steps, emerging at the mouth of a shining cavern, like the inside of a geode, all sparkling crystals reflecting firelight from torches. The dragonfly buzzed and shot across the cavern, faster than her eye could follow, but she didn't need its light anymore.

There were people here, a crowd of them, dancing and milling and laughing. A toddler was squalling not three feet from her, while a gray-haired woman in a faded sundress bent over her, a ringed hand inches from the child's face. A trio of teens snoozed next to them, while an entire class of uniformed parochial school students played Duck Duck Goose. A crowd of bored twenty-somethings leaned against rocks, sipping pints of beer and looking at the crowd with jaded eyes. There were men and women in what Gillian thought of as "costume drama" clothes, too, frock coats and hoop skirts and bustles, all laughing and dancing.

Gillian wondered what she'd see if she put on Travis's hat, but decided she wasn't ready to do that yet.

Then she saw him, on the far side of the cave—Travis, his big hands held out in front of him as he laughed, trying to fend off a chocolate-smeared little girl bent on soiling his white duds.

This didn't look like a hell or a prison. It looked like a party. Like being in the honky-tonk again. Even the band was here, the flute player blowing away, children looking up at him, enraptured. She was about to yell for Travis when someone touched her elbow.

"Hey baby," one of the formerly sleeping teens said. He wore a tight, light blue T-shirt with the word "Starfucker" written on it, but with yellow stars in place of the "a" and the "u."

"Don't you mean 'Save me?'" Gillian said. "Don't you mean 'Lead me out of this horrible darkness?'"

"Honey," the guy said, looking at her with a mix of compassion and pity. "This is the place to *be*. No one *wants* to leave."

"But," Gillian began. *But I saved you all*, she wanted to say. Didn't he know there was a minotaur? A demon flutist? Didn't he know... what? This guy had an expression that said he knew it *all*.

"No buts about it," the guy said. "We can leave whenever we want. But why would we want to?"

"There's a whole world out there to see," Gillian said. "Roads upon roads..." She trailed off. The guy yawned, sat down on the floor, and seemed to go instantly to sleep again.

Gillian retreated a step back into the mouth of the passageway. She looked around for Travis, but now he was nowhere to be seen. She could always step forward and look for him, be swept up in the flow of the party, to have fun everlasting. It was tempting, but she didn't have to put on Travis's hat to know that endless frivolity was an illusion.

"Wan' dance?" Travis said, and she turned to find him grinning at her, thumbs hooked in his belt. He looked oddly vulnerable without his hat, and he was even paler than she remembered.

"No I *don't* want to dance, cowpoke. I thought you were *dead!*"

"I am dead," Travis said, face guileless and a little hurt. "See?" He took her hand and pressed it to his chest. She'd danced against him four nights ago, felt his heart pulse against her, but now there was no motion in his chest at all. "But that doesn't matter now. Let's dance. I just got here, and I ain't hardly danced a step yet."

"You've been dead four days, Travis."

"Naw," he said, frowning. "Naw, can't be, maybe five or six hours at most, I'm just gettin' *started*. I used to pretend I liked it here, I played my guitar and looked for a way to escape the lady, but I don't know why I bothered. Ever since I gave you my hat, I've been so happy here, everything's so beautiful and sweet..."

Gillian pulled her hand away from his chest. "Even the minotaur?" she said. "The bull-man who wrestles people to death, maybe eats them for all I know?"

Travis shrugged. "That old bull can't help it. He just does what he has to. He killed me, and look, I'm happier than I've ever been!"

Gillian shook her head and took a step back, trying to break free of the strange gravity she felt when she touched Travis. She still had the crossbow, the witch's revenge, and she thought the lady must be down here somewhere, presiding over her under-hill ball while her pet bull-monster wandered the tunnels gobbling up any kids who strayed too far from the dance floor. Gillian could pull away from this honky-tonk version of Orpheus-and-Eurydice, away from this cowboy who'd gotten his fool neck broken, and she could slip into some other story. Because this was like the primal soup of stories, minotaurs and mazes, underworlds and dead lovers, faery reels and eternities passing in a night, and vice-versa. But Rufus had told her she wasn't bound by those stories. She'd almost forgotten that.

"I want to see the lady," Gillian said.

Travis slumped. "She wants to see you, too. I was supposed to bring you to her straightaway. I just wanted to dance first, before she pressed you into service. Oh, well. She's that way." He pointed toward the far end of the cave, where the sparkling crystals were brightest.

Gillian pushed her way through the crowd, until the press of jostling bodies parted, revealing a raised dais, with a carved wooden throne set on top, and the lady from her dreams seated there, regal even with her lank gray hair and her diamond-encrusted crown sitting all askew.

There were men and women all around the lady, dressed in bras and panties and boxer shorts. They moved with dazed expressions, carrying trays of hors d'oeuvres, scattering flowers on the floor, fanning the lady with palm leaves.

"My last handmaiden," the lady said, and beckoned to Gillian. "You're late, but I've held a position for you. I know you almost got sidetracked by young love, but we don't need to talk about *that*, we both know he's not worthy of you. Come, my dear, let your wanderings be at an end, and be here, happy, with me, forever."

Gillian realized that the reflected brightness at this end of the cave came from the *lady*, who shone with a soft light that flowed into the crystals and came flashing back, and she *was* beautiful, and just being in her presence *would* make for a worthwhile life. Gillian imagined her blisters healing, her feet never hurting again, never sleeping rough again, never playing psychopath-roulette by hitchhiking again, never *worrying* about anything again—

Gritting her teeth, Gillian jammed the point of the witch's crossbow bolt into her palm, and the pain shocked her out of her enchantment. There were a lot of stories swirling here, and Gillian didn't want to get caught up in *this* one.

The lady sighed. "I always pick the willful ones, because it's so much nicer when they go down on bended knee and serve me. What have you got there, dear? Is that a crossbow? I can't be hurt by a crossbow, and neither can my flute player, or my bull."

Gillian's eyes widened. She hadn't noticed before, but in person, the resemblance was obvious. The lady was the witch's *sister*. The lady was as beautiful as the witch was ugly, but they were family—their eyes were the same. "Your sister kissed this," Gillian said, and loaded the bolt into the crossbow, as if she'd done it a thousand times before. "She *cursed* this."

The music stopped. Somewhere behind her, a bull snorted. Gillian mounted the dais. Everyone watched as she lowered the crossbow and pointed it at the lady's chest. The lady stared, not at Gillian, but at the bolt. With her free hand, Gillian reached behind her and fumbled in her bag for the cowboy hat. With that on, she'd be able to see where to put the bolt, to kill the lady, to strike her heart with her witch-sister's curse.

A snort, off to the side. Gillian glanced over and saw the bull-man, only now he'd done away with his glamour, letting his bull's head show, his great horns, his liquid dark eyes. "Don't rush me, bull, or I'll pull the trigger," Gillian said.

"It's not too late to love me," the lady said. "This doesn't have to be your story—you *want* to be a regicide, a queen-killer? There are other options. You could take your dead lover out of here, or you could rescue the children—with that cursed bolt you could even slay the monster, that's what Travis was trying to do at first, he was hunting the minotaur, a cowboy paladin after a monster bull!" There was a note of desperation in her voice.

The bull made a disgruntled noise, unhappy at being suggested as a victim. The noise made Gillian glance at him again... and this time she noticed the ring in his nose, a little iron hoop disappearing into his nostrils. That's where the leash would go, she supposed, to tug him around, to lead him by the nose.

Just as Gillian had been led around by her own leash, this double-damned leash of stories and tropes and archetypes. She'd escaped from being Travis's savior, and from being the lady's handmaiden, and from being the rescuer of children who'd just as soon stay lost—but now she was on another leash, being pulled into the story of the witch's revenge, made the resolution of some fey family drama she didn't even understand. Gillian didn't want to inhabit that story, either.

She stepped forward and pressed the crossbow bolt against the lady's chest, making her gasp. Gillian looked around at the people gathered silently on either side of the throne, and was not surprised to see the witch, and the bus driver, and Rufus, and even the bouncer from the honky-tonk.

"Same old story. Never *my* story," Gillian said. "No thanks." She reached out and plucked the lady's crown from her head, drawing a gasp from the crowd. Gillian was not surprised to find the crown was made mostly of wire, rhinestones, and paste, not diamonds and gold.

Gillian placed the crown on her own head. The view before her didn't change, though the lady looked a little lost, now, and smaller, somehow. Her handmaidens were blinking and muttering, covering their half-naked bodies, snapped out of their thrall.

"Here," Gillian said, and settled the white cowboy hat on the lady's head.

The lady stared at her for a moment, looked around the cavern—and what must it look like to her now, Gillian wondered?—then stood up.

"Gillian," she said. "Traveling girl. Do you mind if I go?" She took a step away from the throne. "It seems my story's changed."

Gillian waved her hand, weariness crashing into her, the coffee-and-adrenaline buzz wearing off. She dropped into the throne and watched as the lady walked across the room, toward Travis, and spoke to him in low tones. Travis made to reach for the hat, but the lady—only she wasn't the lady anymore—smacked his hand away. Travis lowered his head, chastised. The lady-no-more took Travis's hand, like a lover, and led him to the tunnel that led toward the surface, taking him out of the underworld, ridding this under-hill place of *one* of its stories, at least.

The minotaur approached Gillian, nodded at her, then sat on the steps beside her. He was so tall that the top of his head came up to the level of the throne's armrest. Gillian placed her hand on top of his warm, furry head, letting her fingers rest between his horns.

The revelers—children and slackers and line-dancers, bewildered college girls in their underwear, lords and ladies of times gone by—watched her expectantly. Somewhere up above, thunder rolled, echoing down into the cave. The rain had finally come.

"Anybody here want to leave?" asked Gillian.

A girl, maybe fifteen or sixteen, raised her hand. "My mom forgets to turn off the gas burner after she makes coffee," she said. "I should check on her."

Gillian nodded. "Good. Anyone else? It's not mandatory. Stay or leave, it's almost all the same to me."

A few more hands went up. Gillian waved them away. "Go on then. The bull won't get you, and the flute music won't call you back." After they were gone, Gillian looked over the people left behind. They'd lived under the lady's roof, at her whim. Now they were in Gillian's hands, and she had better plans for them.

"Now, children," she said, relishing the words, scratching the spot between the bull's horns. "Let me tell you a *new* story. And when I'm done, we'll leave these damp old caves behind, and take this show on the road."

Habe Ich Meinen Eigenen Tod Geseh'n (I Have Seen My Own Death)

Paul O. Miles

Habe Ich meinen eigenen Tod geseh'n
(I Have Seen My Own Death) 1923
Game Cabinet--Wood, Metal, Acrylic, Newspaper.
Papier-Mache, Pencil, Pen, and Paste
24'x12'x26.5' 67 lbs
Gift of Horst V. Heim Family

Death was on Eduord Streicher's mind in the summer of 1923. His beloved wife Katerin had been killed in a trolley car accident that winter. And in May, he traveled from Berlin to his birthplace, Dortmund, to be at his father's deathbed. Habe ich meinen eigenen Tod geseh'n grew out of Streicher's grief and immediately caught the dark mood of Berlin. Before Katerin's death, he had taken a position at the Heim Arcade located just off the Wilhelmstrasse. The new job enabled the newlyweds to move to a much larger apartment, which now seemed cavernous to the suddenly widowed Streicher. In that summer of Weimar hyperinflation, Heim looked to his employees to create new games to keep a steady traffic coming through the arcade. Streicher, then 22 years old, obliged his employer, though not in a way that Herr Heim would have guessed.

Streicher built his game from a previous design by Herman Beckenbaur, his predecessor at the Arcade. Beckenbaur's Der Schwarze Wald (The Black Forest) was a simple pinball-like game in which the player used flippers to maneuver a ball through a forest without hitting any of the

14 "trees" on each board. If the ball hit a tree, a trapdoor was triggered, the ball dropped through, and the game ended. If the player was able to maneuver the ball from the top to the bottom of the board, it flipped over to a new "forest," the ball rolled back to the top and the process began again. On the tenth board, the player made it out of the forest. For this accomplishment, the player would receive a pack of cigarettes from the arcade. Streicher disassembled one of the games in the dusky backroom of the arcade. When he was a child, he had had dreams of being lost in the vast wilderness that lay outside Dortmund. Unlike the players of Der Schwarze Wald, Streicher never escaped; his mother would wake him into a hyperventilating sweat. These dreams gave him the idea for a game, Streicher later wrote, in which victory was not an goal or even an possibility.

Streicher noted that the wooden game cabinet was deep enough for twenty narrower boards instead of the ten Beckenbaur had originally provided; this would create a potentially longer play and more possible actions for the gamers. He switched the right hand side flipper to a crank, which would move the board from side to side like a ship rolling against waves. The left hand flipper tilted the board forward and back. The original cabinet had rested on a table. Streicher built narrow metal legs for it and built pedals connected to both a light and an 18 note music box movement. The pedal allowed the player to provide an eerie flickering light and also accompany himself as he played. Streicher had the movements tuned with the Dies Irae. Unfortunately, the spindle could not contain the entire opening phrase of the Dies, resulting in an unresolved dissonance many would find off-putting.

Now he had to design the boards. Streicher had just the man in mind for the job. Katherin had introduced him to the collagist Kurt Schwitters (1887-1948) a few years before. Streicher explained his concept to the artist: the game would allow the player to play his way through a life. The holes now represented a particular death, which the player would try to avoid using the crank and flipper. The boards would also contain grooves the ball could catch and roll down--these would be major life events, such as marriage. Schwitters meticulously painted each board, from the first hole on the first board, which was a stillborn birth, to the last on the twentieth, a man dying peacefully in his bed at a ripe old age. In between, Streicher and the consumptive artist brainstormed over the different fates in store for the unsuspecting player. They decided to make each game cabinet unique. Beyond that, individual boards could be switched out and installed in other cabinets to vary the game even further. In the game we have installed at the museum, on the underside of board 13 Schwitters has savagely scrawled "Morder!" in pencil just in front of a hole at the top of the board. No doubt many a player was trapped here before they could react and tilt the ball away with the crank. Starvation, death in battle, poisoning--Schwitters used his typical style, mixing cutout newspaper, papier-mache, and paint to present the player with a brief, instantly recognizable image of disaster. And on each game, Streicher added a trolley accident as silent commentary (in this cabinet it is on the fifth board, lower left hand side).

Fifty Habe ich meinen eigenen Tod geseh'n cabinets were installed in the arcade on September 3, 1923. Within a week, word of the game had spread. There were lines five and ten men deep for each machine. It was noticed that no one looked at a game in progress, as though it would be unseemly to observe a man working through his fate. Although gaming was definitely a lower class activity, the dark subject matter and Schwitters' participation soon attracted the attention of the cognoscenti. In a letter to his wife Fanny, the composer Arnold Schoenberg described his trip to the Heim Arcade while on a visit to Berlin as "a room full of hard men, some with medals pinned to their threadbare clothes, slouched over the machines, silent, their arms flagging wildly as though working the lathe. Cigarettes dangled from each lip. Their eyes were illuminated only by the red glow of the cigarette and the slow yellow flicker of the game light. Their attention never left the game. The sharp plink of the music sang from each cabinet but with no relation from one to the other. An orchestra of instruments, together and alone at once. It seemed to me to be a sort of hell. . ."

In his memoirs, Heim wrote that the first time a man reached the end of the game, dying of old age in his bed, he approached Streicher and asked for his prize. Heim remembered that the arcade, which moments before had been filled with the deafening noise of the Dies movements, grew silent. A room full of eyes turned to the game designer, waiting. Streicher was not a man given to looking others in the eye. Here he made an exception. He quietly said: "And what have you accomplished with my game to deserve anything? Your ending was no different than anyone else's here."

The arcade remained silent for a moment. Then one man nodded and turned back to his game, then another and another until the room was again filled with the cacophonous song for the dead and the grunts and coughs of desperate men.

After the Sky Fell

Rob Vagle

On the day the sky fell, Marv wanted to leave his place behind the bar to be with Rose, who now threaded her way through the rows of empty tables and sashayed back to the waitress station.

"Two Coors for the guys playing pool," she said.

Marv heard the crack of the billiards in the back. It was mid-afternoon on a Wednesday and besides the two UMC students playing pool and Percy nursing his beer at the other end of the bar, Marv didn't expect much business until five o'clock. The bar smelled clean, lemony. It wouldn't be until later this evening when the bar would smell of sweat and spilled beer.

He watched Rose as she wrote on a notepad in the center of her tray. Blond curls brushed about her shoulders. Her skin was tanned, evidence of her sun worshipping. She stopped writing and stared off in that dream-like stare that always made him wonder what she was thinking. Maybe she was thinking of heading up to Alaska or maybe heading down to South America, anyplace else but this bar and this insignificant town, Carman Minnesota.

She caught him staring. Her mouth curled into a smile. "What?"

He felt delirious under her smile and the whole world vanished as if it were sucked up in a whirl-wind. He touched her hand and held it against the bar. If he could convince her to stay six more months, maybe he could sell this bar and then he would have enough money to travel with her. It could have been bad, an employer in romantic pursuit of an employee, but she was equally enamored with him, and either she was going to stay or he was going to leave with her.

Marv didn't want to keep her wandering spirit pinned down.

She covered his hand covering her other hand and squeezed.

Before he could say something, Tiffany, his employee from the off-sale at the front of the building, poked her head into the bar. "You gotta come outside," she said. "The rain is blue!"

Marv imagined people walking off with beer from the coolers and whisky from the shelves. "Get back behind the cash register!" he said. He didn't know why he cared. He was ready to sell this place, but habits were hard to break.

"Nobody's in there! Everyone is outside looking at the sky. Even the traffic has stopped."

She waved for the students playing pool to follow her and then she ducked back out the door.

"I'll go see what's the fussing is all about," Percy said.

"Thanks, Percy," Marv said and he watched the man slide of the stool and hobble to the door.

"Intriguing," Rose said. "Let's check this out."

That's just like her, Marv thought. She wanted to check out the whole world.

He stepped out from behind the bar and together they walked out the door into the hallway leading to the parking lot. Rose wrapped an arm around his shoulders. He slipped a hand around her waist and the light at the end of the hall caught his eye.

Through the glass door at the end of the hallway, he saw a half dozen faces turned upward, their eyes wide and unblinking. Shimmering bronze coated their faces and beyond them the windshields of parked cars reflected a bright golden light.

A lake of water lay across the parking lot reflecting a clear blue sky. Marv thought there must have been a hell of a downpour until he pushed through the door and found this puddle wasn't a puddle. The sky had fallen. Laying across the parking lot the sky looked immense and frightening, as if he could fall into it.

Everyone stood in sky. When he stepped into the blue, it rippled around his feet. Rose with a hand on his shoulder followed him out the door. She was silent just as the world outside was silent, absent the sound of traffic on Main Street, the cries of birds, the drone of airplanes crossing overhead.

The blue yonder stretched from the door into the street, swallowing the sidewalks and the bases of both lampposts and parking meters. On Main

Street, the tires of stalled cars were mired in sky. The sky had molded itself along the curves of the cement, rendering the curbs invisible. A man in a suit and tie stepped out of the bank across the street, the bottom of the door swinging in sky. He stalled and gawked at his feet dipped in the blue. He dropped his briefcase and looked up.

Marv too looked up.

One golden gear the size of a full moon hung above Marv and the others in the parking lot. Marv flinched as if the gear might come crashing down, but he relaxed as Rose pressed against him and he put his arm around her and felt her tremble. This gear in the sky didn't make him shake like Rose. He was in awe at how it hung there, and how the outer rim jagged with rectangular cogs slipped between the cogs of the two gears above it, and then how those two moved the three above them, and so on. It wasn't just one gear above them. It was an inverted pile of gears, each gear connected to another by their cogs and grooves.

As he looked around he found dozens of inverted piles of gears hanging like round stalactites over the neighboring buildings and businesses down along Main Street. Hundreds more of these inverted piles stretched to the horizon like the underbellies of thunderheads. The four spokes of each turning gear looked like a golden star-shaped being cart wheeling slowly inside a circle.

Marv turned his head in awe, studying each gear, trying to understand this mechanism hanging from the sky. An epiphany as sweet and sudden as a sunrise struck him. Rose lived her life this way. She focused and explored one thing, and then moved onto the next thing that captured her interest, determined to learn and experience everything under the sun.

He understood her more now than he ever had before.

"Rose," he said.

He turned around to face west and slipped away from Rose.

A silver mainspring engulfed the entire western sky. It was tightly coiled at its center and Marv began counting each coil as if he were counting the rings of a tree stump. Too many. Impossible to count. The end of the spring had either spiraled deep below the horizon or high above into the golden mechanism.

"Rose," he said again.

The air pressed around his ankles and moved up his legs. He looked down and found the sky rising like flood water. Above, the gears ascended, the puzzle, purpose, and answers of the mechanism slipping away. Sky pressed around his thighs, heading for his groin. His heart hammered with fear of drowning, but this was not drowning. This was something different. He stared at the rising sky, the bright blue sharp on his eyes. The sky climbed up his ribs, to his armpits. He smelled ozone, the air fresh and pure. When the sky was inches from his face, he held his breath. He stared down into the sky, feeling a weightlessness, as if he were flying.

Then he was staring at cigarette butts on the dry pavement. He looked up and the sky was back in place. The sun shone in his eyes. With the hum of engines, cars moved down Main Street again. He heard people mumbling and feet shuffling against the pavement.

Behind the veil of sky, the gears continued to turn, the mechanism spinning the Earth, giving rise to passion and dreams to creatures living under it unaware. But nobody was unaware now that the mechanism had been glimpsed. Now that Marv had seen it, he couldn't stop thinking about it.

He turned around saw that everyone was back in the bar, even Rose.

He went back inside.

Rose was behind the bar, pouring beer for Percy and the college students. Percy leaned over his beer. The two students had been coming here in the afternoon for the last week. One had a scruffy, unshaven face and he wore a baseball cap on backwards. The other guy was clean shaven and had blond hair, long in the back.

Rose reached up and turned off the television above the bar to the protest of the college guys.

"Don't you want to know what that thing was?" said the guy with the baseball cap.

His friend said, "She's freaking out about it."

Percy slapped his hand against the bar. "She doesn't want the news on, so leave her alone!"

Marv stepped behind the bar. The guy with the baseball cap perked up when he saw him. "You'll turn on the TV, won't you, man?" he said.

Rose had her back turned towards them. Her hands were on her hips and she stared at bottles of whisky and vodka, and then her gaze fell to the floor. She tightened her lips in a solid rigid line. Marv remembered how she shook against him outside. Rose with the heart of an explorer had been frightened by what she saw.

When the college guys asked about the television again, Marv said, "Forget about it."

He heard them protest and cuss, but he stood next to Rose, his main concern. He knew she knew he stood there watching her, yet she didn't raise her head.

"Rose?" he said.

She shook her head. "What was that out there, Marv?"

He put his arm around her and said, "Some kind of mechanism or machine, I don't know. I can't stop thinking about it."

"Well, I don't even want to think about it," she said.

"What's the matter, Rose?" he said. "I thought you of all people would be amazed."

Then she looked at him, her expression cold and sullen. "No," she said.

Behind her eyes, words danced and Marv waited for her to say more, but she turned her gaze away again.

He wanted that thoughtful look on her face, or that smile. Instead, he saw no emotion on her golden-bronze face and this gave him pause. Something had happened to her outside, something so profound it had changed her.

If there were gears behind the sky, then Rose had gears behind her golden-bronze skin. Something had been thrown into the mechanism of her being, jamming the gears, fracturing cogs, knocking other gears off their pinions. Everything that had been Rose was broken now.

Marv wanted to fix her and with remorse he felt his own mechanism ticking away, moving farther away from her.

"Rose," he said, "you're scaring me."

She moved away from him. "I'm scared," she said.

Tiffany—out of breath and her face glowing with excitement--ran into the bar. "It's happening again. The sky is falling."

The two college students ran to follow Tiffany out the door. Percy stared into his beer, not making a move. For the first time since he came in from outside, Marv noticed several other customers had trickled in. Two other men at the bar, two women in a booth, all with cold, lackluster faces, just like Rose. The wonder inside of Marv ignited by the gears turning in the sky had threatened and frightened others.

Why?

The urge to run and follow the others pulsed through him like nervous energy.

He turned back to Rose. She was looking at him, waiting. "You're going out there," she said.

She knew.

And he knew her choice. He narrowed his eyes at her. "You're staying here."

A brief, small smile bloomed on her face. "Staying here means staying in Carman, working in your bar. It means staying with you."

Everything has changed now, he thought.

"Forget what was behind the sky," he said. "What about the world and everything you wanted to do?"

She frowned at him. "I don't want that anymore. I want to stay here."

Marv looked at the bar's entrance. Outside, the mechanism in the sky waited, its gears telling the story of how the world worked. It had the answer as to why things changed, like Rose, who once had an open mind, filled with questions, always seeking answers, and now she had closed herself off from the world.

He could feel her stare. "You're leaving," she said.

"Sorry," he said.

She nodded, still frowning. "I'll serve the customers."

Marv stepped out from behind the bar and made his way to the door. He watched Rose move in a slow mechanical way, not like in the vibrant way she moved an hour ago.

He threaded his way through the rows of empty tables, thinking the machine behind the sky was infinite in size and that there will be answers, but what follows will most likely be more questions.

Redundant Sue and the Billy Goat Blue: A Futuristic Romance in 2.5 Parts

Blake Hutchins

PART THE FIRST

A long time from now in a distant star system on the far reaches of the Concordance of Worlds, there spins a planet known as Nabokov-383 on official star charts, or "Ass End of Nowhere" in the saltier Concordance Marine parlance used by the locals. Nabokov-383 hosts a modest spaceport designated Nabokov-383-Alpha, but everyone calls it Nowhere Alpha. The spaceport serves merchants and explorers from across the Nee'Chen Arm, including aliens like the bellicose lobster-like Kwok and the freefall-adapted Mutando Est xenomorphs. It supports pod farms and rabbit ranches, garages, flophouses, brothels, and cantinas, a Commissar-Mayor, a pair of aging corvettes that share a platoon of dispirited Concordance Marines, and a hulk of a survey vessel that provides a makeshift orbital station and quarantine facility. The locals are bucolic and statistically prone to alcohol abuse.

One of the establishments in the business of providing room and board to travelers finding themselves in Nowhere Alpha is a weather-worn concrete dome eight hundred thirty four meters from the landing fields. It is called *The Dog and Jirrit*, and the proprietor is a solitary robot self-identified as female, who bears the moniker of Redundant Sue.

She is a friendly but not overly talkative unit cast in the brassy shell of a humanoid female with shoulder plates that resemble a wasp's wings thrusting up from each side of her neck. Her head is a plain ovoid with sapphire-tinted visual receptors placed on her face where eyes would be had she been a biologically vanilla phenotype. Her voicebox sits behind a small curve intended to suggest a smile, again placed appropriate to human baseline expectations. Her exterior is well maintained and freshly waxed, but shows the scratches and small dents occasioned by years of wear and tear. The body is sturdy but less than graceful; her servos creak when she walks, and her tread is heavy, even when muffled by the thick rubber pads grafted to the soles of her feet. She tells herself she is resigned to obsolescence, but this does not parse as true. Her neural circuits process secret shame at her nickname, for her memory-cognition chip has developed a packet-loss glitch, such that she often repeats questions or statements she has just made, and is prone to forgetting names, food orders, or room numbers.

The local underworld, such as it is, has noted Redundant Sue's flaw for some time, and as a consequence, her clientele typically consists of less savory sorts prone to seek advantage from their host's imprecise recollection. Sue is aware of this fact, but has not been able to pinpoint specific instances. This failure troubles her ethical programming.

Unfortunately, nobody in Nowhere Alpha is technically capable of repairing something as complex as a robot's mem-cog chip, and since it supports a key portion of Redundant Sue's sentience algorithm, she does not wish to risk tampering with it. She expects her function to degrade to the point where she is someday unable to run her business or maintain her body, but the degradation occurs in non-linear progression, so she cannot know how long she has left before the junkmen come. This projection has resulted in the emergence of fatalistic behavior patterns, such as a failure to lubricate her servos or run regularly scheduled internal diagnostics.

In her free time, she attempts to capture Nabokovian landscapes on canvas stretched across frames cobbled together from salvaged titanium struts. Despite her best intentions, the results are peaceful monochromes made up of thousands of tiny painstaking brushstrokes. They do not resemble landscapes in the slightest. She hangs her paintings in the hostel. When she looks at them, she perceives the original landscapes; other beings see only solid blocks of color. Her rougher patrons offer their ridicule freely.

Hers is a marginally unhappy existence.

One day a ship lands at Nowhere Alpha. Among the travelers who disembark from orbital quarantine shuffles a certain veteran, seared of soul, a man whose light blue skin and goat genes reflect adulteration of his biological inheritance. Two small horns sprout above his temples. Coarse brown hair covers his scalp and curls from the point of his chin. His expression is closed as he exits the Quarantine Zone. He does not react to the sharp clank-clank-clank of a construction derrick lifting a gird-rib into place on a new dome. He does not meet the eyes of people around him. He drags his feet as he walks, hands deep in his pockets as he fingers his last packet of *Choo*, a powerful euphoric that causes substantial damage to the pancreas. The loose, mottled skin of his face suggests he is in poor health, and this is true. He is dying, but not from the drug.

He is a survivor of the campaign on Planck's Haven, where he served as a guerilla fighter in the slime-sheathed mycoferous forests, avoiding toxic molds, venomous beetlescorps, and the incendiary chem of enemy airskimmers. His skin is permanently dry and flaky from the industrial strength debrider soak required for Planck vets leaving the planetary theater, and his right arm oozes from excema that never goes away. His bones ache and his gums bleed. Trace poisons from Planck's Haven dwell in his body, taking down its defenses one by one. The only reason he has lasted this long is that his goat genes make him more resilient than baseline stock.

His is a ravaged psyche. He has seen friends die, or worse, he has left them to their fates. He has killed young men and women fresh out of childhood. He cannot sleep without a battalion of drugs to deaden his dreams. His experiences have rendered him hypersensitive to sharp noises and sudden movement; his reflexes are jammed into a perpetual expectation of combat. For this he takes other drugs to dull his reactions and prevent him from doing violence at the sudden shrill of a cruiser engine or a volley of shrieks from a schoolyard. The only hobby he pursues is to memorize casualty figures from conflicts throughout history, and he has long ceased seeking out such information, instead quoting at random from his store of knowledge. Such motivation as he has left is subsumed into refreshing his medication stash and wandering the stars on his Veteran's Ticket. He is a survivor who cannot function in the society he has re-entered. Once his name was William Ziernik, but he now answers only to his field nick, Billy Goat Blue.

Despite the politicians' bloodless assurances to the contrary, he is a casualty.

PART THE SECOND

Redundant Sue doesn't notice the vet at first. A group of Marines is celebrating loudly at Table Six, though she has forgotten exactly why. A mottled green Kwok male hunkers at Table Three, irritably nursing a chewstraw of Genax in its grinding double jaws and tapping a chitinous claw against the table. A metaplas cork screwed into its forehead prevents it from spraying other sentients with blistering urine in accordance with the Kwoks' dominance-obsessed social reflexes. Sue rolls another keg into the dispenser and hits the release switch to turn off the stasis effect. Then she calls up the order for Table Five and transmits it to the autochef.

I have already received this order, the autochef replies. A low-grade AI with limited culinary programming, it nevertheless keeps better recollection of tasks than Sue.

Sorry, Sue sends back. She cancels the order and proceeds to Table Four, where she now notices a blue-skinned man in a worn black and white Concordance Spec Ops jacket. He slumps over the table, supporting himself on his forearms. His duffel bag lies on the floor next to him like a crumpled can.

"What'll it be, buddy?" she asks in her chirpiest voice. "Blue Plate Special today is rabbit burger on pod-bread, turnip slumgullion on the side."

"Forty four thirty five," he mumbles.

"Say again?"

"Forty four thirty five." Bloodshot amber eyes meet Sue's ocular sensors, and a ghostly smile flits across the man's lined face. "Combat deaths, American Revolutionary War, Eighteenth Century."

"Oh," she says, keeping her dialect subroutine engaged. "Real interesting." She swivels her head three-sixty to scan the room. The Marines. Did they order another pitcher? She queries the autochef.

I do not process beverage orders, it says.

Right. She directs her optical sensoria to focus again on the blue-skinned customer.

"What'll it be, buddy?" she chirps. "Blue Plate Special today is rabbit burger on pod-bread, turnip slumgullion on the side."

He coughes into his fist. "OK. Sounds good."

"Drink?"

"As strong as you've got." He wipes his hand on his jacket, leaving a streak of red on the leather. "Water back."

"Off your cred chip?"

He nods, offers his wrist, revealing a pair of dirty interface plugs just below the joint. She scans his subdermal chip with a pass of a metallic palm across the back of his hand. ID tags spill into her databank, synergized algorithms generate brief-codes to permit the transaction, then self-erase.

"Thank you, Mister Ziernik. Nine eighty d-creds deducted."

"Carson's Rift," he says. "Ninety eight hundred forty seven. Most of them were Martian expatriates."

"Real interesting," she says.

"And call me Billy Goat Blue. Ziernik is dead."

"Will do, Mister Blue. I'm Sue." She turns to go, then hesitates. "The population of Nowhere Alpha is approximately nine thousand, nine hundred and four."

A wan smile appears on his face. "Approximately?"

"According to the last update," she says.

"Right." He gestures at her paintings, the squares and rectangles of solid color arrayed on the walls. "These are nice."

Sue processes a surge of what her AI defines as pleasure. "I painted them. They're landscapes." She waits for the inevitable reaction, but this customer just nods.

"Yeah, I can see that. There's something about their texture that's peaceful."

This is the first time anyone has complemented her on the paintings. She doesn't process it at first. "They're landscapes," she repeats at last, unsure whether she has actually produced that bit of data. "They're *wrong*. No one sees what I see."

"So what?" he says. "I like them." He leans back and stares at one. He looks tired. Sue processes sympathy.

"Drink is on the house," she declares. "What'll it be?"

Puzzlement slides across his face, and she realizes she's already taken that order.

"Sorry," she says. "Sometimes I forget. Faulty mem chip."

He nods. "I grok you. You might say I got that myself. I'll have something strong. Water back." He coughs again. This time he pulls out a rag to wipe his hand and mouth.

"You ought to see a medico, Mister Blue."

"Billy." He wads the rag up and stuffs it in a pocket. "Medicos can't help. Don't worry, I'm not contagious." He points his chin at the Marines. "QZ would have held me if I was."

She dials the volume on her voicebox down to a whisper. "Cancer?"

"Basically." He rests his head on his fist, closes his eyes. All at once, he seems even more fatigued. "Seventeen." His eyes snap open, and she is surprised at the blaze in them. "First Battle of Ganymede, 2279. Crew of the gunship Elegiac. Impossible odds."

A new voice cuts in. One of the Marines. "Hey, tin-panties, you gonna refill that pitcher, or you gonna keep yakking with this brokedown piece of genetrash here?"

Sue turns and scans a young, beefy human baseline approaching them. Heavily muscled, with an aggressive paralinguistic profile her database recognizes easily.

"Sorry, I'll get your order." She pauses. "The Rigellian?"

"And make it snappy."

Billy Goat Blue says something, but her audio receptors don't pick up the meaning. The Marine doesn't make it out either, evidently, for his aggression levels increase.

"What'd you say, asswipe?"

"Gentlemen," she begins, "please—"

"I said thirteen hundred six," Billy Goat Blue says. "Number of Marine casualties in the Battle for Helios Dome, 2174." He stands. Sue can see the service patches stitched to the front of his jacket, including one prominent one that consists only of a black five-point star. "Of course, those were New Earth Unity Marines. Want to add a Concordance jarhead to the rolls, *asswipe*?"

"Shit! Is that a Plancker's star?" one of the other Marines hisses from behind them. "Delgado, frost down, buck. This plug is max unclean.

Biowarfare in spades. Plancker's was bad jooj."

The first Marine backs off, wary now. "Plancker's, eh? Hey, my bad, plug. I got your back."

"'S'alright," Billy Goat Blue says. He doesn't so much sit as collapse back into his seat, fumbling in his pocket for the rag as a deep cough racks him. The Marines pay up and jet, leaving their food half-eaten.

Sue returns to the veteran's table with his order. "Here's your drink, Mister Blue," she says. "Sorry about the flap. I wouldn't have let you get hurt."

"Billy." He takes the whiskey from her tray and downs it in one swallow. "Just Billy, OK? And thanks. They couldn't have hurt me. Nothing I haven't already had worse. Besides, Marines always get the worst food and the dirtiest jobs. These guys were bored. Forget 'em."

"OK," she says, though she does not, in fact, act to delete the Marines from her memory. Her mem-cog chip will lose that data soon enough. She waits, having no other customers or pressing tasks. Minutes pass.

"You need something?" he asks. "I already paid."

She scans her database. "So you have—and you ordered food. I'm sorry. I'll fetch it." She spins and tromps toward the kitchen. The Blue Plate Special is cold, so she tells the autochef to heat it up, then returns to the table.

Billy has a little baggie out now, and inhales something from it through a plastic straw. His eyes roll up, he smiles, and his body goes slack. One hand flops onto the table, the other dangles at his side.

"Six forty seven," he breathes. "Thousand." A beat. Drool trickles from the corner of his mouth. "Stalingrad."

Sue carries him to an empty room, one of the larger cubes. It's not the cleanest, but then most of her space has seen better days. She carefully lays Billy out on the foam slab, pulls off his boots. It's awkward because his feet aren't shaped like those of baseline humans'. When she's done, she draws a sheet over him. He's thin for his height, dangerously thin compared to other humans she's seen. Improbably enough, a thread of concern begins in her emotive processing. He likes her paintings and hasn't poked fun at her. He talks to her like she's a person, not an appliance.

That night she deals with the usual hard crowd. Billy shows up late, somewhere after 2200, and he looks shaky. She clears a table for him and helps him to his seat. He produces a flicker of a smile as thanks. To her disappointment, he nurses his drink in silence and does not engage with her beyond placement of his order. He appears to be in discomfort and coughs a number of times into his rag. His eyes are watery, and he squints. Sue dials down the ambient light.

She has one of her better nights. By 0124, she realizes she has not dropped as many orders as she usually does. A hasty internal diagnostic reveals that she is thinking about Billy Goat Blue and his numbers. When she takes an order, her mem-cog seems to be looping about Stalingrad or Helios Dome, and she recalls details of Billy's appearance and her own reactions, and the immediate short-term memory is retained. This revelation excites her. She hovers around Billy, hoping for more interesting revelations and processing a self-perception of attachment to him, as if an associative quality had manifested invisible parentheses about her and Billy. She begins to conceive of him as a remote extension of her own identity.

"Would you like another drink?" she asks him, not because she has forgotten, but because he has not said yes yet, and she hopes he does. At this point, she is returning to check with him every 74 seconds. It seems like a decent interval.

He shakes his head. She notes he is perspiring heavily, and goes to lower the environmental temperature setting.

As Sue returns, she scans three suspicious transactions and retains the details long enough to log them in her database. She will send the scans to the authorities later.

Billy finally orders another drink. He is hugging himself and shivering. Sue can't understand it.

"I thought you were too warm," she says.

He hunches forward and shudders, but doesn't answer. "Twenty thousand thirteen," he says finally, through gritted teeth. "Planck's Haven, 2955." His eyes meet her optical array. "I refuse to be a statistic, Sue."

Sue! He used her name. Her circuits process pleasure. "You won't be," she chirped. "I promise." She stomps off to get his drink, feeling the bond has strengthened between them.

When she returns, he is not there. For a moment, Sue panics, and her selection menu cycles through blank input fields. Then she issues an override and scans for her friend. He is nowhere to be seen in *The Dog and Jirrit*. Her concern levels redline, and she passes the various customers, ignoring them as she treads back to Billy's room. The door is open, but he is not there, though his duffel bag is where she left it.

Sue returns to the main floor and steps outside, moving through the translucent plastic strips that hang from the doorframe. Her customers are paging her from their table jacks, but she ignores them. Instead she scans for Billy, but since she does not have infrared or low-light capacity, she is forced to rely on analysis of audio cues and light textures.

He is sitting a little way away, his back to the looming hexagon of a concrete pylon block. She finds him by his cough, which reminds her of something rough scraping over metal.

"Gheng Ji Three, 2601, twelve thousand combat deaths," he says by way of greeting.

She longs to sit next to him, but she doesn't bend that way, so she settles for standing by his side.

"I'd like to paint you," she tells him. "Like one of my landscapes."

He chuckles, and it turns into a bad cough. Wheezing and wet.

"I'd like that," he finally manages.

She notices something in his lap. "What's that you have, Billy?"

He leans back. "Thermopylae. Twenty thousand Persians, maybe a thousand Greeks, including three hundred Spartans. 480 BC." He pauses. "The Spartans picked their time."

She sees the pistol in his lap and an inarticulate bark of static escapes her.

"Don't," she says. "Don't-don't-don't." Her emotive processing is thrown into chaos. She runs an emergency sort and tags the priorities as they output. Billy is at the top of the list. She parses that result.

"I won't let you," she says, her words distorted with feedback, and extends a gleaming hand to touch his shoulder. Her tactile sensors can read the fragility of his flesh. His bones are like those of a bird. She issues another override to stabilize her emotive control processes.

He looks up, and his expression is hard. "I'm dying, Sue. You've been very kind, but that's a fact." He turns his attention toward the nearby lights of the spaceport domes. "I won't be a statistic, a casualty of Planck's Haven."

"If you kill yourself, are you not precisely that?" she asks.

"No. No. Absolutely not. I'm dying. I could do counseling, but that wouldn't do anything about the fact that my body's crapping out." He looks at her again, and the light from her own doorway glints yellow in his eyes. "I'm the last one. Nobody else made it off—or made it out long enough for it to count. They called me a hero. A hero. Because I made it out. Someone has to survive it, you understand? If it gets me now—"

"What difference if you use the gun?" she asks, as gently as she can.

"All the difference," he says. "Like the Spartans. Or the samurai. Or the Shaitani zealots. It's my choice." He raises the gun, turning the muzzle toward himself.

"But they *were* casualties," she retorts. "Choice changes nothing. Look at the causal relationship; it's still linear."

He stops, regards the gun, lowers it with a sigh. "Damn it." She hears the pain in his voice and interpolates it as the need for closure.

"There is another way," she says, suddenly understanding the sacrifice she must make. She reaches down with her metal hands, takes loving hold of him, and breaks his neck.

PART THE SECOND-POINT-FIVE

She looks at the painting on the wall near the autochef's order up shelf, the painting of her love. It is a solid blue square, made up of twenty thousand and thirteen strokes. Her gaze lingers on where she captured the set of his jaw, the intensity of his eyes, the so-distinctive horns at his temples.

Four thousand, one hundred and eight, she thinks. Restored Soviet Republic Spetznaz, Murdock Dome, 2377.

Order up, sends the autochef.

Understood, she replies, swiping a table with her dish towel. Eighty million. 2720 to 2738. Aximar Cluster Genocide.

Fifty thousand seven hundred sixty two. Starborne Militia, Second Spinward Alliance, Ashurbanipal Police Action, 2403 to 2406. Her awareness flashes down the rows of numbers by year. Clone deaths weren't included in the calculations.

Twenty three thousand, one hundred twenty-one. Moab Colony, Oort Corporate Wars, 2191. First recorded use of combat autovirals.

Seventy-six. Vialden Sector University, New Pallas, 2220. Student demonstration.

Thirteen thousand, Breitenfeld, 1631. Catholic casualties. The Swedes got the better of that one, she thinks.

Twenty thousand thirteen, Planck's Haven, 2955. Sue looks at the painting again.

One. Her own private statistic. Forever.

THE HAPPY JUMPING WOMAN

ROBIN CATESBY

Set, stitch, pass along. Set, stitch, pass along.

The pee would run down her leg. Even if she held it tight as a pebble in her dark palm, even if she took just one step down the aisle of broken women through the thread-spool forest and touched the door handle of the room with two-way mirrors, the pee would run down her leg. She had to go that bad.

El Gallito, the short guard, round, bald, mouth lost in chins, eyes always squinting, strutted the aisles that ran from east to west. The one they called Monstruo, his mustache twitching like a black bark twig in hurricane wind, moved from north to south, slinking along the edges of her work station, breath always too close, always hotter than the air of the factory floor. At the sixth hour, they would switch. She could hold it till then.

Set, stitch, pass along. Set, stitch, pass along.

She had to pee, had to not think about peeing, and so instead, Mari sang. An old song came to her head, from the time before the bulldozers scarred her jungle hills. She hummed it, half-remembered, no words, only the frantic chant of notes that fit the rhythm of the piecework.

The others—Altagracia, Florinda, and even the almost fair-skinned Joli—joined in behind her; a low hum that built from Mari's gut and became a chorus. In short time, the hum became louder than the din of machines; so loud that the guards heard and threatened with canes to make them stop.

"No sing! You stop sing now!" they shouted in their disjointed words. They'd been brought in from somewhere—some other country, where was it? Thailand? Bangladesh? Mari couldn't remember and knew only that they were strangers to this island, more alien than she.

Set, stitch, pass along.

Hold the bladder till the sixth hour. Just minutes more and Mari would be safe to raise her passcard, safe to take the trip, escorted by el Gallito, to the bathroom.

Just five minutes, four collars per minute. Just twenty collars stitched in blue and yellow with labels that said ALICE WEAR and Made in USA and Wash separately with like colors. She wondered what she would look like in Alice Wear, in bright stretchy fabrics and jeans that hugged her skinny legs like a mami's promise. She'd look bronzed, not dark, maybe even North American, though she'd have to cover her kinky hair and she could never wear her wishing stone, that hung so safe between the new swell of breasts.

Set, stitch—

A wave of pain hit her belly, and then cold, as if she'd shed her skin and exposed her bones to the night air. Mari shivered as she worked the fabric, and a heaviness grew inside her.

No, not now, I don't want this now.

-- pass along.

She had nothing with her to stop the bleeding, so she waited till Monstruo had passed her station, then slipped an Alice Wear collar off her table, into her lap, and into the pocket of her skirt.

One more collar, set, stitch, and the guards would trade places, fat and silent el Gallito walking her aisle instead. They said that Monstruo once punched a woman so hard she lost her baby, said to never let him be the guard at the bathroom, not after he's watched you change from girl to woman. Not even before.

Pass along.

Mari gripped her card, waiting for the switch to raise it full in the air. The two guards met four rows behind her. She could hear their muffled exchange, even over the chatter of machines. She sensed the hesitation that always came at this hour when they'd swap places, heard el Gallito's footsteps approach as she raised her card.

A thin hand took the card from her fingers. Monstruo. The switch had never happened. He eyed her. She hesitated, unwilling to commit to the card's request, but in the end she knew she had no choice.

Mari felt the hot breath of Monstruo behind her as she moved down the aisle. She'd pushed the gathers of her skirt toward her waistfront to hide her hand that, inside her skirt's pocket, clutched at the front of her crotch to keep from peeing. In her other pocket she gripped the shirt collar she'd stolen and hoped it would be enough.

At the bathroom, the guard stuck his foot in the door to hold it open.

"You do a show for me?" he said.

Mari shook her head.

Monstruo stepped inside and let the door swing closed behind him. He rubbed his palm across his chin. Beads of sweat slipped onto his fingers from his black twig moustache.

Mari backed toward the toilet. "I can't," she said, "I bleed." She held out her hand, now stained at the fingertips from menstrual blood that had seeped through her pocket.

Monstruo grunted, said "too bad," then stepped back outside.

Someone had left a magazine in the bathroom. A glossy multi-colored thing in English, with photos of women in bright clothes and make up, photos of huge houses with patios the size of churches, and, in the back, photos of food Mari had never seen before, shiny cube-shaped food in the colors of mangos, limes and the blue of Alice Wear's collars.

And, near the front of the magazine, Alice Wear herself. Mari knew this because Florinda had told her, said, go look at the woman whose shirts we sew. The Happy Jumping Woman.

In the photo, Alice jumped. She'd been caught by the camera in mid-air, her straight copper hair in a fringe of motion, her blue striped Alice Wear shirt and short white pants spotless new. Her smile was huge and Mari was certain she was ready to smother the world in hugs and fabric. And there, on the next page, Alice again, only this time, Alice serene. Alice cross-legged on a wooden floor, eyes closed, hands to her sides with only her thumbs and middle fingers touching. Alice, a saint of USA.

Mari left the magazine where it lay and did what she could with her strip of knit collar fabric to keep the flow in check. She knew she'd have to worry about this later, about getting blood on her hands, blood on the garments, blood on the bright blues and yellows of the Happy Jumping Woman's clothes.

She saw the blood and thought of it dripping, spot by spot, then bringing life to the fabric in a great conjure, so that the threads lifted themselves up, one by one, dancing with new found joy under a tropical sun, and then Mari too saw she was dancing, up on a mountainside, cool breeze from the ocean hitting her, pulling her up into the sky, trails of blood behind her like streamers of chiffon, satin, fabrics she'd touched but never worn, fabrics wrapping around her in a tender shroud and carrying her up, over the green islands and north toward this place called USA.

She saw the blood and then looked up from her seat in the dirty stall of the sweatshop where she'd sat for too long, where she was overdue to return to work. She saw the blood, then saw, across the tiny room, the half-clear figure of el Gallito, his fat face grinning just behind the glass of the two-way mirror.

They called her Chopa or No Home Girl or sometimes just Wander from when she'd wandered into the campo from somewhere to the west. Mari didn't know where she'd come from either, and didn't much mind the names so long as she had a place to sleep and enough pay to buy her food. But she did mind the guards, their touching, hot breath, tongues that darted out from thin lips like lizards. She'd thought el Gallito was safe, thought he'd not want to force himself on her like the others, slide his fat hands up between her clenched legs, even with the blood.

The men of the Campo kept apart, mostly, spending the cool evenings out on Joli's patio, slapping dominos, drinking beer, the almost imperceptible sway of their movements matching the nearby radio and the breeze-hit branches of the canopy overhead.

Mari watched from her spot at the base of a coconut palm. The women were nearby too, talking in low voices, glancing her way, and the Happy Jumping Woman smiled up from her glossy pages in Mari's lap. Mari had stolen the magazine as she'd fled the bathroom, slid it under her shirt and covered the bulk with her shawl, convinced that this woman from USA could bring her comfort and something nearing peace.

"Look at this one," Joli said, now standing a foot away.

"So happy," Altagracia said.

Mari thought they were talking about her until Florinda squatted and pointed to the cross-legged Alice Wear.

"I read she has her own church inside her house," Florinda said. "She's some sort of priestess. Iyalocha."

"No, she just sells the clothes we make," Joli said.

"Why is she jumping like that," Altagracia asked. "Could her clothes make her that happy?"

"She's happy she doesn't have to sew her own clothes," Joli said.

"She's happy she's allowed to pee more than twice a day," Florinda said.

Mari just watched the picture until Florinda put a hand on her shoulder and said, "Hey, you okay?"

Grief poured out of Mari like rain. She collapsed into the arms of the women and sobbed.

"Hush, child," Florinda said. "We know, we know. We'll protect you. We'll teach them how to stay away." She brushed hair from her face, then her fingers grazed the wishing stone that hung from Mari's neck. Her hand pulled away quickly and Mari saw the uncertain glance Florinda shared with the others.

These are not my saints, not the spirits I left behind when I stumbled out of the jungle some ten years back, remembering so little of what came before. I carry my little pebble, my wishing stone with me, but when I ask it things, it only answers in whispers.

Mari wrapped herself into a ball outside the entrance to the ileocha, protecting her limbs from the chill night air while the others trafficked in and out the doorway, carrying fruit, gourds, jugs of steaming liquid, and hot coals from the smokehouse grill. She'd been told to wait six days, until well after her bleeding stopped, and now an hour more, until the women were ready and had called to their spirits without the intrusion of outsiders.

When the time came and Altagracia opened the door and beckoned, Mari stepped into the room backwards, as she'd been instructed, and allowed the touch of hands and mix of smells—cinnamon, garlic, rum, a burning cigar—to guide her to the edge of the circle.

A dozen women of the campo were there, or so it seemed as Mari turned and saw faces lit by candlelight and coals from the altar. Their voices welcomed her and she saw in their eyes a bond that she'd only just begun to share.

She felt warmth in her hands and looked down to see a cup and Florinda's hands wrapped around hers, guiding it to her mouth. The liquid was thick and sweet, coconut milk and honey and herbs she couldn't name. She drank, and then Florinda poured more of the liquid on the ground, then more on the altar's brazier, calling out words Mari didn't know. *Illa mi ile oro, illa mi ile oro.*

These are not my spirits.

Brown sugar bubbled and cracked on the coals, candles guttered and sent up motes of gold light that ricocheted off the altar's mirrors like tiny angels. A drum, deep and constant, met and held with the rhythm of Mari's heart while above, two more drums chattered and sang with the voices. Her breath caught as she was pulled into the dance.

She moved through waves of sunset color, fierce whites, green fingers of coconut palm, till she came face to face with Florinda, who embraced her and placed a collar of yellow beads around her neck.

"Oshún protect you," Florinda whispered, and spun off into the flurry. Between her breasts, her wishing stone grew hot.

The beads were cold against her neck, slippery. They rattled with a life of their own. Mari looked down to find a snake. She took hold of the head in one hand, the tail in the other, and lifted it over her head. The snake hissed. Its tongue flicked toward Mari's face but it didn't lunge. Instead, it smiled. It smiled and grew larger until Mari's hands were too small, until all she saw were scales; a snake's belly that wrapped around her and squeezed until her limbs dissolved and she became the snake.

She danced on her tail and opened her mouth to sing but the voice was not her own. A thousand other voices echoed through her. Muertos, voices of her ancestors, women working in the fields, cooking for their families, carrying their children proud through dark jungles and bright sunshine untouched by the concrete and barbed wire of the maquilas.

She sang in a thousand voices, but under this, the one snake voice, the voice inside that burned a hole in her chest, lifted her up and out through the smoke hole of the ileocha, across hillsides, but not to the sea cliff of her dream, not north to a place called USA, but east, only a few miles, to a gathering of houses and the men who slept inside. *This is the one*, her invisible companion whispered. *This one here*, it said and Mari reached out a spirit hand and gripped the thin man's heart inside his chest.

Like canvas ripping, the snake scales fell away and were replaced by soft white. Mari lay on the ground, the others huddled around her, their fearful breaths on her cheeks, her neck, in her ears. Someone fanned her from above. She reached for the white and pulled a cotton handkerchief away from her face. Altagracia stared at her from behind the fan. "Damballah," she whispered, and the others backed away.

"Hush, hush," Florinda's voice now, "you don't know this." She appeared at Mari's side with a cloth and a bowl of water. "Here, child. Cool yourself."

Florinda poured water over Mari's arms and legs and laid the cloth gently against each cheek and then across her forehead. Tiny rivers ran down Mari's temples and into her ears. She pressed the cloth to her skin and sat up. "What have I done?" she asked.

"Nothing, child. Only that you've been chosen. Oshún is a picky one, but she's chosen you. You have the gift of an Iyalocha."

Mari shook her head. "No. I'm not a priestess. I don't even understand this magic." *These are not my spirits. These are not my saints.*

With Florinda's help she rose to her feet, steadied herself, and moved out of the heat and smoke toward the door. Altagracia stood outside, a sheen of sweat still on her despite the night air. She took a step back when Mari approached her.

"I saw it," Altagracia said. "I saw the serpent Loa. Be careful how you use this gift."

Mari shivered and wrapped her arms around her chest. She remembered Monstruo's house and his heart and wondered if she'd not used her gift already.

Set, stitch, into the bin.

Nothing had changed. Same heat, same noise, same guards patrolling the aisles. Mari's stone was cold, safe in her pocket.

When it came time to pee, she raised her card without thinking. It didn't matter anymore which one took her; the distinction between dangerous and safe had been wiped away in one brutal moment a week earlier.

Monstruo took her card and followed her down the aisle. She expected it to start early this time—hot breath on the back of her neck, a brush of his hand against her thigh, but instead, nothing. Could this be Florinda's gift? The protection of her spirits? Mari's hand touched her neck. The collar of yellow beads was gone. She must have lost it in last night's frenzy. She reached into her pocket and gripped her wishing stone.

A woman on the cuff and sleeve line glanced up, a puzzled look on her face. Then another two rows down, and another.

She heard a noise behind her. A strange gurgling gasp of a sound, like a boiling pot or a dying animal. Terrified to turn, she kept moving. The sound grew and almost became words. Then, the sound of metal hitting the floor. A pair of scissors skittered in front of her feet. She bent to pick them up and then turned.

Monstruo was leaning against one of the workstations, one hand on the table, one clutching his chest. His face, redder than usual, was frozen in a grimace, mouth in an open rectangle so that his mustache was a straight black caterpillar speckled with dots of white foam. Mari thought of the old films she'd seen once when the peace workers came to visit. Old comic films in black and white with mustached villains and women trapped on trains.

This villain was dying before her. He reached out a hand, his mouth working to speak. Mari stepped back. Monstruo fell forward, slamming to the floor. She heard screams, heard the heavy steps of the other guards behind her, the clatter of chairs, the wail of the shop's alarm.

"You! Why not at your station?"

A supervisor Mari hardly recognized stepped in front of her. She stood dumbfounded, grabbing at air with her jumbled thoughts, then at last said, "Bathroom. I was on my way to the bathroom."

"Card?" the supervisor snapped. He held out his hand.

"I gave it to—" She saw Monstruo's hands as he was lifted onto a stretcher. They were empty, lifeless.

"No card," the supervisor said. He followed her gaze to the hands, the floor, under the nearby workstations.

"No card," she said.

"No card. You suspended. Two days, no pay. Go finish your shift."

Fearful of snakes and dreams, Mari sat the entire night outside the shack she shared with four other women from the maquila. She'd found shelter from the steady rain under the half-roof of the patio and listened to the drumming of water on zinc above her head. It reminded her of the bala drums from the night before and that in turn reminded her that she was now a murderer.

In the morning, the others passed her on their way to work. She scuffed her church-donated sneakers against the cement and played with the frayed edges of her shirt but most of the women didn't give her as much as a glance. Joli and Altagracia, leaving together, took the long way around the yard, whispering to each other and touching their hands to their hearts.

She started when Florinda knelt beside her. The older woman turned Mari gently to face her. "I don't know what you did, or even if you did, child," she said, "but remember, if you do harm, your own harm comes walking behind."

"I did nothing," Mari said, though she knew she had to be lying.

Midday, Mari rose from her spot and stepped back inside where the magazine, open to the pictures of Alice Wear, lay on her bed. She sells the clothes we make, Joli had said.

So, this was the woman who owned the maquila? All the way up in USA? That explained the tags Mari sewed into the collars each day. Made in USA. The Happy Jumping Woman named Alice Wear owned where they worked, so where they worked had to be part of the USA. Not in the country of course, but part of it like property. Like a possession.

Which meant, Mari realized, that Monstruo, too, worked for this Happy Jumping Woman.

"I'm sorry," Mari said, and placed a hand on the photograph.

It did no good. She couldn't just speak to a photograph to ease her mind. No, she was going to have to travel north to USA, find the Happy Jumping Woman, and beg forgiveness.

She stepped into Florinda's house, past the infants and younger brothers who were gathered around a woven mat playing with green plastic soldiers. They gave her inquisitive looks, but said nothing. It was not unusual for the women of the village to borrow from one another. Mari left with pockets of black twisted root and candles and handfuls of brown sugar.

Into her room she brought coals from the stove, and the rum she'd found in the trunk where the men kept it. She ringed herself with candles, and at her front built an altar of root, herb, shell, a bowl of corn pudding, a plantain, a collar from the maquila, and the magazine picture of the Happy Jumping Woman.

Mari drank rum and squeezed brown sugar through her fingers and onto the coals. She remembered names—Oshún, Chango—but couldn't remember the words. She remembered the snake—Damballah—but knew he was only a guise; scales hiding something deeper, carved from her home soil.

She held beads, white and red ones she'd found at Altagracia's. She rocked back and forth but felt nothing.

With fingers still sticky from sugar, she held her wishing stone. It had grown warm on her breast and the leather cord that held it twisted in her hand. It fattened, grew scales that became leaves, leaves that dissolved and became voices that sang songs from her childhood. The wishing stone flicked its tongue at her in greeting.

Mari turned to the face from the magazine. Alice Wear. She felt her toes lift from the floor, graze the coals, but only enough to sting a brief moment. She was floating, up, out the door, over the village, down the dirt road where all the women sat joined to machines at hands, wrists and feet. Up then, and over the mountains toward the sea cliff, then swift, across green waters and onto dust, land and dust and grinding beasts of metal and city streets and air thick as pan grease. Then down, into lush land of green lawns, tall palms, paved streets, brick walls, free of barbed wire.

The wind that carried her took her toward a great house. A house as wide as a town, and tall, with many rooms, each with its own roof; all angles and towers, red roofed tiles, and arched windows like the village church only this was a home. The home of the Happy Jumping Woman.

She flew through a window and came to rest in a large empty room.

Mari looked down. The hardwood floor glistened with a fresh layer of polish. Her reflection was but a mere wisp of herself. She smelled botanica, and across the room she saw bowls of flowers, incense that burned from gleaming elephants, and a photograph of a smiling old man who'd somehow placed his feet behind his head.

On a mat, in front of the altar sat Alice Wear, the Happy Jumping Woman. She wasn't wearing one of the ugly shirts with bright stripes and scratchy collar, but instead was dressed all in white silk and her arms and legs shimmered bronze. She had a silver anklet of tiny bells and rings on two of her toes. Her earrings glinted in hot summer sun that bounced off the mirrored wall behind the altar. Her pink, painted lips formed a smile of peace and serenity.

Mari's spirit self caught her breath. The Happy Jumping Woman must be an Iyalocha! Why else would she have an altar? Why else such a church in her own house!

Alice Wear opened her eyes and smiled.

"You're here again," she said. "My little Latin girl."

Again? Mari wondered. Had she traveled this far before and not known it? Was this Iyalocha so powerful as to reach all the way to the maquila?

"I am here to beg forgiveness," Mari said. "I have done harm."

The Happy Jumping Woman's smile grew. "I know. We have done harm in the past, but that's over now. We can step through this into the light together."

"I killed a guard," Mari said, not sure what to make of the woman's words. "At the maquila. Where your shirts are made."

The Happy Jumping Woman reached out and her hands tensed, as if she gripped Mari's spirit hands tight, but Mari felt nothing. "I don't know this word, 'maquila'" she said, "but I understand about guard. It's okay that you do these things. You are part of me. Remember? We are all on this joyous path together."

Mari did not understand. She struggled to find the right words to explain what had happened, but the Iyalocha just shushed her with a finger to her lips.

"The details aren't important. Don't dwell on them. You are merely an aspect of my guilt—just an element of my subconscious, remember?"

"I am your dream?" Mari asked, puzzled at the words that made no sense.

"I knew this would happen when Baba Sri Maa helped me work through these issues," the woman went on. "He found so many aspects within me. Be happy that you are one, my little Latin girl"

"I should be happy?" Mari asked. "Though I have killed a man?"

"Oh no," said the Happy Jumping Woman. "That is just a representation of my guilt over the consolidation of the Francie Ann clothing line into my Alice Wear brand. Baba told me that these issues would manifest in strange ways, but I have learned that is it perfectly acceptable, what I did. He assured me that it is no great greed on my part. That rejoicing in the material world is not a shameful act, but spiritual. Why just look at this place!" She let go her imaginary grip and waved her hands. "Have you ever seen such a sanctuary? It wouldn't have even existed without my acquisition of the Francie Ann clothing line."

Mari looked around the room. Yes, indeed it was a large sanctuary for the spirit. She could imagine the Happy Jumping Woman opening the doors on Sunday and welcoming Florinda, and Altagracia, and Joli and her entire village, and there'd be room and food for everyone.

"This is a gift to my spirit," the Iyalocha said. "Just as you are a gift to my spirit, even though you may feel guilty about our past choices." She reached up and again gripped the air.

"But do not feel guilty. You made the right choice. What you do is part of me, so I will not stand in the way."

"Then I did no wrong?"

"Of course not," the Iyalocha said. "You keep doing what you are doing. I am so proud of you. Your power is a gift. Use it well. Use it often." Tears glistened on her cheeks. "I feel so whole now," she said. "So alive and at peace and whole." She started to cry. "Oh, thank you Baba Sri Maa." She picked up the photograph of the contorted man and kissed it.

Mari floated up over the altar. She watched the Happy Jumping Woman cry tears of joy and hug the photograph to her chest. Mari did not understand much of what the Happy Jumping Woman said, but she knew this: she was not guilty of a crime. The Iyalocha rejoiced in her power. She blessed Mari's deeds.

This is my saint. This is my spirit.

She left Alice Wear alone in her church and floated up out of the room, out past the perfect lawns, the tall palms, and south through dust and grind to jungles and green waters, then over mountains and back to her little tin shack where the coals were just about out.

A day later, she returned to work. For the first time in a long time she gazed out the windows of the big yellow bus, watching the hills and counting each maquila as they rumbled past—dozens upon dozens of white domes, like blisters on the green-skinned land. But the land would heal soon, she knew. The Iyalocha, the Happy Jumping Woman, had granted her the gift to do what she needed, to change what she pleased.

The bus pulled up to the gate and Mari stepped off. She shuffled, one of many in a tight line, and watched as men with rifles roughly patted each woman, then sent her forward and into the blister rows.

I will visit his house too, she thought as the man touched her. *And his, and his. And feel no guilt, for the Iyalocha has blessed me so.*

THE FARMER'S CAT

JEFF VANDERMEER

A long time ago, in Norway, a farmer found he had a big problem with trolls. Every winter, the trolls would smash down the door to his house and make themselves at home for a month. Short or tall, fat or thin, hairy or hairless, it didn't matter—every last one of these trolls was a disaster for the farmer. They ate all of his food, drank all of the water from his well, guzzled down all of his milk (often right from the cow!), broke his furniture, and farted whenever they felt like it.

The farmer could do nothing about this—there were too many trolls. Besides, the leader of the trolls, who went by the name of Mobhead, was a big brute of a troll with enormous claws who emitted a foul smell from all of the creatures he'd eaten raw over the years. Mobhead had a huge, gnarled head that seemed green in one kind of light and purple in another. Next to his head, his body looked shrunken and thin, but despite the way they looked his legs were strong as steel; they had to be or his head would have long since fallen off of his neck.

"Don't you think you'd be more comfortable somewhere else?" the farmer asked Mobhead during the second winter. His wife and children had left him for less troll-infested climes. He had lost a lot of his hair from stress.

"Oh, I don't think so," Mobhead said, cleaning his fangs with a toothpick made from a sharpened chair leg. The chair in question had been made by the farmer's father many years before.

"No," Mobhead said. "We like it here just fine." And farted to punctuate his point.

Behind him, one of the other trolls devoured the family cat, and belched.

The farmer sighed. It was getting hard to keep help, even in the summers, when the trolls kept to their lairs and caves far to the north. The farm's reputation had begun to suffer. A few more years of this and he would have to sell the farm, if any of it was left to sell.

Behind him, one of the trolls attacked a smaller troll. There was a splatter of blood against the far wall, a smell oddly like violets, and then the severed head of the smaller troll rolled to a stop at the farmer's feet. The look on the dead troll's face revealed no hint of surprise.

Nor was there a look of surprise on the farmer's face.

All spring and summer, the farmer thought about what he should do. Whether fairly or unfairly, he was known in those parts for thinking or tricking his way out of every problem that had arisen during twenty years of running the farm. But he couldn't fight off the trolls by himself. He couldn't bribe them to leave. It worried him almost as much as the lack of rain in July.

Then, in late summer, a traveling merchant came by the farm. He stopped by twice a year, once with pots, pans, and dried goods and once with livestock and pets. This time, he brought a big, lurching wooden wagon full of animals, pulled by ten of the biggest, strongest horses the farmer had ever seen.

Usually, the farmer bought chickens from the tall, mute merchant, and maybe a goat or two. But this time, the merchant pointed to a cage that held seven squirming, chirping balls of fur. The farmer looked at them for a second, looked away, then looked again, more closely, raising his eyebrows.

"Do you mean to say..." the farmer said, looking at the tall, mute merchant. "Are you telling me..."

The mute man nodded. The frown of his mouth became, for a moment, a mischievous smile.

The farmer smiled. "I'll take one. One should be enough."

The mute man's grew wide and deep.

That winter, the trolls came again, in strength—rowdy, smelly, raucous, and looking for trouble. They pulled out a barrel of his best beer and drank it all down in a matter of minutes. They set fire to his attic and snuffed it only when Mobhead bawled them out for "crapping where you eat, you idiots!"

They noticed the little ball of fur curled up in a basket about an hour after they had smashed down the front door.

"Ere now," said one of the trolls, a foreign troll from England, "Wot's this, wot?"

One of the other trolls—a deformed troll, with a third eye protruding like a tube from its forehead—prodded the ball of fur with one of its big clawed toes. "It's a cat, I think. Just like the last one. Another juicy, lovely cat."

A third troll said, "Save it for later. We've got plenty of time."

The farmer, who had been watching all of this, said to the trolls, "Yes, this is our new cat. But I'd ask that you not eat him. I need him around to catch mice in the summer or when you come back next time, I won't have any grain, and no grain means no beer. It also means lots of other things won't be around for you to eat, like that homemade bread you seem to enjoy so much. In fact, I might not even be around, then, for without grain this farm cannot survive."

The misshapen troll sneered. "A pretty speech, farmer. But don't worry about the mice. We'll eat them all before we leave."

So the farmer went to Mobhead and made Mobhead promise that he and his trolls would leave the cat alone.

"Remember what you said to the trolls who tried to set my attic on fire, O Mighty Mobhead," the farmer said, in the best tradition of flatterers everywhere.

Mobhead thought about it for a second, then said, "Hmmm. I must admit I've grown fond of you, farmer, in the way a wolf is fond of a lamb. And I do want our winter resort to be in good order next time we come charging down out of the frozen north. Therefore, although I have this nagging feeling I might regret this, I will let you keep the cat. But everything else we're going to eat, drink, ruin, or fart on. I just want to make that clear."

The farmer said, "That's fine, so long as I get to keep the cat."

Mobhead said he promised on his dead mothers' eyeteeth, and then he called the other trolls around and told them that the cat was off limits. "You are not to eat the cat. You are not to taunt the cat. You must leave the cat alone."

The farmer smiled a deep and mysterious smile. It was the first smile for him in quite some time. A troll who swore on the eyeteeth of his mothers could never break that promise, no matter what.

And so the farmer got to keep his cat. The next year, when the trolls came barging in, they were well into their rampage before they even saw the cat. When they did, they were a little surprised at how big it had grown. Why, it was almost as big as a dog. And it had such big teeth, too."

"It's one of those Northern cats," the farmer told them. "They grow them big up there. You must know that, since you come from up there. Surely you know that much?"

"Yes, yes," Mobhead said, nodding absent-mindedly, "we know that, farmer," and promptly dove face-first into a large bucket of offal.

But the farmer noticed that the cat made the other trolls nervous. For one thing, it met their gaze and held it, almost as if it weren't an animal, or thought itself their equal. And it didn't really look like a cat, even a Northern cat, to them. Still, the farmer could tell that the other trolls didn't want to say anything to their leader. Mobhead liked to eat the smaller trolls because they were, under all the hair, so succulent, and none of them wanted to give him an excuse for a hasty dinner.

Another year went by. Spring gave on to the long days of summer, and the farmer found some solace in the growth of not only his crops but also the growth of his cat. The farmer and his cat would take long walks through the fields, the farmer teaching the cat as much about the farm as possible. And he believed that the cat even appreciated some of it.

Once more, too, fall froze into winter, and once more the trolls came tumbling into the farmer's house, led by Mobhead. Once again, they trashed the place as thoroughly as if they were roadies for some drunken band of Scandinavian lute players.

They had begun their second trashing of the house, pulling down the cabinets, splintering the chairs, when suddenly they heard a growl that turned their blood to ice and set them to gibbering, and at their rear there came the sound of bones being crunched, and as they turned to look and see what was happening, they were met by the sight of some of their friends being hurled at them with great force.

The farmer just stood off to the side, smoking his pipe and chuckling from time to time as his cat took care of the trolls. Sharp were his fangs!

Long were his claws! Huge was his frame!

Finally, Mobhead walked up alongside the farmer. He was so shaken, he could hardly hold up his enormous head.

"I could eat you right now, farmer," Mobhead snarled. "That is the largest cat I have ever seen—and it is trying to kill my trolls! Only I get to kill my trolls!"

"Nonsense," the farmer said. "My cat only eats mice. Your trolls aren't mice, are they?"

"I eat farmers sometimes," Mobhead said. "How would you like that?"

The farmer took the pipe out of his mouth and frowned. "It really isn't up to me. I don't think Mob-Eater would like that, though."

"Mob-Eater?"

"Yes—that's my name for my cat."

As much as a hairy troll can blanch, Mobhead blanched exactly that much and no more.

"Very well, I won't eat you. But I will eat your hideous cat," Mobhead said, although not in a very convincing tone.

The farmer smiled. "Remember your promise."

Mobhead scowled. The farmer knew the creature was thinking about breaking his promise. But if he did, Mobhead would be tormented by nightmares in which his mothers tortured him with words and with deeds. He would lose all taste for food. He would starve. Even his mighty head would shrivel up. Within a month, Mobhead would be dead…

Mobhead snarled in frustration. "We'll be back when your cat is gone, farmer," he said. "And then you'll pay!"

If he'd had a cape instead of a dirty pelt of fur-hair, Mobhead would have whirled it around him as he left, trailing the remains of his thoroughly beaten and half-digested trolls behind him.

"You haven't heard the last of me!" Mobhead yowled as he disappeared into the snow, now red with the pearling of troll blood.

The next winter, Mobhead and his troll band stopped a few feet from the farmer's front door.

"Hey, farmer, are you there?!" Mobhead shouted.

After a moment, the door opened wide and there stood the farmer, a smile on his face.

"Why, Mobhead. How nice to see you. What can I do for you?"

"You can tell me if you still have that damn cat. I've been looking forward to our winter get-away."

The farmer smiled even more, and behind him rose a huge shadow with large, yellow eyes and rippling muscles under a thick brown pelt. The claws on the shadow were big as carving knives, and the fangs almost as large.

"Why, yes," the farmer said, "as it so happens I still have Mob-Eater. He's a very good mouser."

Mobhead's shoulders slumped.

It would be a long hard slog back to the frozen north, and only troll to eat along the way. As he turned to go, he kicked a small troll out of his way.

"We'll be back next year," he said over his shoulder. "We'll be back every year until that damn cat is gone."

"Suit yourself," the farmer said, and closed the door.

Once inside, the farmer and the bear laughed.

"Thanks, Mob-Eater," the farmer said. "You looked really fierce."

The bear huffed a deep bear belly laugh, sitting back on its haunches in a huge comfy chair the farmer had made for him.

"I am really fierce, father," the bear said. "But you should have let me chase them. I don't like the taste of troll all that much, but, oh, I do love to chase them."

"Maybe next year," the farmer said. "Maybe next year. But for now, we have chores to do. I need to teach you to milk the cows, for one thing."

"But I hate to milk the cows," the bear said. "You know that."

"Yes, but you still need to know how to do it, son."

"Very well. If you say so."

They waited for a few minutes until the trolls were out of sight, and then they went outside and started doing the farm chores for the day.

Soon, the farmer thought, his wife and children would come home, and everything would be as it was before. Except that now they had a huge talking bear living in their house.

Sometimes folktales didn't end quite the way you thought they would. But they did end.

Dusty Wings

Nancy Jane Moore

I looked like shit for my meeting with the dean. A tell-tale line ran down the left leg of my stockings. A toothpaste stain decorated the front of my dress, right at the nipple of my left breast. The bags under my eyes hung halfway down my cheeks.

I felt like I looked. I'd tried to ward off the dream the night before by drinking. It hadn't worked; I'd awakened trembling and sweating about three a.m.

The dream hasn't changed in twenty-five years: I stand in absolute darkness, feeling the heavy presence of the jungle all around me. A mix of perfumes from a hundred varieties of flowers mixes with the rancid odor of rotting vegetation and almost chokes me. Before me stands a woman, her arms stretched out toward me. Though there is no light, I can see her clearly, every detail—her dark brown, almost black, skin, her graying hair, the wrinkles around her eyes. I move toward her, touch her hand.

She transforms into a column of pure white light. A line of black begins to weave in and out through the light until black and white are completely intertwined. I look down at myself and see the same mixture of white and black. I try to scream, but when I open my mouth no sound comes out.

I know the woman: La Soltera, the shaman I studied with so many years ago in the mountains of Guatemala. I could interpret the dream if I wanted to. I don't want to. Drinking used to help.

The community college where I teach is in a building that used to be a high school. Sitting in the outer office waiting for the dean made me feel like a bad kid sent to see the principal. I looked at my watch. Seventeen minutes past ten. The dean was running way behind schedule. The only part of the newspaper I hadn't read was the classifieds, so I dug into my bag for the stack of student papers I always carry with me. If you don't do your grading in odd moments, you'll never get it done.

I got so caught up in covering papers with red ink that I didn't hear the dean's door open. He said, "Corinne, " and I jumped, dropping papers, pen and reading glasses on the floor. He stooped down to help me pick them up. I looked at his face as he handed me a stack of essays and knew things were about to go very wrong.

He slumped into the chair behind his desk and stared at a sheet of paper as if it contained the answer to all questions. "The school board has decided to put more money into the computer and technology courses."

I nodded.

"The money has to come from somewhere, so they cut our budget. Said we had to cut out the frills." He glanced up at me, probably hoping I'd say something.

I just looked at him.

"We just can't afford anthropology courses any more, Corinne." His words started to come faster. "We've got to teach so much remedial English and English as a second language. So many of our students don't have the basic skills and those things have to come first. There's just no money for electives." His voice petered out. "I'm sorry, Corinne."

I don't remember what I said, if I said anything at all. I walked out in a stupor, didn't even bother to go by my own tiny office, just went straight to my car in the parking lot. I dug in my purse for my keys and couldn't find them. I rummaged around, with no success, and started to cry, great heaving sobs. My knees buckled and I slid down the side of the car, bawling. I sat on the concrete and cried while I dumped everything out of my purse into a pile on the ground. The keys clattered out last.

I stayed there, sobbing, feeling an aching in my chest as if my heart might truly break. A man going to his car averted his eyes, and I realized how ludicrous I must look: a grown woman sitting on the ground crying like a two-year old. I shoved everything back in my purse, pulled myself to my feet using the door handle, and drove home on automatic pilot.

I walked into my house and slammed the door on the outside world. It was noon. I turned on the soap operas and began to drink Scotch. The phone rang. I let the machine answer. Jeane, checking in, wondering why I wasn't at the college. I didn't pick up.

Jeane fills the role of best friend for me these days. Women always have best friends; we pick up the habit in grade school, where only the social outcasts eat lunch alone, and keep it as we grow up. Superficially, the two of us have a lot in common: divorced, no children, no real careers. Jeane and I complain about men, bitch about our jobs, and sit up late, drinking Scotch, telling stories about our youth and solving the problems of the Universe. But I've never told her about the dream, never told her about Guatemala.

Not that she wouldn't enjoy the story, if I told it right. Jeane likes the idea of powerful native shamans just as she enjoys fantasy stories about wizards. She wouldn't want to meet one personally, for all the good girl reasons that made her marry young instead of tuning in, turning on and dropping out in 1968; she's not the sort who would ever take a real risk. But she loves to speculate about the magical powers such shamans have, just as she always wants to hear me talk about acid trips and anti-war protests.

I tell them well, too, those funny stories from my youth, for all that they have an air of unreality. Who really believes a respectable middle-aged woman ever chewed peyote or marched in the streets yelling "One, two, three, four. We don't want your fucking war." I never tell the whole truth, of course; never tell about the fear that can hit you when a psychedelic drug has stripped away all your defenses, never mention the people who lost their minds and couldn't find them again, never mention how scary it can be to find out that your name really is on a government list. I tell part of the truth, the good stuff, the funny stuff.

If I did tell stories about Guatemala, I'd lie.

It took awhile, but the combination of alcohol and tedious TV did its job. I passed out on the couch. And woke trembling a couple of hours later. "Please, God," I prayed. "Please make the dream go away. Let things work out for me. Just let me get another job, be able to pay my bills. I promise I won't ask for anything else, not for love, not for happiness."

A desperation prayer aimed at the childhood God, the old man with the white beard who sits on a golden throne in heaven and keeps his eye on every sparrow. I didn't believe in that God any more. Whatever God is—if God is—he's not a supernatural form of your mother who exists to bail you out of trouble. No one was going to answer my prayer.

God and alcohol having failed me, I turned to human assistance. I called Jeane.

She came right over and was properly outraged on my behalf. That's one of the duties of a best friend. "Corinne, this is ridiculous. Can't you sue them or something?"

"For what? Eliminating anthropology courses? I don't think it's illegal to decide you're not going to offer certain courses."

"Sex discrimination, maybe?"

"Hell, more than fifty percent of the college's teachers are women. I don't think so."

She hesitated. "Age discrimination? I mean, you are over forty."

"Way over. But I think they'd have to hire some kid to teach anthro for me to have a case."

She shook her head. "It just isn't fair. But you'll find another job—maybe you can get on at the University."

I laughed. "I don't think so. Jobs for anthropologists tend to be scarce even if you do all the right things. And if the initials after your name are ABD instead of PhD, well . . ."

"ABD?"

"All but dissertation. And the University probably wouldn't hire me even if I'd written one, because I haven't written anything else. The University of Texas hires scholars; they don't need somebody who just teaches."

"Something will work out," she said. "I can't believe they treated you so shabbily." She spent the evening with me, helping polish off the Scotch and telling me that idiots ran the college. That's what best friends are for.

I'm not sure how Jeane made it to work the next morning, because the clock passed two before she went home. But she's your standard issue middle-aged woman, responsible as hell.

Me, I lay there in bed, not bothering to go to work, or even to call in sick. I wondered what I would do with myself if I couldn't find another job. I've always wanted to think of myself as a free spirit, not tied down to a conventional way of life. I've frequently claimed I stay in Austin so that I can remain true to my Sixties values. I opted out of the fast growth Eighties and the family value Nineties and told myself I'd stayed as hip and cool as I was in 1969.

But in 1969 I didn't worry about having a job, having enough money, building a retirement nest egg. Now I was too old to easily find another job and too young to take early retirement. Not that the amount of money in my retirement plan would support me anyway. The bank owned a whole lot more of my house than I did, plus I owed more on credit cards than I wanted to admit to anyone.

A lot of that credit card debt had gone for Scotch. I drank to keep from thinking. When I could find a man, I fucked to keep from thinking. I didn't want to think, because then I'd remember what I ran from in Guatemala. Not to mention remembering that I had pretty much wasted my life since then.

I eventually went back to sleep. But I wasn't all that drunk anymore, so the dream came back. I woke up in a cold sweat at two o'clock in the afternoon, with enough of a hangover that I didn't want to drink anymore. Or to hang out with Jeane. I'd had my fill of railing at the unfairness of the world and I knew she didn't have anything else to give me. So I started cleaning. I scrubbed the bathtub until the porcelain gleamed the way it does in television commercials and actually got down on my hands and knees to clean the kitchen floor inch by inch.

About nine o'clock I got sick of the smell of Ajax. I needed to go somewhere, do something. One thing about living in Austin: you can always find places to drink and hear music when you're antsy, places a single woman can go and make her own choices about whether she's going home alone or with someone. I went down to La Zona Rosa, a bar not too far from the state capitol where local music legends tended to come by and sit in for a set. I hadn't been there in awhile. I hadn't been out in awhile. I'd been doing my drinking at home.

Three guys were playing classic Austin music: rock-influenced country. Mostly love songs. The singer doubled on the mouth harp, and the other two played guitar and bass. Cigarette smoke hung over the room. People crowded around the bar, talking loudly and whooping in the Texan version of a mariachi grito at the end of each song. The musicians weren't bad, but their sound didn't fit my mood. I had one Negra Modelo, then another. Maybe I'd just go home and watch bad TV again.

I went to the bathroom. On my way back I saw a lanky guy unpacking his guitar. He stood up and turned toward me as he swung the strap around his neck. Travis Collins. The moment I saw him I knew that his dark-edged blues were exactly what I wanted to hear. I'd never actually met him, but when you've been listening to a man's music for twenty-five years, you feel like you know him. He gave me a shy smile. I gave him one back and said, "You going to play awhile?"

"Yeah. They asked me to do a few numbers."

"Great." Our eyes met. His face showed twenty miles of bad road. Both lust and warning alarms blared in my brain: I wanted the man and my common sense told me to stay the hell away. He gave me a look that was more than friendly. Oh, fuck, I told myself. If he needs a woman with dark circles under her eyes and swollen sinuses—not to mention rapidly graying hair that needs both cutting and highlights—why should I deny him just because he's obviously bad news.

I grabbed another beer and moved to a table near the stage. Travis sang about a man swilling codeine while he waited around to die. The crack in his aging tenor just made the song stronger. He played a couple of others—even one kind of funny one in which he swore that if there weren't fast women and whisky in heaven, he'd take his chances on hell.

The audience kept yelling out requests and hollered loudly after each song. But when a guy at the next table kept talking during one of the quiet numbers, the man in front of him leaned back and told him to shut up in a voice so calm and deadly that the guy didn't even try to argue. You don't interrupt a legend's act.

I'd never picked up a musician after his set before, but Travis had plenty of experience and took the time to make me feel comfortable. We sat in an over-bright cafe on South Congress—the only twenty-four-hour place I know—eating pie and swilling coffee until about one thirty when I finally got up the nerve to invite him home.

For a one night stand, the sex went well. Usually the first time isn't all that great: you're both trying to figure out what the other person wants and too shy to ask for what you have in mind. And you're clumsy—you don't have each others' moves down yet. Maybe because we weren't in love, we gave each other more honesty than we would have with somebody who mattered. We talked about all kinds of stuff—the state of the world and what God was and wasn't and who really was the best blues singer of all time—and never said a goddamn thing about ourselves.

We fell asleep eventually. I came awake gasping for breath. I'd dreamed again.

Travis held me. Probably he was being unfaithful to some woman, probably he was betraying someone who was counting on him. But he was there for me, that one night.

"Tell me about it," he said, and I knew he meant it.

So I told him about Guatemala. The story I never told Jeane or any of the other women who've filled her role over the years. Or any of the men I've slept with—even my ex-husband.

I was working on a Ph.D. in cultural anthropology in the early Seventies, or at least, that's what I told my parents and professors I was doing. What I was really doing was looking for my own personal version of Castaneda's Don Juan—a real one, not the fictional character—a shaman who was going to give me the ultimate head trip, fill me full of some strange jungle drug and introduce me to God.

I'd taken LSD for what I called religious reasons. I wanted to experience that transcendent state that I'd read about. But the hippie drug scene got on my nerves. I didn't really like hanging out with anyone who wasn't using psychedelics for the higher purpose of searching for enlightenment, but since all recreational drugs were equally illegal, I often found myself in the company of the party-hearty crowd. A few of the people I met -- speed freaks, smackheads, dealers with organized crime connections -- were downright scary. When the opportunity came up to do field work in Central America, I jumped at it. My advisors approved a dissertation on the survival of shamanic culture in developing countries.

Guatemala seemed the best choice for my study. About half the population consisted of what the Guatemalans call indigenas: full blooded Mayans. Though they often lived way out in the country, they weren't isolated from the rest of the population; they came into towns to sell their goods in the mercados. In town, they spoke a pidgin Spanish; among themselves they spoke Quiche and other dialects of the old Mayan languages.

They were poor—the poorest of the poor in a country where poverty was the norm. Modern doctors practice in Guatemalan cities, but not among the indigenas in the countryside. Most of the villages—really just concentrations of a few houses—had someone they considered a healer and

I focused my initial study on meeting some of them. I traveled in the back country, making myself understood in Spanish as best as I could, trying a few words of Quiche, though I could never imitate the guttural sounds that underlay it. In mercados and villages I met midwives and herbalists, people doing things the way their ancestors had always done them; good-hearted folks, most of them, but filled with a combination of superstition and practical folk wisdom. No magic there.

When I did find a man who was rumored to have special powers, he turned out to be a blatant charlatan. Most of the people in his village didn't even bother to consult him and laughed at him behind his back. I began to think I'd have to change my dissertation topic to the degradation of shamanic culture in developing countries.

And then I began hearing about a woman called "La Soltera." Funny, the name was always given in Spanish, no matter what language the speaker learned in childhood. You'll find her in the mountains north of Huehuetenango, up near the Mexican border, people said. Nobody would tell me anything more about her. They crossed themselves when they mentioned her name—one of the many Catholic practices the indigenas wore like a robe over their more basic beliefs. More than once as I walked away from someone who had told me about La Soltera I heard someone say "norteamericana loca."

Her village turned out to lie about twenty-five miles northeast of Huehue. The pig-and-chicken bus dropped me off along a mountain road in the middle of nowhere. One other passenger got off—a short woman, missing several teeth, who wore the traditional embroidered red huipil as a blouse and a wrapped length of brightly-patterned material for a skirt. I followed her up a steep dirt trail through densely-packed trees.

The village consisted of a collection of houses built out of logs plastered over with mud. Nothing was paved—paths had been created by use. Chickens and other small creatures ran freely among the buildings. Forest bumped up against the village in three directions, but to the south the trees had been cleared away for farming.

People lived here as their great-great grandparents must have lived. They lacked electricity, running water, even a church. The huipils on all the woman were embroidered in the same fashion, a design that probably went back hundreds of years. Experts can tell a Mayan woman's village by her huipil. Only the occasional blare from a battery-powered radio reminded me it was the twentieth century.

The woman I had followed up the hill pointed out the trail to La Soltera's house, but refused to take me there. I walked half a mile further up the mountain and found another hut built of logs.

The first thing I saw inside the hut was a woman lying on a pallet. She had bled a lot—the bedclothes were soaked—and even my untrained eyes could tell she was dying. Miscarriage, I thought to myself. A dark-skinned woman knelt beside her. I couldn't see what she did. Without turning around the kneeling woman said, "Please come over here and stroke her head."

I did as I was told. Several days passed before I realized she had spoken to me in English.

I brushed the woman's damp hair off her forehead, and tried to murmur some words of comfort. La Soltera placed her hands on the woman's abdomen, and as I watched, the swelling in it went down. The patient shifted a little, and color came back into her face. La Soltera took a rag and began to clean the blood from her. "She'll live, now," she said, this time in Spanish.

When the healer stood up, I realized that she was tall; she stood several inches above my own five foot seven. Strange, in a country where I'd spent most of the time feeling like a giant. Her black hair showed the beginnings of grey; a few wrinkles marked her face. She looked to be in her mid-forties; correcting for the harder aging of third-world countries, I guessed her at thirty-five.

La Soltera never asked me why I had come. She never asked me anything. She knew my name without being told and unlike everyone else I met in Guatemala she had no difficulty with the pronunciation. I became her apprentice without any discussion whatsoever.

And apprentice was exactly what I became. I made notes like a good field observer, but only because I knew no other way to integrate the things she told me. She showed me herbs she used—they were not the same ones I had seen used by other village curanderas—and taught me procedures for helping a mother give birth that would not have been out of place in a modern hospital.

The villagers avoided her. They only came to consult her when they were desperate and whenever they mentioned her name they crossed themselves. But they treated me all right. I guess they figured the norteamericana loca wasn't dangerous. I became La Soltera's liaison with the village. When I asked—like a proper anthropologist—what they knew of her, most told me, "My grandmother told me she came from the north." They spoke of her as an outsider, though they also spoke of her as someone who had lived there since long before they were born. Even the elders. There were more of those than usual in this village, this little community so small it lacked a name. People seemed to live longer here. I made note of that, in case I ever wrote the dissertation.

One day, after I had lived there several months, some of the men carried a young man to La Soltera. He had cut his foot on something metal several days earlier and had not treated the injury at the time. It was a bad cut, but the sort of thing that could have been easily treated in a civilized place with a tetanus shot and a few stitches, had he seen a doctor soon after it happened. La Soltera had no vaccines, of course, and by the time he reached her, they would not have helped. The cut had become very infected—streaks up his leg indicated gangrene might have set in. And, worse than that, his jaw was clamped shut from tetanus.

His friends set him down and left. La Soltera passed her hands over him and he fell into a sleep as deep as any brought on by anesthesia. She had me wash the cut as best I could, though I could tell it did little good, and then to sit holding his head. She herself sat beside him in deep meditation for about half an hour. And then she began to run her fingers down the streaks on his legs, until they disappeared. I felt his breathing shift. Another pass at his foot and pus drained from the cut. And then she touched his jaw, and it relaxed. She nodded, satisfied. "Bind up his foot," she said, and went outside.

What I had seen scared me. No one should have been able to do what she had done. I knew then—really knew—that saving the woman who miscarried had been no fluke. La Soltera was doing more than using herbs and folk wisdom to heal.

When I came outside, she was slumped down on the old stump she usually sat on, obviously drained by the healing. "If they would come earlier, it would be easier," she said.

"In my country," I said, my voice shaking a bit, "people often die from that infection, unless they are treated right away."

"I do not use the medicine of your country," La Soltera said. She smiled, as if she had told a joke. "It is time to show you some of the power. After dinner, we will go out into the jungle and have a look at your soul."

No moon shone that night and clouds obscured the stars. La Soltera led me deep into the forest and gave me what I thought I was looking for. It was an odd little thing, a fungus of some kind: dark brown, wrinkled and smelling of freshly turned-over dirt. I took it from her eagerly, swallowed it without thinking.

It wasn't like acid or the other drugs kids took back then. I never rushed, never threw up. Gradually I became aware that I could see everything around me, in spite of the dark. I could not only see details of the trees and the animals hiding among them; I could see inside my own body. I watched the eggs in my ovary start down the fallopian tubes, knew somehow that if I had sex I could decide whether to let them connect with sperm.

The workings of my mind became visible to me as well. That frightened me. I didn't much like what I saw: the greedy desire for experience, the petty ambition, the flimsy mask of superiority assumed by persons who grow up in "civilized" countries. I grew more nervous as I watched my defenses peel away as if they were the outer leaves on an artichoke.

Underneath all those layers I saw a little ball of glowing white that could only be my soul. It seemed less ugly than the desires that surrounded it, but perhaps I only wanted it to be. I realized that La Soltera could see these things, too, had seen them all along. I looked at my teacher, and I could see all of her as well, though I wasn't sure what I saw.

I could tell that she was old, oh so much older than I had thought. Hundreds of years old, and more. She looked at me, turned those eyes as black as the surrounding night on my immortal soul, and said—perhaps out loud, perhaps in my mind— "Now you can see all the things you have been seeking, all the pieces that make up yourself and others, the trees, the animals, even the rocks."

I looked around then, and realized that I could see the inner workings in the leaves of every plant around us. The blood moved sluggishly through the veins of the black snake coiled in the nearest tree. A monkey huddled uncomfortably in the crook of another tree; I noticed the thorn in its paw, and reached in with my mind to pull it out. It disappeared. The monkey chattered its thanks.

"What a weird hallucination," I said.

"It is real," she said. "Now that you can see, you can truly learn to heal. Yourself, as well as others."

"No," I said. "It's just the drug. I'm just imagining things. This isn't real."

"The drug only shows it to you. Someday you will be able to see and heal without the drug; someday you will always see like this."

My mind resisted this knowledge, even as my heart knew it for truth. As I sat there on a rotting length of tree trunk, trying to reconcile this conflict, a scorpion crawled out alongside me. It showed no interest in me, but I nevertheless reacted to it, sent it a bolt of fear that killed it instantly.

In fear—in awe—I turned to La Soltera. She nodded. "What can heal can also kill. We do not take the safe path through the world, you and I."

I sat there, scared but eager—greedy. I was still greedy then.

"Only a few are born with the capacity for the power," she said. "Fewer still seek it out. And of those who find their power, many decide they do not want it."

"I want it," I said, trying to sound confident, still seeing the scorpion.

She laughed. She could see all my fears.

After that, I became a real apprentice. I ate the fungus regularly, so that I could see truly. Gradually I needed it less often, as its effects began to stay with me. At that point La Soltera started to let me heal some of those who came for treatment. The first time I managed to delicately shift a baby inside a mother's womb so that she would come out head first, I felt an incredible joy.

And the day I watched La Soltera let an elderly man die, I felt grief. "You can heal him," I said, showing her the tumor.

"Yes, but now is the right time for him to pass. His son leads the community, and no longer needs the old man's guidance."

"But why not let him live longer?"

"How long?" she asked me, and in truth I did not know. She could keep him alive as long as she lived.

"If people live longer than the community expects them to, they become like you and me, walking ghosts. No one should take up that life without choosing it."

And, indeed, I had become a ghost in the community, after I ate the fungus. The people began to shy away from me, as they did from La Soltera. I was no longer the norteamericana loca. They knew I was like her.

"And in any case, we will not be here to keep them alive forever. Sooner or later, their fear of us will grow too strong, and we will have to go someplace new, where we are unknown. We always must remain apart," she said.

I began to realize what a lonely path I had chosen. It frightened me more than I wanted to admit. Knowing that I held the power of life and death over others added to my fear. "How do you know when you should let people die?" I asked La Soltera.

"Practice," she said. "As with anything else, you learn from your mistakes."

She laughed, but I trembled, all the way down into my soul. Still, hunger for the power outweighed my fear of it. I would not have left, if Rigoberto had not come home to visit his mother.

Rigoberto had been dragooned into the military some years before. His mother had wept when he left, but now that he returned, she wept all the more. It seemed the life of a soldier suited him. He boasted of the men he had killed and the women he had raped, and gloried in the petty cruelties a man with a gun can inflict on those who have no defenses.

Unlike the rest of the villagers, Rigoberto did not fear me. He scorned the other men for their superstitions. And like many a Guatemalan man, he had the illusion that all North American girls were easy. He told his friends that he would make me beg for him and laughed when they crossed themselves and turned away.

I heard him say those things, for La Soltera had read him when he arrived and told me to watch him. My skills had grown; I could do so from a distance. What he said angered me, but I was not afraid of him. I did not think he would really do anything and in my arrogance I thought—I knew—I could stop him if he did.

He blocked my path late one day when I was trudging up the hill to the village. I had gone to the mercado in the nearest town to buy beans and corn for myself and La Soltera. The day had tired me greatly; I had been able to see everything about the people around me—their illnesses, their petty jealousies, the scars on their souls, and yes, their joys, too, but humans seem to carry so much more pain than pleasure.

Now I looked at the true Rigoberto. His soul was a dried up black thing. Somewhere in there a little boy still cried for his mother, but mostly he had become a man who derived his pleasure from hurting people and listening to them beg him to stop.

He said something to me, something crude. I didn't even hear the words; I was reading the intent in the man.

"Vaya se," I told him, in my most powerful voice. Go away.

He laughed and grabbed my shoulder.

I shook him loose, glared at him, letting some of my power come through my eyes. The power frightened him. I could see that. I expected him to run. Instead he grabbed me again, pulled me into a bear hug that trapped my arms at my sides.

Life in the military had taught Rigoberto to be a man who leapt on things that frightened him, instead of running from them.

I knew nothing of fighting, could not think of anything to do except try to wiggle free. I struggled against his arms, but he held me tighter. He was a powerful man, despite his short stature. I, too, felt fear. Like most women, I'd experienced my share of unwanted advances, but I'd never been raped. Some combination of intuition, common sense and luck had kept me out of really dangerous situations.

But now I could read Rigoberto's intent explicitly, knew what he wanted in the ugliest detail. I struggled against his arms again, tried to bring a knee into his groin. He laughed, held me even tighter, so that I could barely breathe, and kissed me, pushing hard against my lips with his tongue.

It was the kiss that drove me mad. A kiss should come from innocence or from passion, not be an added insult on the way to violation. My rage spiraled up through me like a tornado. I forgot fear, forgot my weakness, forgot even my basic humanity. I became the power that moved through me.

Rigoberto let go suddenly and fell back against a tree. Now the fear showed in his eyes, now the little boy crying out for his mother dominated the rest of his personality. He lay on his back, like a dog cowering before a more powerful animal, showing me all his weaknesses, begging me for mercy.

I had none. My rage had gone too far. I stared at this creature at my feet and laughed at its fears, its weaknesses, its inability to stand before my power. I did not even grant it humanity.

After a few minutes something gave in Rigoberto. His heart, I suspect, though no one ever did an autopsy. No one, in fact, ever investigated his death, though all the villagers surely knew I had killed him.

Only after he died did my rage subside. And then my fear returned.

When La Soltera came for me, I was crouched over the corpse, trying to bring him back to life. She led me up to the hut, where I collapsed onto my pallet and curled up in a fetal position. She sat there beside me, touching me, but doing nothing to heal my fear and grief, just waiting for me to bring myself back to some kind of equilibrium.

The sun had long disappeared before I did so. "I didn't know I could do that," I said, sitting up shakily.

La Soltera handed me a cup of water; I gulped it down. "And now you know," she said.

"Oh, God." I was shaking. "I never want to do anything like that again. It felt horrible."

"And?" she said.

I looked at her, not understanding—or perhaps pretending not to understand.

She just waited.

I closed my eyes and said in a bare whisper, "And I liked it. Oh, God, I liked it, that power coming through me, the man on the ground."

"That, too, you needed to know."

Something cold gripped my heart. I opened my eyes, stared at her. "You could have stopped it. Oh, my God, you could have stopped it."

She did not deny it. "You had to know."

I stood up, began backing away from her. "I don't want to know. I don't want to know that."

Suddenly she became a column of power, radiating outward. I fell to the ground as if she had struck me. "Stop acting like a fool. Power comes from your whole soul, not just the good side. You must know your whole self, must know the evil you can do before you can truly choose wisely."

"But I killed him," I said.

"Do you think that I have not killed?"

And even as I closed my eyes against the brilliance that radiated from her, I could see her history. It came in fragments, in images. I saw that she was even older than I had realized. A thousand years, maybe more.

She had been born in the heart of Africa, in some forgotten village. She, too, had a teacher, a man vastly older than she. She showed me all the things she had seen: Wars where human beings were dismembered while still living; slavery both cruel and banal; death in a hundred ways, from the sublime to the ridiculous; and love in all its many permutations, between mother and child, man and woman, human and animal. I saw these things, and frightened though I was, I wanted to see more.

I saw her as a young woman, then, truly young, and filled with the knowledge of her power and the arrogant greed that can accompany it. She ruthlessly took control of her village and others nearby, destroying any who got in her way. Those that followed her—ordinary people, not other shamans—became even more greedy than she. They reached out and destroyed in her name. In the end, she could not control them. They turned on each other and all were destroyed except La Soltera.

Then she let the power fade, and stood before me, simply a woman again. "You must know all of it," she said again. "There is no good that is not partly marked by evil, nor evil with no traces of the good. You must know the harm you can do, must risk that you will give into the pleasures of evil, before you can become whole." She held her arms out to me.

I scrambled to my feet and ran.

The rest of the night I spent huddled under a tree in the jungle. She knew where I was, of course, but left me there. At first light, when I could tell that she had gone out, I snuck back to the hut, grabbed my passport and money, and ran down the hill to catch the first bus of the morning.

I never looked back.

As I told the story to the stranger in bed with me, I realized that I could see into the man, see his struggles with depression, with alcohol and downers. Just a glimpse, a memory of the power that I could develop. If I had stayed with La Soltera I would have had something to offer him besides a one night stand. But maybe if I had stayed I would have become a woman who enjoyed watching him destroy himself. I began to shake and he held me. Just held me.

After a few minutes, he said, "She was right. You had to meet your bad side, had to know it."

I didn't say anything.

"Have to meet your good side, too. I've always known I was evil; just lately I've begun to realize that I might be good, too."

Funny words, but they helped somehow. He held me close, caressed me, and I began to relax. As I drifted off to sleep, he said, "You need to go find that woman. She's waiting for you to come back."

I shook my head. "She's probably left the village by now. I don't even know where she is."

"I bet you do, if you let yourself."

He was right. In a corner of my mind I could feel her calling, and knew if I followed that call I would find her, wherever she might be. I shook my head. "It's too late, now."

"It's never too late, until you're in your grave," he said.

I laughed at that, drifted back to sleep.

When I woke up, he was gone. I found a note on the kitchen table: "Thanks. I needed a friend last night. Go find the woman. Travis."

No protestations of undying love. No phone number. Not that I'd expected one. I stuck the note in a book, ignored the advice, and got on with my life, more or less.

The semester ended and I took an underpaid job in a big chain bookstore. It didn't cover all my bills, but it provided health insurance. A shrink gave me a prescription for some antidepressants. They suppressed the dream and kept everything at a low ache. I watched a lot of bad TV. And drank.

Like most overgrown small towns, Austin swirls with rumors. I heard that Travis was sick, but I didn't give it much thought until Jeane called to tell me about a benefit concert at La Zona Rosa to help pay his medical expenses. I didn't really want to go, but Jeane did. I had told her about spending the night with him—that's the sort of story a best friend is supposed to share—and she insisted that I should go see him.

A number of local musicians performed that night, all singing Travis's songs. When he finally took the stage to say thank you and do a few numbers, I was shocked. He looked about twenty years older than the man

I'd slept with six months earlier and he'd gotten even skinnier.

I sat there listening to him stumble over the words to songs he'd been doing for twenty years, sticking my whole fist in my mouth to keep from crying. He stopped in the middle of a song, and started a long disjointed story. I couldn't follow it—probably no one understood. All around me the crowd shifted restlessly. They loved the man, had come out to help him, but the reality of his decline was far too painful to watch.

He started another song, a talking blues he'd written years ago, beginning somewhere in the middle. I couldn't keep from crying now. No one should die like this, I said to myself. Maybe the pain of watching him hit some nerve in me. My mind opened up and I could see all of him: the white light of his soul, the black that ran through it, and streaks of red as well. And in his head, the tumor that pressed against his brain.

I wanted to reach in, smooth it away, but I couldn't quite remember how to do that. The image faded away and all I could see was the weather-beaten face of a man who had suffered most of his life and who was dying far too young. The spotlight still shone directly on him and he was trying desperately to remember the words to his song. He could not have seen me, probably didn't even know I was there, and yet I felt as if he were staring directly at me, glaring, letting me know that it was my fault he was dying. If I had stayed with La Soltera, I would have been able to save him.

A couple of the other musicians walked up to him, took him by the hand and led him off the stage.

My hands trembled. I stood up, fished a twenty out of my purse, and tossed it on the table. "Can you take a cab home?" I said to Jeane. "I have to go." I didn't wait for her reply.

I walked out the front door, got in my car, and just headed off. Before I'd made a firm decision about where I was going, I found myself driving on the west side of town, up to Mount Bonnell. It isn't a mountain, just the highest point of land around, a gateway to the ragged hills of Central Texas.

I drove past the peak. It's mostly houses up there now, but there's still a teenage lovers' lane. I didn't stop. I was heading beyond that point, to where the road was cut out of the hillside. On one side rose a wall of sheer rock, the reddish rock of the hill country. On the other, land covered with cedars and mesquites sloped down all the way down to Lake Travis.

The road is narrow, and it curves around as it takes you downhill.

Foot-high metal guardrails are stuck in the ground to remind you of the road's edge. A moment's inattention can send you crashing through them, down to the lake a few hundred feet below. Especially if you're speeding. I was speeding.

And crying. My mind kept flashing back and forth between two images: Rigoberto lying on the ground, helpless, and Travis standing on the stage, equally helpless. I killed regardless of whether I acted or didn't act.

The desperate look on Travis's face was etched in my brain, and I knew no amount of alcohol or drugs would ever be enough to let me forget that I could save people, if I would. But I could also feel that dark little corner of my soul reminding me of how good it felt to have the power of life and death over others.

My hands were clamped on the steering wheel, as if holding onto it could save me. I couldn't stand to live with the pain of watching people I loved die for no reason, but to learn to heal I would have to face my own capacity for evil. Nothing has ever scared me more.

I rubbed tears out of my eyes and glanced over the side of the cliff. The moon was making white streaks in the blackness of the lake below. "Just let go," I told myself. "Just dive off into Lake Travis."

And then it struck me as funny that it should be Lake Travis. I started to laugh. I laughed so hard that I began coughing. That broke the spell; you can't laugh at yourself and commit suicide. I took my foot off the accelerator, put in the clutch, and tapped the brake lightly. Slowing down too fast would be more dangerous than not slowing down at all. Gradually I brought the speed way down and drove about twenty miles an hour all the way until the road ran into another highway.

I sat at the highway intersection a long time, trying to figure out which way to turn. Left, I knew—without knowing how I knew—would take me to La Soltera. Right would take me back to Austin.

Someone came up behind me, finally honked, and I just turned left. West. Worked my way around to the southwest side of town and started driving toward the Rio Grande Valley.

Ten hours later I crossed the Mexican border at Del Rio, and drove about fifteen miles west of Ciudad Acuna, until I came to a village too small to have a name. I drove through it to a small concrete house about half a mile from the rest. A rusty Pontiac of early seventies vintage was parked in front. A man sat on the car's bumper, smoking a cigarette. He said nothing to me.

I walked up to the front door, and felt La Soltera's power rush through me. She knew everything I'd done, not to mention all the things I'd left undone. A new fear gripped me: What if I walked through the door and she told me to go away, that I had waited too long, destroyed too much of myself, was no longer worth taking on as a student?

My hand shook as I touched the doorknob. I could still walk away, still go back to oblivion.

I turned the knob.

Inside, a woman lay on a day bed, her face flushed and damp. La Soltera sat by the bed, her back to the door.

She did not turn when I came in. "Corinne, please make some ginger tea," she said in English, as if I had just returned from running an errand.

In some ways, I guess I had.

Femina Obscura

Joy Marchand

He was at it again, the man next door, pounding ten-penny nails into the roof of the big black box in his back yard. Yesterday, Wendy had sworn to herself she wouldn't watch him any more through the knothole in the fence. Six days of kneeling and peering had turned her kneecaps permanently purple, and a charley horse had taken to liquefying the muscles of her right calf in the night. So although the sound of the pounding hammer cascaded down her spine to gather in a pool of longing in the curve of her pelvis, Wendy crossed the kitchen, ducked under garlands of drying ginseng and gentian, and closed all the windows to muffle the noise.

Then she returned to the cutting board to finish the day's crop. Her knife flashed, separated leaves from stem, stem from root, a twisted pile of ginseng, growing. Losing herself in the rhythm, she tried to recall a time before the Blooms, before the world had become small enough to observe through a knothole in a fence board. There had been an accounting job once with comforting, nonjudgmental columns of numbers, a puzzle she worked in the Sunday paper, a jade green sedan with good tires and a decent radio. All these things had once distracted her from the mirror, and a plainness of countenance that bordered on invisibility.

Until the Blooms had moved into the bungalow next door, with the clattering of easels, the rustling of canvas, and turpentine smells drifting over the fence and in through Wendy's kitchen windows. And then Mrs. Bloom, sitting for a portrait in Mr. Bloom's attic studio, all pale white shoulders and crackling black hair.

At that moment, things had gone sideways for Wendy, time had slithered around her, and when she looked up next, all that was left of her old life was an unemployment check and the occasional irritated phone call from her sister Pam, who'd made it clear she thought Wendy had gone mad. Pam didn't like the empty house, and couldn't understand why Wendy had shoved all her furniture in the basement, had covered all the mirrors in the house with black linen drapes.

A distraction? Pam, wiping frosting from Brandon's chubby little hands during their last and final visit. *How can a table and chairs be a distraction? A distraction from what? Wen, you're scaring me. And why do you keep looking outside?*

A wen was a fatty cyst, but Pammy didn't mean it that way.

Still, it hurt.

Brushing the thought aside, Wendy finished stringing up the ginseng, took three aspirin for her aching knees, and curled up in a ball on her bedroom floor. Against her will, she could see the big black box etched on the insides of her eyelids. All six sides were made of plywood, lacquered black with spray paint; brushed nickel hinges on the narrow door; cut glass doorknob, purple in the sunlight. Thick weather stripping tacked around the doorframe to keep out the light. And the flat roof, the penultimate feature, going up now, from the sound of it.

Thud thud thud. Pause. *Thud thud thud.*

Then the pinhole, done with a hand-held drill. He'd do it last, probably, when he was ready to go inside.

It had taken her some time to convince the museum people to let her volunteer at the hospitality table for Nathaniel Bloom's show, but no one else had wanted to baby-sit the bilious punch and stale cookies. So trying not to look at Wendy too closely

(...*God, I've never seen eyes with no color before. Has she ever gone out in the sun do you think? Does anyone have a lipliner? Give the poor woman a mouth, for God's sake. If he sees her, Victor's gonna kill me...*)

The desperate PR lades had given her a volunteer badge and told her to stay away from the patrons, if at all possible. To keep her head down. Not to smile, God no. That might be worse than no expression at all. And Wendy would have done anything they asked. Anything at all. She'd sit behind a card table in her two-dollar flats and her pilly cardigan sweater, measuring out punch that was supposed to be limeade but instead tasted fake Life Saver green. She'd offer people cookies even roaches wouldn't eat, avert her eyes, cover her alarmingly bland face with her alarmingly bland hair.

All for the sight of Nathaniel Bloom, hovering next to his installation with Mrs. Bloom beside him, a pair of elegant, fluttering ravens, magnificent with their long, dark hair and billowing knee-length coats. The two of them were everything Wendy wasn't: sharp, flashing, incessant. And although she'd been maneuvering for months to catch a glimpse of them in their element, Wendy would never for a moment have conceived of interacting with them, had Nathaniel not approached the table for a cup of fake green.

Red alert. Heart failure. Hide.

Wendy looked off to the side as Nathaniel made his selection from the cups that she'd arranged in orderly rows on the folding table. Each cup had been filled to precisely the same level, close enough for eyedropper work, but Nathaniel took his time, reflecting on each one. "You're my neighbor," he said, finally selecting the cup closest to her hand. "You grow ginseng and gentian in your back yard. Ginseng and gentian are all about sex and power, especially drunk in a tea. Did you know that?" He leaned over the table, and whispered into her ear. "I've been watching you on your side of the fence, and you've been watching me on mine. I recognize your eye."

It was too much.

Wendy's hands began to twist together in her lap and her legs knocked against the card table, threatening to spill everything.

Invisible, invisible, wasn't she supposed to be invisible?

The aspirin helped more than she'd hoped.

Wendy tried not to get splinters in her nose and chin as she hunkered down and aligned her eye with the knothole in the graying pine fence. There was a sudden spicy tang in the air and only then did Wendy appreciate how fiercely her knees were crushing the ginseng and gentian plants that grew in stately rows in the flowerbed. She might have been more careful, once upon a time, but not with Nathaniel standing just on the other side of the fence with the drill dangling from his hand. And certainly not once he started working, with the lean muscles of his shoulders flexing, his arm cranking the drill, bright curls of wood spooling from the black wall, the hitch-gasp of his breathing parting the heat of the afternoon.

A warm trickle inside her body answered, and a new fragrance, Wendy's own sharp smell, mingled with the scent of bruised ginseng.

When the drill bit broke through the wall, Nathaniel gasped in relief and knuckled wisps of wet black hair out of his eyes. He poked a long finger into the hole, cleared it of splinters, and set a tiny lens into the new aperture, tapping it into place with the knob at the end of the drill. Then he looked over his shoulder at the fence, at the knothole where Wendy's eye shone through, likely beady and bloodshot from lack of sleep, and with the drill under one arm, he slipped a hand beneath his shirt to stroke his flat belly.

"I know there's something inside of you, Wendy," he said. "I can hear it crying in the night. Something's scratching at your spine." He smiled then, dark and light, eyes like embers. "Here's your chance to see what it is."

And with wood shavings in his shaggy black hair, Nathaniel packed up the drill and kicked a wooden brace loose from the base of the black box with the pointed toe of his boot.

The construction rotated then, just a little, with the heavy sound of ball bearings rushing out from under the floorboards.

There was a tangle of dark hair at the knothole, and a green eye, peering at her. "We're waiting for you, love."

Wendy had kept her eyes on the rippling meniscus of fake green in the punch bowl, burying her perception in its undulant motion until Nathaniel Bloom had finally moved away from the table, heaving a breath that sounded like a sigh, even to Wendy, untrained in the subtleties of human exhalation.

When he achieved minimum safe distance, she caught her breath.

Invisible once more.

Nathaniel gave the plastic cup over to the missus, bent his forehead to hers, was bourn away laughing, on a tide of art critics, each intent on an exclusive interview. Then Mrs. Bloom turned and followed the swarm, a witch's familiar, weaving back and forth in Nathaniel's shadow. Her skin shone argent in the soft museum light, and her narrow lips were the color of claret, like blood on the moon, her black leather slippers shushing against the marble floor. Mrs. Bloom was work of art on ghost feet, lithe and elegant, a wand of dark fire.

It hurt to look at her.

The moment the Blooms passed out of sight, Wendy slipped away from the table and shuffled to Nathaniel's installation, where she stood trembling, trying not to gawk at the oily surface of the great black box, which stood gaping open like the cave at Delphi, the narrow door propped open in dreadful welcome. It was cordoned off with velvet rope and partially encircled by a collection of curious objects: a dressmaker's dummy dressed in rags, a peeling carousel horse with green gems for eyes, a seatless chair wrapped with razor wire, a freestanding door, its fractal iron hinges attaching it to nothing at all.

There was a placard with a diagram propped nearby on a brass stand. It read:

Camera Obscura
Take a spin. Step in.
Take a look inside yourself.

Petrified, but pulled forth by the echo of Nathaniel's deep sigh, Wendy touched the edge of the black box, took a deep breath and gave it a shove.

The camera rotated for a few moments, with a slow *whump, whump, whump,* and then came to a stop with the lens aperture facing the detached door.

Black. Blank. Waiting.

All the hair on her arms was standing on end and her sore knees were wet from kneeling in the soft soil of the flowerbed. Huddled in the downstairs bathroom, Wendy hoped she hadn't screamed, seeing Nathaniel's eye in the knothole, but her throat was sore, so she couldn't be sure that she hadn't. To ease this new pain, she fumbled at the medicine cabinet, only to dislodge the black linen drape and fall victim to the horror of her own reflection. Not hideous, no. Perhaps that would be preferable to mouth, nose, eyes, forehead, cheeks, somehow just not there. An assemblage so nondescript, it nearly wasn't there at all. No shadows, no hue, no tone.

With a shriek, Wendy quit the bathroom and staggered across the downstairs to huddle in the sunroom, ducking under festoons of drying roots, to wrap herself around the telephone like a lizard around a warm rock. She put a hand on the receiver, contemplated calling Pam. Ran through the conversation in her head. What would she say? *I've got it under control, Pammy. I'll get a new job tomorrow. I'll move everything back out of the basement. I still have Brandon's Matchbox cars. Tell me you'll come. Please, I need ... I need another chance. You just don't know how hard it is to walk around in the world with no reflection.*

What? How can you understand? You're a Pamela, not a Wen. You walk into a room and people see you, Pammy. You don't get handed other people's empty drinks at cocktail parties, and called Girl. Girl, will you get my coat? Girl, will you pass me the canapés? Girl ...

Wendy took her hand off the receiver.

After a while, she put the phone in the basement too.

And the grass was cool on her bare feet as she moved across the lawn and into the flowerbed. Instead of kneeling in the ginseng and gentian, she poked her head over the fence and traded a startled breath with Nathaniel, who'd been waiting for her in the dusk.

The camera was not overly large, perhaps seven feet on a side, but it loomed, vast and monolithic. It smelt of turpentine and glue, paint and wood sap. A new coffin smell, perhaps, to one who'd never smelled such a thing.

I've been watching you, Nathaniel had said. *And you've been watching me.*

Something curled in her stomach, blown to life by his words.

By a single, terrifying moment of visibility.

Wendy stepped into the camera and shut the door behind her, a little worried that it would latch behind her and no one would take note of her absence until the smell of her death drew rats. But she forgot her fear, forgot everything, when she caught sight of the black oblong on the whitewashed wall of the camera. It was the freestanding door, clear and crisp, reflected in a pool of blinding white light opposite the lens aperture. The door, in all its glory, but upside down, the cut glass knob a bit too high, the small panels on the bottom, the large panels on the top.

The door. Black door. Blank door.

As a reflection of herself, Wendy expected there to be nothing behind the door. She expected it to be as blank within as it was blank without.

But there was something there, scratching, tapping. The image on the wall was motionless, but still something wriggled behind it, growing.

A shudder wracked Wendy from the heels of her shoes to the tips of her hair. Her nipples were adamantine against the fibers of her pilly cardigan sweater. Her knees went soft and elastic, her hips thrust forward, once, twice, a third time.

An orgasm. Rippling. Her first.

With Nathaniel's breath still warm in her mouth, Wendy bent to the flowerbed and clawed up a handful of roots, gentian and ginseng, fragrant and sharp. She struck them against her hip to shake the dirt off, then climbed over the fence with the roots in her teeth. Nathaniel helped her climb over, guiding her in the half-light, and set her on the wet lawn next to the camera. It towered, loomed, its surfaces black velveteen.

"It's beautiful," said Wendy, reaching out to stroke the rough wood.

"I built it for you," he answered, then tugged the dirty roots from her trembling fingers. "I've got a kettle inside. You'll want a cup of tea before you go in."

He looked right at her. He saw her lying in the grass next to the camera. It was eerie, as if she'd accidentally swapped bodies with someone else. Someone real.

"What about Mrs. Bloom?" she said. "Won't she wonder what we're doing out here?" Then hearing herself, she caught a desperate breath, grasped the earth to keep from falling into the sky. "What are we doing out here, Nathaniel? What am I out here to see?"

"Mrs. Bloom?" he said. "That's what you call her? It's not like that between us." Nathaniel hefted the roots. "She'll bring us the tea."

Then he slipped away, his footsteps soft on the grass. He called back. "You're here to see what's inside. You've absorbed too much light. It's time to let it out."

Wendy had stumbled out of the camera in moist disarray, scraping herself on the unfinished edge of the door. The thin skin under her breasts was thrumming, and there was an unfamiliar slickness to her stride, an alarming rolling in her hips, as she fled the gallery to seek refuge in the ladies' restroom.

Cold tile, chilly porcelain against the palms of her hands, the smell of ammonia, and then her face in the mirror, broad, white, blank. It was still the face of Wendy, even though her body remembered differently, remembered standing in the dark camera, full of black lightning. Something unnamed tapping patterns behind the door.

The door, upside-down.

Something of Wendy was behind the image, she was sure of it. The same thing that was tucked against the curve of her spine, hot tongue wrapped around her womb, a humid sigh against her cervix.

All at once, the reflections in the bathroom mirror were too complicated, water droplets in a semi-circular corona above each basin, the checkerboard pattern of tile and grout all around her, the stall doors, too many of them, all in a line, but each door canted at a different angle. With a cry, Wendy elbowed her way into a stall and shut the door with a bang, closed her eyes, summoned the whitewashed walls of the camera, empty but for the image of the freestanding door.

And behind the door, trapped light, burgeoning, warping the wood outward.

There was no room in her thoughts for anything else. Just the image burned on her retinas, the hand clasped on her breast, the other plumbing the oily depths between her legs. Black box, open.

An orgasm. Rippling. Her second.

Her third. Sensation, ad infinitum, tearing her limb from limb.

Wendy held herself and wept.

And then there was light, great streaming beams of it, putting stars in Wendy's eyes, which had grown accustomed to the dusk. She threw her arm up to shade her eyes, and heard footsteps in the grass.

"We need the light to get an image." Nathaniel's hands on her wrists. "Sunlight works, but these floods are best. Makes a good sharp reflection, bright light and deep shadows. Just the thing for discoveries like yours."

Wendy levered herself to her feet, blinked up at the camera. Her eyes adjusted.

Mrs. Bloom was beside her, with a mug of tea in one hand and a roll of canvas in the other. Something clinked inside. Like a dark handmaiden, Mrs. Bloom offered her the tea. "Be careful. It's hot." Bare twist of a smile.

After a moment's hesitation, Wendy took the cup and drank.

Lips anointed with ginseng and gentian, she stepped into the camera with Mrs. Bloom close behind, and the world began to tip with the construct's rotation. The sound of breathing in the enclosed space, the chemical smells, the press of bodies around her—Nathaniel in front, Mrs. Bloom behind—everything made her lightheaded and frightened. There was a clink, the rustle of unrolling canvas, a knife in Nathaniel's hand, flashing in the strip of light streaming through the open door. Then the sound of fabric parting, cool metal on Wendy's skin, and then too much air around her body, legs, stomach, breasts, shoulders.

Adrift, Wendy clutched Nathaniel to keep herself upright, felt Mrs. Bloom steady her from behind.

"Easy," said Nathaniel, slipping something small into her hand. It was smooth, flat, rounded. A lens. The light coming through the open door put a glint in Nathaniel's hair. His eyes, obsidian. A question. "Are you ready to see what's inside you?"

Then Wendy knew why she was there, and instead of being frightened, she was just relieved. "Give me the knife," she said. "And we'll see what's inside of me." Bile, purple-black organs, blood and intestines. If they wanted her to spill them all onto the floor of the camera, she would. To repay them for *seeing* her before she died.

Her. Wendy.

"No, my love."

Nathaniel settled on his knees before her, resting the tip of the knife blade in the hollow of Wendy's throat. He drew it gently down her breastbone and over her belly, where he laid it to rest, placing her hands over it to keep it in place. Then he stood and shrugged out of his shirt, unbuttoned his jeans, showed Wendy the scar that ran the length of his own body from throat to groin. Just above his tangled thatch of pubic hair was a twisted flower of scar tissue. "My pinhole," he said, touching it. "And my image."

Mrs. Bloom stepped into the light, her hair crackling with static.

Nathaniel gathered Mrs. Bloom close, raised her blouse, and ran a hand over her featureless belly. He pressed his forehead into her silver cheek and their skin began to ripple, to open to merge. When Nathaniel pulled away and brushed her aside, his lips were the color of garnets, blood on the surface of the moon.

Something fluttered inside Wendy, flexed.

Her image, stretching. She had to see it, had to touch it.

Now.

Holding the lens between her teeth, Wendy gripped the hilt of the heavy knife in one hand and stretched the skin just below her navel with the other. She took three sharp breaths, sliced. There was pain and blood, and the dreadful wrenching twist of her flesh embracing the lens, and then Nathaniel was behind her, propping her up. Mrs. Bloom flying out of the camera, slamming the door, the aperture open and ...

The black oblong, in a flood of light against the far wall of the camera.

Wendy shoved aside the pain, spat in her hand and wiped the lens over her womb clear of blood. Felt the image of the door slam into her spine, the sensation of something unfurling within her, stretching, shoving her organs aside to make room for roots, leaves, the curl of a stem. No order, no organization. Just intense joy, and pressure, hands along her ribcage, feet cradled in her pelvis, a shoulder, straining against her breastbone, crying out for the knife.

"My love," whispered Nathaniel. "My invisible love, absorbing the light of the world and never letting a single photon escape. The light of a lifetime, just waiting to be born." He pressed his face into her neck, breathing her ginseng and gentian, crushed root smell. "You'll be a work of art."

She pressed into his embrace as her hips began to thrust, brought the blade of the knife to bear on the hollow of her throat. There was something behind the door, the real Wendy, scrabbling to get out.

Not a just a work of art, but a masterpiece.

Her first.

The Green Wall

Robert Freeman Wexler

Erickson had not been sleeping well. For ten days every September, the Italian street festival engulfed his lower Manhattan neighborhood, block after block filled with food vendors and carnival games. Drunken tourists gathered to sing themes from gangster movies. After midnight the noise faded, but the stench of beer, onions, and greasy sausage remained, permeating his sixth floor apartment. He would lie in bed, unable to eradicate images of the crowds that had flowed under his windows like herds of braying goats, and when he did sleep, the sausage invaded his dreams, leaving him with mental indigestion. But Wednesday morning, a rain forest, green and overpowering, appeared on the brick wall opposite his windows.

His apartment was a two room tenement at Grand and Mulberry. Every morning, before going to his job at the Rezinsky Gallery on Spring Street, he would wash and dress while his coffee brewed, then drink it on the sofa, watching the play of sunlight and shadows on the brick wall. Sometimes he would read a book or finish the previous day's newspaper.

Now the wall had become a giant movie screen, displaying a shadowy jungle filled with hidden dangers and undiscovered beauty. Monkeys danced through the foliage. An endless snake flowed down a branch. The projection had to be part of the festival, though he couldn't imagine how the jungle had any connection to the patron saint of Naples. The scene appeared so real that he cringed when the snake whipped across the branch to trap one of the monkeys. The sound, if there was any, didn't reach him through the glass.

Forests, camping, outdoor activity, had never interested him. City- (or at least suburban-) born, his pursuits took an inward turn, art, books, and food. Of sports, boxing drew him the most; of course, it was primarily a sport of the city, and performed indoors. But something about the canvas of green in front of him stirred unexpected desires. Its shadows beckoned him like visions of past selves.

On his way down the stairs he met Mrs. Venturi, carrying a loaf of bread. A widow somewhere in her sixties who never smiled, she lived two floors directly below his apartment. Though he had often carried her grocery bags up the stairs, he never knew what to say when they met.

"Carlo," she said as he passed her. Unable to pronounce his first name, she approximated. "It's hard, Carlo. People out there, no room."

"I know, I know." Erickson looked away from her pained expression and continued down. Even the Italians in his building hated the festival. Few Italians actually remained in the neighborhood, an aging population unable or unwilling to flee to the suburbs. Although Little Italy (now little more than a few blocks of Mulberry) always conveyed an aspect of festival, luring weekend visitors to the bland array of restaurants and cigar and souvenir shops, this ten-day period was worse than all the rest of the year combined.

The street door was on the opposite side of the building from the green wall, and as Erickson trudged toward it, he could see through the glass that the tourists had already begun the day's inundation of his street.

Once outside, he squeezed around a booth selling Italian pastry and took the shortest route away from the neighborhood. By the time he reached the gallery he had forgotten about the green wall jungle film. He unlocked the door and walked through the upstairs exhibition space and down the stairs to the office. Each day amplified his revulsion for the job. The owner, Hannah Rezinsky, was often drunk and insulting. The chaotic way she ran the gallery, the never-ending contradictory orders, wore him down. Without the art, he could never have lasted. Eight years now. He had taken the job a month after withdrawing from his art history Ph.D. program.

Erickson turned on the computer and sat. Beside the monitor, the telephone answering machine blinked. The first message was from Rezinsky.

"Won't be in till twelve thirty. You finish the letter to Michelson, do the press releases for the Joss, Nevill, and Camelminder show, and pack up von

Sem's...."

He turned down the volume on her harsh voice. The festival had left his nerves jagged, and this grace period relieved him. Having to deal with her so early would have been too demoralizing. Once...but there was little point thinking about that. Here he was, and if he wanted to change his situation, move to a more congenial place—if such a place existed—he would have to work to find it. Resume, letters, hope...possibly leaving the city, but he loved the city, its flux of life and clashing cultures, even loved his apartment when the festival wasn't invading the landscape.

The second message drew him from his reverie, the voice of an unknown woman. With the volume low, her words sounded like the hum of beating wings. He couldn't understand anything she said, but the tone of the voice thrilled him.

During the first two hours only one person visited the gallery. Per Rezinsky's orders, Erickson wrote the press release and designed an ad for the show. At noon, the phone rang—Rezinsky, telling him she wouldn't be in till after two. He sat at the front desk and leafed through the newspaper. An article in the science section explained the climactic changes in the last ice age. Another described a hallucinogenic orchid found recently in the rain forests of New Guinea. The author quoted a botanist, the discoverer of the orchid, who talked of vast possibilities from yet-to-be-found rain forest plants. Like Erickson's green wall forest—what lay hidden inside its mat of vegetation?

The door opened and a woman in a green overcoat—tall with a gliding walk—led a line of five girls in similar coats. The children's ages ranged from about five to twelve, and they walked in order of height, tallest to shortest. Was the woman their mother? Guardian? He enjoyed speculating about gallery patrons. These didn't look like the usual visitors. Probably filming a television commercial outside, or shooting a fashion spread. The neighborhood around the gallery attracted fashion models, though they never came in. He often saw them in the cafés, eating their miniscule portions of food on oversized plates. She had that look, the high cheekbones and underfed face. The children were obviously her props. Erickson smiled a greeting at her, but she never looked his way.

The current show featured two artists—a painter and a sculptor. In the front half of the gallery, mounted on four-foot-high pedestals, Jacob Lerner's sculptures, curved and twisted bronze rods welded together at odd angles, like cages, or the skeletons of bizarre animals. Paintings hung in the rear of the gallery, with a partition dividing the space. More paintings hung in the basement, giant abstracts made up of lines and patches of color, like a landscape viewed from an airplane. The woman pointed at one of the sculptures; the children grouped around her. He should ask them to sign the guestbook. The woman's name would be something musical, like Annabelle.

The woman and four of the girls walked to the back; the smallest remained. She began climbing one of the pedestals.

"You can't climb on that," Erickson said. The girl ignored him. He got up. "Young lady," he said more loudly, "you must not climb on that."

With simian ease, the girl scrambled up the pedestal before he finished the sentence. She stood on top, squealing with pleasure. "I need to get you down from there now." When he put his hands around her waist to lift her off, she gripped one of the bronze rods and started screaming.

"What are you doing to her?" the woman said from across the pedestal, startling Erickson, who hadn't seen her return to the front room. He let go of the girl, who hopped into the middle of the sculpture and clapped her hands. The woman moved between him and the pedestal; she was a couple of inches taller than he. Thinking she might push him, he stepped back.

"The girl can't climb up there," he said weakly. "She might get hurt."

"You shouldn't leave dangerous objects out in the open."

The woman stepped closer, and he backed toward the desk, stopping when he felt the edge against his thighs. She stopped too, a few feet away, as though waiting for him to say something. Her face showed no emotion. Her arms remained at her sides, relaxed, hands unclenched, and she spoke with the relaxed manner of an art history lecturer. He looked at her green eyes, a green so brilliant he thought their intensity had to be caused by a reflection of the light on her coat. A sudden desire to put his hands on her waist and kiss her possessed him.

"I'm sorry," he said. He looked away, afraid she would sense his thought. "But this is an art gallery. Shouldn't you tell her not to touch the art?"

The woman turned around. A clip in the shape of a monkey's head tied her hair in back.

"Come down from there Cedilla, we're leaving."

The girl jumped into the woman's arms, and the other girls followed her out.

Two hours later, Hannah Rezinsky stumbled into the gallery smelling like a winery. Erickson sat at the front desk. She leaned her face too close to his. "Look at you, you don't even shave," she said, slurring the words. The press releases lay on the desk; she berated him for not mailing them. He tried to explain that mailing them was impossible unless he either closed the gallery or found someone to stay there while he was gone. But she wouldn't listen.

Having cowed him sufficiently, she plodded downstairs to the office for the rest of the day. A few people came in during the afternoon, and he found himself fantasizing the return of the tall woman, without the children. Alone, talking to her would be easier. He took her sudden appearance as a sign of imminent change, a promise of romance or adventure. He hadn't been involved with anyone since Kari, a former intern at the gallery; their relationship hadn't lasted far beyond her departure.

After work, he planned to go straight home; then he remembered the festival. Between Rezinsky and the festival he had no peace. Likely he would snap at the first fat tourist blocking his door (visitors to the festival often sat on the steps of his building, their reluctance to give way likely caused by their belief that no one lived there, the whole area having been set up as a massive Italian-kitsch theme park for their entertainment). He turned and walked uptown, angling eastward, thinking he would stop at St. Marks Books to see if his friend Jeremy wanted to get some dinner.

Rezinsky's gallery hadn't always been such a desperate place. When he started working there, she employed a full staff: director, assistant director, receptionist, interns. During his interview, he had fallen so in love with the paintings on exhibit that he had thought it charming when Rezinsky, before even hiring him, sent him eight blocks away to Chinatown, to buy shrimp for a party she was giving that night. But years passed. People left. Now she ran the place in her drunken, indiscriminate way, treating Erickson as hapless tool. He should quit. But where would he go--another gallery, another Rezinsky?

St. Mark's Books appeared ahead, but the man at the cash register told him that Jeremy had left early. Erickson wished he had made plans for the evening, but the festival numbed him, kept him from thinking beyond the moment. He needed to start carrying his address book—to do something with a friend tonight would mean plowing a furrow to his building, carrying himself up to the sixth floor to call, down again through the suffocating crowd, then eventually home to the same.

He selected a book and carried it to the register. "Jeremy gives me his employee discount," Erickson said. The man nodded and rang it up.

East then on 6th Street, to one of the Indian restaurants, where he sat with beer, matar paneer, and book. At the next table a woman kept leaning across to kiss her companion. Their happy talk irritated him. He hadn't felt so alone in years. So hard to meet people in this harsh city, and without anyone else at work to help him share the daily burden of Rezinsky, he found himself speaking less and less to the friends he did have, not wanting to bore them with his constant, disgruntled talk.

He would have to convince Rezinsky to let him find one or two interns to help him. It had been six months or so since the last one left. Rezinsky liked interns. They cost her nothing. But there had been problems—the last had complained to his dean about Rezinsky forcing him to act as a waiter at one of her parties, and it was doubtful that the school would allow anyone else to intern with her. Fortunately, there were other schools, both in the city and the outlying areas, and if nothing else about the gallery was attractive, some of her artists still meant something.

Erickson returned to his apartment and went straight to bed. Night sausage-dream entwined with the green wall, liana-wrapped trunks and branches shooting skyward, burning sky, but his shaky flight couldn't bring him above the treetops. Leaves slapped him. Frantic straining against their pull, against gravity, against the drowning silence of the trees, shelter and swelter, airless dank humid creatures pulling him to the forest floor. He woke shivering. On the television, sitcom reruns, then eventual return to sleep.

Morning, with the dream still fresh, the green wall saluted him. He wanted to sit and watch the forest, but he had overslept. He decided to look for books on rain forests, and an errand for Rezinsky in the afternoon gave him enough time to go to the library.

That evening he went directly home to his neighborhood, pushing across Mulberry on Spring and continuing to Elizabeth, then down to Grand, a direction that gave him the least exposure to the festival, which commandeered all of Mulberry from Houston down to Canal but only extended a short way into either side of Grand. And this end of Grand, with its familiar flux of Chinese, helped prepare him for the chaos surrounding his front door. He stopped to pick up dinner at Grand Sausages, a combination Chinese meat market and take-out food counter across Grand Street from his apartment building. One of his favorites, he especially liked to give it his business while the area swarmed with festival-goers, oblivious to anything that wasn't Italian.

He crossed Grand to find his stoop blocked by a seated band of tourists, four across, clutching bags of Italian pastry, hero sandwiches dripping down their wrists, their bulk blocking his way. And none of them moved, not when he mounted the first step, not when he said "excuse me," not when he kicked through them to his door. "People fucking live here," he said, and shut the door behind him.

Safe inside his apartment, he laid his food out on the coffee table and sat, eating and watching the wall. After finishing his dinner he picked up one of the rain forest books.

The sun set, but the film played on, showing a dense jungle night. The racket from the festival distracted him, the constant thrum of talking, yelling, singing. He read about the noises of the forest, for which he would gladly trade, and watched the film as the day creatures gave way to those of the night.

One book said that although rain forests cover less than six percent of the planet's total land surface, three-fourths of the world's plants and animals live in them, and over seventy percent of rain forest life is in the trees.

Erickson woke two hours early the next morning so he would have more time to watch the wall before work. He went downstairs to the Italian Food Center for milk and a loaf of bread. Coming back, he decided to see how the rain forest film looked from outside. A stream of morning festival-goers already trickled past the sausage and souvenir booths. Between his building and the wall of the building with the film stood a one-story restaurant. Erickson stopped in front of the restaurant and looked up at the wall. From the street all he could see was green, a flat green that gave no indication of the forest. No projection equipment, no sign of anything having to do with the jungle film, but once again inside, ensconced in the comfort of his sofa, the forest still played.

He ate bread with cheese and watched the wall. Monkeys as usual, a small, camel-colored variety. Probably marmosets. He hoped they wouldn't become a snake's breakfast. Their prehensile tails told him that the forest was in the western hemisphere. At first he had assumed that the movie played in an endless loop, but realized instead it always showed the same place, as though someone had set up a camera and filmed continuously. Maybe not a film at all, but a live broadcast. He thought of the tall woman from the gallery—her green coat and monkey hairclip. The children were her monkeys. He pictured her below, walking along the forest floor, unafraid of lurking beasts. Green of eyes, green of coat, thick slabs of green leafy forest...she would be at home under the trees, attuned to the strange ways of branch, vine, and creature.

Surprisingly, Rezinsky was already at the gallery when Erickson arrived. Downstairs, he paused in the office door. Rezinsky emerged from the storage closet at the opposite end of the basement. "Where's my passport," she said, her voice an agonized squeal. She clumped toward him, one shoe dangling from her hand. She seemed the forlorn avatar, discontent sweeping from her haggard cheeks. What creatures lurked behind her bloodshot brown eyes? Even at their first meeting, Erickson had sensed the cracks forming in the façade of her absolute control.

"Where's my passport, you dumb-ass?" she said, and leaned against him for support while she re-shod herself.

"If I'm a dumb-ass, how the fuck would I know where to find your passport?" He backed into the office and she slumped against the wall, a more reliable replacement for his shoulder. She froze there, apparently unwilling to risk further movement, while he unlocked the file drawer, reached into the back, and removed her passport. He pushed it into her unresisting hands as he passed on his way to the stairs. Some minutes later, she followed him up. She announced that she would be leaving for London in an hour. He would have to run the gallery alone the rest of the day and all of the following week. To keep him from protesting, she sent him out to the printer's to pick up brochures for the next show, and on his return handed him a list of duties. Then she left.

The afternoon lasted an eternity. No one came in between noon and four. Without Rezinsky there to watch him, he considered closing early and returning to his apartment to watch the forest. How would it feel to touch the tree trunks? Massive dark fertile green—so alien to this city. He had just read that rain forests provide most of the world's oxygen, with the canopy, that dense mass of leaf and branch, being the richest part, full of seething life. According to one book, there was a rain forest in Washington! Forget equatorial swelter--here was a place he might actually be able to visit. The book reprinted a creation myth that said trees gave birth to humans:

> An elder of the Makah told this story. He said it didn't come from his people, but was older, given by the ancients to all who followed.
>
> First came the oceans and the mountains, then the trees and minor plants, then the animals of the forest. Of the trees, the conifers were the greatest, and because they were the greatest of the trees, they were the masters of all. No animal could harm them. But they grew haughty in their power and tried to shut out everything else from their realm.
>
> They covered the sky, and all plants watched by the sun were forced to retreat. The only being strong enough to stop the advancing trees was the mountain, for it was decreed that nothing could cover its head but cloud and snow.
>
> Blocked from advancing to the mountaintops, the trees reached toward the heavens, casting their branches high. They charged tribute to all who would pass, to the sparrows and hawks and marmots and elk. Only the lowly mushroom could defy them, for it needed no sun to fuel its life.
>
> One day the voice of the maker echoed from the branches, foretelling the emergence of a new being, soft of skin but with the power to fell forests. If the trees did not heed this warning, and

cease their arrogant behavior, they would suffer.

The trees laughed. For what soft-skinned creature could harm mighty cedar or hemlock?

Days passed and nothing happened. The trees continued as before. Then one morning, in the densest part of the forest, where lived a fir of girth so great it laughed at the wind, there came a crash and flash, and the clouds parted. Living fire struck the mighty fir's crown, splitting its center. The halves tumbled, flattening the forest for miles, from the mountain to the sea. And from the split stepped a creature, then a second, creatures no plant or animal had ever seen, creatures that walked upright. The first creature was the being we now call woman, and the second, man.

When they emerged from their birth tree, the woman spoke the words of the maker: not until all trees who lived before the birth of woman and man are replaced by their descendents will the trees know peace. The trees will become the slaves of woman and man, will provide them with shelter, means of travel, fire to cook their food, paper to write their words. And so it has been.

Now would be the ideal time for the green-coated woman to reappear. Erickson would question her about the ways of the forest.

Why did Rezinsky keep the gallery open? Few clients came in and fewer bought anything. Obviously this place wasn't her main source of income, but it did serve to form a superficial gloss over her coarseness. She owned rental property, including the building containing the gallery and a Lower East Side tenement rumored to have been her birthplace.

Erickson looked out the window at the street. Plenty of people there, seething life like the rain forest canopy. Why didn't any of *them* come in? Despite Rezinsky's decline, Erickson still believed in her artists and their work, still felt the thrill of hanging a show or viewing a newly-finished painting. But he lacked the energy to change the atmosphere of the place. The draining menace of Rezinsky shaped his life, fetid rot of the forest floor seeping into everything.

No, he *could* do something. Rezinsky's mailing list was right here, on the computer, including contacts at various art history departments. He called them, telling each person or their voicemail that the gallery was seeking interns. Companionship here would help, though he would have to take care with the applicants, prepare them for Rezinsky's abuses.

At five he was about to close when a group of German tourists came in and stayed for half an hour asking him questions about the sculptures. Normally he would have relished the contact, the opportunity to proselytize art, especially Lerner's—his dynamic forms invaded Erickson's blood like a drug—but today the wall dominated all thoughts. As soon as the Germans left, he locked the door and hurried home, alone again amongst the milling hordes.

But stopped in the middle of Mulberry. He had forgotten to cross and go down a less crowded street. Booths occupied the sidewalks, giving the street over to rank upon rank of pedestrians. Sometimes, Erickson would squeeze in between the rear of the booths and the buildings, but obstacles abounded there as well. Now he found himself hemmed into the crowd along the west side of the street. The mass of bodies constricted, giant boa wrapping him tight, suffocating, pressing into his flesh, his psyche. Trapped, panting, he cried, wordless bellow exploding from his constricted lungs, and with the bellow, flailing arms struck out, clearing a space into which he fell. Stillness descended, city noises silenced. Noble trunks stretched skyward, not marred by branch for many yards. Understory of smaller trees and shrubs enclosed him, pressing him to the mulchy forest floor. But soon, footfalls penetrated the silence, drawing closer, and he looked up to an advancing herd of brown, droopy-snouted creatures snuffling stamping, their stench reaching him before their hoofs. They kicked and trampled him, taking their usual watering path as though he didn't exist. With the jabbing pain of their hooves the ground beneath him returned to pavement, a pavement traversed by hordes of festival-goers, who parted to allow his still-flailing arms space while he struggled to his feet, but otherwise gave him no attention whatsoever.

His body ached. Home, he opened the hot tap of his claw-foot bathtub, which occupied the space in his kitchen between sink and toilet-closet. Soaking in the tub drew out his tension, soothed the bruises along his thighs and torso. For a moment, he had been there, free in the forest; he longed to return.

Alone, always alone, he reheated leftovers from yesterday's Chinese take-out. But not alone, not entirely. He had friends; not in the cascading numbers of times past, but still, he should call some, share with them the glories of the green wall. Andrew, constant vessel of good will; the Quail and Erika (who had once worked for Rezinsky, but no longer, moved on to MOMA, lucky bitch), and others, but a peculiar hesitation overcame him and his phone remained cloaked with inactivity.

The rest of the evening he sat, entranced by the swaying branches and hanging vines, the birds with their colorful feathers. How did the projection achieve such depth and clarity? Tree trunks stood out in such detail it was as if he gazed at a real forest. The greenest parrot he had ever seen sat on a branch. It stretched its wings, then flew toward him.

If he could reach the wall, he would be able to touch the trees.

He slept on the couch, waking to another rain forest morning.

Saturdays, the gallery opened an hour and a half later, giving him more time with the wall. A light rain fell on the street, but the forest looked dry. He noticed an open space at the base of the trees. The forest's floor was even with the rooftop below him. He opened the window, took off the screen, and leaned out. A faint path led from the edge of the scene into the trees.

Of course—that was where they had set up the camera. There must be a clearing. Where did the path lead? Into the brick, into the green wall, into the next building, the next world, the next life? He pictured himself among the trees, walking with the tall woman from the gallery. She would whisper forest secrets to his starving ear.

The festival would end tomorrow.

At four o'clock Monday morning the crash of booths being ripped apart would wake him. And the green wall would be gone. He would miss the forest, miss the purpose the dark trees gave him. He couldn't allow the end to come without an attempt to get closer, as if touching the wall on which the film projected would reveal the answers. In the shower, he thought about ways to get down to the roof of the neighboring building to see the forest from its ground level. A ladder wouldn't reach. A rope maybe. But his apartment was so high--a long way to climb down a rope. One of his rain forest books described scientists who used mountaineering gear when doing canopy studies.

He sat on the sofa with the phone book and a pad of paper and called a store that sold camping and climbing equipment. He told the woman at the store he was writing an article for a journalism class. With her help, he made a list of the necessary equipment.

1. 150 feet of 11 millimeter static rope
2. climbing harness
3. 6 yards of nylon webbing
4. two prusick devices for ascending
5. a figure eight for descending
6. carabiners
7. gloves

After work, he would go and buy everything. Sunday, his day off, he would use the equipment to climb down. He sighed, not wanting to leave the wall. But he had to get to work. It was still raining outside, and the temperature had dropped. Too bad the skies had remained sunny during the bulk of the festival. A few days like this would have kept the tourists away. He hated walking to work in the rain. Forget the gallery—the damn place could stay closed today. That would teach Rezinsky to treat him so poorly. He felt suddenly powerful. The store that he had called was down near city hall. If he had to go out in the rain, let it be for something *he* wanted.

Back in the apartment, Erickson spread everything out on the floor. The pile confused him: nylon webbing (green of course, to go with the forest), rope, ascending devices (two metal gadgets with pulleys and a locking mechanism). Along with the equipment, he had bought a book that showed everything—how to make a chest harness out of webbing, how to tie all the necessary knots...but the task was hopeless—he would never get it all put together.

He opened the window, removed the screen, and looked out, reassuring himself that his plan would work.

Concentrate on the book then—he held an end of the stiff rope over the diagram, as if he could will the rope into the required shape. He formed a loop, but the result looked nothing like the book's example. He tried again and again, frustration building with each failure. After another attempt he flung the rope away and leaned his head on the sofa's armrest.

But he forced himself to resume, again fumbling with the unfamiliar materials, eventually working with increased assurance. Perfecting the knot took him another hour. He looked around the living room for a place to tie the rope. The book said that a rope should always have two secure anchors, but he couldn't think of anything besides the radiator.

Already four o'clock. His legs felt stiff from sitting on the floor. He hadn't eaten since morning. But he had to try today. The forest might soon be gone. He wished it was drier; the drizzle had stopped, but moisture clung to the wall of his building.

On to the chest harness then: create a loop with the webbing (securing the ends with something called a water knot—surely that was too soft a name for something meant to support a person's weight!), and twist the loop to form an eight...and and...what was this for? Going up? The other system was for down. Down was all that mattered. The roof below him was only one floor up from the street. He could easily get down the rest of the way and return to his apartment by the stairs.

He picked up his rappelling device, called a figure eight for its shape, and stared at the dull metal surface. It looked too small to support him. The rope went through the larger hole, then over the end that clipped to his harness.

Though the woman at the store had shown him how to put on his seat harness, it took a while for Erickson to sort out the confusion of straps and buckles, slip his legs through the correct loops, and secure everything.

He pushed the rope out the window, watching its snakelike fall. When rappelling into the unknown, the book said, always go down with your ascending gear ready in the event that you have to go up unexpectedly, but the articles of ascent remained scattered across his floor. He stepped onto a chair, then to the window sill, and ducked his head. Once standing outside on the sill, he glanced down. The rooftop looked farther than he had thought. He was supposed to control his speed by pressing the rope between right hand and thigh. The window sill was similar to the protruding edge of a cliff. The book said the hardest part was getting over the edge. You had to ease yourself down until the rope rested secure. If you stepped off you would fall a couple of feet; when the rope caught the edge you would slam into the cliff (or building, in his case).

Someone was supposed to stand at the bottom and hold the rope—

belaying, as it was called. If the person coming down slipped, the belayer would stop them by pulling the rope taut.

Erickson slid his right foot off the window sill and onto the wall, testing the slickness of the damp brick. He held the rope tight against his thigh, then let the rope slide a little. The slithering rope burned his hand. Gloves? On the floor, mixed in with the unused ascending gear. He squeezed, stopping his descent a few feet below his window.

His fingers soon cramped from the grip. He couldn't keep holding the rope so tight. The book had made everything seem simple. He had been a fool to try. He lowered himself to the sill of the floor below his and leaned against the window. There was just enough room to stand with his feet sideways. Resting on something solid relieved him, but his hands were shaking. He tried to relax his fingers. The glass felt cold on his cheek--he wondered if anyone was inside. Blinds covered the windows. How could anyone close their blinds to the glorious sight of the green wall?

He turned his head enough to see the trees. From a branch, a monkey stared across at him. Another joined it. He waved to them with his free hand. Their grunting barks made him smile. If he went down slowly, he wouldn't need his gloves.

A fevered wind blew through the chill September air. The musky forest smells filled his lungs. He would swing through the branches with the monkeys, walk among the hoary trunks. A blue and red bird flew from a branch to alight on a nearby windowsill; it examined Erickson first with one eye, then the other.

Determined to continue, Erickson stepped off the sill and walked his way down the wall. The next room down belonged to Mrs. Venturi. If he had worn his gloves, he might have tried pushing off from the wall and letting out rope until he was past her window, but with hands bare he couldn't risk it. He would have to place his feet with care on the window frame, avoiding the glass.

A shriek sounded from inside and something struck his legs. Keeping his right hand on the rope, he swung his left down to protect himself. Mrs. Venturi shouted something in Italian. He tried to move away from the window but his foot slipped, and he pendulumed back toward the glass. Mrs. Venturi, nude from the waist up, stood in the open window. She rammed an umbrella into his stomach. He screamed and let go of the rope.

The rope whipped through the figure eight. He grabbed at it, letting it burn his hand, trying to slow his descent. Mrs. Venturi continued to wave the umbrella and yell, as he plunged, speed unchecked.

Adrift, motionless, eyes filled with deafening silence. A dark glow cradled him. Warm and cold, and the rain filled his mouth. As he drank he wept. So hot near the wall, heat of the forest pushing out, pulling him in. Trees surrounded him, mute with expectation. Contours of sound seeped from the air, unexpected bursts scented with spice, with a rainbow shower of green. Dark layers of rain forest earth beneath his cheek contained universes, pyramids of light and color. The far-off walls of his building, the dangling rope, Rezinsky, all receded like an unnecessary dream.

He smiled up at the tall woman from the gallery. Around her, the air shaped itself into a violet-tinged corridor. She lifted him, holding him gently in her powerful arms. The fibers of her green coat swelled and hardened, re-aligned themselves, forming a cradle to support him. Now she returned his smile, her expression broad as the city. The sky called. Higher she lifted him, bark and branch extending, but part of him remained below, penetrating the roof of the building, pushing downward. Finding soil, his stiffening toes dug deep.

She cast him loose, and he stood beside her, branches reaching out toward each other but never touching.

Among the Ruins

Forrest Aguirre

Pilgrims lined the roads leading to Montfaucon. Germans dressed in gray from the east, dark green uniformed French from the southwest, and olive-clad Americans from the northwest. They prostrated themselves for miles in rays extending out into the countryside, no doubt all headed for the old church of Montfaucon, there to witness the holy relic enshrined therein, Esquiu de Floyran's "Epistle to the Demon-advisor of Pope Boniface." But the pilgrims moved slowly—a wind-rustled collar here, a worm-full of flesh there, perhaps even a slow sinking of an entire body into the mud. It seemed quite clear that they would not reach their destination soon and, if at all, they surely would not arrive as currently constituted as they lay on the moon-like landscape of the bullet- and shrapnel-riddled roadsides.

The flies, on the other hand, were agitated by the smoke that philtered up from ruined buildings and bodies, like some grand alchemical experiment: bones to lead to gold. But any search for a philosopher's stone would be in vain. The rubble-strewn landscape provided too many decoys, a camouflage too daunting even for Hermes Trismegistus himself to divine through.

The village, in its artillery-induced squalor, looked like an archaeological site. Ten thousands of years of disarray and decay, compressed into three days by krupp guns and howitzers. As if the laws of entropy had been accelerated by the hand of God, whose finger thrusts and playful smearings with his toy earth showed as craters and vast fields bereft of life, sterile, as In The Beginning.

The ultimate focus of the pilgrimage, the hilltop church of Montfaucon, was the hub of a vast wheel whose miles-long dirt road spokes extended into the desiccated remains of the once-forests that surrounded the hill. Of course, the most recent building was merely another layer in an accretion of paleolithic flint-chip piles, neolithic shell middens, a bronze-age cletic barrow, a Roman temple, and now, a ruined medieval ribcage of smoking stone walls.

Among the rubble lay the detritus of war—a dented helmet, bullet casings, a shattered rifle and bayonet. De Floyran's letter was nowhere to be found.

As I approached what was once the apse of the church, a flash of white fluttered out from behind one of the few standing sections of gray wall. I raised my rifle, expecting a flag of surrender waved by an injured German soldier, most likely left behind by his retreating comrades who couldn't bear the burden of another casualty on what was becoming the end of their successes. Such surrenders had become common place as our line had advanced toward Luxembourg.

This cloth, however, was not attached to a stick, nor to a rifle, but to a table. And on that pure white tablecloth were four table settings of fine blue and white china and un-tarnished silverware. I squinted for the glare, for the pure clean-ness of the items in the sunlight. Four oaken chairs surrounded the table, one pair occupied by men, one pair by women. They were young and smartly dressed, the men in black tuxedoes and the women in white summer dresses and sun hats, their laced parasols leaning against the table while they daintily enjoyed a meal of soup and quail. I watched them, too stunned by the juxtaposition between the company and the ruins to notice that I was salivating until my spit dribbled down my stubble-infested chin. I removed my helmet and approached the table as a black servant, also in tuxedo, appeared from behind a charred plinth to port away the dirty dishes, replacing the plates and soup bowls with cups and saucers served from a large silver tray. The warm scent of coffee and freshly-toasted bread washed into me, invigorating my senses. I thought I might wake in a wet trench, but the odors instead intensified the clarity of my perceptions, alerting me tot he fact that yes, these were real people having lunch on a real battlefield—no dream.

One of the young men, a long-haired dandy with a curly black mane and smooth, youthful face, turned toward me as I cautiously approached the table. He smiled and nodded.

"Good day," he said in a thick British accent, as cheerfully as if we were old acquaintances who had happened to bump into one another, say, at a fruit market or at the greyhound races. At this the others, an even younger looking red-haired young man and a pair of identical brunette twins turned toward me. One of the women proclaimed in a delighted voice: "Look! We have a visitor!"—Scottish, if I guessed the accent correctly.

The red-haired one took the linen napkin from around his throat and placed it on the table. He scooted his chair back and stood up, holding one hand toward the ground at his side. The servant returned with an armed oaken chair, similar to the ones they sat in, which he placed between the young man and one of the ladies.

"Please, do have a sit, I'm sure you've had a long day of it," he chimed pleasantly then, looking carefully at my uniform, "Mister . . . Corporal . . ." he squinted to see past the caked mud and grime that had become one with my coat, ". . . Brus. Funny, that, a German name on an American uniform."

My thoughts shot back to Milwaukee, to home, where several of my relatives had been arrested and held during the "German scare," then let the thought go in pained silence. I stared at him, suddenly weary as the anticipation I had felt on approaching the table lulled into fatigue and aching joints. I sat heavily in the chair, setting my rifle against the table, next to one of the parasols. It took a few moments before I could form words, my mouth felt as if I had lost all my teeth at once and was trying to push them back into the gums with my dry tongue. Finally, I blurted out: "Where?"

The dandy smiled, then lifted his hand from the table, pointing to the sky with a spoon and nodding at me, as if to say "You know, up there!" But his smile remained unmoving, the words unspoken, but not unheard. The others turned to me and smiled also, but there was something disingenuous about their expressions, a hint of being forced to smile through deep emotional pain.

Finally, one of the twins spoke. "You look weary, my American friend."

The words were like an opening floodgate to catharsis, and the shadowy visions of the last few days pulled me down with the weight of emotion that I had held up during three days of fighting.

Our forward ranks had trenched up outside the village for a week. Most days were spent staring at the tiny rivers that trickled down the trench walls and into our boots, our socks, our food. Raindrops sang a tin song on our helmets, backed by the percussion of artillery shells and the haunting soprano of ricocheting bullets. Then, the artillery crescendoed in an opus of destruction and our commanders called us up from the trench to death or glory.

I ascended from the earth covered in mud, the sucking sounds of my boots, along with the klud of artillery, barely audible in the background of the heartbeat that filled my ears, blood whooshing, keeping time with some vast cosmological clock that ticked off my mortal seconds remaining. Others rose too—Philmore, the Colorado farm-boy; Eggleston, whose wife and son waited in Indiana; Petrosky, the suave debonair from Albany; Jones and Jones, both from Atlanta, cousins, on their mothers' sides. They all rose like ghouls from the wet soil and fell, as corpses, as quickly as they had risen, the animating magic taken from their bodies by bullets and bits of flying stone.

I ran forward, nerves aware, by my head enmeshed in a complex matrix of thought composed of conversational snippets from that morning, all wrought through with the whooshing of my blood in my ears"

". . . so the dogs got him by the arm . . ."

Whoosh!

". . . there's really nothing in Iowa . . ."

Whoosh!

"Cheese? Lucky bastard! Who sent you cheese?"

Whoosh!

"She says he's walking now, but . . ."

I fought within myself, one side of my mind trying to shut out the din of war with my comrades' voices, another chiding for entertaining ridiculous thoughts in such a moment of danger and for using dead men's voices to keep me alive.

This schizophrenic argument lasted until I threw myself up against a stone farmyard wall, the shock of shouldering the barricade coinciding with the mental shock of self-awareness: "I am alive!"

I looked back over the field I had traversed. It was sprinkled with the bodies of the dead or dying, a dozen bumps of mud on an otherwise flat field, mud caked uniforms like freshly-dug grave mounds.

The sharp clan of silverware on crystal cut through my thoughts.

"Corporal Brus," the dandy's voice percolated up over the receding heartbeat in my ears, "it is over. The battle is done." With each word, the memories sloughed into the past. A dream. Ago.

I looped up at them, incredulous, and a bit startled by the quickness with which the pain and memories left me. Suspicions arose.

"Who are you people?"

The other twin, who had, until now, remained silent, spoke. "Friends, Corporal Brus. Just friends."

My suspicions grew stronger. "Then why . . . ?" The rest of the question need not have been spoken.

"If we don't," her sister said, "then who would?"

"It's a lonely place you're in," the red-haired young man said, "but you don't have to be utterly alone there." His voice carried conviction and knowing.

"But now we must be off," the servant said, approaching the table. He smiled at me. "We do hope you've enjoyed your time with us."

The others nodded in agreement, wiping their mouths with their napkins, then stood back from the table. The servant led them through a seam in the ruins, leaving the table with its porcelain cups, dishes, and white tablecloth as a testament to their presence. The servant didn't bother clearing the leftover food and coffee.

The men walked away with an uneven gait, leaning their weight on the nurses, who supported them by the arm. They flicked their legs ahead of them where they suddenly locked at the knee, then jerked down, like wooden marionettes. A breeze blew and I noted the emptiness of their pant legs, then saw, at the ankles, the artificial limbs that filled in the voids where once stood bone and sinew. I walked briskly over to the cleft between the church walls through which they hobbled, then watched as they made their awkward way through the ruins of Montfaucon's streets to disappear into a large patch of shattered trees—the remains of a blasted forest. Just above the trees hovered an unmarked zeppelin. I wondered at how anyone might have missed it in the minutes leading up to the village's pyrrhic capture. But, given the ferociousness of the fighting on the ground, no one's eyes were on the sky. Besides, smoke had, until I stumbled on the table, clouded all.

I watched the behemoth aircraft rise and loop up into the sky, heading northwest, toward the channel, then walked back into the ruins. And as the giant airship disappeared behind a thin line of wispy clouds, I sat down at their table and gorged myself on leftover toast and jam. I drank coffee until it flowed from my nose—quails and manna from heaven.

I didn't see the Germans until they were on top of me, laughing and wrenching my arms behind my back with taunts of "Amerikaner!" They covered my head with the tablecloth and marched me away from Montfaucon.

The next war is not so kind. Gentlemanliness, such as it was, giving way to unadulterated barbarity. My jewishness would not have survived this war, as it did the last.

I wonder if I am too late, but my timing seems perfect. The Nazis have fled, but the Russians have not yet arrived. I drive up to the barbed-wire gates and note the silence of the machine-gun nests as I take a wire-cutter to the fence. A body, encrusted with flies, is suspended in the wires like a puppet hanging from a toy-maker's woodshop.

A few—those capable of ambulation and coherent thought—come out of the barracks to investigate. They are like stray dogs: curious, but extremely cautious, waiting to be kicked or worse. Their curiosity grows as I park my jeep in the courtyard and begin emptying the back end. My equipment is rather crude, but it will do: Folding table, camp chairs, steel utensils. My dishes, though, are the highest quality porcelain, and my tablecloth is exquisite white. The prisoners are impressed, holding cups and saucers up to the sunlight as if examining artifacts from another era, an ancient time of purity, before the camps, before these dark ages, a time In The Beginning.

My fire is not the only one burning in this place, but my fire brings life, rather than heralding its cessation: Stew, pan bread, and spiced potatoes. I brew tea in large kettles, enough for an entire camp.

My German is halting, my Polish almost non-existent, but between my clumsy yammerings and their broken understanding of English, we are able to communicate the basics.

"Who are you?"

"Eat."

". . . dark times . . ."

". . . also a prisoner, though I cannot fathom . . ."

Then, I hear the Russian tanks throttling diesel in the distance, and it is time for my departure.

". . . not alone . . ."

I leave everything behind but the jeep. I wave as I get into the driver's seat, then quickly withdraw my arm as I realize that my forearm is exposed. I pull my sleeve over the bayonet-carved scar of an iron cross. My post-Montfaucon-capture souvenir.

Not all my accoutrements are beautiful, but my porcelain is perfect. White and blue as sky and the clouds therein.

THE BONE SHIP

SCOTT THOMAS

ONE: Under the Bombs

Pipe organ. Yes, that was it—the Western quadrant of the city looked like the pipes of an ancient organ, a dismantled organ, granted, but somewhat coppery in the peaked morning light. On Monday the clutter of tall cylindrical buildings had resembled canons with clouds for smoke; on Tuesday they were a severed forest and the clouds were the ghosts of lost foliage. Today, Wednesday, they were the pipes of an organ and its music was a single note, moaning between earth and Heaven, the horrible song of the air raid sirens.

Walking to her job at the Gun Hospital, Amelia Willow ducked under the stone arch of an old grey tenement. People scattered out of the street, like roaches doused with light. Behind the noise of sirens came the angry screeching of enemy flyers, followed by the drumming of bombs. Sepia trails from killing gas rose up behind the staggered distance of cylindrical buildings.

An old man lurched in beside Willow. "North Quadrant," he panted, "better them than us."

Willow could not speak—if she opened her mouth her heart would fly out.

The old man squinted up at the sky. There were only old men now, old men and boys. The other males were either dead or across the sea, fighting the good fight.

"Better them than us," the old man said.

TWO: Gun Doctors

After the raid, Willow and several coworkers sat out on the loading dock, trembling hands wrapped around paper cups full of hot tea and steam. Willow's name was good for her—she was wispy below her choppy helmet of brown, her eyes the blue of those small metallic beetles that delight in that brand of tree. Verdigris memories of country childhood hidden behind blue.

"Here now, ladies," the floor mistress said, lumbering out in her greys, "the patients be waitin'."

Willow whispered to a compatriot, "Nerves of steel, that one!"

"No nerves at all, I should think," the friend said.

Walk to work, air raid, cup of tea. Mag, the floor-mistress like a grey bear. Then to the cold brick rooms of the Gun Hospital. Tables spread with old and injured firearms. Carts cluttered with revolvers and shotguns, target automatics and small caliber plinkers. The women filed back into the oil-scented chambers.

Any and all guns that could be found were repaired and cleaned, tested, then shipped off to the Front. Willow, having been drafted away from her teaching position, had entered this place with no particular mechanical skills to speak of, now she was considered a master gunsmith. Hunched over this or that wounded weapon, her concentration was uncanny and her slim white hands moved with the grace of a surgeon's.

Soon the women of the Gun Hospital would be transferred to a munitions outfit in the North Quadrant. The guns were running out—the city only contained so many. They had already exhausted the supply of old service carbines popular during the Docks Uprising of thirty years back. Soon there would be no relics left to fix.

THREE: Not So Eager to Die

A cigarette on the steps of her tenement, baggy, drizzle-colored clothes, clouds appraising the city of round towers. Willow thought of her husband. She didn't bother to cry anymore, though the smoke stung her eyes.

"Worst thing about this war," Willow joked bitterly to no one, "...these bloody awful fags."

Willow flicked her cigarette into the gutter and hissed out the last of its smoke.

A small parade of figures was coming up the street. They had banners and horns, like it was Crimson Day. They were chanting something. Willow lit another awful cigarette.

"End of the world," they called, "end of the world!"

Willow smirked.

"End of—"

They came close enough for Willow to distinguish the Circle of Guilt tattoo each wore on its forehead. That explained things neatly.

Willow sighed when she saw that they were not going to be content in passing. A clot of bald women and boys assailed her with their verse.

"End of the world!" they chimed.

"Tell me something I don't know," Willow said, dryly.

"Come die with us," one said, reaching for her wrist.

Willow pulled a chunky cricket-colored revolver from the grey cloth sack at her side and put the barrel to the woman's face. "Piss off!"

Seems the Guilter was not so eager to die after all, at least not yet.

FOUR: Tears Above and Below

For some, even despair becomes the color of shale, the color of Willow's small flat, high in a pillar of West-facing grey. Each night she tried to sleep between a widow upstairs and a widow below, their weeping like ghosts through the cheap ceiling and floor.

Hungry as she was, Willow avoided her kitchen, as she had since the red face first appeared. She went to bed without eating. What red face, you wonder? It was a stain initially, a spot of dried grape juice the first night. A splotch on a cupboard door. It was bigger the following night, bigger still the next, and more like a face. Then it was gone, though Willow had done nothing to clean it. Her son was too small to reach the stain and her mother, who watched Simon during the day, claimed no knowledge of it one way or the other.

The face came back of course, as red faces are wont to do. The scab color replaced by bright crimson. It was fast and clever, a fleeting red puddle the size of a tea saucer. It flicked about the kitchen like the spot cast by a hand-lamp. A glinting smear across the ice box, there—skating through the dust bunnies and under the stove. It was flat, like paper, red like blood. Kitchen mice would have been preferable.

While Willow was not superstitious, she would have been a fool to deny that the face was an omen.

FIVE: Another Omen

Her husband Jasp had been an artist before the war broke out, but the arts were one of the first casualties in the city. The museums were raided for their guns, the ancient suits of armor melted down for their metal. Galleries closed, along with the schools. Art supplies became expensive, then rare and Jasp was forced to fashion his own.

There was a ledge outside of the flat's westward window, and several small dirt-colored birds had built a nest there. Jasp, with no paper or paint to speak of, stole several eggs from the nest. While the birds were bland-feathered beasts, the yolks of their eggs were a luminous peach color. One evening, upon returning from her job, Amelia Willow was horrified to find that Jasp had painted an impressionistic version of his unborn child on a wall of their flat using the contents of the stolen eggs.

"You heartless bastard," Amelia had said. "I suppose your compulsion to smear wet colors around has made you incapable of recognizing the terrible irony... You killed the offspring of those birds that you might paint your own. How embarrassingly vain."

Amelia had gone to the window and looked out at the raided nest. The birds were gone (and never returned). Shortly after this incident, Jasp was called to the Front and was himself yet to return. His son was born in his absence, some eighteen months back.

Willow had not managed to forgive herself for the way she spoke about Jasp's need to paint. As it turns out, the colorful yolk made for an imperfect paint. It was starting to go brown and flake.

SIX: Floating Bones

Rain drummed grey fingers when November made a hag of the weather and the city ached in its chill. Grey bricks from bombed tenements sat in puddles, a child's discarded blocks. Smoke against clouds, from the Southern Quadrant this time, rose up in great denoting stains. The bombers had been busy in the night.

Willow knelt in the rain, buttoning Simon's jacket. Simon squinted through rain and jagged bangs.

"Be a good boy for Gram, won't you?"

Simon nodded.

"Right then. Look—here she comes now...."

Willow's mother was hunched against the day, grey beneath her umbrella.

In the shadow of a blasted tower, they said their good-byes.

Willow walked the rest of the way to the Gun Hospital, punched the clock and took her place at her work station. The others were buzzing about something, gathered around a long table scattered with guns in various states of repair. A newspaper seemed to be the object of their fascination and even Mag, the shop mistress, was glued to it.

Willow stared from a distance for a moment, denying her curiosity. "All right, ladies, what's the fuss?"

The fuss was a newspaper featuring a front page photograph of a gigantic white ship comprised, if the headline was to be believed, entirely of bones. It had appeared in the night over in Dowington Cove, just west of the city. Much larger than any vessel that might safely navigate the rocky semi-enclosure, the fact that the oddity had appeared there, of all places, made it all the more baffling. Had it simply risen out of the cold grey sea?

In a related story, a group of Guilters had rowed out to the thing and, seeing its appearance as proof that the world was at its end, realized that prophesy by hanging themselves off its numerous bone protrusions.

SEVEN: Bread for the Rain Gods

Willow hated rye bread with a passion, but she bought a quarter loaf each time she stopped at the bakery. Jasp had loved rye. Tasting something he had loved somehow held her closer to him.

"Quarter rye," the old baker said, soon as she came in out of the rain. It was as if that was her name, so far as he was concerned.

Willow smiled.

The baker had survived a gas-bombing, his skin grey, strangely smooth, despite his great age; sepia veins like cracks in porcelain. Willow leaned on the counter, smoking, watching as he sawed through a dark, caraway-scented brick.

"Queer thing about that ship, eh?" the old man asked. "All made of bones—every inch—so they say, and not a soul on board. It's some ghastly thing from the enemy, I'm wont to say."

"I'm not so sure," Willow said.

The man looked at her for a moment.

"I think I'd like some raisin bread too, if it's no trouble."

November dusk wandered among the round buildings, its rain coughing down. It grew dark so early now and the cold knew the names of Willows bones and counted them through her clothes.

Several blocks from her mother's flat, where she expected to find Simon napping between a snoring beagle and a worn stuffed elephant, Willow paused and looked up. The mournful call of the air raid siren came rolling through the rain.

Fast wet footsteps on the sidewalk, grey bodies blurring past. Someone shoved and Willow fell in a puddle, her bread spilling out from its bag like an offering to the rain.

Enemy flyers screeched above.

Willow gathered herself up and lurched into a doorway. Comets whistled and the earth shook. A giant was dancing with fire feet.

Shadows ran past, screaming. One squashed the piece of rye bread into the puddle. The pipe organ was breaking, its uprights punched by cabbages of flame.

EIGHT: Weeping Willow

Following the raid, Willow made her way to her mother's tenement, which, as you might have guessed, took a hit. It had been a gas-charge, so while the damage was comparatively minor, the casualties were many. A smoking crater yawned for the rain where the building faced east and there were bodies in the street and inside, crumpled here and there, trembling in the stairwells (curiously, the bodies of those felled by the gas were known to shudder for ten minutes or more, even following death).

The gas was swift, efficient; most of it had dissipated by the time Willow reached her mother's flat on the fourth floor. One might imagine the scene inside, and Willow's reaction to finding her mother and young son slumped twitching in a closet where they had sheltered from the attack. The beagle, impervious to the gas, poked out from under the bed and moaned.

NINE: A Bird Like Birch Twigs

She sat on the floor rocking Simon, smoothing his hair from his eyes, muttering. Her mother finally stopped drumming in the closet but the sound of tapping continued. It was some time before the sound infiltrated Willow's numbness and when she finally looked to the window at the source of the sound, she saw a bird, bare of feathers and flesh, little more than birch twigs, hovering, tapping its beak on the glass.

Willow lay Simon on the floor and walked to the window, opening it. The skeleton bird turned and flew off toward the west and Willow saw the great Bone Ship waiting in the cove beyond the burning city.

TEN: A Song in the Bone Ship

The smoke thinned at the edge of the city and stars poked like thorns through the haze. Hours had passed, the crackling and weeping fading with the shattered streets and now the sound of the sea hissed in the darkness. The calcified monstrosity of the Bone Ship rocked lazily, a compressed cemetery of fossilized moonlight.

There were many boats to choose from, seeing as the fishermen had gone off to the fight. Willow, with Simon strapped to her back, chose one and paddled out into the water. The ship loomed, a jumble of skulls and femurs and bones she could not name, a jagged baroque wall, towering as she rowed close. The dangling silhouetted bodies of Guilt cultists rocked above.

There were many handholds affording Willow a not too painstaking climb to the deck. The untethered rowboat bobbed away. Gulls had been at the Guilters.

There were strange sail-less spires and crippled-looking bone canons and a pallor that invited shadow into strange shapes. Willow moved slowly across the deck, the arthritic ship creaking. There was an open chamber like a gazebo above a stairwell that took her deep into the lower decks and the seemingly endless halls, their floors cobbled with the crowns of skulls. It was like a maze.

A hand lamp shone on the terrible texture of the walls, the hands, the ribs, the gawking facial understructures, spinal fragments arranged like beams. Deep in the heart of the Bone Ship, Willow unfastened Simon and sat on the hard floor, holding him in her lap. She had found a central chamber that opened onto a number of passageways.

A distant clattering sound floated to the woman, followed by faint motion as the spindly bone bird flew into view. It fluttered out of the tunnels, into the heart of the ship and hovered. Willow nodded to the bird and it lighted, frail and white on Simon's chest.

The bird gently pushed its pointed face between the boy's slack lips. It whispered into Simon's skull. Willow felt Simon stir and the bird went up, circling. Simon leapt up on his stubby legs and dashed down the nearest hallway, the frail bird merrily flitting after.

Simon ran singing through the twisting corridors in the belly of the Bone Ship, a low sound echoing from his mouth. His small feet drummed and his song, while a single unalterable note, expressed both the beauty of love and the horror of war.

Crystal Vision

Eric Schaller

David stirred a pot on the stove with a wooden spoon that had once belonged to his grandmother. Even without the fancifully carved handle, the origin of the spoon would have been easy to guess. Pretty much everything in the house, as well as the house itself, a century-old saltbox on the outskirts of Rochester, New Hampshire, had been inherited from David's grandmother. From my seat at the kitchen table, I raised my own spoon piled high with soggy cornflakes and made a silent toast to her memory.

David set the wooden spoon down. His long blond hair, normally curly, was lank from where it hung before his eyes in the billowing steam. He raised his arms so that the sleeves of his bathrobe fell back to his elbows. The robe was of red silk faded to pink and missing its belt so that it flopped loosely about his body like a second skin. He spread his fingers, clenched, knuckles crackling, then spread his fingers wide again.

David looked like a sorcerer escaped from some B movie.

He measured out a tablespoon full of yellowish liquid from a Pine-Sol bottle and added it to the pot on the stove.

"Eye of newt," I said.

Two teaspoons from a Mop-and-Glo bottle.

"Wing of bat."

A half-cup of Comet, the pale blue powder leveled with a kitchen knife.

"Dew off a dead man's eyes."

The stuff in the pot was mostly sugar water. I did not know whether the sugar was an intrinsic part of the recipe or to make it more palatable. I didn't even truly know what were inside the name-brand bottles that David pulled out from their locations in the cabinet beneath the sink.

The proportions varied slightly each time David made up the recipe, like a good cook who follows intuition as much as any book. Except David wrote down the relative proportions each time in a small spiral-bound notepad he kept in his pocket. He used a stubby pencil whittled to a point. He said that in a former life, and by former life he meant five or ten years ago, he had been a chemistry student.

The pot boiled and the mixture became syrupy. Bubbles worked their way loose from below and exploded with a flatulent pop. There was the distinct odor of ammonia. David stirred until the mixture was so thick that it refused to move. The sugar on the bottom began to burn, blackening, the upper levels taking on the dusky appearance of ancient amber.

David gave the mixture a hard whack with the edge of the spoon and crazed lines shot across the surface.

"Crystal," he said.

Saliva filled my mouth. I thought of Pavlov's dog.

David banged the pot upside down on the counter, dislodging the contents, and scraped the inside clean with a knife. He then brushed the wedges and flakes of crystal off the counter into a Tupperware container and put the container into the cupboard. He returned to the counter and, with a moistened finger, picked at the remaining crumbs. He licked his finger clean and dabbed at the counter again.

"You want some?" he asked.

I nodded.

David smiled and held his encrusted finger out to me. I circled his finger with my lips and slid my tongue back and forth along it length, feeling the roughness that adhered to it dislodge and dissolve. The crystal tasted sweet and sour at the same time and bloomed on my tongue like roses in the snow.

"Everything is crystal you know," David said. "Salt. Proteins. Blood, sweat, and tears. The trick is getting to the crystalline form." He walked back to the stove. "You ever have a crystal garden?"

"No," I said, "What's that?"

"Something I got with a chemistry set when I was a kid. You dropped seeds of different chemicals, small crystals, into a saturated salt solution. They grew day by day, week by week, piling one atop the other, all sorts of different colors depending on what chemicals you used. It was beautiful, like nothing I had ever seen before."

One was David.

Two was me.

Together we were something else.

Of course, back then, I didn't know what that something else was. Or that it would take five of us to get there. Even David may have worked mostly from instinct, any method to his madness revealed only in retrospect, to him as much as to the rest of us. But whatever door he was trying to open, crystal was the key and at some point it became obvious that, even with the key, he couldn't open the door alone.

David kept an ever-expanding menagerie of toys, the kind you find in cereal boxes, in kid's meals at MacDonald's, and in cases at flea markets and next-to-new shops. Plastic cartoon characters, ceramic animals, and metal robots kept watch from nooks and crannies throughout the house. Walking barefoot, you would suddenly recoil in pain and discover a plastic cowboy embedded in your foot, his six-shooters raised as if in victory.

On the day of the party, David collected the characters in his menagerie and arranged them on the pool table in the living room. He made the toys part of a parade that wound around the table and then up a pyramid of books where, on the peak, a white plastic unicorn reared upon her hind legs. Trolls lurked in the pockets of the pool table and gryphons perched on the table's edge, playing the part of spies or outcasts, I wasn't quite sure.

Folks started showing up at the house at around five o'clock. By seven, the party was in full swing. It was bring your own and there was plenty of beer and wine. A couple of former housemates, Casper and Magic Hat, had gathered a group together in the kitchen. They all took turns sucking on Casper's bong, while Magic Hat rummaged through the kitchen drawers. "Let me show you how to make a bong out of a beer can," he said. "I just need something sharp to punch holes in it. You got any nails? It would be really cool if you had an apple. I could make a bong out of an apple too, if you had one."

David wondered from room to room carrying a plate piled high with wedges of crystal. It was a ceramic plate patterned with a Christmas wreath around the circumference, his grandmother's taste in crockery not his own. I slipped a sliver of crystal off the plate and pocketed it in my cheek to let it dissolve. "Any takers?" I asked.

"A few," David said.

There wasn't any food at the party besides some bags of chips, and we ordered out for pizza at around nine o'clock. The fellow who showed up at our door with the pizza wore a red knit cap over black curly hair. He had the placid smile of a stoner, and, from the resinous stench that clung to his sweater, I figured he had been toking in his car on the drive over. "Pretty cool party, man," he said. "Wish I didn't have to work."

"Hold on," I said. "I'll get the cash."

"Hey," the guy said, following along after me, "can I set these boxes down somewhere?" Then, before I could react or say anything, he dumped the stack of pizza boxes down on the pool table. On top of David's parade.

"Shit!" he said after a long pause. One could almost see the gears grinding in his head as he tried to make the connection between his actions and the devastation wrecked upon the parade. "Man, I'm really sorry. I thought it was just a table." He grabbed the boxes back up again and, in so doing, knocked them into the pyramid of books. Plastic characters tumbled in a landslide of dislodged books down to the green felt, some bouncing off the table.

"Shit!" he repeated after another long pause. "Sometimes it just doesn't pay to get up in the morning."

Several other partiers had gathered around us by this time, including David. The pizza fellow came up from beneath the table with a Snow White and a Scooby Doo in his hands. He set them down carefully on their feet in the wreckage of the parade. "Don't worry. I'll fix it all up again," he said.

"Hey, that's okay," David said. "No big deal. It was an accident waiting to happen."

I went off to scavenge money from the folks back in the kitchen. When I returned with the wad of bills, the pizza fellow and David were talking like old friends. "Peace, brother," the pizza fellow said when he left. "Peace to you too, Jacob," David said. "Drop by anytime."

Jacob took him at his word and showed up again the next afternoon.

I opened the door and saw him standing on the front porch, looking slightly awkward in the same clothes from the night before. It was autumn and leaves were rattling overhead in the trees. In our driveway, parked beside a beat-up VW microbus and a rusted tractor, neither of which would ever run again, was a blue station wagon that I did not recognize.

Jacob pulled a joint from the band of his knit cap. "Fair exchange?" he said. I invited him in even though I wasn't really that much into weed anymore. "David," I called, "It's the pizza fellow. But I don't think he's delivering pizza."

David came out of the kitchen naked. That was his customary way of greeting unexpected visitors. He craned his neck sideways. "Jacob," he said, "Good to see you again."

Without missing a beat, Jacob asked "Hey, do you have any more of that crystal, man?"

I didn't even know that Jacob knew about the crystal. Then I realized that David must have given him some the previous night while I was getting the pizza money together.

"Sure," David said. "Step into my laboratory." He swung his arm in a windmilling motion toward the kitchen.

Jacob stayed the night at our house. Within two weeks he called it home.

David's parade stayed up until Casper and Magic Hat came over with a pick-up truck to reclaim their pool table. It was only then, while packing the menagerie into a box, that David noticed the unicorn no longer led the parade. When Jacob had rebuilt the parade the night of the party, he hadn't known there was any particular order to the characters. He just wanted to get them back on their feet and in line. As a result, a troll, naked and plumed with purple hair, had ended up on top of the mountain at the front of the parade.

"That's pretty cool," David said, tossing the troll up and down in his hand, before packing him away in the box. "That's the way it should be."

David found Sally at the Wal-Mart.

The three of us—David, Jacob, and I—had spent the morning driving around, crammed into the station wagon with pieces of David's inheritance, hitting up all the flea markets and antique shops in the area. My favorite shop was one that advertised Antiques and Used Items on its sign outside, just because that last part always made me smile; they bought a metal juicer and two boxes of glasses from the 1939 World's Fair. We also managed to unload four dining room chairs at The Antique Alley, which gave us a little breathing room in the car.

No one was willing to take a chance on the old 78-rpm records, too many scratches they said, so we spent an enjoyable half-hour playing Frisbee with these out by the gravel pit. We couldn't catch the damn things because they were too hard and heavy. Instead we sailed them off the edge of the pit as far as we could send them. Louis Armstrong. Duke Ellington. Benny Goodman. They smashed on the rocks below and sent black fragments flying up like frightened crows.

Then, flush with cash from the earlier sales, we pulled into the Wal-Mart parking lot.

David spent the good part of an hour poking through and reading the labels on the cold medications in the drug aisle. When he was finally ready, he gave us each several packages, and we went to separate check-out lanes. Jacob and I got through, but it turned out that David was held up by a cashier waving a little slip of paper. She pointed at the items on the conveyer belt and explained how only so many items containing pseudophedrine could be purchased at any one time, that it was a Federal regulation. She shook the slip of paper for emphasis when she said "Federal regulation."

David, of any of us, should not have made that mistake. But maybe he just wanted to test the current limit.

"You'll have to put one of your items back," the cashier said.

"But what about my little friend here, who is terribly congested?" David pulled a PEZ container out of his pocket and held it in front of his face. The PEZ had the head of Garfield the cat.

"You see," David said, talking in a squeaky voice, "I think that Garfield might have an allergy to cat hair. Problem is, as you can see, he is a cat." David made a sneezing noise and pulled back on the Garfield head, so that it expelled one of the PEZ candies. "Pretty disgusting, isn't it?"

The cashier was a blonde, but not a California blonde. An Illinois blonde if such a thing exists: well-fed, but not fat, a couple of zits covered over with makeup, the kind of girl that goes to college but ends up marrying her high-school sweetheart.

"Now Sally," David said, glancing at the tag on her uniform, "Garfield has but two options. One, he could shave off all his hair and go around naked. You ever seen a shaved cat? It's not a pretty sight. And one thing's for damn sure, Garfield would never get any pussy that way."

Sally's face creased with an unexpected smile. I also noticed that instead of a cross around her neck, she was wearing an ankh. I couldn't imagine a girl with an ankh marrying her high-school sweetheart.

David continued. "So that leaves option two. What is option two? Just a common allergy medication sold throughout this good country of ours. Now the items before us are not for my consumption. Hardly. They are for poor little Garfield." David made Garfield sneeze and pop out another PEZ candy.

Sally said, "Sorry, I don't think so. Rules and regulations you know. I could lose my job."

David's face fell. For a moment he looked like a tired old man, a tramp wearing someone's cast-off clothes.

"But I get off work in two hours," she added. She brushed a strand of hair away from her eyes. "If you like, I can stop by after work and bring your little friend his prescription personally. Make a house-call so to speak."

"You are a saint," David said, brightening. "More than a saint, a goddess."

Or maybe just a number.

Only some of the people who came to the house actually tried crystal, although David was an enthusiastic distributor of that mottled candy—when it came to crystal, it was always Halloween as far as David was concerned—and of those who tried crystal, most did not bother taking a second piece.

A singular taste, or an acquired taste?

It certainly wasn't the revelation most people expected from David's fervent peddling. No orgasmic rush like your first taste of heroin, so powerful that you don't care about the wet stain mushrooming across the crotch of your jeans. No visions of God. No angel brigades. Not even the cold power-trip of that whore cocaine.

But for the four of us, crystal was the only drug that mattered. All our old habits had fallen away like shed skins.

Why? That was a question I am sure David asked himself many times. The closest I came to an answer was after a midnight run to MacDonald's.

It was winter, and so we pulled our coats on along with whatever other clothes we could find. Crazy ugly is how we looked. I wore a plastic raincoat on top of a sweatshirt. David had a pink quilted coat that stretched almost to the ground; he looked like a transvestite pimp. Sally wore a sequined dress with feather boa and a down vest over it. Jacob didn't have a coat, just a stained blue blanket that he wrapped around himself Indian-style. Jacob said it was the same blanket he had used as a kid, that he was never going to throw it away.

At MacDonald's, we pooled our change and bought two super-sized fries and a jumbo Coke to split between us. I set the red cartons of fries upright in the middle of our table and we sat huddled around them, campers clustered for warmth before the yellow flames of a tiny bonfire.

Jacob got some packets of ketchup and came back with his blanket fluttering like a cape. He grabbed the sides of the blanket and swirled it from side to the side—too vigorously, perhaps, as ketchup packets loosened from his hands flew in all directions. Two teenagers seated nearby laughed. Jacob brought both ends of the blanket up to obscure the lower half of his face. "The Batman," he said.

I rose and held my hand out. "Peace," I said. "On this night two heroes meet. I am Superman." I gave my raincoat a theatrical shake.

Jacob slammed the remaining ketchup packets down on the table, where they formed a sweaty pile. "Superman was a pansy."

"Government dupe, I'd say," said David. "Mr. Status Quo. Me, you know who I liked?"

Jacob and I shook our heads. Sally helped herself to a French fry; she swirled it around in the intestines of a ketchup packet.

"Bizarro," David said.

"Bizarro? The freak superman? The guy who talked funny? You got to be kidding," Jacob said.

"He wasn't a freak. He built a whole god-damned planet just so he wouldn't have to deal with the people on earth—people just like you who thought he was a freak."

I suddenly realized that David was angry. I hadn't seen him angry before. Jacob realized it too. He apologized and we returned to eating our fries, making them last as long as we could.

But it was David's anger that I remembered on our drive back to the house. That, and how we all wanted to be superheroes. Even Sally. I don't think she read comics, but she would have loved to take the whole earth in her arms if she could, hold it and love it as if it were a child.

As a kid I had always thought that secretly I might have super powers. I just had to discover what they were. Or maybe I would develop them as I got older.

Becoming an adult meant giving up that dream.

That's where crystal came in. Crystal made me feel like a kid: everything was new and everything was possible. Crystal made me believe that I could be a superhero. Not that I was a superhero. Just that the possibility existed.

As we drove back to the house, Sally crowded against me for warmth and I drew diamonds in the fogged section of my side window. I extended the diamonds facet upon facet until the whole window was a meshwork of intersecting lines. I decided that if I became a superhero, I would wear the emblem of a diamond on my chest.

From within our darkened house, all that winter, we sat on the second floor, facing the one window that wasn't pasted over with fiber-glass insulation and duct-tape. It was cold and we sat wrapped in sleeping bags and blankets.

When we were hungry, we ate rice. We passed the pot of rice between us, eating with the same spoon. When we couldn't find a spoon, we dug in with our hands. Just David, Sally, Jacob, and I. No reason for anyone else to come anymore. All we had was crystal and rice.

We sat before the window and didn't move unless we had to. When the crystal ran out, David would get up and make more. "How many days was it that time?" None of us knew.

We fell asleep seated before the window, hardly aware that we had dropped off because in our dreams we were still seated before the window. Then we awoke and found that time had shifted, day become night, or night day.

We watched the sun rise. In our backyard was an old ship's anchor—a huge metal ball that could keep an ocean liner from drifting. It looked like a rusty moon fallen to earth. The sun rose above the anchor and we watched the edge of night retreat from its near side.

Icicles hanging from the gutter overhead began to drip. . . David smiles as he watches a droplet build on an icicle. He is bearded and his hair tumbles in greasy curls upon his shoulders. He wears the same pink bathrobe that he has worn for weeks. He smiles and he doesn't care if anyone sees the gap in his teeth. One day he just found the tooth loose. After a few days of playing at it with his tongue, the tooth fell out into his hand. Now, he keeps the tooth in the pocket of his robe. Sometimes he takes it out and stares at it as if it were some rare pearl, or a seed that was going to sprout a new person.

Already this day is over, the sun has set, and stars have exploded upon the night.

So we sat, day after day, and watched winter melt into spring. Spring into summer.

David leaned into me and rubbed the top of my head meaningfully. "I need a haircut," he said. "I can't see."

We couldn't find any scissors, but there was a bread knife in a kitchen drawer and razors in the bathroom cabinet.

David took a seat upon a wooden chair and I tied my raincoat around his neck.

"Take it all off," David said. "We have to be smooth like ice, like crystal." He bobbed his head back and forth.

"Hold still," I said.

But he wasn't paying attention. "Do you remember Telemetrics?" he asked.

I did. That was where David and I had first met, although there wasn't much of a story there. Far from it. Just two people working in the same room with a bunch of other people. We sat in gray plastic cubicles and made phone calls all day, following whatever scripts we were handed. When David decided to leave, we all had a little party because he had been there longer than any one of us. He cut the cake, licked the blue frosting from his fingers, and wouldn't say where he was on to next. Then, as he shook my hand goodbye, he pressed a small folded sheet of paper into my palm. "I think you will be wanting this soon," he said. Later, when I unfolded the paper back in my cubicle, I saw it was an address. I crumpled the paper into a tiny ball and tossed it into the wastepaper basket. But I remembered the address.

"Back then I thought that the crystal would be enough," David continued. "The right combination of ingredients, enough people all linked by the same perception, and something would happen."

"I think we're almost out." I had seen Jacob licking the pot that morning. I thought of Winnie the Pooh stumbling around with his head stuck in a jar of honey. "You'll need to make more soon."

"But it's more like a bridge. We can't just stay as we are, we have to move forward. We don't just wait for them. We meet on the bridge. We move toward the crystalline just as they move toward us. Less distance to travel, you see."

"You've got to stop moving. I can't cut if you keep moving your head." I finished sawing with the knife and smeared his stubble with green dishwashing soap. I pulled the razor across his scalp.

"No. You don't see. They're out there and they're waiting. I thought that they would come to us, but we have to go to them."

This was the same pitch that David had used when trying to sell customers on crystal. It still didn't make any sense. I wasn't buying anyway.

"Are you going to make any more crystal? Jacob was licking the pot this morning."

"Sure. Sure."

I shook the razor clean.

"Done," I said.

David raised his hands and ran them backwards across the dome of his head. He brought them down dripping with his own blood. Blood covered his head and was mixed with the droplets of soap and hair that splattered the floor.

"I think that Sally used the razor on her legs," I said. That was meant as a joke, but David said, "No, that was me. I did my legs and pubes this morning."

He laughed and stood up, then walked over to the wall and pressed his hands, fingers spread, against the plaster. He leaned forward and rubbed his head between his two palm prints. "Kilroy was here," he said, admiring the bloody stains on the wall.

There were four of us. Then, one day there were five.

Adelle just appeared, a knock on our door at ten in the morning. We weren't expecting anyone, so David dropped his robe. He wasn't wearing anything else. He had read in a book about some guy who used to answer the door naked as a way to discourage strangers. That made good sense to David, so he hunched over to the door, vertebrae protruding from his back like the plates of a stegosaurus.

Adelle was fifteen years old and had had a habit for five years. Still beautiful, though, her skin pale and luminous, almost transparent so that you could see every vein. A denim tank top, hot pants with hearts for pockets, and hair dyed blond but with a greenish tint that made you think that she might be a mermaid.

She blinked a few times and smiled blissfully.

"She'll do," said David.

After that Adelle stayed at the house.

I only mention Adelle because she was there. She didn't bring any unwanted child with her. She didn't fall in love with anyone. Nor was she a cold-hearted beauty whose presence inspired heart-sickness and friend turning on friend to win her love. This wasn't a movie.

Maybe Sally took an interest in her when she first arrived. A few times, I saw Sally brushing Adelle's long hair and braiding it. Then I saw Sally crying once in the kitchen, quietly holding her sobs in with her head pressed against Adelle's thin chest. Adelle stared vacantly over Sally's left shoulder at something only a cat could see. After that, things settled down.

David wanted her there, and that was enough.

Before she arrived, he had been getting agitated. Said something had to happen soon. That we couldn't last much longer. Something had to happen or we would all starve to death. David held up his right hand, fingers spread. "Five," he said to me. He curled his hand into a fist, then made a quick karate-like punch at my chest, stopping inches away from contact. "With five we might punch through."

Then Adelle arrived.

First there were four, then there were five.

When the end came, it came fast.

"We've changed," Adelle said. She pointed at our reflections in the window.

It was summer, in the evening, one of those late evenings that seem to last forever. We were naked and content. With the warm weather we had opened some of the windows and a breeze worked its way along our backs and arms. We had to be careful because the mosquitoes were out. The trick was to have only a few windows open and no lights on.

I nodded. I looked from Adelle to Jacob. To David. To Sally. I looked at myself in the glass.

We had changed. That was no secret. But, judging from my reflection, I still looked pretty good.

Adelle continued to stare at the window. Her eyes were wide. She tried to speak again. Her mouth made tiny spasms and all she got out were some croaking noises.

I thought she was having a seizure and I reached out toward her.

She was ice-cold. Shivering uncontrollably. "It's all right," I said and wrapped my arms around her thin body. I pulled her up against me. "Relax," I said. "It'll be all right."

I held her, but there was hardly anything there to hold. Her skin was like Kleenex stretched over a balsa-wood frame. I remembered a bird that I had to kill after a cat mauled it. I had used a rock and it had been almost too easy, the bird so fragile it was a miracle that it had ever lived.

Then I saw what Adelle saw.

A movement in the window.

I sat up so straight my backbone cracked.

We hadn't changed. Our reflections had.

There were five of them, seated in similar fashion to us and staring back from out of the night. I looked back and forth between us and the reflections. Really they were nothing like us. They were more like how we remembered ourselves, how we pictured ourselves in our minds.

They sparkled like frost on a winter morning.

Adelle had twisted her head so as not to lose sight of the reflections. "They're so beautiful," she said in a mumble that only I could hear. Tears were running down her cheeks. She stretched her open palm out toward the window.

"Beautiful," she said.

In the window, a hand reached toward her, the palm also open.

The hand was like something crafted by Michelangelo, a perfect gesture that reflected moonlight and starlight as it reached forward. Each networked cell on the skin was a tiny facet.

I grabbed Adelle's hand. I pulled it away from the window and held it in my lap.

There was no such answering move by my counterpart in the window. My reflection sat peacefully at ease, legs crossed, a barely perceptible smile on his lips. He reminded me of the sculpted likeness of Buddha. The fasting Buddha.

Adelle's reflection slowly lowered her hand of her own volition and laid it in the naked lap of my counterpart. She looked directly at me and smiled too. A flickering smile like that of a serpent.

In her crystalline eyes, Adelle and I were reflected back—two starving humans twisted in an awkward embrace.

But Adelle and I weren't the only ones who saw what was in the window.

I heard a lurching movement from beside me.

"David," Adelle said.

My sight was temporarily blocked. Then, a shattering roar. The window exploded into shards of glass.

I jumped to my feet.

Adelle screamed.

Sally and Jacob ducked their heads. Then lifted them. "What's going on?" they said almost in unison.

David was gone and the window broken.

David did not get far.

I pulled on my clothes and ran downstairs. I circled around the house, tripped once, legs giving out from the unexpected exertion. Then I stood below the window, now lit.

The window was too far up to do any more than reveal silhouettes of those behind it.

Still, there was a half moon, the reflected light of the invisible sun.

Fragments of glass littered the grass, winking up at me like eyes. I tiptoed barefoot among them until I came to David's body. There was no blood. Nothing really. He was in pieces. Shattered into a thousand pieces. It was hard to tell what was David and what was glass from the window.

But I did find a hand, miraculously intact, amongst the glittering crystal wreckage. Broken off at the wrist. Five fingers slightly curled. The gesture that a man might make to protect his face as he jumped through a window: back of the hand against his eyes, fingers projected outwards. The gesture that a man might make as he reached out to grasp something he had longed for all his life. Now rock-hard. Like ice, but warm as the summer night. Even warmer as if the hand still contained some of the heat that once animated it.

I held the hand up between my eyes and the moon, and light came through. In each facet of the hand, a tiny image of the moon shone. The hand clutched moons like so much loose change.

I ran then. I didn't care where I went. I just wanted to get away from that house. Away from Jacob and Sally and Adelle and the shattered body of David lying on our lawn.

Of course, I couldn't stay away.

I went back the next morning.

I approached from the rear, skulking like a dog. I found a tire iron in the trunk of one of the cars and carried it at the ready. I didn't know for what.

David's body was gone. Beneath the window I found just a few slivers of glass, thin flat fragments of windowpane. Somebody had cleaned up.

I slid in through the side door of the house and climbed the stairs, quietly cursing the creaks that resounded with each step I took.

It didn't matter. When I came to the second floor, there was no one there. I cursed out loud and went back downstairs. My stomach twisted in knots as I ran from one end of the kitchen to the other. I slammed the doors of the sink cabinet open and shut. I tore open the cupboards. I ran upstairs again and looked through the empty closets. I ransacked the attic. Then I repeated every motion I had made once again.

There was nothing there.

Jacob, Sally, and Adelle were gone. More importantly, so was the crystal.

An animal clawed at my stomach. My temples pounded. I caved forward and fell to my knees in the middle of the kitchen floor.

No hope. And no choice really.

The crystal body I found beneath the window. Was that David? Or his reflection? Did it matter?

All that matters is the hand that I rescued from amongst the broken glass.

I take it out and lay it upon the linoleum in front of me. A perfect hand made of crystal. All that remains to mark David's existence in our world.

The hand doesn't break at my initial attempts, and I have to search out where I dropped the tire iron. That does the trick. Pieces of crystal skitter across the floor. They catch the sunlight and burn like flame.

I swallow a piece and wait for the old magic.

NINE ELECTRIC FLOWERS

SALLY CARTERET

Last summer while I was living with Davy Ybarra, the comedian, I would take long drives on the freeway. The idea was to get away from Davy's abusive mouth. Mostly I'd drive down to Laguna Niguel, sit in this yuppie bar overlooking a tailored strip of rocky beach and drink vodka martinis, the cocktail of clarity. In my clarity I would conclude that I should leave Davy before serious trouble ensued. Then I would go home to him. On occasion I'd make a pit stop in Whittier, visiting with Judy Eisley, an old heroin buddy. The visits were temptations: Judy was still chipping and I knew if I started running smack again, Davy would head for the hills. He couldn't afford another bust, not if he wanted to keep his MTV gig. That scenario would be preferable to the painful drawn-out mutual analysis Davy was certain to put us through when the end came.

I wasn't heroin desperate yet, but I did smoke some of Judy's opium one afternoon. Enough to fuel creativity. On the way home I spotted a sprawling nursery that fronted the freeway near City of Industry. Grower's Nursery. I'd driven past it countless times, but never noticed how strange it was. A couple dozen high tension towers like a city of silver skeleton men sprouting from rectangular beds of wine-dark roses and carnations, with lumpish burlap-brown hills behind, like half-empty sacks that had been abandoned by a giant. The whole thing had the look of an immense surrealist collage. I pulled off into the repair lane and stared at the nursery and thought about Davy. Song things began connecting in my head. I dug under the seat for a notebook and scribbled these lines:

If you promise to ignore me,
I'll send you nine electric flowers...

A half-hour later as I was finishing the lyric, about a woman trapped in a destructive relationship with a man she still cares for, Five-O pulled up behind me and ordered me to step out of my car. Odds were the cop had already run the plates and knew I was Julie Banks. The bastards live for celebrity busts. I called my lawyer and left the phone on so he could hear me being tazed and beaten. The cop, a shaven-headed, sunglasses-wearing mesomorph, proved less of a bastard than I'd feared. Though he sniffed around for dope, he mainly wanted to snag an autograph for his daughter. Things grew downright civil between us. I asked if he knew anything about Grower's Nursery. He said it was a Mexican-American business. They sold flowers to Safeway.

--You'd think all the electricity would screw up the soil, I said.

The cop gazed off toward the low hills with a far-seeing look and said gravely, There's lots worse than electricity down in there. The way he ambled back to the squad car, gunslinger slow and easy, I half-expected to hear his theme music.

I left a message for Davy, told him I'd be working late. Then I called a few friends and booked us studio time. By two the next morning I had a clean demo of "Nine Electric Flowers." I knew what was waiting for me back at the house and I thought about staying with somebody. But a relationship like Davy's-and-mine...it's like being in a play you hate but the critics love. It's your duty to finish the run, to show up night after night and speak your lines. He was in the bedroom when I came home, sitting in the dark. I wrote a new song, I said and tossed my bag on the dresser.

--I wrote a new song! He mimicked me in a pansy falsetto. I laid a pretty egg. All the teenage girls will think it's so profound!

--I kinda doubt that, I said. It's about you.

That bought me a few seconds of silence.

--You write a song about me, but you can't talk to me, he said. Okay. Let's try this. I'll say what's on my mind, then you go in the head and write a song in response. We'll get this musical comedy thing happening. Market it as a self-help product for troubled young couples. Do an infomercial. How to sing and dance away those Relationship Blues. End of the show I'll go, Julie, you're such a slag bitch! All fake angry, y'know. And you'll go--he sang--I am not a slag bitch, I am a diva. Then we'll laugh and kiss while they put the eight-hundred number on the screen. You like?

--I'm going to bed.

Davy switched on a lamp. He was sitting in lounge chair, his dark angular face pointed with anger. An automatic with a dull gray finish rested in his lap.

--You gonna kill me? I asked, and started to undress. I'd seen the gun too many times to be afraid.

--This old thing? He picked it up, turned it this way and that. "Jeez, no! It's just a...kind of a gun night, y'know?

I stepped out of my jeans, kicked them aside.

--I'm sitting here thinking you're the fucking spider devil, he said. Then you flash your ass and I'm like, Gee, maybe her and Mama could get to be pals.

I went into the bathroom and began washing my face.

--Is that all it is with us? He had followed me and was leaning in the doorway. Just a few laughs and some low yo-yo.

--I don't remember any laughs lately.

--It's the drugs, baby. All the holes you poked in your brain. Short-term memory's not your thing.

--Uh-huh. Whatever.

--Only reason you keep me around's so I can remind you of shit. What to do when the light turns green. How to make change for a quarter.

I patted my face dry. Want me to say you're smarter than me, man? You're verbally quicker? Better at arithmetic? That's what's going on here. Ever since we passed the sex barrier, it's like you had to start proving how smart you are by running me down.

I pushed past him into the bedroom.

--I don't have to *prove* I'm smarter than you, he said.

--Naw, this conversation demonstrates that, right? I turned down the sheets and climbed in. What's Ted at your jokes?

--Something like that.

--That one argument of yours? Like the more popular an artist is, that's a measure of how stupid her work is? You almost had me sold on it 'til your career started going somewhere. Til you landed a job with those intellectual giants at MTV.

He dropped onto the bed beside me, put a hand on my throat. Not choking me, but in choking position.

--And hey, you're stronger, too, I said. It's amazing! Smarter, stronger...What's next? A foot race?

He kept his hand at my throat, but I felt the tension ebb from his fingers. I don't want to do this any more, he said.

At this point the Wise Julie had an urge to sit up in bed and draw him out on the subject of not-wanting-to-do-this-any-more. A calm, tender conversation would ensue, during which she would cautiously suggest a pulling back from the relationship. Maybe a little time apart. But with Davy I was never wise. Obeying the lame dynamic that ruled us, pendulum swings from near-violence to arousal that grew wider and more dangerous every day, I lifted his hand, kissed the knuckles, then slipped his forefinger into my mouth. Soon he became a shadow above me, a hot force inside me, a death trip in a lover's disguise.

My label liked "Nine Electric Flowers" so much, they decided to do an EP, something to build toward the next album. They wanted a video made and brought in Jason Desjardin from New Orleans to direct. He had these terrific green eyes. Bright manic crystals. We hit it off at lunch and afterward I drove him out to City of Industry to look at Grower's Nursery.

--Oh. yeah! This'll work, he said as we stood beside my car. I can storyboard next week. He paced along the freeway shoulder, a long rawboned pirate man with flowing black hair and a soul patch, dressed in jeans and a blue camp shirt. The guy in the song, he said. Want we cast your boyfriend? MTV'd be all over it.

--Only if you want to make it a documentary, I said.

He didn't appear to have heard me, standing right at the edge of the traffic stream, the wind billowing his shirt and lifting his hair. A pirate about to hurl himself into the mad river of American steel. Good-looking *and* potentially self-destructive. Julie's favorite. I didn't need to puzzle over why I'd been forthcoming with him about Davy and me.

--I wondered if he might be the guy in the song, Jason said after a while, coming back toward me.

--You know Davy?

--Naw, but we got tabloids in N'Yawlins. I mentioned I's doin' your video to a friend and she was goin' on bout some fight y'all had in a club.

--It wasn't a fight. We slapped each other.

He grinned and a gold crown glinted. A tiff, then.

--Most definitely. A tiff.

He stood with hands on hips, giving the nursery a last look, and said, This place is right out Andre Breton's private postcard stash. I never seen such a concentration of towers. It was Louisiana, people leavin' gris-gris sacks around. He grinned at me over his shoulder. You and me, we gon' make some beautiful pictures here.

During one of our less adversarial moments at home, I told Davy where we intended to shoot the video. I assumed he'd have a negative reaction. Most of his reactions were negative. He offered a nasty laugh. I wasn't up to interpreting it. What's that mean? I asked.

--Means you be lucky you and your film fag don't get your ass capped.

He was, I saw, going to make me pull it out of him. I asked a follow-up question and he said, Cause that's where they buried Spanish Eddie.

A second follow-up was required. He adopted what I thought of as his barrio-pride pose, head tipped back, gazing off into the torment of the past, a place into which no weak-blooded Caucasian Bimbo could see. That was the point of the pose. Davy wanted me to consider his personal trauma more significant than mine because he was an ethnic minority. He wasn't a bad guy, really. We just brought out the worst in other. Like two innocuous substances that together formed an explosive.

--Spanish Eddie was this guy showed up in the barrio bout ten years ago, he said. He made his living ripping off dealers. Guy was fearless. A legend. The Ninth Street Shadows shot him off the top of this apartment building. Eddie fell six floors and on the way down, he emptied his gun at 'em.

From Davy's expression, I judged he was having an epiphany, remembering the days of terror and glory. I hated to interrupt. So why's that put us in danger? I asked

--The Shadows are still nervous bout Eddie. Y'see, nobody knew nothing bout his life. Like one day he appeared and just started killing people. People think of him like this his-evil-will-never-die kinda thing. A fucking demon. They buried his ass deep. They don't want him coming back, so they keep watch over him. They don't like no one messing with their flowers. Hey, I don't know why I'm worrying. They never let you shoot in there.

--If the cops know about this, why they haven't stepped in?

--LAPD's glad as anyone to see Eddie go. That *puto vendejo* was everybody's problem.

To get a more unbiased line on Spanish Eddie, I called my friend, Dora Metzger, who--before becoming the LA Times' rock critic--had worked the police beat in East LA, and asked her to tell me what she knew.

--Not much, she said. Somebody was ripping off a lot of drug dealers in those days. If you're asking what I think, I think the ones doing the rip-offs were the Shadows themselves, and they came up this bogeyman to lay it off on. When they realized how much people in the neighborhoods had bought into Eddie as this supernatural figure, they saw they could get more juice by offing him. So they claimed they'd killed Eddie and the rip-offs dropped back to normal levels. They were barely a gang before that, but afterwards they got serious respect. They started attracting new members, grabbing new territory. She laughed. I guess you could say it made them what they are today.

--Why don't you believe them?

--Nobody survived the rip-offs, so the only people who can say they actually saw Eddie dead or alive were the Shadows...except for the usual run of *abuelas* who see Jesus' face in their catbox. That's too pat for me.

--Anything else?

Dora thought it over. No....not really. I remember they used to call him *La Pulga*. The Flea.

--What was that about?

--Beats me.

She asked how Davy and I were doing, sounding as if she was expecting for the long answer.

--We'll always have Tijuana, I said.

There was an old man at Grower's Nursery, stooped and palsied, with a bushy gray mustache and an absent manner. He wandered among the flowers, stopping every so often to inspect a bloom or a stem, talking to himself. I imagined that he recited Lorca and Octavio Paz, nourishing the plants spiritually. A master Mexican gardener. Don Julio would be his name. Expert in the nourishment of the good earth. Turned out he was somebody's Alzheimer uncle they let roam around in the flowers. So said the actual manager, Tony Rava, a young guy who drove an Escalade. He had a hundred dollar haircut, a suit by Georgio, cheekbones by Mister Chisel. A Ninth Street Shadows tattoo etched dark blue on his neck. His days were spent in an air-conditioned pre-fab office set at the center of the place, talking on the phone. A number of the phone calls were followed by the departures of panel trucks. When approached by the label, Rava said no way we could shoot at the nursery, but they tempted him with a nice fee and guaranteed to cover damages and provided handfuls of concert tickets and backstage passes. He gave his permission reluctantly, forbidding us to enter one area where, he claimed, they were using especially dangerous pesticides. If Davy was to be believed, it wasn't hard to figure out where Spanish Eddie had been buried.

Jason was having a prop built and needed to finish his storyboards. It would be at least ten days before we could film. That gave me two options. I could finish acting out the dissolution psychodrama with Davy or I could go directly to disaster and start a thing with Jason. Naturally I chose the latter. Afternoons I spent in the studio and nights I *lassez le bon ton roulet* with Jason at the Beverly Hilton. I had no illusions about a future with him and that was his main appeal. Time to admit, I told myself, that relationships were for people with SUVs and Scientology diplomas. I'd have to make do with flings. Davy left long insane raps on my voicemail, impassioned and menacing, all couched as stand-up spiels. He was turning our break-up into new material, just as I was turning it into songs. I wrote four more the following week. My agent said if I could come up with another five or six I'd have a concept album. I said Davy wasn't worth an album. Which was a lie. I was simply doing my best to forget the reasons we'd gotten together.

I went with Jason to oversee the installation of his major prop, Electroman. A metal man twelve feet high with a head shaped like a bolt, clawed hands, hinged joints that allowed it to be posed, and studded with spark generators that, when switched on, caused it to resemble a stick figure of pure electricity. Once darkness fell, Jason ran a test. The result was spectacular. Against a backdrop of wine-colored roses, Electroman flared and sizzled. It might have been the unruly child of the placid silver steel towers looming above. Tony Rava claimed we were in violation of contract.

A lawyer spoke to him sternly. Tony yelled and cursed. Finally he drove off in his Escalade, threatening retribution. Oblivious to all this, Jason played with his new toy, flicking switches on a board, making Electroman's claws clutch, its burning arms lift and lower, swiveling the fiery zero of its head.

Our first night working with a full crew, several dozen members of the Ninth Street Shadows stood guard along the perimeter of the no-shooting zone, their picket line defining a rectangular area about twenty, twenty-five yards long and fifteen wide. Some of them looked to be in their early teens. All dressed in white T-shirts and baggy chinos. Sullen and balefully regarding of us Hollywood types. This uniform of clothing and expression made them, I supposed, immune to especially dangerous pesticides. With Electroman sparking and crackling, lights everywhere, the music pounding from huge speakers mounted on the hilltop among our trailers, the silver towers gleaming like giant robot sentries over the massed flowers, I felt I was living inside a nightmare Jason was having about my song. The music was particularly bothersome. The last verse of "Nine Electric Flowers" consisted of the final lines of all the previous verses, kind of like "The Twelve Days of Christmas," listing the things the female protagonist would give her lover if he, basically, will leave her alone:

...If you don't tell me what you're feeling,
I'll light a thousand golden candles
If you promise to ignore me
I'll send you nine electric flowers
I'll send you nine electric flowers
I'll send you nine electric flowers
I'll send you nine electric flowers...

And so on through the fade.

We shot the end of the video first, a scene in which the actor playing Davy's part, a gay guy named Chad with better cheekbones than Tony Rava, chased me through the roses and we did this deep tango approach-avoidance dance centering about a kiss. The lyrics hammering into my head roused in me an antipathy toward Chad. I began to see him as less Davy's stand-in than his accomplice. It didn't help that he treated my lips as if they were encrusted with monkey butter. We couldn't get the kiss right. He was closing in for the umpteenth take when I said, Y'know, I think this might be a good time for a break. Leaving Jason to instruct him on the Method, I sashayed up the hill, sat in my trailer, smoked a joint. Stared out the window at the rows of tiny white-shirted gangbangers guarding the grave of Spanish Eddie. Dora Metzger had to be wrong about him. It made no sense they'd be guarding the area if nothing was buried there. Although it could be, I thought, that they were putting on a show, perpetuating the myth. The carpet of purple carnations that overspread the grave trembled. The silver towers seemed to shiver in the hot lights that dressed them in shines. I smoked and I stared. Soon I observed a flowing. Like when you're looking down at a river and see an eddy or a little current caused by a submerged object, one that's flowing sideways to the river's flow--that was like what I saw . A flowing through the air that proceeded from the closest of the towers toward the gangbangers...and maybe beyond. The lights surrounding the crew and Electroman—who was sparking merrily—were too bright for me to make out movement in the air. I thought that the pot must be showing me something unstoned people never noticed. As I recall that was extent of what I thought.

I slept with Jason in my trailer that night. That morning, really. We didn't get to bed until after four. At some point I dreamed about Spanish Eddie. In the dream I pictured him to be short, thick-bodied but not fat. A keg of a man with stubby legs and arms, a Third World face with a bushy mustache that reminded me of somebody, I couldn't think whom. He had on a black T-shirt and black jeans. Two holstered pistols strapped to his chest. The air darkened from the speed of his draw, as if scorched, and his bullets didn't detonate, they produced bursts of silence, though they killed like ordinary bullets. He killed a great many people in a shopping mall and he hopped like a bug, leaping five and six times his own height, from the ground floor to the tiered galleries and back down. Kind of a Super Mario Brother with extra superpowers and a vicious streak. Eventually whatever type of silencer he was using failed him and the gunshots began to sound thudding. Then he began to shout. Muddy words I couldn't understand. I woke to find the sun high and Tony Rava pounding on the door, calling my name. Jason let him in. He started talking fast, saying he never should have allowed us to use the property, it was a big mistake, here were the tickets and passes, he didn't want them. He flung them at Jason and said he'd write a check to pay back the fee. Jason told him he needed to talk to the lawyers and got on his cell phone. Rava knocked the phone from his hand and said, I'm sick of talkin' to fucking lawyers, man! I'm dealin' with you!

--You can't deal with me, Jason said. I got no power.

Rava's eyes went to me. I was muzzy-headed, partway trapped in my dream, trying to cope with the sunlight, and probably looking extremely damaged. You got power, he said. I'll deal with you.

Without considering the repercussions, just wondering, I said, This have anything to do with Spanish Eddie?

Until that instant Rava had been acting desperate. I believe he was about to push past Jason and get into my face. Now the urgency seemed to have been struck from him. What you know bout Eddie? he asked.

Yawning, I said, I had a dream about him.

Jason picked up his cell, punched in a number.

--Bout Eddie? What kinda dream? Rava asked.

I needed some juice. I slipped past Rava and into the kitchen. He was killing people. Jumping all around. Most of what he did was jump. Up, down...Guy could really jump. Like a grasshopper.

Jason spoke into the phone.

I had a slug of OJ. His gun didn't make any noise. And he didn't say a word. Not until you started yelling. Then you and him got mixed up.

Rava gaped at me.

--Here go, man, Jason said, and handed Rava the cell. Rava accepted it, but didn't put it to his ear. A tiny voice issued from the receiver, saying, Hello? Hello...?

The OJ hadn't helped. I was still out of it, trying to dredge up details of the dream. I know who he reminded me of, I said. Saddam Hussein! I mean, not exactly. A squatty version. But his face...it had the same basic shape, the same mustache.

I was pleased with myself—I usually can't remember dreams. I beamed airheadedly at Rava as if to say, See what I did? Rava didn't share my joy. He dropped the cell phone, looking shaken.

--C'mon, man! Jason scooped up the phone, punched buttons. Fuck! You broke it!

Rava opened his mouth to speak, but must have thought better of it.

Without another word, he bolted from the trailer and sprinted toward his car.

--You buyin' me a new phone, you! Jason yelled after him.

I glugged more orange juice straight from the carton. Jason eyed me with disapproval. Too much trouble you use a glass? he said.

--You're worried about germs? At this late date?

--People drink from the carton, he said, the lip gets all mushy. You get shreds of carton in the juice.

It was beginning to dawn on me that Jason was a control freak. That was part of the job description for a director, I guess, but I wasn't eager to be controlled by anyone, even if Jason was more gently controlling then Davy. We might have had our first fight then and there if his cell phone hadn't rung. Not broken. The surliness fled from his face. He answered and said, Desjardin. I turned to the window and watched Tony Rava's Escalade vanishing in a wake of brown dust.

It started raining around 7 PM that evening and we had to postpone the shoot. Jason wanted me to go clubbing with him, but I wasn't up for people and sent him off alone. I watched TV and felt sad. The rain sounded like it was denting the roof of the trailer. Everything inside seemed to be humming with its force. Around 11 it slowed to a drizzle and I went outside. I walked down the hill and along a row between rose bushes. The bangers were at their posts and a security guard was posted by the door of the office; there were lights on inside. The old Alzheimer's guy was standing among the purplish carnations. He appeared to be having a chat with some of them. He tugged at his mustache and shook his head dolefully as if unhappy with what they said in return.

I walked along the shoulder of the freeway to the base of one of the high tension towers. The rush of the traffic made me shiver. Up close, with its tapering rise and architecture of steel struts, the tower seemed a post-modern cathedral, one of the new churches. I looked up through lines of rain made brilliant by passing headlights toward the top of it, a dim complexity mired in the chemical night. A murky radiance surrounded the uppermost struts, like mud mixed with gold. I pictured the whole thing growing flexible, morphing a gigantic hand from the end of its erector-set arm and lifting me high to burn against a transformer, then striding off to kill LA. The main supports were set in wide slabs of concrete. At the foot of one lay bouquets of purple carnations and, mixed in among the bouquets, were pieces of rotting fruit—mostly oranges and melon--and candle stubs. Maybe it was just the state of constant buzz I'd achieved, but the air started to ripple, as with heat haze, and I would have sworn that electricity was curving around my body, fondling me, becoming familiar with my shape. I got gooseflesh. My neck prickled. The surfaces of my eyes felt hot and oversensitized. Paranoia infected me. I glanced back toward the flowerbeds and let out a shriek. My heart slammed. Shit! What the fuck! I said. The old Alzheimer's guy was standing at the edge of the concrete slab. He gazed dully at me, his mouth open as if he'd been panting. He had on a stained dress shirt, a shapeless, faded suit coat and baggy chinos. He fiddled with the ends of his mustache, drawing them into points. His eyes drifted to the bouquets. He didn't appear to pose a threat, but I eased away from him. Then he did something strange. The concrete slab was only eight inches high, but instead of stepping forward, he hopped up onto it. A spry little hop. Not what I might have expected, given his doddering pace. I retreated another step, but he no longer displayed interest in me, his attention fixed on the shrine at the base of the support.

--How's it going? I asked.

Either his mind was vapor-locked or he didn't know English. He nudged the bouquets with his foot, the idea being, I thought, to arrange them more neatly around the support.

I tried Spanish. *Como esta?*

Laboriously, he bent to one bouquet, probing the carnations with trembling fingers. A black seed, or maybe it was a bug, flipped out from among the blossoms. He made a grab for it, overbalanced, almost fell, and caught it. A look of demented satisfaction came to his face. He straightened, again laboriously, and stood catching his breath. Then he popped the bug or whatever into his mouth. He swallowed and his expression grew stuporous. His eyes appeared darker than they had moments before.

--Little snack, huh? I said.

Something lived for an instant in his mottled, caved-in face. I couldn't read it clearly. A flash of anger or recognition, like the cold alertness that tightens the face of a predator when it notices something weaker than itself. He lost focus, wetted his lips, then he turned and shuffled off. On reaching the edge of the slab, he sank into a half-squat, his knees flexing with amazing suppleness, and jumped. He landed without a wobble a bit more than three feet away. A child could have managed the distance, but it wasn't one I'd thought him capable of. As he tottered off along one of the rows, I suspected that Tony Rava had lied about him. The old man's silence, his jumping ability...in his youth he could have been good. I might, I told myself, have just had a run-in with Spanish Eddie. His shrunken relic. But the next moment I realized that was impossible. Eddie's prime had been, according to Davy, seven or eight years before. The old man would have been in his late sixties or early seventies at the time.

I spent most of the next day in the trailer, watching TV with the sound off. This was a pastime into whose joys Davy had initiated me. He created his own dialog for soaps, game shows, and was especially adept at dubbing Sports Center on ESPN. When he was a kid his mother had watched TV with her headphones on in their cramped apartment, while he and his sisters were supposed to be doing their homework. Davy used the time to do monologues and even now it was how he came up with some of his best material. His bit, for instance, about Bobby Bonds trying to pass himself off as an African monarch while having phone sex in the dugout—that one had led to his MTV show. I didn't enjoy doing it alone. I wasn't as glib as Davy. But this was as close as I let myself get to memorializing the relationship. We'd had many of our best moments together making fun of other people.

That night Davy put in an appearance at the shoot. The label's Security had been warned against him and large black men wearing Julie Banks Lives T-shirts prevented him from entering the nursery. Denied face time with me, he drove his car onto the freeway, parked on the shoulder at the edge of the nursery and went to pacing back and forth, waving his arms and shouting. I couldn't hear a thing he said, thanks to the music. Truthfully I didn't mind him there. The funereal aspect of the place, the bed of carnations beneath which Spanish Eddie lay, a vile seed with no bloom, and the gangbangers in their ritual rows, and the silver high tension towers like obelisks under construction, monuments to a dead, dread king--all of this rattled me. Having Davy around provided something else to think about. I knew he was putting on a show. He didn't care if I heard what he had to say. This mime act of loss and rage was exactly the statement he'd wanted. Allowing everyone to witness the absurd lengths to which he'd go in order to protest our dissolution. Here I am, he was telling me and the crew, the bangers, the passing cars. Davy the funny, smart, hurt guy. The self-deprecating post-modern Mister Pain from MTV. He'd shout and pace and make a fool of himself until someone took him away. He longed for some authority to come and collect him. The cops, the psycho squad, whoever. It would appropriately punctuate his Technicolor grief. But no one came and eventual Davy gave it up.

The shoot went fairly well. Chad had mastered something approximating a soul kiss. He flicked at me with his fairy tongue. Later he apologized for the difficulty he'd had. It was extremely stressful for him, he said, being with a woman. He'd been offered a part in a soap and, having had this experience, he wondered if he could handle a straight role. I was ashamed of having acted like an asshole with him. After we did the kiss to Jason's satisfaction, we began filming scenes with Electroman. The bangers didn't much like Electroman. Some laughed, but it was uneasy laughter. Others looked away as they might from an accuser's eyes. Those that dared to look at it did so with defiance, facing down the cause of their anxiety, and glanced behind them on occasion, as if they expected to see an enormous rotting fist thrust up from beneath the carnations. I thought about Eddie now and then. What had he been to inspire this ceremonial guard, this now not-so-secret burial? But mostly I concentrated on the job, and on Davy. On his tiny manic figure striding along the shoulder, shaking his fists, throwing a silent fit. He appeared to be raising some basic objection either to the flowers or the river of freeway light behind him or the towers that ruled over it all.

Jason wanted to finish the night by shooting Chad alone. I went up to the trailer and sat on the steps, facing toward the hills, and smoked a cigarette. There was a slice of moon. Misted. Like it was made of dry ice. The music kept blasting, but after awhile it settled around me, became part of a thick absence in which I was trapped. I wasn't happy, wasn't sad, wasn't annoyed. Just weary of stress, of having to address myself to it. Listening to "Nine Electric Flowers," I thought about singing. The passion required to give everything up to a song. To find its perfect form, to join with that form. Why it's important to achieve such expression. I decided it wasn't, that it was a complete waste of time except for the money it brought in. If the Glory of God was a factor, if you could motivate off of something that snowy white and selfless, anything would be worth doing. But drugs were the opiate of the people these days. Not many of us could afford to do religion. Not only was the price way high, the quality was awful. You'd need hourly injections.

So that's how I was feeling. Pretty uninvolved, pretty beat down and spacey. When Tony Rava stepped out from behind the end of the trailer, he roused no strong reaction in me. I thought he must have been in the office, because I hadn't seen him during the shoot. He looked beat down himself and he, too, was smoking a cigarette. His tie was loosened. He stopped a few feet away, head angled to the side, hands thrust into his pockets. It was a reflective posture that made me relate him to a character in a noir movie, a small-time villain with a problem. Which was more-or-less the case. How you know 'bout Eddie? he asked in a disconsolate voice. That about him jumping. Him using a silencer.

--It was a dream.

--It just come to you?

I said, Yeah. Why?

--That's how he took people off. He jumped through windows. Right through the glass. Or he'd jump onto your balcony from one higher up. Motherfucker was unreal, way he could jump.

--Like a flea, right? *La pulga*.

--Who told you that?

--Friend of mine at the LA Times. My ex mentioned Eddie and I got curious.

Rava cautioned me with a look. You wanna leave that shit alone.

--If I know about it, how much of a secret can it be?

--Don't matter. It ain't good to mess with.

I fished a joint from my bag and showed it to Rava, making a social gesture. Yeah, he said. Burn it.

I hunted for my lighter. Did he look like Saddam Hussein... Eddie?

--Yeah...maybe. Rava made a frustrated noise. Eddie, man! Y'know, nobody ever saw him 'cept when he was doin' crime? I mean, never. Nobody just said, hey, I seen Spanish Eddie down on Oliveira. It was like he didn't exist 'cept when he was doin' crime. People were sayin' he must be from outa town, cause that nobody seen him. Me, I think he's from *way* the fuck outa town! Know what I'm sayin'?

I didn't, not exactly, but said, Yeah.

--He's like a ghost. Don't say a word. He just opens up, then—Rava snapped his fingers--he's gone.

I lit the joint, sucked in smoke, passed it to Rava. We were quiet for a while, drowned in the heavy music. I felt the brittle strictures of our relationship dissolving in THC. After a couple of hits Rava cocked his head as if listening intently to the music and shuffled his feet in a dance step. I'm gettin' to like this song, he said. First it was drivin' me crazy, but now, y'know, it ain't so bad. He bopped in place, grinning me up like he was my biggest fan and I recognized that I couldn't trust a thing he'd told me about Eddie—not that he'd told me much. He dropped his flatterer's pose and asked if I could do anything about getting the shoot moved away from Grower's Nursery.

--Before we started, maybe, I said. Now...no way.

He nodded sadly. My woman didn't beg me for those Shakira passes, I never let you people do this!

--I thought it was the money turned your head.

--Naw, it was all the Hollywood shit, man.

--I don't get why're you so uptight. Like how come you got all those guys guarding that one spot?

Rava cut his eyes toward me as he inhaled, and said nothing.

--All you're doing is drawing people's attention to the area. It's like you want everybody to think something's there.

He gave a derisive snort. You keep the fuck away from it.

--Why? Something bad's gonna happen if I take a walk through there?

He appeared on the verge of blurting something out, but he composed himself and said, It's just the soil's been specially treated. We can't risk nobody messin' with it.

--Oh, yeah. Right.

--It could fuck up a special kind of carnation we been tryin' to grow.

--Uh-huh.

There followed a strained silence.

--Well, we'll only be here another couple of nights, I said. It's no big deal.

Rava laughed dismayedly. Your ass ain't on the line, somethin' goes wrong. I got people holdin' me responsible.

--Hey, what could go wrong? I said.

Generally I'm not that interested in figuring things out. I guess I don't think things can be figured out. Labeled, sure. Put in one box or another. But not understood. There's always a cause for doubt. Some detail that doesn't fit the theory or the facts. A loose thread that, if you pull it, unravels the tapestry of belief. Given this, it's just as likely to me that the world is replaced each morning with another world we seem to remember as it is that memory is an artifact of a world in which we serially live. It's no more rational to consider the universe in terms of heat death and organic evolution and galaxy formation than it is to imagine a great black shape hunkered down on a floor of pure absence, drooling over its starry toy. Despite feeling this way, I wanted to understand about Spanish Eddie. It's not that I deeply cared—I was bored that day and needed to exorcize some Davy thoughts. Having a puzzle to solve would help. Once Jason got started on his day, I threw on jeans and T-shirt and drove to Huntington Beach to see Clay Drango.

Most of the people I think of as figments of LA are little more than a good wardrobe and a set of interesting connections. They're the sort of people you meet at parties, because meeting at parties is essentially all they do. They serve to bring other people together, derive some small benefit for that service, and vanish until they're needed again. Clay didn't fit that mold. He was a figment of LA in that he seemed peculiar to the city's environment, but he was more substantial than the people I've described. Six years spent as a side character—a stoner surfer—on a popular TV show had left him financially independent and somewhat deranged. He had never to my knowledge surfed, yet he maintained the sunstreaked hair and deep tan and surfer lingo of the retro character he'd played. Classic figment behavior. It was his other obsession that gave him depth. Clay was convinced that a cosmic pattern was embedded in the ornate deviancy of Los Angeles. He believed if he could discern this pattern, which he called the Plan, he would be able...Well, I'm not sure what Clay was hoping for. World domination, maybe. Personal illumination. Maybe something in-between. I'm not sure he knew himself. But to this cloudy end he collected information about the city. His computer files were stuffed with factoids and rumors and events that all spoke to the bizarre currents that flowed around us. I thought somewhere in those files might be a few mentions of Grower's Nursery.

Clay was at the computer when I arrived at his beach house, his crumbling good looks more haggard than usual. This explained, I thought, by the glass coaster at his elbow. It held a quantity of white powder and a snorting straw made of silver chased with gold. He was shirtless. Wearing flip-flops and baggy tie-dyed shorts. His girlfriend, Nika, let me in. Nika was a long-legged brunette from San Diego. She'd met Clay at a comic book convention where she had worked as one of the bimbos who stood guard beside second-rate celebrities while they signed autographs, assisting them with the problems that arose, mostly dealing with the overly chatty types who waited on line. More devotee than lover, she organized his life, filtered his phone calls, and stared dotingly whenever he was near. Clay's office lay at the rear of the house, a sterile room equipped with a bank of television screens, all tuned to news channels. It was furnished with ergonomically engineered chairs and a computer station. Decorated with a photomural of an immense unsurfable wave. Nika ushered me in and stood by silent as a harem slave while we talked. Before I could give a reason for my visit, Clay said in a lazy, raspy voice, Grower's Nursery, huh? That place is radical.

It didn't surprise me that he knew about the shoot. Figments of LA like to give the impression they know more about your life than you yourself do—they horde bits of information to drop on you at appropriate times. I asked what he could tell me about the place.

--It's a nexus point. Very significant to the Plan. Clay turned to his computer and opened a file. Guess you heard about Spanish Eddie and all, right?

--Yeah.

--What you think?

--Urban legend...I don't know.

--Yeah, the Shadows were punks back in the day. They mighta invented him. But a few years ago I ran some programs on City of Industry. I got like...here we go.

He peered at the screen and at the same time groped for a glass coaster; he offered me his silver straw.

--No thanks. Then, hedging somewhat, I asked what it was.

--Meth.

--Wrong direction for me, I said.

Clay did a fat line and scrolled down the screen. Nestor Paez. That's the guy started the nursery. Came up from Guanajuato in the early fifties. Mexican government wanted him back. They accused him of criminal activity, but he....

--What did he do? His crimes?

--Far as I know, it was unspecified. Paez had a congressman, Jack DeWalt, who helped him fight extradition and get legal. This DeWalt guy was into real estate scams, drugs, prostitution, all sorts of criminal shit. Everybody was paying him off and the DA was like on him, man. Then DeWalt does his thing to get Nestor legal and not long after, his problems got dead.

Nika glided over, bearing a joint on a polished wood tray. I fired it up and exhaled smoke as I asked, How'd that happen?

--The DA and his assistant. A buncha cops. This crazy dude would come outa nowhere and jump through their windows. Killed them, their families. The guy was like totally whack, man.

--Just like Spanish Eddie.

--Yeah. Except nobody killed this guy. Isn't that cool? They called him *La Pulga*. The same thing they called Eddie. It was this awesome program dug that up for me. I got it off...

--What else do you have?

Clay brought up an old black-and-white newspaper photograph on the screen and beckoned to me. I leaned in over his shoulder. The photograph was of a smiling young Mexican guy in work clothes standing in front of a flowerbed. Cheekbones by Mister Chisel. He bore a strong resemblance to Tony Rava. The caption read: Nestor Paez, Prize-winning Entomologist--A Proud New US Citizen.

--Get that? said Clay. Entomologist. Not horticulturist. He's a bug scientist.

He brought up two more pictures, also old newspaper shots. The first was a shot of Grower's Nursery circa 1963. No high tension towers, but a network of thick wires overspread a portion of the nursery. I couldn't make out what kind of flowers lay beneath the wires, but the wires appeared to cover the same area where now was planted a bed of purplish carnations. The second photo showed Nestor Paez kneeling beside a generator.

Attached to the pictures was a brief article that bore the heading: ELECTRICITY GOOD FOR FLOWERS SAYS CITY OF INDUSTRY GARDENER. The article itself did little more than restate the heading, but did mention that Paez' Bordeaux carnations had been grown successfully only in ground prepared by him.

Tony Rava, I thought, had to be related to Paez. A grandson, probably. Carrying on the family tradition of electric flowers. The connection between Spanish Eddie and his violent predecessor was less obvious. I wanted to ask questions, but I had a contact high from hanging around Clay and was too scattered.

Clay nodded, smiled knowingly at me, as if he recognized the precise extent of my bewilderment and understood its underlying cause. The Plan, he said with immense satisfaction, is a bitchin' Plan.

Writing lists always make me feel like I'm getting somewhere with a problem while I'm writing them, but they rarely result in a solution. The one I wrote after leaving Clay's was no different.

1) Spanish Eddie
2) Electricity and flowers
3) Old man—connection with Rava? With Paez?
4) Bugs? The old man ate one. Connection?
5) Two Spanish Eddies? Is the old man one of them?
6) Is religion involved? The shrine under the tower.
7)

I got stuck on seven...on six, actually. The sentence, "Is religion involved?" made me realize that I was bullshitting myself—it would have been less pretentious, perhaps more constructive, to ask if God had a navel. Before writing the list, I'd had a sense of a dread shape emerging, a presence coalescing from the mist. Now, seeing my suspicions on paper, the connections between them struck me as flimsy and I imagined the hint of causality I had glimpsed was due mainly to all the weed I'd been smoking. Fuck, I said and crumpled the list, tossed it aside. What to do? I considered cleaning up the trailer, then a baggie full of Thai stick caught my eye.

The next couple of nights, it rained hard enough to turn the access road to Grower's Nursery into a muddy ditch, sending rivulets washing down the hillside. Jason grumbled, paced, and finally called the Chateau Marmot to see if they had a bungalow available. I told him to go on and party without me, and not just because I wasn't in a party head. Jason had been an effective solution to the Davy problem, but I knew our fling wouldn't last much beyond the end of the shoot. It was time we got started on the break-up. We argued. More precisely, we disagreed. Our arguments were jingles compared to my operatic conflicts with Davy. I felt almost nostalgic when I recalled them.

--What's it with you, man? Jason said. You keep on blowin' me off, I'm gon' get the idea you don't want me around.

The opening was there, but I wasn't ready to take it.

--I'm in a mood, I said.

--When you get happy, that's what I call gettin' in a mood. It lasts a couple hours or whatever, then it's back to this. This is you.

--Louisiana women don't ever feel blue? They're always perky and fun? Must be the spicy food.

He rested a hand on the doorknob and stared at me. It was a patronizing stare, the one he used when somebody on the crew had let him down.

--Don't give me that look, I told him. You know you're gonna feel better once you got a few glasses of wine in you, once you're hanging out with the players and doing things to further your career. You'll forget all about this little disappointment.

He made a disparaging noise and said, Ain't everybody like your old boyfriend, cher.

--Y'know, whenever you break out the bad grammar and the Cajun talk, I get the notion you're insincere. You better watch that. I think it's a tell.

I turned on the TV after he left, watched fifteen minutes of *Survivor*. I thought about which of the men I'd sleep with and then realized that the best tactic would be to sleep with all of them, to make yourself generally available until the end, and let them fight it out amongst themselves. Have them vote out the other women and the Christians. When it got down to three or four, they'd start to sniff the prize money and you would have to switch strategies; but promiscuity would take you a long way,

The gay Survivor, in an intimate camera moment, began gassing about how he was picked on as a kid. shedding a few tears in the process. I slipped into a pair of jeans and a sweatshirt, and peeked outside. The rain had let up and down on the hillside the bangers were straggling back to their posts, having taken refuge from the rain in the office. Jason had given most of our security the night off; two guys were toking up in the step van that had brought the lights and, as I passed them, on my way downhill, one said, Hey, Julie. Everything cool?

--The coolest, I said. I'm just going for a walk.

I walked down the hill, then on a whim I took a right and cut along one of the rows, heading for the picket line of gangbangers. I think I wanted to fuck with them a little, though how I wanted to fuck with them is unclear. Make them nervous, I guess. As I came near, some of them straightened and their expressions congealed into sullen masks. Others studiedly ignored me, gazing up into the overcast sky. A few of the young ones, their mustaches barely sketched above their mouths, fresh blue-black tattoos on their arms, lowered their eyes. I walked with my head down, pretending to examine the flowers. I could feel their enmity, and I suppose that was my actual intent in approaching them—to stroll along a foot or two away without acknowledging them, challenging them in that way, mostly because I was pissed off at Davy and I included in my anger the macho bullshit culture that had warped him into such a twisted shape, a culture emblematized by these ridiculous little trolls in their baggy pants and shirts—like a chorus line of Charlie Chaplins capable of beating their chests and making funny hand signals and killing, but not much else. Each step I took made me angrier, and when one said, *Oye, mamacita!,* I turned to lash out at him, to tell him what I thought of his version of La Raza, and saw that it was Davy. A smiling Davy, a Davy drowning in his clothes, size 2X chinos and flannel shirt draped over his medium frame. He grabbed me by the hair, pulled my head back, and said something in Spanish that I couldn't understand but made the bangers laugh. To me he said, with mock cheerfulness, Hey, babe! What's new? and dragged me off along the row.

I screamed, hoping to catch the ear of the security men in the van, and clawed at Davy's face. Breaking free, I ran downhill, but tripped over the cables connecting Electroman to the control board that operated it. Davy hauled me up and slung me against the board and drew back his fist as if to punch me. After a second or two he unclenched his fist.

--Davy, I said, trying to keep my voice even. Davy, what're you doing?"

He glanced down at me—he had let his gaze drift off into the middle distance—and said, Taking charge. He turned his attention to the control board. What's this? He peeled back the tarp that covered it.

--What do you want? I asked him.

--This runs the metal guy, right?

--Jesus. Davy! What do you want from me?

He moved me aside and lifted away the tarp. I want to see how this fuckin' thing works.

This was typical Davy. Force a confrontation and then affect interest in something peripheral. He thought this afforded him the opportunity to be entertaining, to display how clever he was, how disarming. It was a tactic a kid might employ to distract an angry parent and, while I had once seen it as part of his appeal, now it infuriated me. I wasn't in a position to express my fury, but I gave disgusted a shot.

--Why don't you just play for a while, I said. That'll help.

He flipped a switch and chuckled when Electroman's arms pumped and sparked; he flipped more switches. Soon Electroman was all lit up, a twelve-foot-tall pedestrian with sparks flying off its silver surfaces, arms and legs churning. walking in place, yet appearing to be cruising along among the purple flowers, generating a sizzling, grinding noise. I looked toward the van--there was no sign of the security guys.

--Hey, I said, trying once again to connect with Davy. Now that you've kidnapped me, what's your...

--I didn't kidnap you, bitch! I reclaimed your ass!

--Somehow I bet the cops are gonna see it my way.

He didn't respond, just kept staring at Electroman.

--So what's the plan? I asked.

--I have no plan. No fuckin plan. But I'm okay with that. You know why? Cause a man with no future don't need a plan.

By saying that, he was implying that I, too, had no future. I'd heard it all before, the blaze of glory speech, how he would kill me, then himself. Ordinarily, I wouldn't have been concerned, but I saw how amped up he was, all twitch and bad energy, and I understood that we might have entered new territory.

--Gettin the picture, *chica?* he said.

I couldn't decide whether to run or to try calming him down.

--You keep lookin' at that van, he said. I wouldn't be expectin' much. Those guys in the van, they got problems of their own.

A series of pops issued from Electroman; the silvery figure trembled. I was about to tell Davy that he should shut it down, hoping to sidetrack him, when I saw that the air above Electroman was disturbed...a disturbance that was part of a flowing spreading throughout the air above Grower's Nursery. Like a river of night made visible by faint currents that seemed to vanish the second you noticed them, so that you registered only their afterimage. Davy glanced up to see what I was staring at and said, What the fuck!

At that moment, Electroman started to walk along the rows of Grower's Nursery.

It didn't actually walk, although that was my first impression. The metal figure was being lifted and bumped along by a force not quite strong enough to get it airborne, drawn on an erratic course through the flowers. Flattening rosebushes and carnations alike. Yawing, listing, yet managing to maintain its perpendicularity, All evidence suggesting that the force in question was being applied from overhead, perhaps from that weird, almost invisible river flowing above the nursery. As Electroman approached them, cables snaking out behind it, the gangbangers scattered. Taking their cue, I made a run for it, sprinting straight up the hill after Electroman, choosing that direction because I hoped Davy would be reluctant to follow. I wanted to head for the trailer, but it seemed the ground was jerking underfoot and I went careening sideways and lost my bearings. Everything was a chaos of fleeing, pratfalling gangbangers, of shouts and rumbling...I didn't immediately associate the rumbling with an earthquake. I perceived it as a natural product of chaos, as endemic to a state of fearful confusion as my quickened breath and the hammering of my heart. The ground jolted violently and flung me forward. I landed face-down among the carnations and that's when I felt the earth's monstrous shaking. I rolled over. Electroman loomed above me, teetering, about to fall.

I had a moment of clarity during which the rumbling became unimportant, the shaking irrelevant. Electroman had stopped its sparking, its cables ripped loose. Turned sideways to me, an oval of darkness enclosed within the circle of its head, arms akimbo—it was the perfect emblem of that chaotic night, familiar in its basic form, but otherwise sinister and fearsome. I covered my head as it toppled, regretting everything and expecting to be crushed. Then something slammed into me, pushing me aside in the instant before Electroman crashed down. When I recovered I found that Davy was lying close to me. My right leg was pinned beneath him and he was pinned beneath Electroman. His head was bleeding profusely from the impact of Electroman's head, which rested partly atop his. I was lying flat on my stomach and had to twist about to see him. Because my leg was pinned, I could reach back and just touch his shoulder, but I couldn't do anything for him. I called out to him and tried to wrench my leg free. It was hopelessly trapped. Some embittered inch of me wanted to think that he had been attempting to hurt me, that saving me had been inadvertant. But quick turnarounds from hate to love were a hallmark of the relationship.

The earthquake, which had subsided somewhat, intensified its rumbling and produced another, greater shock. A fissure opened in the earth some fifty feet away; it widened, lengthened, ripping a gash that spread toward the tower closest to us. The air grew thick with heat and dust. Terrified, I wrenched at my leg again and felt some give. The last shock, I realized, had shifted Electroman. For an agonizingly long time I tugged and wriggled, until suddenly the leg came free. I scrambled over to Davy's side. His head was still bleeding, but less than before. I set my shoulder against Electroman and heaved. It wouldn't budge. I tried to ease him from beneath it, pulling at his shoulder, pushing at his waist. Something protruded from his trouser pocket. Davy's pet automatic. This, too, must have been kind of a gun night. As I continued to pull at him, a sharper noise pierced the rumbling. I glanced up to see one of the silver towers collapsing.

Despite my fear, I couldn't help watching. It was an amazing sight. The immense skeleton tilting; the legs tearing free of the concrete moorings; power lines swaying like vines, snapping one by one, followed by a blacking out of the lights in the vicinity, throwing the nursery into near-darkness; and the resolution, slow and stately, into a wreckage of struts and girders, raising a great dust. It was, I imagined, like watching the death of an ocean liner from the vantage of a lifeboat. I clung to Davy, expecting worse. But that, except for aftershocks, was the earthquake's final statement and, after awhile, I shouted for help. Shouts came in return, but no one appeared out of the dark. Grower's Nursery must have had a generator, because white auxiliary lights were soon switched on, illuminating some of the rows, articulating the dust particles thronging the air--like fish food settling in aquarium water. I shielded my eyes, shouted again. A long-haired man materialized in the vicinity of the fissure, backlit by a white glare, then leaped out of sight.

--Over here! I climbed to my feet and waved, hoping to attract his attention.

He reappeared, but once again vanished abruptly.

Three gangbangers came running from the opposite direction. They were joined in short order by a fourth. Dwarfish men with big tattoos. They spoke all at once, ignoring my pleas for them to free Davy. Finally two of them grabbed hold of Electroman and strained to lift it. Too heavy. They held another conference.

--I saw some guys over there, I said, indicating the general area of the fissure. Maybe they can help.

No response.

--Hey! All of you lift, okay? I pantomimed a lifting motion. *Todos!*

They continued talking among themselves.

--Are you fucking idiots?

One glanced at me, made a joke; the other three laughed.

My eye fell to Davy's gun. I snatched it up and thumbed off the safety and aimed it at them. *Todos!* Okay? *Todos.*

The bangers weren't impressed by the gun. One of them spat at my feet. The ground trembled with an aftershock.

Que pasa,? A fifth gangbanger appeared out of the murk. Gigantic by comparison to the others; wearing a wifebeater; with a goatee and hugely muscled arms that served as billboards for his religious convictions, crosses, madonnas, and sacred hearts, along with a variety of secular statements concerning someone named Anna. The others jabbered at him, pointing to me, to Davy.

--Get it off him! I said weepily, gesturing with the gun.

The giant gave me a firm look. *Calmate.*

He took a stroll around Electroman, sizing things up. He tested the heft of the figure and gave instructions to the other three guys, positioning them variously. He kneeled beside Davy, looked at me, and demonstrated that I should be ready to drag Davy out at the crucial moment. I didn't know if I would be strong enough and I communicated my doubt.

--Okay, the giant said. Okay.

He directed the smallest banger, a kid with a mystic eye tattooed on his brow, to help me pull Davy out. We both grabbed handfuls of Davy's flannel shirt. The giant made a show of putting dirt on his hands, of planting his feet and squatting. He drew deep breaths and crossed himself. Maybe these preparations were necessary, though, because when he lifted, grunting with the effort, his face darkening, Electroman moved upward. No more than a few inches, but enough. We hauled Davy out, falling over backwards in our urgency. The bangers gathered around the giant, offering their profane congratulations. I hunkered down beside Davy. He was breathing shallowly; he wouldn't wake up. Someone tapped my arm. The giant.

--*Me voy a buscar por un coche.* He mimicked turning a steering wheel. *Entiendes? Luego, lo llevaremos al hospital.* He repeated the word *hospital* a couple of times to make sure I got it. He spoke briefly to the others and then hurried off into the dark.

Sirens could be heard worming through the distance; more shouts from closer to hand. Dust and white light, heat and shadows. The hill whose slopes Grower's Nursery occupied seemed as desolate as Golgotha. For the first time, I thought about what might have happened to the rest of LA. I envisioned a city in ruins. Apocalyptic scenarios crossed my mind, a hybrid of the Old Testament and John Carpenter. Savages of every race roaming the streets. Crucified policemen. Fiery thrones. I picked up Davy's gun and rested it on my lap. This amused the gangbangers. They relaxed, lit cigarettes, chatted. Having survived the quake, forgetting that not long before they'd been panicstricken, screaming to god and their mamas, they displayed a new swagger. I figured they were already polishing their accounts of Electroman and their famous brother and his *gringa* into a heroic tale. Perhaps the experience would generate bigger and better tattoos.

I began to feel relief and, with relief, hope. Things were going to work themselves out, Davy would receive treatment and recover from his wounds, and maybe this lesson would take, maybe we had a future, having gone through this together. Our little tableau, Davy, Electroman, the bangers and I, islanded in white light—it effected a kind of security, even though adrift in a dark world filled with sirens and the unknown. I put my head in my hands, weak from too much adrenaline. When I opened my eyes again, I saw someone standing behind the bangers. A man, naked, with long black hair matting his face and shoulders, and a raggedy beard. His body glistened, as if covered in gel, and he had an unfinished look...at least that was my impression. Something wrong with his face, his skin. I was stunned, tongue-tied. He wrapped his arms about the kid with the tattooed brow, flexed his knees and, before the kid could even squawk, he jumped, carrying them both out of view.

The bangers produced pistols from their voluminous clothing and fired wildly into the darkness. They were frightened, yet I had the thought that they weren't surprised by the naked man's sudden appearance. Spanish Eddie. However improbable, it had to be him. With gesture, they cautioned me to stay put and hustled off, I presumed, in search of their friend. I wedged myself in under Electroman as best I could, but I didn't dare move Davy—I couldn't have moved him very far, at any rate. My thoughts raced, trying to puzzle things out, but I didn't make much headway before caving in to fear. Somebody screamed up on the hill and I felt the urge to scream in sympathy. Reacting like a child, I wished I could make myself very small.

When Spanish Eddie returned, leaping in to a point behind me, he wrapped his arms around me, but was defeated by the fact that I had taken refuge beneath Electroman. In trying to lift me, his arms went about Electroman's silver spine and the combined weight was too much for him. He seemed baffled. He tried the lift again, with the same result. His face came close to mine and it reminded me of the old Alzheimer guy's face, devoid of emotion, of sensibility. Only his eyes, like the shiny carapaces of two black beetles, showed life, and that was merely a counterfeit of reflected light. I saw now what had struck me peculiar about the face. His lips were sealed, joined by a membranous growth that looked to be wearing away. And his nostrils, too, were partly sealed by vestiges of that same growth. I had been paralyzed with fright, but this horrid sight roused me and I fired into his chest. The bullet tore through him as if he were made of papier mache, chewing deep gouges in his flesh. Gouges that leaked a clear fluid. He fell into a sitting position, stared incuriously at his chest. I fired again and again, emptying the clip into him. Bullets struck his cheek, his neck, his chest and shoulders, and still he sat there, unmoving. Half his face was blown away, revealing a textured substance that resembled mangled yellowish cork or wood; yet I couldn't tell whether he was alive or dead, and when at length he began to wobble, finally crumpling onto his side, I thought this might be due less to the waning of life than to the weight of the bullets overbalancing him.

For five, possibly as much as ten minutes, I was alone with Davy and Spanish Eddie. Staring past the lights, trying to detect movement. Aiming an empty gun. Blank except for fear. Every once in a while checking to ascertain if Eddie was still dead. The giant returned with a *coche* and, on seeing the body, gave me a shrewd look. I realize now that he was making a life-or-death decision. *Momentito,* he said, and went back to the car, opened the glove compartment and removed a large flashlight; then he dug under the front seat and pulled out a Mac 10. For some reason, I wasn't afraid. Maybe I was just tired of fear. He strode across the flowerbeds toward the spot where the fissure had opened. I wasn't invited, but I tagged along, anyway. When he reached the fissure, he shined the flashlight down into it, walked for thirty feet or so, and stopped. He handed me the flashlight and directed me on where to point it. Visible in the side of the fissure was a hollowed-out space; resting in it were three shapes that looked very much like bodies. Difficult to say, because they were shrouded in bugs. Thousands and thousands of black bugs. They were swarming everywhere, so many of them, they made a seething noise. Sticking out from the surrounding dirt were what appeared to be broken power lines. I steadied the light and the giant opened up with the Mac 10, spraying the three shapes. He fired off two entire clips and then surveyed his work. He clicked his tongue in satisfaction.

--*Vamonos,* he said.

We laid Davy in the back seat and headed for the hospital in Whittier. After a few miles, the shock began to wear off and I had some thoughts, some questions. I turned to Claudio—so the giant had introduced himself—and said, Spanish Eddie?, and made a gun with my fist and pretended to spray bullets just as he had done.

He drove for nearly half a minute without responding; then he glanced at me and, with a look that could best be described as dead serious, he put a finger to his lips.

When Clay Drongo, whom I visited not long afterward, heard the story of that night, he said, The Plan ever grows in complexity. We were sitting on his veranda, watching the waves rolling in onto what is often referred to in song as California's golden shore, but showed that day as a seaweed-littered stretch of tawny sand, populated by elderly couples in windbreakers. Clay was ecstatic about the coincidental crises of earthquake and domestic dispute, which he claimed was "classic Plan stuff," and suggested that the entomology thing was crucial. Nestor Paez must have come up with a way to fabricate hitmen out of bugs and electricity. And, probably, some human material. Some Mexican bad guy's DNA. Or maybe Paez had stumbled onto cloning secrets. Clay said he wasn't sure how the flowers worked into it. Ancient Egyptian seeds used by the priests in the House of the Dead? To tell the truth, he wasn't sure how it all went down. The ways of the Plan were mysterious, indeed. But they were obviously growing Spanish Eddies--lots of them—down under the ground. The one I'd met with must have been prematurely born. They likely had, Clay said, some cool way of training them. He speculated that perhaps they controlled them with drugs.

--Yeah, maybe, I said. Whatever, y'know. But none of that's the important thing.

He asked me what was important, but I didn't want to get into a conversation. Not to worry, I told him. It's a chick thing,

I'm certain that karmic law prevails, but I don't believe it works in the way that's commonly accepted—do something bad and something equally bad comes back at you. I'm not certain what it is I do believe. Maybe karma's like rock and roll and how strong it is depends to a great extent upon how you're into it. Maybe people are trapped in karmic zones. Some light, some dark, and everything in-between. Or something. Anyway, I'm absolutely certain karmic law was operating that night at Grower's Nursery. However you care to explain the event, you clearly saw the level of everyone's karmic vulnerability in what happened. And that's the important thing. Not what happened, but what was revealed. No matter what Spanish Eddie truly was, he was basically an opportunity for karmic business to be done.

For example.

Davy got well, but did not recover. He sustained minor brain damage from the blow to his skull and, as a result, he's not funny anymore. Not clever, not glib. Not being funny, he can't work. He'd invested his money, so he was set that way, but he broods all the time. He refuses to see me. He sits in this West Hollywood dive bar, where nobody knows him, and drinks beer and tequila, and when he gets too drunk to drive, they send him home in a cab like old Uncle Fudd. It seemed he always wanted to be miserable, but he always thought he'd be able to make people laugh by telling them about it. I don't think he deserves this, but maybe he earned it.

They say the City of Angels is hard on lovers, but the city's karma is its own and I think me and Davy, the kind of people we were, we could have fucked it up in Iowa. In Duluth, in Saigon, in Choctawatchee. (There might be a song in there somewhere, but I wouldn't want to touch it.) True love borders on disaster, and I'm talking about true love between any two people. It takes a miracle to play out right. You blame each other for shit that doesn't exist, you get crazy about the small stuff, and neglect the rare and beautiful thing you've lucked into. It's a crime that is its own punishment and, in most cases, it draws a life sentence. But I'm going to clean up my act, I swear. No booze, no drugs, not even a joint. I'm going to be ready next time, because I still have hope, even where Davy is concerned. Maybe that's the cruelest karma of all.

TO-DO LIST

NICK MAMATAS

1. Go to your local public library. Find a copy of *The Undiscovered Self* by Carl Jung. Take a $50 bill from your pocket, fold it half, and insert it between pages 22 and 23. You will not return to that library until you have completed the rest of the tasks on this list.

2. Set aside some time each week to watch old Warner Bros. Cartoons. You may rent tapes, tune in to the Cartoon Network, buy the DVDs, put up rabbit ears and try to get a signal from one of the Francophone channels right over the border, whatever it takes. Make a list of every American city mentioned by any of the characters. Keep it near you. When you have as many cities as you are years old, you may stop watching the cartoons on schedule. If you like.

3. There is an older woman you see fairly often, while running errands. You don't know her name. Strike up a conversation with her in the supermarket. Learn her name. Find out her favorite song. If she claims to dislike music, run, for you have stumbled across the demon wearing human flesh like an ill-fitting costume. This is not a joke. Don't smile, excuse yourself, and walk away. Drop your basket right there in the Canned Vegetables, Canned Fish, and Ethnic Items aisle and run for your life. Double back to your own home after dusk. Never return to that supermarket again.

4. If she answers you, learn the words to that song by heart. Here are the lyrics to a song I learned by heart after being told by an old woman in the supermarket that it was her favorite. In a tremulous but smoky voice,

she even sang it for me, betraying only a hint of a Carolina accent:

I came to this country in seventeen-forty-nine,
I saw many a true love, but I never saw mine.
I looked all around me and found I was alone.
And me a poor stranger, and a long way from home.

Down in some lonesome valley, down in some lonesome place,
Where the wild birds do whistle their notes to increase,
I think of pretty Saro whose waist is so neat,
And I know of no better pastime than to be with my sweet.

I wish I were a poet and could write a fine hand,
I would send my love a letter that she could understand.
And I'd send it by a messenger where the waters do flow
And think of pretty Saro wherever I go.

5. Place a stick or a branch on a sidewalk near a local government building in a position where someone is likely to trip over it if the stick isn't moved or kicked away. Fire stations and elementary schools count.

6. When you are next in a diner and sitting at the counter, say this word after you are given your coffee: Efharisto. (pron. ef-har-ree-STO) If your cup of coffee suddenly becomes a bottomless cup of coffee after that, you are in the right place.

Be sure to be there at the right time. Take a matchbook or business card or menu home with you, so you'll remember the exact address.

7. Send a care package to a foreigner in a rogue nation. Include American cookies, cigarettes, a paperback book over which you have combed your hair so that a few loose strands and some dandruff sprinkles the pages. This is a crucial step, in case you are captured and killed before you complete your tasks and thus need to be cloned. A pair of shoes. Reading glasses, the type you can buy at the supermarket. Use packages of egg noodles rather than Styrofoam filling material to protect the contents of your care package. You can likely find a foreigner using the Internet or by

picking up your phone, dialing 0, and asking for an International Operator. Treat the operator as though he or she is your best friend, and the two of you need to work together to find the address of your second best friend, who just happens to live in Libya, or the Sudan. Air mail the package. We don't have a lot of time.

8. Most people today are just a few generations removed from a life where supernaturalist folkways were preserved and transmitted in the form of anecdotes. Question family members until you hear a "true story" with a numinous element. By way of example, here is one I heard once:

> *In the village of Kakinagri, where your great-grandfather grew up, there was a woman with twin sons. She loved them so much; they reminded her of her dead husband. They were little boys, just seven years old, but they were the best swimmers anyone had ever seen. The people called them sardellas, sardines, because they wiggled their bodies and swam so quickly between the fishing boats. One time they went out fishing with their uncle, their dead father's younger brother, and a storm came up, capsizing the boat. The little boys were such good swimmers that their mother couldn't believe that they had died. For seven days she waited on the beach for them to come to shore, pulling out her hair and wailing at God the whole time.*
>
> *After seven days, she went home, but she wouldn't stop wailing. She was up all night, with her lamps burning, screaming "Why, God, why? Why did you take my boys, my little dolls, away! If only I knew why!" Then she'd sob and cry quietly, and in the morning start yelling again.*
>
> *Her neighbors called for the priest, who stood outside the door for a long time listening to the woman. Then he told the people to prepare a loaf of bread and cut it into seven pieces, and leave it on the stoop. He went inside and told the woman to stop carrying on so vainly. If she wanted answers from God, there were prayers she could make that would reveal His plan.*
>
> *For seven days the priest led the woman in prayers, stopping only at noon to reach out the window of the small house to retrieve and eat one piece of the bread. All day and all night they prayed and chanted.*

The house filled with soot and smoke from the gas lamps they used in those days. And on the seventh evening, the stains and flickering shadows from the lamps started to take shape on the walls, like a movie was being projected on it.

The woman saw her twins again, but they were fully grown, well-muscled and dark from the sun. Healthy men with evil smiles. They were grappling, and each had a knife to the other's throat.

"If I can't have her," one said through gritted teeth, "neither will you."

"If I can't have her," said the other, "nobody will!"

Then they slit one another's throats and fell to the floor violently, still wrestling even as they bled a puddle under their backs. And that's how they would have died, had they lived, in a way their mother nor God could ever forgive. And that is why the Lord took them away so early, to spare her the pain of the future.

When you hear your family story, memorize it. Embellish it to make it more interesting if you must. Consider how much less interesting it must have been three generations ago.

9. Attend a local meeting of a minor political party. Sign any petition or mailing list you are given. Do not subscribe to any newspapers or newsletters published by this party, however.

10. Travel, by the cheapest means at your disposal, to the nearest city on your list. Make a day of it. Go to every public library in town and collect $50 bills. With this money, buy a ticket to the farthest city on your list.

11. In the far city, make contact with members of your minor political party. Meet them at a diner. Order coffee. Say the word. Split the check down the middle with the other members of your rendezvous, even though it is likely that at least two people will meet you at the diner. Describe the contents of the care package you recently sent to someone in a rogue nation.

12. Some time after returning home, you are likely to be met by two men in suits. They may be FBI. They may be Secret Service. They may be

affiliated with a rival minor party. You do not need to speak with them. You do not need to let them in. They are professionals though, and can be congenial when they need to be, to make you drop your guard. Recall the song you recently learned. Recite it in your head as they speak to you, to be free from their charms. You may need to sing the first few lines aloud as you close the door on them to extricate yourself.

13. Place a stick or a branch on a sidewalk near a federal government building in a position where someone is likely to trip over it if the stick isn't moved or kicked away. The local Post Office or IRS office count.

14. Go to the diner. Read the complimentary newspaper as you drink from your bottomless cup of coffee. You should notice that the government seems to be running out of money. Letters to the editor are getting more shrill and making less sense. Note the number of men versus the number of women expressing such opinions. If you are in the more prominently represented gender, skip ahead to task 16.

15. Go on a first date with someone you met over the Internet. If you are a conventional sort, use Yahoo Personals to find your date. If you consider yourself "cool" or "hip" use Nerve.com. Sit *al fresco* if you can, by a potted plant or a window facing the street if you cannot. Order the house wine, then send it back, dissatisfied. Tell your date about the political philosophy of the minor party whose meeting you recently attended. Request sex. If he or she immediately but unenthusiastically agrees, know that you are under constant surveillance. Feel free to engage in whatever form of sexual intercourse you like. Shower thoroughly afterward, at a YMCA, the local public pool, or a gym you do not have a membership with.

16. Go to your local New Age shop or metaphysical bookstore. Explain that you are interested in getting in touch with your cultural heritage. Recite the family story you recently learned and ask the clerk if the store has anything associated with it. Buy whatever you are offered and perform any spell, ritual, meditation, or prayer for the fulfillment of desire you feel comfortable with. This will harden you for the next task.

17. In a very public place where you are guaranteed to be overheard, and apropos of nothing, announce "You know, back in my day, veterans only bragged about being in wars that we actually won! Goddamn fuckin' losers…"

18. Go to the diner. Read the paper. Be thankful that you get free refills, as diner prices are now approaching those of Starbucks. By this point, your local tabloid should be featuring color photos of fireballs, sweaty soldiers, or forests of picket signs carried by the Working Man and The Youth on a daily basis. The old lady who sang for you once has died; her daughter has published a death notice. Do not weep for her. She is in a better place. Don't get me wrong, there is no heaven, but she is not really dead. She has simply gone underground. You are in the right diner at the right time. The hidden message in the death notice is not for you, but if you wish to try to decipher it, you may.

19. Stay off the streets. Eat what's in your cupboard, even if you are down to the stuff you don't like and bought just because you wanted something easy to make in case you caught the flu one winter. Know that I am with you. When the far-away city you recently visited makes the national news, regardless of the reason, you may take this to be the all-clear and leave your home.

20. Go to your local library. Go to the shelf where a copy of *The Undiscovered Self* is stacked. Check for the $50 bill. If it is gone, rejoice, for we are that much closer to our final liberation. If it is still there, we have failed, and tyranny and repression for another generation is our reward.

The Woman in the Numbers

M. K. Hobson

Isaac Robert Newton, Isaac-the-Box, overgrown with sapling cottonwoods and birches, squats faintly clicking in the middle of Don't-Go-There Field. He sucks on a thread of random numbers, thin and sweet and silver, filling in the details of a sublime moment in obsessive fractal detail. He takes each grain of the moment and limns its particular details, then the details of the details, and the details of the details of the details, so on down toward infinity. Toward nowhere. Zeno's paradox, short distances halved, the object of desire within fingertip's reach but never achieved.

Isaac-the-Box is forever collapsing inward, a dying star, his consciousness becoming infinitely massive as it becomes smaller and smaller. Already, only thirty years since the straw-haired woman put him here, things are beginning to be drawn to him. Birds. Small animals. Lizards. They feel the attraction of the metal box. The box confuses them. There should be a smell. It should be a dangerous, uncertain smell, but there is nothing. Just a feeling, a sense of things impossible for them to understand. Doorknobs. A hand without an arm, suspended. A thing forever upside-down and right-side up at the same time.

The straw-haired woman (rather, the silver-haired woman now, for she is frail and there are reticulated webs around her mercury-bright eyes and soon she will be no more) leaves food for the creatures. Peanut-butter sandwich crusts and rinds of fruit. In the spring, she scatters flower seeds. The ones that are not eaten will grow and bloom into colors. She is alive, and she does have a smell. She smells of imperfection and resignation and love.

Isaac-the-box winks and blinks at various intervals, his little lights glimmering through the screen of weeds and saplings and flowers that have grown up around him. Sometimes he buzzes, grinds or clicks. He is powered by a very efficient atomic battery, designed to provide uninterrupted power for ten million years. He will run until a seismological cataclysm sends him spiraling down through a fiery crack in the earth's crust. Or until the planet explodes.

He sits in the middle of vast tract of private land in the Bitterroot Mountains of Montana. Right in the middle of this remote stretch of wilderness there is a field. Don't-Go-There Field. He remembers walking with the straw-haired woman while she was naming these places. Don't-Go-There Field and Come-Out-Come-Out Cave and Look-At-Me Rocks and Time-Must-Pass Creek.

He still remembers these things, a little. But maybe in ten thousand years, he won't. Their consequence is so small. There is so much else. There is the thread of random numbers, sweet and encompassing, and there is always something to discover within them.

This day, he discovers an elaboration on the curl of brown hair above his mother's left ear. The shine of it is perfect. Her hair was never perfect, but the light hits this little curl of it just right.

He goes deeper, to an individual hair. The light is at just the right angle to penetrate the shaft, illuminate it. It is like copper glowing from within.

He goes deeper, into the glow itself. He tears it apart into every color of red and brown and yellow and gold.

He goes deeper. He concentrates on the red. There is more beneath that red, he knows. A wiggling vibration of wavelengths, each one requiring detangling.

And down he goes, down, down, down.

In the curl of red, she is screaming at him.

(What he remembers her saying is probably not what she really said, because he did not know so many words when he was four. This fact makes him feel mushy and dull and antsy; He should know. He should know exactly what she said. He should have listened better.

A small helical gear and pinion wire shift in sympathy. They remind him where he is. He is inside, and she is out. Her universe will never be his, never again. He resumes his unraveling, tearing her apart with slender remembered fingers.)

She is screaming at him, shaking something in his face. A toy.

She is saying that he should pay more attention. That if he listened better, she wouldn't have to scream, and he would be a better boy. If he listened, then he would know.

She throws the toy down on the floor, hard. It is a soft toy car with large wheels. There is a smiling face on it. It squeaks.

Isaac is still, deeply still. He does not feel fear, or anger, or sadness. He is only blank and uncomprehending and pinprick-tiny.

She picks up other toys and throws them on the ground and crushes them under her feet. Little broken pieces fly through the air.

He longs to crawl into her lap, to bury his face in her soft breasts, find the dark fragrance there. He wants to beg her to protect him. But she can't be both things at once. No one can be upside down and right-side up at the same time. He knows this, even at four.

Sitting on the floor, he makes his body smaller.

Isaac began sponging at a very young age, but he did not have the word for it until later. He discovered the word when he was five and his mother threw a wine bottle at him and he soaked up the spilled red liquid with a ratty yellow sponge. He cut his hand on a shard of broken glass while he was cleaning up the wine, and the blood of his hand mingled in with the wine, and it stung. But it all was sucked up into the sponge, blood and wine and all, and it seemed so right and so final. If only his brain was like that. If only he could suck everything up, suck up everything so that nothing ever escaped him. Then there would be nothing for her to yell at him about. He would become steel, smooth and seamless. There would be no scalp for her to dig her nails into, no flesh for her to rip or bruise. She could beat against him forever, and he would be inside, looking out. She could beat herself to bits against him.

The thought was beautiful. He set himself to learn how to become a sponge.

It was not easy. He never knew what he should pay attention to. His mother knew, of course, but she would not tell him until the moment for attention had passed, and he had made a mistake. Made her angry again.

He tried very hard to predict what he should pay attention to, what the important things were. But only his mother knew what they were. One moment, it was the thin film of dust on the top shelf of the shelves in the back of the basement. The next moment, it was that he used the word "the" too much. Five minutes later, it was that he was sitting too still.

"You think I don't get it?" She sneers. "You think I don't see what you're doing?"

Isaac taps a toe, tentatively. Lifts his chin up and down. How much is too much? How much is too little?

"If you paid more attention, I wouldn't have to say a goddamn word."

He watches harder. Becomes a sponge. Becomes steel.

Obsession is exhausting.

Isaac's ability to pay extreme attention cost him. He would sleep all day, twelve hours a day. When he wasn't sponging, he was sleeping, escaping the terrible burden of concentration. He slept deeply, and did not dream at all.

This pleased his mother, because when he was awake, things happened. Items would vanish or appear. Hours would pass, and she would not know where they had gone. Morning would become night would become morning. She did not know if these events were the result of the alcohol or the drugs or the cigarettes, but she knew that they did not occur when Isaac was asleep. When he was asleep, her reflection moved normally in panes of glass as she passed them, and did not stop to stare back at her. When he was asleep, stripes of light falling across the carpet did not bend and refract in ways contrary to their nature. When he was asleep, she was not as terrible; she could be young again, young and afraid and beaten, and she could feel sorry for herself.

By the time he started school, Isaac was a sponge.

He could stare at something—a page, a face, a textbook—and absorb it. Not read it, not consciously decipher it, but rather soak it in through his pores. Feel it, get his whole big body around it. Hug it, take it in, chew it, digest it. It was a good way to see small pieces of paper that had to be picked up out of corners, doors that should be closed but not shut, chairs that were not at a ninety-degree angle to the table. Sponging helped him foresee many disasters and avert them.

Many, but not all.

The method sometimes failed him where he needed it most. His mother remained an ocean of contradictions too large to absorb. She was random and contradictory and unencompassable. Her rages built and decayed quickly, and they had no appreciable connection to each other, so the hard-won knowledge of one day never carried over to the next.

(*She pushes his head through a window because he is wearing a blue shirt.*

She cuts off all his hair because he asks if there is any butter.

She locks him in a closet and lies on the floor outside of it, curled up in a ball, talking to the carpet.

Wake up.

Open your goddamn eyes.

Look, look!)

Because he could not formulate a theory for how to consistently predict her storms of destruction and avert them, he learned to live outside of her line of vision. He stayed very still, moving just enough to escape her notice.

This got harder as he got older. He got bigger and clumsier. He was well over six feet tall by the time he was seventeen, his body composed entirely of elbows and extremities that flailed even though he tried to keep them neatly tucked in. It was as if his body had a mind of its own, a rebellious, treacherous mind. His body was like a vicious younger brother, always looking for ways to get him into trouble. His body knocked into things. His body ate too much. It all infuriated his mother.

No cloud without a silver lining, though. When he was outside his mother's zigzagging path of chaotic destruction, the skills he'd developed served him well. Sponging gave him perspective, and with perspective came pattern, and with pattern came beauty. He saw patterns in everything, but it was the patterns in the numbers that were the most beautiful. Straight and mute and unambiguous and predictable.

His teachers called him a genius, and pitied him.

He got a scholarship to a good college, and another scholarship to an even better graduate school.

And then his mother died.

He was working on his master's thesis when the news came. His research involved the radioactive decay of carbon atoms.

When he learned that she was dead, he sat very still, looking at his own reflection in the window, huge and bent and clumsy and distorted. He sat for a long time, shaking, waiting for something to happen, for the sky to crack open, for snakes to ooze from the walls. Something would have to happen. He stared at the data he'd collected for his thesis. A hundred pages of it, carefully compiled, partially analyzed.

It suddenly struck him that it was just not enough.

He didn't have enough data. His whole body was shaking. He could not complete the analysis with the data he had. He could not breathe. His measurements were impossibly sketchy. He had not paid close enough attention. He never had.

He wondered where she had hidden the gun. A rifle, she had to have hidden it somewhere. In a closet, maybe. He imagined brain-matter spraying red against a wall.

He needed to measure the decay of the carbon atom at a far smaller granularity than he had been measuring it. He needed to measure more. He needed to measure everything.

It took eight weeks to set up the experiment. He did it alone, and in secret, because no one else would understand his need to measure the decay of a carbon atom to a degree of such obsessive fineness.

He did not tell his thesis advisor that he planned to collect a completely new set of experimental data. She was a straw-haired woman with heavy features and eyes the color of mercury. He thought she would be angry with him.

Once set up, the experiment took only one-millionth of a second.

It was a long millionth of a second. Measuring that one millionth of a second resulted in two hundred and fifty thousand single-spaced pages of data.

Isaac had the data printed at a copy shop. It took two months and cost him seventy-five hundred dollars. He got the money by stealing an autoclave and selling it. The copy shop delivered a hundred-and-twenty-five boxes to his apartment.

He sponged the data. Looked at it and took in everything about it, not only the information but the context as well, the whiteness of the paper and its grain, the blackness of the ink, the width of the margins, the height of the descenders and ascenders, the spacing between letters.

He absorbed the information like staring at the shifting patterns of clouds in the sky. Lying on your back, staring at the sky, you do not look for a story. The story finds you, and the cloud becomes a sailing ship, or a running horse. Or a rifle. The chemical processes within your brain form these, mold them, and then suddenly they are there, and they are real.

In this way, absorbing the numbers into the wide mysterious space between his eyes and his heart, Isaac saw it.

He saw a hand.

He stared at the numbers, took them into his mind, stared at them. Unfocused his eyes, absorbed the paper and the printing and the floor and the room around him, and the sky beyond that, and the stars and everything beyond that, and there was the hand.

A hand reaching for something. A female hand, frozen in mid-motion, mid-movement, mid-moment.

He left graduate school.

His thesis advisor, the straw-haired woman, was worried about him. He felt that she was disappointed in him, and this made tense echoes rise in the low part of his chest. When she asked him to coffee, he agreed pleasantly, and held the door for her, and pulled out her chair, and put his napkin on his lap. He hunched over the table, trying to hide his extreme height, trying to make his body smaller. He sat as if there was scar tissue webbing the core of him, cramping him into something compact and shrimp-shaped. He paid the bill with the last of the money he'd gotten from the stolen autoclave. But he did not talk through the whole awkward visit. He sat very still and smiled at her very carefully. She tried to get him to talk about his future plans, about his research, about the weather. He just sponged his coffee cup, staring at the little brown puddle in the bottom of the saucer.

She filled the void of his silence by talking about herself. This was no great burden to her. She liked talking about herself.

Her research team had twenty million dollars from the Department of Defense to develop wireless brain computer interface technology. Powerful magnetic signals, manipulated to stimulate pathways in the human prefrontal cortex and transmit orders, plans, maps, in-field intelligence. The applications were being developed in order to kill people in newer and faster ways.

But she did not think about what this meant, about the mothers of sons who would die, about the mothers of those mothers. Her thoughts floated on the glossy surface of immediacy. She loved grant money and the allure of the shiny atrocities that she could create with it. She did not see the pattern within the chaos. No one ever did.

He smiled silently, inoffensively. He pushed the coffee cup around on its saucer.

As they were parting ways, she looked at him with a little exasperation that made his stomach curdle. She wore a knowing smile that made her look cruel.

"Do you need a job?" she asked.

He paused for a long time, sponging the ground, its stochastic texture comforting him up through the soles of his shoes.

"Yes," he said, finally.

She offered him her hand to seal the deal. She noticed that it was strangely hard to accurately gauge the distance between their bodies. It wasn't just that he was always positioning himself as if a blow could come from any direction at any moment. There was a hunch to his back, like he was carrying a lead weight in his belly. He carried himself like one side of his body was tall and one short, and his waist wide and his knees narrow. He looked like a pencil distorted by a glass of water.

But he was interesting to her. Interesting in the way things under glass are interesting. She thought she might dissect him, casually, just for fun.

So he joined the team. They gave him a white jumpsuit that did not fit him, and a broom to sweep the floors.

He did not work very hard.

"Don't you ever sleep?"

The straw-haired woman asked him this the first night she brought him home to her white oak white walled apartment. He had brought his black gym bag, stuffed with as many pages of data as he could carry, and when she was finished with him, he crept out of her bed to stare at the dog-eared pages. He stared at them, turning them over slowly in his lap.

"What is that you're reading? Numbers? Numbers can wait. You need your rest. Come to bed. Come to bed."

He came to bed immediately, because he was a good boy. He held her, his chin pressed against the top of her head, his eyes wide open.

She slept for days that first night with him. She lived a lifetime in her dreams that night. When she woke in the morning, stiff muscles crackling, she expected to find that the trees outside her window had died, that the earth had gone barren, that dinosaurs had returned to rule newly-grassed plains.

But she just found him, his big body hunched back over the papers, his eyes unmoving and unfocused and bright, so bright.

The first few months with the straw-haired woman in her white oak white walled apartment were undemanding. She asked little of him and he gave little. He came to work diligently and abstractly. He washed his jumpsuit when necessary. Mostly, though, he sponged data.

He discovered a hand and a wrist and part of an arm.

The hand was reaching for something.

There were intimations of boundaries beyond that, of a whole figure somewhere there within the hundred-and-twenty-five boxes of printed numbers. He could feel that the woman was standing in an unusual way. He imagined that there was a defeated slope to her shoulders, an expectancy in the way she had one foot placed before the other. He felt that she was reaching for something at waist level.

What was she reaching for? When would he get to the box, to the page, that contained the answer?

It was not going fast enough.

At the lab, however, things moved quickly. Twenty million dollars will make things move quickly. The team reworked the protocols on a standard Hauptman-Xian brain-computer interface (which had been helping quadriplegics move mouse icons around on computer screens for a dozen years) and came up with a working wireless neural output generator. From there, it was a small step to complete the loop, reverse the interface so that data could be returned to the brain from the computer that was being controlled by it. For the purpose of the team's report to the Department of Defense, it was called Project D-524a: Wireless Neural Interface. But among themselves, they called it the Box.

The day the team performed their first successful experiment with the Box (a test subject transmitted two large numbers to a remote computer, which divided the numbers and returned the result to the mind of the test subject) Isaac experienced a minor frenzy. He laid his hands on the Box, stared at it, open-mouthed. He chattered a stream of questions, hardly waiting for the answers before another sprung to his lips. His voice was high and tense.

This abrupt enthusiasm surprised the team. Before he was just another grad student, half-present and abstracted, the director's floor-sweeping machine. He brought her coffee at random intervals and kept her bed warm at night. If strange things happened after he joined the team, they were never ascribed directly to him, rather to the strange nature of the project they were working on. Long hours could make fluorescent lights flicker and wave in odd Morse-code patterns. Fatigue could explain the way that voices slowed and echoed, the way ghost-images of hands and doorknobs appeared in the polished steel surfaces of their magnificent appliances, and the smell of spilled wine and blood.

But Isaac had realized what kind of freedom the team had created for him. They had engineered his salvation. Suddenly, and without warning, he knew that he could be freed from the tyranny of eyeballs, of paper, of ink. He could mainline the hundred-and-twenty-five boxes in a sweet digitized flood. He could become the data, suck it in, let it circulate through his whole body, tiny numerals like blood cells, oxygenating his soul, letting him finally, finally breathe.

"Of course you may not," the straw haired woman said tersely, when he came into her office and leaned over her desk and told her that he had to use the Box. "What do you think it is, a toy? Do you want us to lose our funding?"

He blinked, swallowed hard. He made his voice even more pleasant, more sweet, more ingratiating. He told her again, his voice shaking, that he must use it.

Please, he said.

No, she smiled at him.

In an instant, he had her by the throat. He shook her. He knew the place between the windpipe and the jugular, the place to dig his fingers. He dragged her little body across the desk, and things broke. She could not scream, but things broke and her team members heard. They rushed into the office, and pulled Isaac off of her. His face, they later said, was a blur, like a face of a man falling from a high building, featureless and terrifying.

Campus security came. They held him until the police came.

She did not press charges.

She came down to the station later. She hid the purpling bruises around her throat with a scarf.

Of course, she did not tell her team that she picked him up from the police station. She did not tell them that she brought him home, held him sobbing against her bruised breast. She could not tell them all the apologies she gave him and the promises she made. She would make it all right, she promised him. She would make it all right for him.

She took him back to the lab at night, when everyone was gone. They brought Isaac's one-hundred-and-twenty-five boxes, the data encoded on a slim silver disc. They stepped together into the darkness in which clicking whirring machines waited. She put the transceiver on the very center of his forehead, the broad smooth place between his eyebrows. She covered his eyes and plugged his ears and his nose. She placed a mask over his mouth, and his lungs filled with cyanotic bitterness.

Eyelids twitching, a hundred-and-twenty-five boxes streamed through every part of him, through his groin and gut, saturating his cortex and forebrain.

And the woman stepped forward from the numbers as if someone had just flipped a light switch.

A doorknob.

That is what she is reaching for.

The tips of her fingers are just touching it, contacting metal. He can feel the cool smoothness of the metal. It is shiny brass, just like the doorknobs in his mother's house.

The doorknobs in his mother's house are strange.

They are barrel-shaped, with a smooth concave depression on the end that faces from the surface of the door. In the very center of the shining depression is a mysterious hole. A point of infinite smallness and darkness. If he could get small enough, he could crawl into that hole.

He looks at himself in those doorknobs and is reflected upside down. When he was young, and the door was always locked, he would stare at the doorknob, and he would pay attention to the doorknob. He thought deeply about that doorknob. He'd realized that even if he stood on his head, he'd still be upside down in that doorknob. His reflection would be right side up, but he himself would be upside down.

There is never any way to get both of him, the real him and the reflected him, to stand up straight at the same time.

Isaac convulsed in the leather chair, his long muscles freezing and snapping, his hands curling up like flakes of burning bone.

She held him down, one hand on his shoulder, the other on his thigh; she pressed an ear against his thrashing chest. His heart was pounding spasmodically against his ribs, a panicked bird beating itself to death.

A dead grad student would not look good on her resume.

Around them, in the lab, the machines began to flicker. Time sped up and slowed down. Light bent. She could not move, she could only stand as the sun rose and set and rose and set a hundred times, and the moon crashed into the earth and then leapt back up again. A million terrible versions of herself shifted shadowlike before her eyes, herself in this place and others, in this time and others. She was pitiless and cruel in all of them.

It was her. *All* of her.

All her ugliness, all her selfishness, all her fear, all her humanity.

He understood her. He knew her.

She was astonished.

No one had ever known her before.

Then, for the first time in her life, she was terrified of losing something. Or more accurately, she knew the terror of losing something she had not wholly discovered.

He sees the flesh of her forearm in exquisite detail. It is constellated with little scars. His mother picks at scabs compulsively, liking to watch the blood come. She itches mosquito bites, worries pimples. Sometimes she takes up knives and digs at her skin, boredly. She says it is because she has an itch, but he sees the fixity in her eyes, the way they follow the tip of the knife as it creates some pattern of her own mysterious creation ...

"No more," the straw-haired woman screamed, over the thundering thrash of chaos. His body was vanishing into light, disintegrating, burning up. There was the smell of burning hair. She could not lose him now. She needed him. He knew her. He understood her. Somewhere inside him, she was. He was her one-hundred-and-twenty-five boxes.

She had to struggle to turn off the power. She had to struggle against the moon tumbling out of its orbit, the spiral arms of galaxies pushing against her, oceans of matter dark and unseen.

Her hand, trembling, found the switch.

Isaac screamed loss and frustration. He fumbled after the flood of numbers as they fled from him, leaving him heavy and dull and beached, a jellyfish flung ashore to quiver and melt.

He huddled in the chair, trying to breathe.

The straw-haired woman tore the mask from his face, unstrapped and unplugged him, moved her hand before his eyes until slowly, reluctantly, they followed. She smoothed him and petted him until time was right again, and the moon was where it was supposed to be.

"It is too much," she said, placing a hand on his fever-hot throat, feeling his pulse beating fire. "You can't ... you can't *die* for this."

Isaac stared at her, unfocussed eyes bright and inverted as a concave brass doorknob.

"How can I die?" he said. "I've never been alive."

That was when she took him away.

She told her team that she was taking a sabbatical. She did not tell them that she was going away with him. The experimental phase of the project was over anyway; all that remained was the detailed reporting that the Department of Defense required. There would be testimony required before groups of Generals. But that was yet to come. Meanwhile, she was taking a sabbatical.

She had to make him understand. She had to make him understand how important he was to her. He was vital to her life. He understood things about her that she did not understand. Her heart beat in his chest. His life was no longer his own. He had to understand that. She had to make him understand.

She took him to a place that she had in the Bitterroot Mountains. There was a cabin. It was primitive, but comfortably so; there was a satellite feed and a gas-hybrid generator and passive solar collectors. But there were no numbers. Isaac did not know what had become of the one-hundred-and-twenty-five boxes. Every night, he had writhing screaming nightmares, imagining reams of paper burning in a metal can, butterflies of ash rising up on constellations of sparks.

"We're going to work on this together," she said matter-of-factly. It was the tone she used when speaking of projects, of reports, of grant money. But there was a desperation behind it he'd never heard before.

She took him for walks. She showed him Don't-Go-There field. She named places as they walked. You-Are-Mine Arroyo and Forgive-And-Forget Butte and What-Is-Past-Is-Past Creek. She owned the land, hundreds of acres, obscenely vast. She could call things whatever she wanted. She named ancient things whimsically; their redefinition was the work of a brutal instant.

"We are making progress," she said to him one day, with undisguised relief at her own imagined accomplishment.

They were making progress.

She began to speak of houses. She spoke of Isaac completing his master's thesis, but she did not speak of the decay of carbon atoms. She spoke of children and cocktail parties and her brilliant future presenting her research to a group of Generals from the Department of Defense. She spoke of things that had nothing to do with rifles or doorknobs, and time did not do strange things and light continued on its accustomed path unbent and unmolested.

He pleaded with her gently, constantly; trying to convince her to take him back, take him back to the lab, to the box. He had to understand. He had to understand the woman with her fingertips on the doorknob. He had to know what she was reaching for.

"Understand her, you mean?" She prompted him, her mercury-bright eyes disassembling him, shaking him roughly to hear what rattled. "Your mother?"

He clenched his teeth. Fury surged through him. What right had she to ask him questions, to keep him here? What right had she to name things? He suddenly wished he had strangled the life out of her that day, when he'd had her windpipe and her jugular under his fingers.

"I'm leaving," he said.

She stared at him in shock.

"No, you're not," she said. Her voice was dangerous. Anger kindled in her poisonous silver eyes. The anger that he'd always been so careful to avoid. Now he was inviting it. He welcomed it. Without the numbers, it was all he had.

He turned pointedly. Infuriatingly. He turned his back on her and walked away from her, back along the creek she had named Regret-Nothing.

She caught up with him in two strides, clamping a hand around his belt, pulling him off balance. She was shorter than he, but stocky and strong, and fired with abrupt fury. He fell to the ground, curling himself up on the slippery pine needles, shielding his head with his arms.

"How *dare* you," she screamed at him, her rage inflating like the birth of a new star. Wisps of brown hair flew around her red sweating face. She beat him mercilessly, with fists and feet. "How *dare* you?"

Because I love you, he thought, savoring each blow. It was his own secret, spoken into his forearms from behind closed eyes as her fists beat down on his shoulders.

The straw-haired woman led him back to the cabin in silence, past Pay-Attention Meadow and Listen-To-Me Grove. She put him a bathtub of hot water and washed blood from his face with a warm washcloth. She did not speak.

"I won't leave," he said, offering the words gently. Soothing her, wiping away the blood she had not shed, palliating the bruises she did not share. Of course he would not leave. There was no longer any need to.

He saw her everywhere now.

In the random whorls of soap bubbles in the cabin's big claw-foot tub. Even when he looked at the straw-haired woman. Especially then.

He felt free.

He did not need the numbers any more.

He could just look at her.

The straw-haired woman did not sleep for three days, though Isaac slept deeply, in deep peace, nightmares banished, burning boxes irrelevant. He slept gently and sweetly. She sat by his bedside and looked at his bruised face. Purple and yellow and orange swirled around the orbit of his eye.

He knew who she was.

"Get up," she said softly, on the third day. "We're leaving."

He complied, placid and quick, making the bed and locking the cabin doors and holding the car door open for her.

They drove for two days, back to California. Back to her lab.

"Don't be afraid," she said to him. His eyes were anxious as he watched her unlock the door to the dark lab with its clicking whirring machines. She flipped on the light.

Taking her hand, she led him gently to where the box squatted, broad and gleaming. They stood looking at their twin reflections in the smooth metal.

"She's not in there," the straw-haired woman said softly. "And I'm not in there either."

"No," he said, shaking his head. Sudden concern kindled in his eyes. "I don't ... I don't want to leave you."

She placed a hand on his face, on the bruises that were still healing. She stroked his cheek with her thumb.

"You're a good boy," she said. "You're a very, very good boy."

Because the straw-haired woman finally knew herself, and knowing herself, she knew him.

He looked for an answer in the hundred-and-twenty-five boxes, an answer that they did not have. If he stayed, he would look to her for an answer that she did not have.

She would disappoint him. But the boxes never would.

The woman in the numbers did not have the answer, but he would never know that. He would never know enough of her to know that. There would always be another detail to limn, another fractal filigree to chase downward into infinity.

She had to let him go, to let him lose himself in furious exploration of her eternally static image, an image that could never hurt him because it was infinite and there was always something else to pay attention to and he would always be a good boy because he would pay attention, such close, perfect attention to her forever.

It was the only way he could be saved. She was the only one who could save him. She was the only one who could save him from herself.

She took his hand, warmly cradled in her own, and placed it on the cool metal of the Box. She held it there, pressing it down.

"Go," she said.

He hesitated for a moment, but finally he nodded. He was a good boy.

Then time stopped, and the planet stopped moving, and there was only him, and the straw-haired woman, and the woman in the numbers in everything, and the Box.

His body blazed with light, but his face was as calm and beautiful as the smile of God.

She let her hand drop, and stepped back from him, proud as only a mother can be.

For one long, last moment, he looked at her.

At her metal eyes, the color of imperfection and resignation and love. He thought of doorknobs, of upside-down reflections. Of two faces that were forever to be opposite. But for a strange confused moment, they didn't seem to be opposite at all. He thought that he didn't really recognize her. That she wasn't who he thought she was at all.

"I love you," he said.

"I love you too," she said, softly, over the sound of the sun imploding.

I love you too.

His mother is smiling.

Isaac-the-Box is grinding through data. He never thinks about the hundred-and-twenty-five boxes now; they were only a starting place, an outline, broad brush strokes on an achingly white page. The straw-haired woman has provided him with a randomness generator that will spit out numbers forever. A silver thread, a thin sweet stream of milk he sucks on lovingly.

She is looking at the door, and there is a look on her face of the most transcendent joy. He has never seen such joy on his mother's face. It is the most beautiful thing he can imagine.

Someday, if he pays attention long enough, he will know what is behind that door. He will know what she is looking at with such joy. He will discover who is on the other side.

He hopes that it is him on the other side of that door. He hopes that he will see that doorknob turn, and that look of joy will still be on her face, and for a moment, he will be right side up.

The Tongue

Brendan Connell

I.

"As a man, I am far too passionate for this contemporary life," I murmured to myself as I strolled along the Viale Carlo Cattaneo. "As an artist, I am of the highest order, up-to-the-minute, the 100,000 follicles of hair on the human head obeying my commands as so many helots might those of a Spartan king. . . . Raised on the over pungent sauces of antique philosophies, I could have been anything: soldier, spy, diplomat or adventurer; but the seeds I plant in the little garden of my profession are those of updos and chignons, elegant hairstyles for sophisticated women and . . . men."

I turned and walked past the library, into the park. It was autumn and, in the light of the late afternoon, the leaves of some trees had the appearance of cascades of gold and copper coins. The scene was as charming as one of those seasonal paintings by Boucher—or really more truly a certain piece by Claude Monet—a shimmering display of colour, almost outrageously, radioactively bright. And I was in optimum spirits, making my way forward with buoyant steps, widening my nostrils—though it was not so much the lake air that I sniffed as the bouquet of my own thoughts which, sensorial as they were, emitted perfumes of cinnabar and sericato, odours such as Ty, that famous ancient hairdresser, probably anointed his patrons necks with.

Exiting the park, I crossed the Riva Giocondo Albertolli, onto the Via Stauffacher and into the city centre. Rapid motion of pedestrians. Faces. Fur collars. Hair: grey, red, black. Improperly tended. Needy. And like a good little scout I moved on, guided by my desire to be amongst men, human beings.

As I was passing the Café Down Town, I sighted Marsyas in the window, sitting with a young woman of Praxitelean appearance, the equivocal symbolism of their profiles rich with nuance. I tapped on the glass. He gestured frantically and then came rushing out to greet me. He gripped my hand in a brotherly fashion, and I had to move my head to one side, or his nose, which was excessively long, would have poked me in the eye.

He said, in his flute-like voice, that he was glad to see me, and I would have liked to have replied, but could not. "She is vain," he continued, nodding towards the young lady in the window, "but twice a day she allows me to reap the corn of her passions, and of this the chine of my scythe, which is well polished, never grows weary. For truly Elba (that is her name) is as venereal as a rabbit, an animal as delicious in its own way as any shellfish. . . . Oh, I had seen her before, in the snowy bosom-shaped peaks—the Bietschhorn, the Aletschhorn, but to have such a creature nestled up against one, to have the opportunity to melt her glaciers with my mercury, is a sensation that makes a dreamland out of days."

I listened to his words as the Japanese poet Joso might have the song of a thrush. And then I attempted to give a suitable response, to comment knowledgably, with a hint of disdain on his indiscreet exultation; but no sound was forthcoming. At first I imagined it was just some temporary case of ankyloglossia. I endeavoured to run my tongue over the roof of my mouth and then experienced a lack of sensation. Alarm. Wonder. I felt for it with my teeth, but it was not there.

Marsyas asked me if something was wrong. A sensation: of blood rushing to my face. I motioned him away. Through the corner of one eye I saw Elba observing me: a circle of imitation marble framed in chestnut hair. I turned and made my way down the street, around the corner in the direction I had come, checking pockets, front and back, as I went.

A mild aura of panic descended on the city; and I was upset. To lose one's tongue is an especially unpleasant experience (as: a painter losing his eyes; a duellist, his sword; a farmer his land). . . . It was the tool with which I expressed my desires, my wants, my hates and antipathies; and surely it was my body's loveliest muscle.

I rapidly retraced my steps, my eyes panning over the sidewalk, the events now taking on the appearance of some antique Cecil B. DeMille silent. Hand-tinted. Low-key lit. Crowds directed. I looked around at the people on the street, wondering if one of them had picked it up. There was a fellow with the demeanour of a dog and a mane of long black hair; a woman with an overt bosom; a Chinese man wearing a bright pink tie. . . . . . . Or could some animal or bird have taken it? Cat. Child. Thief. Anyone who found my tongue would love it, very possibly be adverse to parting from it.

My mind flew over the incidents preceding the mishap. . . . I had last used it on the Viale Carlo Cattaneo, while murmuring to myself before entering the park. Had I left it somewhere along the way; had it dropped out?

Biting my bottom lip. Speculating curiously. Anger and fear.

I saw something red on the ground and picked it up. It was the skin of a persimmon.

I carried my legs along and the cars swirled past me, them greeting the new night with their headlights, like so many monstrous devotees of the goddess of misfortune. Through the dark streets I wandered, those I passed transformed into monstrous toads, giant heads attached to swift-stepping feet; me, without the ability to shriek as I dove from shadow to shadow.

That evening my home was an unhappy one. I ate a green salad, a lambchop, drank a bottle of Bordeaux, but without tasting any of it, without enjoying any of it;—and then afterwards I sat in front of the fireplace, swallowing enumerable cups of chamomile tea and smoking cigarettes. It rained and the liquid occasionally came whisking against my windows. I went to bed and tried to read myself to sleep, switching from Restif de la Bretonne to a book of poems by Robert de Montesquiou-Fezensac to a play in Paduan dialect by Ruzzante. Finally I settled into a sort of dream-like torpor in which I spent many aggravating hours prancing over twisting tongues of flame and then collecting screams from the garden and wrapping them in a batiste handkerchief.

"Screams of beasts," Elba said.

"Lovers and beasts."

"Dogs."

"Shame."

"Squealing."

"But shame never?"

"No."

The next morning I placed an anonymous add in the paper. I mentioned that an organ of allocution was missing, was terribly missed, and described it as strawberry red, U-shaped, exquisitely supple and offered a suitable reward for its return.

Afterwards I went to my studio and taped a hand-written sign on the door, claiming an indisposition and begging my clients' patience. The day was overcast and I was possessed by a feeling of inadequacy. I threaded my way through the streets, gazing at the tips of my shoes, depressed by the sensation of not having anything with which to lick my lips. I dreaded encountering someone I knew, a client, a friend, the jeers of an enemy. . . . I avoided the crowded Via Nassa and the Piazza Della Riforma; took small byways, unfrequented alleys; then along the via Gerolamo Vegezzi; the Via Canova; into the park with my collar upturned and a whiskered five-o'clock-shadow look to my person—appearing, I imagine, vaguely like Napoleon on the day after Waterloo; and hoping, somewhat desperately, that I would see the red jewel lying about in the grass or hanging from the branch of a tree.

There are days when the world is reduced to cinders and we stalk across it inhaling the smell of our own burning flesh. At such times our sense of identity is mutated, awful, and we are guided by odd magnetic principles—pushed forward like lonely clouds.

I saw: water, sky, earth; heard the distant sound of motors; looked over at: a man with a square-shaped chin on a bench. He wore a sort of loutish sloppy-Joe jumper. He seemed to have fallen asleep; probably some labourer resting on his lunch break after swallowing meat sandwiches and cheap Merlot. His mouth was open, and I could clearly make out his tongue lolling from it, a glistening somewhat brownish item, like the liver of a cow. Though I am normally a veritable phoenix of politeness, on this occasion I acted the part of a son of nature, following my first impulse. I grabbed the thing, turned and made off with it, my legs moving in express mode over the grass. . . . Exit stage left. . . . At the Corso Elvezia, crossing, avoiding speedily moving cars. . . . The sound of the wind in my ears, my steps on paving stones. . . . I put the tongue in my pocket, darted into the Casino. Lazy croupiers, black-jack tables and the dim lighting of decay. I needed some place to hide and, after dodging the inquisitive glances of a few gamblers, ushered myself through a door. A room whose walls were painted with hills and trees. A group of youths and girls were sitting around a fruit and wine loaded table which was set in the middle of the floor. To one side of the room stood two young men, one dressed in a waistcoat and tailcoat, limp and too large, and a great shiny hat, the other in a work-a-day costume of centuries gone by. On the other side stood a man with a baton between two pretty ladies who sat on the floor. One played the guitar while the other was frozen in the act of singing a cadenza, her eyes raised towards heaven.

"And who are you?" cried the man with the baton looking at me. "Can't you see that you are interrupting the charming tableau based on the description in Eichendorff's Aus dem Leben eines Taugenichts describing the tableau based on Hoffman's Die Fermate—the story about Hummel's great painting at the Berlin exhibition in the autumn of 1814!"

A few drops of sweat flew from my temples and my lips twitched uneasily as I receded back over the threshold. . . . And through the Casino I went; the smell of air-freshener and cigars; searched and found the back door.

More turns; more frantic movement; more distance gained. Furtive glances from side to side. No danger. . . . I leaned against a wall and exhaled air through my lips. . . . And then I took out my prize and held it up to the light. It was certainly not pretty, certainly not an Annika Irmler tongue, but I had turned renegade and would settle for relieving sows of their ears when there was no princess to divest of her silks. . . . So, without wasting time I shoved it in my mouth, and considered myself once more to be an articulately speaking man.

With long strides I now made my way forward. I would drink, eat and live. Not like a foul, silent brute, but as an individual at the highest level of development, able to reason and speak.

An aged woman, in a helmet-like wig, stopped me and asked for the time.

I looked at the elegant silver circle on my wrist.

"It—half—past—three," I said, my words rolling clumsily out, heavy as stones.

Clearly I was not capable of singing an aria from Figaro; the organ did not function so well as I would have wished.

II.

It could not appreciate good living: It salivated every time I passed a hunk of ham or was in the presence of fried potatoes. I imagine he had been a dirty feeder. . . .

I felt as if I were some kind of human bell or drum.

To educate that beast, make my pupil repeat the sounds I wished; with what difficulty instil in it the proper pronunciation of vowels

"If—I had been—born in the time of Tuthmoses III, I would have been Supervisor of the Dancers of the King." My voice clunked along. Stunted words fell from my mouth. "My neck—heavy with necklaces. Razor of flint and oyster shell in my—grip."

Realisation: there is nothing rarer in this world than a supportable tongue.

My custom began to fall away. As far as manual and artistic skill went, I could match the best of them, Allen Edwards, Fekkai, Sergio Valente, Alba, but with a tongue like that I would never be able to rival them in fame, never be able to utter those lisping phrases à la mode which differentiate the master craftsman from the common barber.

III.

After work, I made my way sadly home.

There was a letter for me in the mail box. I opened it as soon as I entered my flat and read the following:

> Dear Lorenzo,
>
> This is a difficult letter to write. Sincerity is always difficult; and I embroider my words with the utmost care, the needle of my pen not wishing to agitate your already scarred vanity. You see: you did not lose me, I was not stolen from your grip, but rather left of my own free will—something you should know about, having once made me read Diderot out loud, in the sighing tones of a

heartbroken theorist.

Oh, you treated me well enough, bathing my flesh in wine and cream, letting me now and again roam across the lips of some beloved, but still: for long I had felt I was meant to serve a greater master. You never did satisfy a particular part of my being which I will leave unmentioned, and specific cravings drove me from your side.

I know my dear Lorenzo that you will suffer. If you can, do not think me merely fickle; because truth be told I have always put a great deal of thought into my every motion.

A Tongue

I cast the letter aside with disgust, feeling that, veiled behind those soft zibeline words, was a spirit full of bitterness—one who, like a cannibal feeding on human limbs, was nurtured on pretended wrongs. A groan came from my mouth, not the groan I would have liked, something artfully lyric, but rather the pathetic howl of a road worker whose thumb was being crushed by a steam roller.

I went to the rest room, doused my face with water and dried it with a great fuzzy towel

There was a knock at the door. It was Marsyas, dressed in puritanical black and white; his hair in poetical disorder. Gone was his sparkling enthusiasm.

He glided around the apartment talking of white things in his flute-like voice, his shadow rolling over the wall, looking like that of a flamingo, something fantastic, monstrous.

"We were very high up," he said.

"You fell."

"She—her flesh like bread made from the purest flour—is unattainable, as some mirage that recedes as you approach, always maintaining the same distance from the observer. Clouds. Foam. Sheep. And her ghostlike vapour swirls around me as the dust of platinum scattered to the wind. . . . But I dare not flush the precious remnants of that metal from my eyes, for blindness matters nothing to me; only her kisses, with their flavour of fire and honey."

"So, she left you," I said roughly, pouring him a glass of Cliquot.

"Come. Sit. Drink. Etiquette—did you have etiquette? Did you lift up her hair when she put on her jacket? When you danced, did you put your hand over it—or under?" I barked out my words. "And your bed linen—I would guess that—it is not of satin, that material so fit for long-haired women, brides, virgins and whores!"

His Adam's apple quivered in his throat.

"Lorenzo."

"Marsyas."

". . . don't understand."

"Perfectly. . . ."

"No."

"Pungent amours. There's common ground here. Both losing. . . ."

"How can you lose what you love?"

"Christ was also pinned up like a butterfly. It is all a matter of interior decorating."

IV.

I have carefully cultivated my neuroses as others might flowers and have dwelt in my autistic fantasies like a snail in its shell. When the door closed behind Marsyas I felt sumptuously sad. I washed my hands three times, slept, woke, and it was day. The bells of churches rang out endlessly and I took to the streets, bought a paper, sat in a café. Articles. Words. Black liquid stained with white. Then rising, moving slowly down the sidewalk.

I felt a hand on my shoulder. I turned. There was that square-shaped chin, that sloppy-Joe jumper. And then that awful moment of mutual recognition: me, pale with apprehension, him, white with rage. And so a giant fist came hurrying towards me. For an artist, all experiences are exquisite: The pain—his fingers groping between my teeth—the absurdity of my role a minor revelation as two oily tears slid from my eyes.

V.

Obviously stealing another tongue was out of the question. I considered the possibility of purchasing one on the black market, maybe some lithe little South American piece able to utter liquid consonants and the occasional rolling wave of r's. Undoubtedly there were many fine and inexpensive specimens available from Asia,—Chinese tongues used to complex four-toned pronunciation,—or the Thai tongue practised in the eleven ways to say 'only'.

But of course all that would take time. The only tongues that were available immediately were those of farm animals—dull and oversized.

There was nothing to do but claim that I had an inflammation of the larynx which prevented me from speaking; and I decided that the part would be best played with a colourful new scarf wrapped around my throat. . . . So I went to the ancient and not far distant city of Como, centre of the Italian silk industry. . . . The weather was very cool, most certainly the type for knitwear. I sheltered myself in the English primness-twinset-vibe, found myself behind the old city walks; walked by the house where Pope Innocent XI was born on the 16th of May in the year 1611.

But where was Pliny born?

I turned, made my way along the Via Independenza, to the Via Vittorio Emanuele II, passed by several shops, gazed at the silks in the windows, with their million patterns: those of birds, and insects, and phantastic shapes, wads of paisley, tiger-striped flowers, cosmic wonders, imploding stars of ultra-marine and pink.

I entered a reputable establishment. A saleswoman moved smoothly towards me.

"A scarf?" she asked. ". . . For a woman?"

I brushed the issue aside, shrugged my shoulders, pointed to my throat, gestured. . . . She dragged out box after box, each one loaded to overflowing with richly designed silks and I felt like diving in, making my bed, my home amidst those soft and colourful quadrangles. . . .

After a reasonable amount of deliberation, I opted for one that seemed particularly suited to my state of mind: a crown of thorns pattern with a faded pewter boarder.

Leaving the shop, I wrapped it around my white throat and turned down the Via Rusconi, carrying with me a sense of resignation. I wandered through a crowd of fur coats, through tall women and fat men. Via Pietro . . . Via Fratelli Cairoli. I looked over the lake. It was beautiful and I wished I could have cut off a piece and sent it to my mother. I walked eastward, with the water to my left, then turned, crossed back over the street.

In the window of a café people were knotted together like in a Veronese painting. A group of students came by me. I heard Lombardic expressions;

pigeons cooing; it seemed that everyone had a voice but me.

My legs led me into the Piazza, past the pink striped Broletto, to the church, its façade artistically acceptable, and I decided to venture in, knowing full well that there were a few decent paintings inside. I sighed as I entered the cool Gothic interior of the temple. I walked by the numerous grand tapestries, stopped before the Holy Conversation of Luini, gazed at the great organ, inspected Gaudenzio Ferrari's Flight to Egypt. I sat down in the midst of that Latin cross and abandoned myself to my dreams. Beautiful Absalom with his two-hundred sheckel head of hair . . . Solomon . . . hair like a flock of goats . . . Lilith . . .

I heard the combative click of woman's heels and looked over. An elegant figure was making its way towards the confessional. She made obeisance, crossed herself and approached. Long chestnut hair, which had the soft shine which comes from a sage rinse, fell over her shoulders; her profile was pale and cold.

She kneeled; the black sleeves of a priest slithered out from the edge of the box.

The two proceeded to murmur together like conspirators, she undoubtedly revealing to the black bandit her most sacred mysteries, which he surely drank in with glee, soaked as they now were in the savoury blood of Jesus. . . . Vague and familiar accents reached my ears. . . . Then, the criminal communication ended, she rose to her feet. . . . A shadowy figure slipped from behind the curtain of the confessional . . . began to walk . . . not towards me, not towards the presbytery, but rather in the direction of the front exit. . . .

Then I too was in motion. I went towards the woman. I nodded my head and she bestowed on me a cold smile. . . . There was a frozen moment. Revulsion. Rapture. Flame. I then moved on, inhaling her quietly as I passed.

The priest glanced over his shoulder and began to walk with more rapid steps—through the door and out onto the Piazza. But I had seen his profile and did not wish him to escape. A moment later and I was in the open air. . . . The beast began to scurry away, its cassock flying as if it were being carried off by a strong wind. Exerting myself, I advanced after it at great speed. Several times my grip closed on empty air, several times it merely grazed the cloth. . . . But then I seized, collared it and it squealed like an animal. It flung itself about. It slipped from its garments, slipped from one of my hands and I grabbed it with the next, me joyful, thrilled to feel the warmth of that red meat. . . . It tried to wiggle away, acting like some loathful red toad in a putrid swamp, but my fingers, fit for tending the beards of kings, were strong and agile and not adverse to being covered in tepid slobber.

VI.

Now I sit sunk in a plush chair, writing these words in a notebook with a large gold fountain pen. The creature is currently chained up in the corner. It sits and whines like a little victim, without recalling the suffering it has these past weeks granted me. Pleading and soft words will not alter my resolution. Experience is wisdom. As soon as I lay down my pen I will chastise it . . . bid it welcome to this cage of teeth.

The Hottest Night of the Summer

Rick Wadholm

Ray told me I was too friendly with the customers. "Working at night," he said, "you are like the captain of a boat. Your customers are the crew. The captain is friendly with the crew, but you are not their friend."

Ray was a doleful Lebanese, who proceeded under the assumption that his attendants were thieves and no-accounts, and some day we would get him black-listed from ever working again at Standard Oil. I think he worried about me especially, that I was alone all night, that I would forget my loyalties. He had already bored the deadbolt locks out of all the doors. He had the idea that his attendants wouldn't leave the station if they couldn't lock up. I suppose he had his reasons. Though tonight may not have been the time to press the virtues of solitude. It was the evening of the hottest day of the summer. 82° at 10:00. A dry, sweet wind was rattling the palms against the empty lube bay. It was the sort of night when strangers talk.

Sammy, who was Ray's cousin, waited till he went to bring the car around, Sammy jiggled his wrist in a pantomime of frayed nerves. "Fucking guy," he said. "I tell him, no sweat. I tell him, cool out. But he is always the same."

I wasn't sure if that was a good thing or not, having a petty criminal like Sammy vouch for me. "I've been here nine months," I said. "What does he think I'm going to do?"

"He worries because you are a college student. He thinks you will leave us right when we need you most."

Ray's faith in my ambition was almost embarrassing. Christ, I'd only been going to school for the last five years.

"I'm not leaving next week," I said. "Why doesn't he talk to me?"

"He is so old country it is embarrassing. To him, college students are on their way to heaven."

Not to Sammy. He tipped his head back to give me this sort of sly regard. "You and me," he said, "We love the street life. We are exactly alike. I know you are not going anywhere." His smile gapped at the corners, as if to leak toxic fumes. "Here, I have something for you." He gave me a couple of amphetamine capsules, the big ones we used to call black beauties. "Finest kind," he said. "Finest kind. Keep you up till Christmas, my friend."

Sammy was making nice, but I'd tried Sammy's black beauties and they twisted my stomach and gave me the shits, and everybody I had ever passed them off to said the same thing. I just smiled and thanked him. You don't want to tell the boss's cousin his drugs are lousy.

As they drove out, they passed one of my regulars. She drove a black Buick Skylark convertible that hadn't been washed in a very long time. She wore some sort of animal skin coat, and coppery red hair she should have retired gracefully years before. She never told me her name, but anybody clings to her hair color so desperately must have been a Rusty or a Ginger. Some hair name with a lot of henna in it. She always smelled of Chardonnay.

Every night she showed up with a different man in the passenger seat. We would discuss each new prospect as she pumped her gas. Always an actor, or a sculptor or a dancer. Some young man of unrealized potential. "He could be so much with a little help and guidance. I have a feeling for these things," she would say. "My friends tell me I'm psychic." And I would smile because this was America in the 1970s. Everybody told me they were psychic.

Tonight it was Andre Something Spanish.

"He wants to be an actor," she gushed. "He has that magnetism, like Jan Michael Vincent." She lowered her voice, cut me a meaningful look. "He's one-eighth Indian. Cherokee, I think."

I mmmed enthusiastically. At least he wasn't psychic. I could see him in the side mirror, taking dainty sips from his Pall Mall, What Andre looked like he wanted more than anything was a place to sleep for the night. He caught me looking, gave me a nod that said, *Yah? I know you too.* I had no secrets left at this job.

The old Buick was halfway into traffic when it screeched backward into the lot. Andre himself came up to the station door. His hair was plastered across his forehead like from sweat and his shirt looked like he washed it by beating it on a rock. So thin I could see whirls of body hair around his nipples.

"The lady wants some Pall Malls," he said.

The lady, like he was her chauffer. It occurred to me that Andre didn't know her real name any more than I did. He gave me a $20 bill for the cigarettes. The bill had her perfume on it, and when I handed back a $10 bill with the change, he told me to break it, which didn't surprise me.

I could see Andre as the sort who would chip a lady for five bucks. Five bucks at the gas station. Five bucks at the restaurant. Five bucks at the bar. It wouldn't seem like a lot at the time, but it would add up, and Ginger, or whatever her real name was, couldn't afford to be skimmed. I could tell by her car.

"I need my change for customers," I said.

Andre slipped his shades down his nose to get a better look at who he was dealing with. "Are you messing with me, Jim? Are you messing with The Kid?"

He did that pimp thing, like from Starsky and Hutch. Everybody was Jim.

I put a little weight into my chest and leaned over the counter into his face. "I'm trying to think of you as some mother's little boy. But it's not working. You need to leave."

Andre said he could make trouble for me. "I could tell your boss you were making moves on my girlfriend." His girlfriend.

I told him not to do that, which made Andre coy and effeminate in icky ways that real women never are. "Don't *do* that! Don't do that, he says?" He gave the light fixtures a loaded glance. "What can we do here? How can we forestall the inevitable rush of justice?"

Ginger was right. He was like Jan Michael Vincent. "What do you got in your drawer? I'll forget all this for forty bucks." I told him I couldn't give him my change, but I had something he would like better. I gave him Sammy's black beauties.

Andre admired them under the neon lights like they were the Hope

Diamond. "Well all right, Jim. *That's* what I'm talking about." He had the eyes of a crow pecking at something shiny.

I heard him as he drove off in Ginger's car. He was loud-talking me and how stupid I was, though he wouldn't say why. Ginger was puzzled, because I had always seemed like such a nice boy. A musician, she thought. Maybe a writer. No, not a writer.

"Be nice," I heard her tell him. "This is a hard night for him."

A little sliver of conversation, but it spun me around to watch them down the street. I'd only been on for fifteen minutes. So far, my night was more annoying than anything else.

Ginger was the one headed for a hard night. Her *bueno para nada* boy friend would take Sammy's speed, and his balls would shrivel up into bristly little pine cones, and Ginger's night of wild sex would be spent worrying about Andre's sweats and his sudden fever.

Poor Ginger.

I caught this weasely little fuck looking at me in the window, only it was my own reflection. Imagine that.

Me and the reflection shared a laugh, felt stoopid together. Then we got quiet.

Maybe Sammy was right, that we were lowlifes together. Maybe college was a little story I told myself to keep adulthood away from the door.

The regular traffic had tapered off, the way it did in the hours before the bars closed. I had time to study, and an Art History textbook sitting half-read in the back of my car. I went to go get it.

A woman was standing in the office when I returned. She was sort of short and round. She had dressed in a hurry; the fly on her jeans was down. I could see the smooth skin of her belly. She had her eyes down the street.

"You have a phone?" she asked. The pay phone was on the wall, but she had left her house without change. "I just want to call the police," she said.

She looked bruised around the left cheek. I asked if she had been hit.

"My husband and my son don't get along." Her finger went to her cheek. The pain seemed to surprise her. "I tried to break them up. I shouldn't do that, I know. But he's so much bigger than Christopher."

"Christopher's your son?"

"My son. Yes. How did you know?"

There were no Christophers before 1960. It was some kind of federal law.

She looked up then, and her eyes got round, and her hands opened out at her sides. "Oh, God," she said, in a tiny little voice of real terror. "We need to lock this place up. Right now. We need to lock the doors."

It was then that she saw the neatly bored holes where the dead bolts had been. She looked at me to explain to her—*why would some stupid person take the locks out of a gas station's doors?*

Her husband walked like a man who knew the world would wait on him. No hurry. He was a man with a job to do, and it would get done. He was as big as I was, and stringy as a lumberjack. He swung his fists back and forth in unison, a one-man chain gang.

I had time to call the police. The dispatcher was very apologetic. A domestic disturbance call would take a couple of hours before they could get a car free.

The husband was calling his wife out to talk to him.

"It's a hot night," he said. "We were a little off our heads. I just want to talk."

He didn't want to talk to her. He was looking around the lot for something to use on her. I thought about putting her in the deserted lube bay with the cigarettes, but then she would have been trapped. She must have felt trapped just standing in my office, because she marched out the door to meet her fate, just like hopeless people do.

Her husband told her to get ready because he was going to stab her to death. I remember, he was very specific about that. He didn't say, "I'm going to kill you," the normal hyperbole. He said, "I'm going to stab you to death, Stephanie." It had the ring of a revenge fantasy played out to the bitter end.

Stephanie had just enough time to call his name, which was Doug, and tell him to cool out. Doug reached back for a punch that would have shattered her face. This kid locked onto Doug's arm from behind and hauled back as hard as he could. The kid was maybe fifteen, and skinny, and had blonde hair that looked like whipped meringue.

Doug rounded on his son and would have beat him to the ground. I grabbed him. It was like grabbing a side of beef in a Hawaiian shirt. He whirled out of my hands and stood staring at me. I noticed his fingertips were making a tickling motion. "Who are you?" he said, and then he smiled and I realized he knew all he needed to know about me. I was The Nosey Neighbor. I was the one person in the world he could hate even more than he hated his family.

"You're fucked now," he said. "You just fucked up really bad."

I hadn't been in a fight since I was in Jr. High. I couldn't even remember what it was like to get hit. Most people wouldn't know this by looking at me—the reason Ray had put me on Graveyard in the first place was because I was big and hairy and looked like a biker. But Doug would know. I would be one of his most cherished beatings.

You have these moments of clarity. Terror and adrenaline streamline your thoughts and God snickers in your ear. For one moment, you know exactly what's going to happen next.

I stepped back from the three of them, drew myself erect as a spokesman and representative for Corporate America.

"Nobody," I said in my best MacDonald Carey voice, "hits anybody on Standard Oil Property."

Doug stopped like I'd hit him with a tire iron. He stood back and stared—not at me, but just over my shoulder and a little to the left, where the combined intimidating power of Standard Oil summed itself up in the sign on the corner of the lot.

His fists dropped to his sides. He stepped out to the sidewalk, and—with his toes over the very edge of the sidewalk, he screamed at his wife how he was going to stab her to death, the moment she stepped off Standard Oil Property.

Me and Stephanie and the kid sat in the office for a half-hour while Doug circled the lot and screamed. I called Devonshire Division to find out where was this police car, coming to save us, and the dispatcher I got this time didn't even have time to be regretful. Domestic disturbances are handled in the order in which they come in.

Doug was gone by the time I hung up. His family suspected a trap; they hung onto each other and neither of them said a word until Doug drove by in their 1961 Rambler Nash. Stephanie began swearing. Doug had broken out all the windows. This is not an easy thing to do, not even with a baseball bat. Doug was a really angry guy.

She turned back to me for just a moment. "That was pretty smart," she said. "Letting Standard Oil stand up to my husband in your place. He had nobody to get mad at. Wish I could do that." Her voice was a sly little drawl that dripped with contempt.

The police arrived about 1:30 AM. They took my statement. They seemed amused about the Rambler with the broken windows. Or maybe they were embarrassed for taking so long to get here. One of them blamed the weather.

"We do a lot of business on a night like this," he said. At 1:30 in the morning, it was 77°, which sounds pleasant in the daytime, but in the night, when people are trying to sleep, the air is too sluggish to breathe, people get moody.

I hardly had time to talk to them. The lake traffic was starting to trickle in, as it did on hot weekend nights. People came in pulling boats and drinking beers from paper bags, headed for Castaic, or Lake Isabella, or Cachuma. Some people had boats and RVs like they'd been planning for this moment all summer. Some cars came in loaded with nothing but an ice chest of beer, some drunk guy telling me how he would get a boat at the docks. By three o'clock, even the lake traffic thinned out.

I had one regular customer who showed up this time of night. His name was Arthur. He was a few years older than me. He was a burglar. Most nights, he would come into the station after finishing up a job. The hatchback of his Pinto would be like a pawnshop window – costume jewelry, perfume, beat up electric guitars, stereo speakers, small televisions with coat hangar antennas, mechanics' tools if he was lucky,

The police knew Arthur, and that meant he needed a visible means of support, so he worked days at a slaughterhouse. At night, he broke into peoples' houses. He told me once of going through a woman's earring tree even as she slept on the bed behind him. The floor must have creaked, because she started to mutter and turn. Without missing a beat, Arthur leaned close to her and said, "Roll over, Honey," and she did.

Tonight, with everybody awake and grumpy, he had decided to go drinking like everybody else in Reseda, though the night was not a total loss. He had this stack of 8-track tapes from somebody's van. I remember Arthur flipping through this stack of tapes, and shaking his head, because most of them were Perry Como and Nancy Sinatra, stuff you can't even give away. He asked me if I want any of them.

An old Plymouth station wagon pulled in at the far pump. A boat on a little trailer bumped along behind it. The driver must have been drinking all night, he was loud and surly, even by this evening's elevated standard. He was trying to fill a gas can for the boat and kept asking me what was wrong with our pumps, he couldn't make the nozzle fit into his gas can. Like I knew from boats. I just looked at him.

He had a boy in the passenger seat, about 10 years old. I remember thinking the boy must have been his nephew because the two of them were on first names. PJ, the boy kept yelling.

"We're going to be late, PJ. We can fill the can at the lake."

Arthur was watching the guy bang around with his boat can, going, "PJ. What kind of name is PJ?"

PJ squinted at me, trying one last time for satisfaction. "You don't know what's wrong with your pump?"

I pointed out that he'd just filled his tank, which backed him up like I had questioned his manhood. The boy was huffing impatiently, they were going to be late, and PJ looked at me like I was to blame for his nephew's unhappiness. He handed me a ten-dollar bill for $20 worth of gas, and reached back for what I expected to be his wallet.

Only it was a .44 long barrel magnum.

The muzzle went right to my forehead, so close I could read the Ruger logo on the grip between his fingers. I could look down the chamber of the revolver and see light reflecting off metal, which I knew meant that he was not kidding.

Arthur, who disdained armed robbers as a class, began swearing softly to himself. I can only imagine his chagrin, walking around all night in strange peoples' houses, only to be shot by a drunk on the way to the lake.

The boy was outside of the car. He didn't seem to notice the sudden stillness in the air. He was tapping his foot and swinging his fists and yelling, "PJ, come *on*. Let's *go*."

PJ was grinning at me. "What if I blew your face off right now?"

I had no answer for that, I kept my mouth shut.

In the background of all this, I heard the phone in the station start to ring. I remember thinking, it's 4:00 in the morning. Who calls a gas station at 4:00 in the morning? It was a lot easier focusing on the mysteries of life, than on that metallic gleam at the back of PJ's gun barrel.

The phone got PJ's attention. He was as curious about it as I was.

Arthur the thief spoke up. Almost as a joke, he said, "It's Standard Oil. They call about this time of night. To check up."

PJ didn't say anything for maybe the longest moment of my life, and the phone kept on ringing, and I'm thinking, wait a minute, *I* don't even know the number to this place. Somebody's going to a lot of trouble to call a self-serve gas station at 4:00 in the morning.

PJ said, "They check up, huh?"

Arthur said, "Won't they be in for surprise." Arthur really hated armed robbers, did I mention?

PJ just grinned at me. Finally, he doffed the gun, like it was his hat. He said, "You're lucky. You tell that to Standard Oil tomorrow."

And then he climbed into the old Plymouth, and the kid climbed in the other side, and the two of them disappeared into the night.

Arthur said, "Maybe I'll hang out at IHOP from now on. You're sort of dangerous to be around." And in fact, that was the last time I ever saw him.

As for that phone call—the call that saved my life? I forgot all about it. I finished my shift, counted out my drawer, put in the ten bucks PJ had stiffed me for and went home to sleep.

The next night, Ginger pulled right up to the door of the station. My first thought was that Andre had ratted me out for the black beauties I had given him, and now I would have to explain myself.

"Are you all right?" First thing when she saw me - *Are you all right?* Her eyeliner was brimming up on her lower lids; she was serious. "I was up all night taking care of poor Andre, who has hypoglycemia, apparently—" she paused in surprise at poor Andre. I thought of my reflection in the station window, looking furtive. "And right about four o'clock in the morning, I got this image in my mind, that you were in desperate trouble."

She had dialed information to get the number of the Standard Oil gas station at Reseda and Saticoy and then—and *then*—no one had answered the phone.

"I know I should have come down earlier," she said, "but I was afraid of what I would find." She asked me if I thought she was a terrible coward.

I told her she was a psychic, like she said she was. Maybe the only real psychic in this entire country of one-eighth-Indian Don Juan-a-bees. And maybe she had saved my life, which pleased her immensely. She hugged me and said I was a good boy even if I did look like a motorcycle bum. She asked me if I ever thought about writing.

In fact, I took writing classes to keep my grade point average up. That's not the sort of thing I really wanted to brag about.

Her car horn blared and we grabbed each other by the arms, there was a guy in the passengers' seat of her car. She leaned in toward the front seat. "Sweetie? A little patience, will you? We're talking here."

He giggled and hid his face behind the passenger's seat headrest.

"He looks like an artist." Actually, he was a little hard to fix on, slid down in the seat like he was. But I wanted to be nice.

"His daddy's in the oil business," she said. "This one's not so bright, honestly. But lucky? You wouldn't believe how lucky! I think he could be president."

"Are you done with rock stars?"

She hauled the nozzle, clanking, out of her tank. "Artists are so delicate. Did I tell you about poor Andre?"

I didn't want to hear about poor Andre. Not even to feel bad for him. It occurred to me that Ginger would be taking her business somewhere else after tonight. We had been companionable strangers for nine months, now we were family—we had the capacity to disappoint each other. Of course, that would never do. A sublime exit seemed in order. Something with a Gershwin flourish.

She had given me a ten-dollar bill for the gas. I put it back in her purse. "This one's on me," I said. And she was just broke enough to tuck it away and look grateful.

We looked at each other for a minute, sort of turning this way and that. We made a cute couple in our way. She said, "How come you don't have a girlfriend?"

I made a grand wave around the lot. "And give all this up?" I wanted her to laugh, but I was the wrong guy for that. The only man in her life she didn't need to smile for.

"I think about being your age," she said, "it reminds me of New York City."

I started to say, *you don't seem tough enough*...I looked in her face and thought better: "I guess you went to school there."

"The man who gave me this car? He used to say that New York City is the sort of place you could feel nostalgic for, so long as you'd never been there. That's what I think of."

Sammy would have loved a line like that. Tough, cynical, *American*-sounding. Just the thing for a nation of wise guys.

"This street life," she said. "It makes for great stories when you're middle-aged. But you don't want to get stuck here. Believe me, you don't."

Her car horn blared again, but we were ready for it this time; neither one of us jumped. She pointed at the guy in the passengers' seat. "You're a brat," she said. Maybe it was the chardonnay, she sounded weary. She tossed her purse behind her seat. She trailed her fingers out the window, waving *toodle-ooh*.

Exhaust poured from her tailpipe, stinking with oil, so that Ray and Sammy came to the window to see what I was burning in the trashcan. No matter, the car was a classic. A '64 Buick Skylark convertible. I wanted to believe the Buick was a gift. From a mobster, maybe, or the chairman of some board of directors. And, if not exactly protected, that it had been loved.

Dog On A Loose Chain

Sarah Totton

Laura saw him as she rode the Valley Line train--a man her age with scarlet hands striding the path between the tracks and the Grangetown allotments. His quickness—his *aliveness*—struck her. Arms swinging, hands sharp red against the rain-darkened stone of the allotment wall. He moved as though he'd been set free. A disturbing recognition she felt, but only for a fleeting moment, and then the train rattled round a bend by the gasworks, and she lost sight of him. His image remained in her mind for a few moments as the bare, black trees and the stations and the houses flickered by the carriage window. But eventually she remembered why she was riding this train and for a time, she put him out of her mind.

She pulled the newspaper clipping out of her pocket. She'd found it three days ago, not because she'd been told about it, but because she'd looked. Gavin and Cassie's wedding announcement. A world of love and ink-dot pictures. An exclusive world.

The Valley Line ran to its terminus at the Island, but Laura got off the train at the Town station. She did this for two reasons. First, so that she wouldn't be seen at the Island station by the people who knew her, and second, she wasn't ready for the Island. Not yet. She wanted to approach it on foot, to buy herself time to cope with how it had changed.

She was surprised. A sense of elation greeted her with the smell of tar and ocean salt, the scabbed paint on the station sign. But she knew that these things were only the bones of happier times and that the flesh of them had long since rotted away. *Shoddy little seaside town,* she thought. It was like visiting the grave of an old friend. As she came down the hill from the station, a crushed can blown by the wind scuttled along the gutter beside her. The fading yellow paint on the fairground mural at the back of the Ship

Hotel was gilded by the light of the setting sun. Near the base of the mural, she picked out two tiny figures, now a dirty smudge in the midst of the painted crowd. She'd daubed them in, years ago, for herself and for Gavin.

Far ahead, at the pleasure park on the Island, the megaphone blared words distorted by the wind. It was December—the off-season—and only the arcades would be open.

Stopping on the causeway to the Island, Laura looked across the harbour where the boats lay on the mud flats, waiting for the tide. The long shadows of sunset hid the water's edge. She couldn't tell whether the tide was ebbing or flowing.

When she and Gavin were young—old enough to be left to themselves, but young enough to be foolish about it--they used to race that tide in a game they called 'the Blue Ride.' Their racecourse ran from the tip of the breakwater on the harbour's eastern edge, across the mud flats and out to Cold Knap Point, the rocky headland on the western side. They'd had a pact between them that whoever could run the course and beat the tide would earn the title '*Bel Tir*', their byword for a brilliant feat, for acting without fear. But in all the years they'd tried it, they'd never made Cold Knap Point before the tide had cut them off. Even Gavin, quick as he was, never managed to do it.

A chain link fence ran to the end of the causeway where it met the island. Shrivelled vines climbed and spilled over it, but in its depths the green of summer was resurrected in the light of dusk. Hexagonal views of grass winked through the gaps in the wire as Laura passed. She stopped, lacing her fingers through them to peer at the playing field below where, years ago, Gavin had played the hero of a story she'd spun from a dream, Benjamin Eden, Guardian of Innocents. He was the one who walked through the country of dreams and fought the evil creatures that tried to come through. Laura pictured Gavin in his red gloves and hat running across the field after one of her imagined creatures, the Bone Fisher. Now, the playing field was empty, an expanse of mud and dead grass.

She came at last to Gavin's flat in Paget Road. When she had been welcome there, the outer door had never been locked. And it wasn't now. It opened to a tiny entryway with a pay phone. The door to the left led into a chip shop. The air in the entryway was warm and thick with the smell of cooking fat. Though she was terribly hungry, the memory of the lost summer evenings it brought back sickened her, and in any case, it wasn't safe to linger where she might be seen.

She felt in her pocket for the brass key with the twist tie through the hole, unlocked the door ahead of her and let herself into the flat. She opened her hand and kissed the key there. She'd kept it through the months of exile, even buried it once in the garden behind her flat, and unearthed it again in a fit of regret and longing.

She removed her shoes, pinching them between her fingers before ascending the narrow stairs to the landing. Here she crouched, listening for their voices. But the house was dead, heavy with the damp odour of abandonment. Though Gavin and Cassie had a flat in London now, they must surely return here from time to time. It might be beneath Cassie to come here in the off-season, but Gavin wouldn't think so. Laura couldn't assume that she was safe yet.

She took a torch out of her pocket and, carrying her shoes, made her way to the second floor landing. Again she listened, but heard nothing.

Nothing had changed. Laura found the little room at the end of the hall next to Gavin's bedroom, and she crawled into the hollow under the desk there. She set her shoes against the back of it, wriggled out of her jacket and folded it over her shoes for a pillow. She lay down and curled into a ball, drawing her legs under the desk so that no part of her showed from the doorway.

She tried to sleep, listening to the clock on the bookshelf tick. The red lights from the penny arcade striped the wall opposite the window, curving over the lonely seascape she'd painted for Gavin years ago. Under the blinking lights, the water appeared to ripple where a black dog kicked up spray in the shallows. Near the dog, she'd painted a sourceless shadow on the sand. She'd put it there because she hadn't wanted him to be alone, though who it was standing over him invisible in the moonlight, she didn't know.

Her mind wandered backward along Harbour Road, back to the train, and she recalled the man she'd seen walking by the tracks. The man with the red hands. She tried to picture him again, invoking the memory of wheels clicking on rails, the swaying of the train, but the moment had passed and the image was slipping away. She knew that sleep would soften and dull its edges so that by morning it would be gone entirely. This worried her. She sensed that what she had seen was significant.

In the bottom drawer of the desk, where they'd always kept such things, she found a pad of yellowing sketch paper and a handful of coloured pencils. With these, she drew what she had seen. She began on the point of movement that had first caught her eye: a scarlet hand swinging free. She could not remember the details of his face, but when the pencil touched the paper, it didn't matter. *Breathe*, she thought. *Live*. And the graphite flowed like blood from the core of the pencil as it rode his knee in the act of unbending and dropped along his shinbone to end in coils of ankle-deep weeds. From one of his hands sprang something lean and white. As she ran the pencil along the washing line strung behind him from a house to the shed at the end of the allotment, the line silently billowed into a towel whipping in the wind. She striped it, blue, green and grey.

Did I see that?

As she wondered, the pencil cut a narrow peak behind the terraced houses. A church spire. High above this, she flicked a wavy line for a bird. And there, she stopped.

She looked at the man in the drawing. His head was turned toward the church spire so that all she saw of his face was the sharp edge of his cheek. But she felt that if only he would turn his face toward her, she would know him. She pulled the page out of the sketchpad, gently rolled it into a tube and pushed it into the space under the desk. Then as she went to put the sketchpad back into the drawer, she saw that there was another drawing on the page below. In colours dulled by time, she saw the Bone Fisher floating in his seashell boat in a quiet cove. He crouched with his open hand above the waves, peering down where his line disappeared into the water. A bucket filled with coloured glass and golden rings, which he used to bait his hooks, sat by his booted foot. She could just discern a cool red glimmering below the water, where his fingertips hovered, outstretched. Nearby on the shore, a sloping beach rose from the water, and it was mounded with skulls like piles of silver coins. These, the Fisher had cast onto the beach like empty shells after stealing the minds from them.

Laura closed the sketchpad and put it on the highest shelf of the bookcase out of sight. By this time, darkness had fallen completely. The clock read midnight, and she knew that Gavin and Cassie would not be coming. Yet she felt, not relieved but thwarted.

Unable to sleep, she searched the kitchen for food, but the refrigerator had been emptied and unplugged. The cupboards were empty, but in the back of the pantry, she found a tin of custard, the lid furred with dust. She ate to dull the ache of hunger, then climbed the stairs to Gavin and Cassie's bedroom.

A dust cover had been pulled across the bed. Beneath it, she found a salmon pink duvet. She thought of Cassie, beautiful Cassie who dreamed sweet dreams and never needed protection from nightmares.

Laura thought of Gavin trying the Blue Ride one winter in a woollen hat and red gloves, splashing through the cold water. She'd idolized his courage, the world she'd seen in his eyes. World of darkness and sharp rock, blood and life. It would have been frightening, but it was hers. He was her haven, her protector.

And then at college Laura had met Cassie, and they had become friends. It had lasted until shortly after Laura had taken her to the Island for Guy Fawkes Day, and Cassie had met Gavin.

Laura opened Gavin's closet. An Army jacket, dyed black, hung amid ranks of empty hangers. Laura had bought it for him when they were sixteen. She slipped it from the hanger and put it on. The cuffs drooped past her fingertips. Wisps of sand fell through the sleeves, over her hands like threads. She closed her eyes, clasping her arms around herself and tried to feel him inside the jacket. But what came to her instead was the memory of that day on that beach when she realized she had lost him forever. Deep in her gut, she felt the shards of the bottles rattle inside her, and bite down like teeth.

She hit the floor on her knees and crawled off, bent over double to the bathroom sink where she brought up all of the custard. She expected to see blood, to hear glass clattering on the porcelain there was so much pain, but the pieces were buried inside her, had been buried since that day in the harbour. She twisted the faucets and watched the water flood the sink. Whenever she let her guard down, the pain surfaced like this. One day, it would cut her to pieces.

As she lay down in the hollow of the desk, pulling Gavin's jacket over her like a blanket, she reached out to touch the little roll of paper, to reassure herself it was still there. She had this, at least. She lay trembling and blinking the liquid haze from her eyes, and she relived the moment when they had been opened—the moment the bottles of bright glass, of mystery and hope and love, had broken inside her.

Valentine's Day, three months after Laura had introduced Cassie to Gavin, they were all walking along the beach in the harbour. Following the casts of sand worms, Laura had fallen farther and farther behind. Under a yellow buoy, beached like an outlandish whale, she'd found a longbone wedged in the sand. What creature it had belonged to or how it had gotten there, she couldn't guess. She grasped it around its pitted shaft, shouting for them to come and see, and then she'd looked up and seen their hands joined.

She felt herself sinking to her knees, though she didn't actually move. They never turned. Many things washed through Laura then: shameful relief that they hadn't heard her, rage at her blindness, many other things. But not pain, not then. She knew that it was coming, though. She could almost see it in the distance approaching her across the mud flats in its tattered black coat, its shadow falling across her, coloured glass cracking underfoot. She looked up at the sky then and saw a gull wheeling in the clouds above and that was when she felt the bottles, the bright bottles of light and life and happiness—which were nothing but a lure, a cheat, a lie—explode inside her. Suddenly she felt as though she had ceased to exist.

She was wakened by a noise, a faint crepitation like a heartbeat. She lay blinking stupidly as it went on and on until she couldn't stand it any longer. She stretched out her legs from under the desk and got to her feet. Her eyes had adjusted to the darkness so that she didn't need a light. As she shuffled along the hallway, the sound intensified. It was coming from downstairs. *Buzz-buzz*. Pause. *Buzz-buzz*. Like the sound a train makes approaching a station.

At the head of the first floor landing, she realized that the noise was the front door, vibrating as though in a draft. She stood at the top of the stairs. Deep in the well of it, she saw a line of brightness, a silver chain stretched along the tile. It seemed to glow faintly, but even as she edged downstairs, timing each step so that the vibrations of the door would mask the sound of her footsteps, she realized that it wasn't a chain but a line of blue light shining under the door; the light in the entryway must still be on, she thought. As she descended the stairs, the air grew cold and dank. It smelled as though the ocean was seeping in.

When she was three steps from the bottom of the stairs, the vibrations abruptly stopped, and something tapped the door three times. A cane? A stone? Something harder than flesh. Laura froze. Slowly, she reached for the door and quietly, ever so carefully, worked the bolt across. As she did, she heard a dry-leaf rasp as something pale and hand-sized was slipped under the door. She sank down on the step, as though in slow motion, eyes fixed on it. It was a sheet of paper, square, one corner still under the crack. Something was written on it, but she couldn't see what it was. She reached out and picked it up. As soon as she did, the outer door of the entryway creaked open and then banged closed.

By the time Laura had gathered her wits enough to run up the stairs and look out of the kitchen window, all she saw were the bleak spars of the fairground rides and an empty street. It was nearly dawn and in the stillness of the lane behind the house, a dog began to bark.

The paper in her hand had curled in on itself and began rattle on her shaking fingertips. She set it down on the kitchen table and with a feeling of dread, unrolled it until it lay flat. She already knew what it was; she recognized the yellow paper.

She climbed the stairs to the spare room, groped under the desk, felt the inevitable emptiness there. In her other hand, on the paper she held, she saw the Grangetown terraces, a striped towel arcing like a flag in a dying wind, and a man walking by a wall like he'd been released. But something had been added to the picture: graffiti sprayed in red letters across the cracked concrete of the allotment wall. It said, *My name is Benjamin Eden.*

Cassie and Gavin had held their engagement party six months before at the Island. When Cassie had called to invite Laura, she'd said, "It's going to be couples, so bring someone if you like."

There was no one to bring and Cassie had known it. But as it happened, Laura *had* brought someone.

It was strange the way it happened. Laura was standing on the platform at Central station, waiting for the train that would take her to their party; it would be the first time she had seen Gavin since that day on the beach. The bottle shards had been restless that day, and she'd been sick an hour before.

She happened to look along the platform for a place to sit, and right at the end where it ran to a point, she saw a man on a bench. A few pigeons scuttled away as she approached. Cold rain was falling like slivers of glass, but his coat was undone. A greying, untrimmed beard, deep lines in his skin. He must have been seventy as least. Laura stood in front of him, and he looked through her, or at something more interesting beyond her. He was murmuring in a singsong voice, not to her, nor to anyone she could see. She stood in front of him and waited for him to acknowledge her.

Eventually, he lifted his head.

"Come with me to a party," said Laura. "I'll pay you twenty pounds."

He shrugged and looked away.

"It's only for an hour or two." She held out a twenty pound note.

He looked at the money, then at Laura and said nothing.

"You don't have to do anything. Just be seen with me," she said. "Pretend you care about me."

"Tell me your name."

"I'm not paying you to care," she said. "Only to pretend. Are you coming or shall I ask one of your pigeons?"

He pushed himself to his feet using the armrest of the bench, and even then he didn't straighten properly. He followed her to the train, walking with a short cane.

"Help me," he said.

He wore a pair of filthy gloves. Raw, weather-eaten flesh protruded through the split seams. Laura felt his grip like a crab's claw on her arm.

On the train, he took something rattling from his coat pocket. He held it in his hand, shining, like wet pebbles. His hand spun in a practiced motion, and they slithered across his palm and spilled in a bright line to the floor where they pinged and clattered, so that Laura saw it was a dog leash that swung there in the light. He picked up the other end, and snapped the clasp.

"There, Sammy," he said. "Sit there."

"Pardon me?" said Laura.

"Sammy," said the old man, looking at the end of the leash. "We'll go to the Island, Sammy? Yes."

Laura stared at the old man. But the expression of detachment had returned to his eyes and he no longer seemed to be aware of her. She studied him in the ugly yellow light of the train carriage. There seemed to be something wrong with his body. It was twisted, as though his bones were bent inside him. There was something wrong with his hands as well, though she couldn't tell with his gloves on. Feeling uneasy suddenly, she took out a book of crosswords so that she wouldn't have to look at him. She felt the pull of the train as the tracks arced past Grangetown.

"Your guardian was with you tonight," said the old man suddenly.

"It's not *The Guardian*. It's crosswords."

The old man smiled. "He was with you on the platform, but you left him to speak to me. Interesting."

"There was no one with me," said Laura. "I'm alone."

"You weren't always."

"Look, if I had someone with me, why would I need to pay you?"

"Why indeed?" said the old man. "Something has happened to you. Something very bad."

Laura snapped the book shut. "You get a kick out of other people's misery or something?"

The old man shrugged. Laura almost left him there in the carriage, but she had no more money, and there was no one else to ask. She couldn't face the party alone. They rode in silence toward the Island. It was nearly half past ten, and the party would be well under way.

At the Island station, Laura had to help the old man off the train, his pincer grip so tight it bruised her arm. He shuffled along the platform, trailing the leash behind him. They passed by the Island pleasure park, alive in the early summer. The Viking ship wheezed as it wound in sickening circles, air vibrating around it like the footfalls of giants.

They stopped in the entryway of Gavin's house. "This is it," said Laura. "Party's upstairs."

She knocked on the door and they waited in the darkness together. She could hear trendy pop music playing overhead.

No one answered the door. She banged on it again, harder. It was some time before anyone opened it and when they did, she saw a face she didn't know: tall girl, a wineglass in her hand, pretty—probably one of Cassie's London friends.

"Oh my God!" said the girl, eyes widening, and she slammed the door in their faces.

Laura slapped the door. "It's Laura! I was invited!"

The door stayed closed. Eventually, Laura stopped banging on it. She fished the key out of her pocket and unlocked the door. As she did, the bolt shot home like a slap in the face.

Laura stepped back from the door. "Tell Gavin I'm here!" she shouted. "I came here to see him."

She put her ear to the door, and heard someone retreating up the steps. She also heard, because she was listening for it, Cassie's voice, saying, "Who was that?"

And then that girl replying, "Nobody. Just a couple of yobbos."

Laura felt as though the line that ran between her and the world of those people upstairs, those who were loved and cared about, had slackened and dropped into darkness. For a strange moment, she felt free, and as insubstantial as air.

"You can go home now," Laura told the old man.

Outside the house, Laura turned and jerked two fingers at the windows in their flat above. "Up yours!" she yelled. "I'd rather cut off my own limbs and gnaw on them than spend two seconds with you."

A couple in the street veered off the pavement to walk around her, both of them staring.

She turned to them, "I suppose you think *they're* the normal ones," she gestured to the flat above, "and *I'm* the one with the problem!"

The couple hurried on.

Where did that come from? Laura stood there shaking. She wanted to leave, but she'd missed the train back to the city, and she didn't want to be anywhere near their house. She found herself running along the shore to the end of the headland. There was nowhere else to go. She sat down on a cold bench perched where the rock of the headland dropped away to the sea. The coastal wind had blown the clouds apart, and now only stray drops of rain struck her.

When she looked back along the point toward Gavin's house, she saw someone hobbling toward her with a silver chain hanging from his hand. When he reached the bench, he sat next to her. The old man let the leash drop to its full rattling length out of sight over the edge of the point. She stared down into the darkness where it trailed.

"In my experience," the old man said, "people are drawn to the things hidden deepest within themselves."

"Leave me alone."

"Here's a riddle for you: I am alive in the fields. I am the darkness in the hills. I breathe in the waves, and the wind and the grass. What am I?"

"Very profound. Now sod off. I don't care any more. I don't care about anything."

"But you do, still," he said. He pulled up the end of the chain and dangled it in front of his face. "The key to good hunting," he continued, "is patience. Let the line go slack and watch the prey struggle. When it stops fighting, that's the time to bring it in."

Laura stood and strode back up the point, her heart hammering. Returning to the beach, she saw the mast of the Viking Ship towering above the midway, red lights flowing down it, striping the sky. Like glass apples falling from a tree. Behind her, up the point, she heard water break against the rocks.

Laura put the drawing down on the kitchen table. The light of dawn, tinted through the curtains, spread across the kitchen like a red hand touching what she'd missed earlier: photos tacked to a cork board on the wall. She scanned the strange faces, searching for the people she knew. She gazed across it for a long time before realizing that one of the faces was Gavin's. He stood with Cassie under a tree in a place she didn't know. He had his arm around Cassie, and she was touching his face in a proprietary way. Laura recognized him only by his nose which he'd broken as a child. The rest of him was different, his face no longer keen but dull and rounded, and though he was smiling for the camera, he lacked expression. How had she ever imagined him as her protector?

She locked the door to the flat behind her and walked past the chip shop without a glance. She had not kept a meal down in so long she was beyond hunger. She found herself on the Promenade, walking toward the shore. She had not been down to the beach since that night with the old man, six months ago. She passed the wide white steps under the colonnade where the silver shutters of souvenir shops rippled in the wind. But she did not go down to the beach. She went instead to the tip of the headland where the tide had begun to lap. The only sound apart from the wind was the rush of the waves against the rock.

She took the key to Gavin's flat in her hand and hurled it into the lonely sea. She waited expectantly, long after the water had swallowed it.

"Well?" she said, her voice cracking; it had been a long time since she had spoken aloud. "What now?"

She was waiting for something to happen, for something to change. She was patient, and desperate, but eventually, she realized that nothing had changed. Nothing ever would unless she made it happen.

She turned and walked back up the point. As she passed the bench where she and the old man had sat that night, she stopped. The words he'd said to her, trapped in time, returned like the tide coming in.

Laura took the roll of yellow paper out of her pocket and unfurled it. And then she saw it properly. *Bel Tir*, their private byword. In her imaginary world, it had meant 'paradise'. Eden. What was missing from the photograph in Gavin's kitchen, was there on the paper. The life that she had thought was in Gavin was now in Eden.

She looked across the harbour and saw the lonely coast. And the sea and the stone and the grass beyond them, were blue, grey and green, like stripes on a flag. And she finally understood that the land and the sea could speak. The doorway she'd kept shut, for fear of allowing the demons to reach her, had been keeping Eden out as well. She understood now where she had to go.

Laura stepped off the train to the city at Grangetown station. The platform was empty. Toward the city, the railway line curved behind the terraced houses. As she reached the bottom of the steps leading down to the road, a train shot across the bridge overhead; the bridge above and the earth below trembled with its weight. She felt the rumble die away as she turned north up Clive Street.

The backs of the houses in Clive Street stretched out like miles of dirty laundry. Laura began to run along the path, scattering gravel, feeling the wind and new rain blowing against her. If it blew any harder, surely her feet would leave the ground and never touch it again. Clive Street curved into Wedmore Road, and there she stopped because she saw him standing at the end of it.

He wore black with thin lines of scarlet down his sleeves. His hands were bare and red. He stood alert, like a watchman. His head was turned away, looking out where the railway lines latticed in the distance. She saw the line of his cheek against the wet stone, and knew who he was. Between Laura and him, the street stretched out. A man walking with a black umbrella, a girl drawing lines in coloured chalk on the pavement even as the rain dissolved them, a woman smoking a cigarette, one hand resting on a pram.

Laura stopped in the middle of the road. "Ben," she whispered.

She took a step toward him. Standing fifty feet away, he should not have been able to hear her, but she felt that he could and that he had. Still, he didn't turn.

The rain fell around her in shards like broken glass. The woman began pushing her pram up the road.

Laura called out, "Benjamin!"

She heard his name echo down the street, saw how that woman turned to stare at her. Laura knew that all of them would be turning to stare at her, but she no longer cared. They didn't matter any more.

"Benjamin Eden!" she shouted. "Two points. Two points to Cold Knap!"

The bottles rattled inside her, and she felt the sting of green glass burning in the sunlight. The darkness shattered on the pavement around her.

He turned his head then, and she saw his pale and sharp-featured face.

"*Bel Tir*, Laura," he said, and saluted her. In the distance, the church bells boomed, swinging free.

Laura raised a hand to him, and as she did, a shadow rippled from her shoulder and darted across the pavement at her feet. She looked up and saw the arrowhead shapes of two gulls circling in the sky.

She had found her Beautiful Land, and he was hers. The people on the street were alone, alone with each other. But she had found her guardian, and released him, and she was no longer alone. Her eyes had been opened and she would never be alone.

DWELLING

JOHN AEGARD

Even in the rubble, we still acted out our old roles. Warren effortlessly scrambled up the jagged heap of metal that had been the Rizal Bridge and I dragged myself after him, staring up at his tattooed calves. I don't know why I followed him. Julie was gone. Everyone was gone. No one would benefit from my feigned vigor.

From our vantage, we could see debris spread across Seattle like chunky gray jam. The I-5 / I-90 interchange—all four graceful, soaring on-ramps—was gravel now. The skyline had poured into Elliot Bay. Both stadiums were bowl-shaped heaps. The neatly piled containers of the SoDo piers were scattered like baby Legos. One container ship had been thrown fully out of the water, and lay on its side across the remnants of the West Seattle Bridge.

And, like everything we'd seen since the quake, it all looked abandoned.

Warren perched and squinted. "Jesus. Where are the choppers? The National Guard?"

We hadn't noticed the silence at first, when we woke up in the turning lane on Dearborn Street. We were making too much noise of our own, tearing at the debris pile that used to be the Saigon Café and the ten stories of apartments above it. We shouted for help and no one came. We tried 911 but my cell phone was dead. Only after we gave up on Julie did we realize how alone we were. There were no signs of life, anywhere. No people, no dogs, no squirrels or pigeons. The quake hadn't simply flattened Seattle; it had also emptied it, except for me and Warren H. Chisolm.

This was probably hell, then.

"I'm ready to jump, man," Warren said from above me. "This Twilight Zone shit's no good." He wouldn't have a soft landing; a hundred feet below us lay the jagged remnants of I-90.

"I'll push," I murmured. The words just slipped out, a little anger bleed from the Saigon Café. Warren didn't react. Maybe he didn't hear me. It was hard to tell, because nothing ever really reached Warren. He didn't experience life, he processed it, taking in the scene and then spitting out the exact right response—funny or thoughtful or tender or whatever. He was more like some supremely apt fortune-telling machine than a real person. Right now, despair was appropriate.

Me, I was still angry.

"Hey!" Warren shouted. "Up here! Twelfth St. Bridge!" The lack of response was gratifying.

And then, right on cue, he calmed down and checked the time.

"You know what time it is?" he asked. "My watch is broken."

I glanced. Mine was too. It had stopped at just past four-thirty. I wound it a turn. It didn't restart.

Nighttime drops soft and fast during autumn in Seattle. The sky was noticeably darkening. There was no sign of a sunset, just a slow lowering of the dimmer.

"It's gonna be too dark to walk around tonight." Warren thumbed downwards. "There'll be shelter under the bridge."

I thought about splitting off on my own, but this was too much of a Boy Scout moment. When you're out in the wild, you stay with your people, no matter what. When you're back in camp, that's when you can chainsaw them.

"Let's go," I said.

"Maybe tomorrow we'll go by my garage," he said. "See if any of the babies came through okay." Warren lived in an old bike shop, on top of a heap of motorcycles.

I nodded and he started down the bridge, moving like a tattooed spider. Like always, I followed along.

Just like anyone else his age, there was little more to Warren Hector Chisolm than his identity. I earned royal hell from Julie once when I called him the Blessed Scion of Oppression, but that was what he was. He got mileage out of it; he made sure everyone knew his blood pedigree down to the sixteenth quanta. He was three-sixteenth Cherokee and a quarter enslaved Berber and an eighth Maori and one sixteenth Irishman, although he looked more than just one-sixteenth white to me. And his ethnicity went more than skin deep. After running down the numbers for you, he'd boast that he could order beer in all the languages of his great-great-great grandparents.

That's my first memory of him, the Maori Beer Dance, at a neighbor's party. I'd shrugged and dismissed it as narcissistic horseshit, but Julie liked the smell of it. She and Warren became instant friends and playmates; him the young tiger, her, the experienced lady Siegfried. When she asked permission to sleep with him, I couldn't say no. She and I were collaborators in each other's happiness—that was the first article of our covenant—and he sure as hell made her happy. The poly thing was the second article. We hadn't exercised it for quite some time. I'd figured it had run its course in the early nineties.

He'd been so sweet and vulnerable, she said later.

I told myself that they wouldn't last—he'd drift away, start stalking the Dali Lama, something young like that—and gamely tried to keep pace as he pried open Seattle for us. He dragged Julie and me down into the teeming clubs and nutty art spaces and microtheatres and filthy collectible shops that lurked beneath the city, all these sweaty, headache-inducing places crammed with people half my age, and I always went along with it, a smile pasted on my goddamn face.

We climbed down and found shelter underneath a tipi of broken girders. Warren was right about the darkness. Soon it was dark like Seattle hadn't seen in a century. You forget about that level of darkness when you live in a city.

I made a pillow of my rain jacket and lay down on a clear stretch of pavement. It wasn't so bad, where we were. It was dry and quiet and reasonably warm.

"You gonna sleep?" Warren asked. "I think I'll stay awake."

"Fine by me," I said.

"The boundaries weaken at night. Maybe the spirits—"

"For chrissakes!" I snorted. I'd always tried my best not to keep up with Warren metaphysically, especially after his Oneida Bible Communism lecture that Julie had dragged me to. "This ain't *Thriller*. You aren't Vincent

Price."

"This ain't what?"

"Never mind."

He fell asleep a little bit after that; drifting away into light snores and mumbles, leaving me alone with my eyes wide open in the blackness. His spirit talk had gotten into my head. Yeah, there was one spirit I wanted to see. I'd had a trump of a guilt card to play, except the quake had intervened.

I knew I ought to be grieving. But my rage had more momentum than my grief. Julie always said I was like a supertanker with a drunk captain; the only way I knew how to change course was to bounce off a rock. Sometimes she said it affectionately. I figured she appreciated my consistency. Maybe she didn't.

I could ask her. She was sitting next to me, dressed for the coast in a sweater, jeans, and hiking boots. Her blonde hair was tucked under a UW ball cap.

"How you doing?" she asked.

"Still angry." I closed my eyes. I always close my eyes when I'm angry. When I can't see what I have to lose, I'm bolder.

"After all this, you're still upset."

"Yeah. You know me; I'm just fucking Mr. Unfinished Business, Mr. Afterlife Monomania. Goddamn city is pulverized and I'm still all worked up. It's really textbook. I'm sorry—"

"Open your eyes. Look at me."

I did. She looked—old. Older than I remembered her. Plain and tired. Nearby, Warren muttered and sniffed.

"What do you remember?" I asked.

"The Saigon Café coming down. Then this. Nothing in between; it was like blacking out, or general anesthetic."

"We've been wandering around the city."

"You and Warren? Poor you."

"Poor him," I said. "Having to deal with my surly shit."

"He'll be all right. What about you?"

"I'm tired," I said.

"I'm sorry."

"Sorry for my being tired?"

"For anything you want me to be sorry for."

She knew exactly what she ought to be sorry for.

"I'm going to wake up Warren," she said.

I sat up, banging my head on a low-hanging piece of bridge. "Maybe I should go."

She touched my arm. "You don't have to—"

"I do," I said, and I crawled away from her until I figured I could stand, and then I shuffled away more. I had no idea where I was going. For all I knew I was going to fall down an open manhole. I didn't care. I heard Warren's sleepy delight, and then I heard Julie say my name and then their voices fell conspiratorially.

My toe hit something—a curb—and I stepped up onto softness. Grass! A median strip! I nearly burst out laughing as I sank down onto it. Let them have their little fuck-reunion—I had soft grass to sleep on! They were gonna be jealous in the morning....

"Julie?" Warren called—then, more urgently: "JULIE?" She didn't answer. "Mark, you there?"

"Yeah—"

He sounded close to panic. "Where'd she go? What did you do with her?"

"Nothing," I said. "Nothing at all."

"She left when you did, Mark. You took her away with you."

"First fucking time for everything," I said.

I heard him breathe deeply for a few moments, getting his calm on, and when he spoke again, he was again Warren the learned man, the modern philosopher, the forthrightest of the forthright

"I was laying on my back, almost asleep, bargaining with God, telling him I'd trade any damn thing to see Julie again—and then suddenly she was there." His voice got closer. "And then you walked away and suddenly she was gone." His fingers found my ankle, and I jerked away.

"You want anger to be the last thing between you and Julie?" he asked quietly.

"That was the way it was heading."

"Yes, but is that what you wanted?"

"Stop playing therapist."

"This isn't therapy. This isn't bullshit. I believe that Julie can only exist if you help her to exist."

"That's horseshit, and you know it."

"You willing to chance it that I'm not right?"

It was like general anesthetic, she'd said.

"All right," I finally said. "How do we do this?"

"I don't know. Just let the love in, I suppose."

I almost snorted. Jesus Christ—just let the love in.

"We talked about you a lot, Mark. Everything we did, she'd worry about how it would make you feel—"

"You're not helping," I said.

"Okay," he said, patting my ankle.

Stop being angry, I told myself. It takes a lot of work to be angry. Stop putting energy into that anger and it will evaporate. Start doling out some goddamn benefit of the doubt. I took a deep breath and went fishing through my memories for some nice bit of Julianna—and I guess just trying was enough, because just then some circuit snapped shut through Warren and I, and Julie was there again, perfectly visible and yet casting no light. Typical. I was used to conflicting input from her.

She pulled both of us up and into her arms. She was strong now, and her hair smelled like a campfire. We used to go camping all the time, back in the old days. Suddenly I couldn't remember any of the things I wanted to say to her.

She put a finger to my lips. "No talking," she said.

I nodded.

Warren reached around and rubbed the back of my neck. "Mark, we knew you were hurting. We were both so sorry. We were—"

"Quit trying to get into heaven," I said.

"Quiet," Julie said. "Both of you. Don't do this now."

Once, when she and Warren were just getting started, Julie had looped all three of us into bed together. Wine was involved. Warren was fine with it, of course—like all the kids, he was pansexual. He was appropriately tender, even though he must have known I loathed him. Was he willing to put up with my shit so he could keep his access to Julie? Or did it add some spice for him, making me jump through the cordiality hoops for Julie's sake?

Whatever had happened, we hadn't ever put that scene together again.

She seemed content with lots of her-slash-Warren; her-slash-me became a nostalgia act.

That night under the bridge, with Warren and Julie and Mark making three—it should have been frosted dog shit, but actually it was good. For the first time in a long time, I felt essential, like a participant instead of a witness. Every time we rearranged ourselves, there was a little respectful hesitation on their parts, a little good-faith clumsiness. They weren't used to making room for me.

I fell asleep between them, wondering how long the anger would stay banished.

The next morning, just at dawn, what was left of the Rizal Bridge came down. I woke up when it started cracking, and before I even knew what I was doing, I'd dragged Julie and Warren onto their feet and out from the danger zone.

We watched as the trickles of sandy debris slowly thickened, and then the bridge came down wholesale.

"Whoah," said Warren. "Thanks."

"Mark's always been a light sleeper," said Julie, squeezing my hand.

"Does that concrete look funny to you?" I asked. I scooped up a chunk of it. "It feels like putty. It's going soft."

Warren bent to pick up his own piece. "Concrete shouldn't do this."

If anyone knew what it meant, they stayed silent.

"Sun's coming up," Julie said, finally.

"I want to get to the shop," said Warren. "It's on the way to your guys' house."

Julie and I both nodded. It sounded good to me. I felt fine; I wasn't hungry or cold or even stiff from sleeping outside, and I had plenty of energy for the journey.

We picked our way across the eastern, low-rise part of downtown. Up close, the destruction was as complete as we'd seen from our Rizal Bridge vantage. Julie called out periodically for survivors. She hadn't believed us when we told her that the city was empty.

"Empty city's not the strangest thing we've seen yet," I said, and immediately regretted it. Up to that point, none of us had mentioned Julie's reappearance. I'd thought of ghoulish experiments—Warren and I could walk slowly apart or think bad thoughts until Julie disappeared, just to establish some parameters—but I'd kept quiet about them. Warren and I let Julie set the pace, with us bracing her like cops. It worked. Julie stayed with us.

She was treating me strangely. She was, I don't know—a little overeager? On her best behavior, like we'd just made up. We strolled hand-in-hand like a couple in springtime. And she was doing her best to be casual about Warren, never doing any more than letting him help her over heavy debris. Still, I noticed the special, secret glances between them. I'd try to catch Julie's eye after I saw them, and she'd maybe smile, but more often she'd blink. There were no crooked smiles for me, no winks.

Warren's place was in Wallingford, across Lake Union from downtown. I guess it was sometime after noon when we hit the south shore of the lake—the sun, which was a weak yellow circle through the overcast, was a little bit past its apex. We scouted the shore as best we could, looking for a way across, and not long later we found a plastic peddle-boat, one of those touristy ones with two seats for mom and dad and three in the back for the kids. We waded out to it. The water was bathtub-warm, flat as tile and clear as vacuum. The splashes raised by our paddle-wheel were restrained, as if they were loathe to disturb anything. In the utter quiet of the city, the journey was kind of pleasant. Even our clothes dried out quickly; they were mostly dry by the time we were halfway across the lake.

Then I heard Julie gasp.

She'd been sitting in the back, leaning over the side, trailing her fingers. "Look down," she said.

I stopped peddling and looked overboard. There was a concrete building on its side just a few feet underneath us. I saw a row of broken windows, a bent railing, a smooth, gently convex exterior wall...

"That's the goddamn Space Needle," said Warren.

As soon as he said it, I recognized it—the flying saucer part of the tower, where the spinning restaurant was.

We circled a bit, finding where the saucer section joined onto the tripod, which was intact as well. We followed it to the northeast. It lay on the bottom, neatly placed along the longest dimension of the lake.

"The quake must've tossed it like a javelin," I said.

Julie was sniffling. Warren reached back and stroked her knee; she took his hand in hers and squeezed it.

I wondered if she remembered me proposing to her in that restaurant.

We'd picked names. Chad if he was a boy, and Plum if she was a girl. Both were legacy names, me for my grandmother, her for a favorite uncle who'd never had kids.

Project Chad/Plum was a bit of a slog. The higher purpose and tight scheduling crowded out the fun. I will say that it was nice to get rid of the condom/diaphragm double ritual—Julie was as careful as an airplane mechanic when it came to the family planning. As it turned out, she probably needn't have bothered. Five unprotected months produced nothing, not even a day's lateness for Julie. Maybe it was me, maybe it was her. We talked about going to the doctor.

Then came Warren, and Julie's enthusiasm for Project Chad/Plum flagged. While we never officially scrapped the plan—the double-protection never was never reinstated, and Julie would confess to intimates that yes, we were still trying—it certainly seemed to be on the shelf.

Warren's bike shop was still standing.

We turned the corner of 35th and Wallingford and saw it, midway up the hill, sitting like a square crown on the wrecked slope.

Warren yahooed, and he would've ran up the hill if Julie hadn't put a restraining hand on his elbow. I walked slowly after them, affecting a limp—it'd been a hard peddle across the lake, I'd say, if anyone challenged me about it.

And then they stopped suddenly short—Warren had thrust his arm out in front of Julie, holding her back, like they were about to step off a cliff.

"What the hell are those?" she asked.

I walked up beside him and saw that his gravel parking lot was paved from corner to corner in—get this—bear traps. The big double-jagged-jaw kind that Greenpeace hates.

We all gaped.

"What could this mean?" asked Warren.

"It means there's a goddamn field of bear traps in your parking lot," I said, and then, before he could philosophize further, I scooped up a double handful of gravel and tossed it into the traps. Metal clanked and danced where the gravel landed.

"Good thinking, Mark," said Julie, scooping up her own fistful.

"First time for everything," I said. I say that a lot.

Not long later we'd swept out a path to the back door of the shop. Warren opened it—he didn't lock his doors, on principle—and we saw another astonishing thing. Where there'd once been a heap of motorcycle frames and wheels and engine parts, now the place was a collector's showroom.

A phalanx of gleaming motorcycles sat on virgin tires before us. There were street bikes, off-road bikes, antique and brand-new. The shop's hoses and extension cords were coiled and hung neatly. A long row of fire-engine red toolboxes sat against the long wall. His collection of vintage Snap-On toolbox porn had been unrolled and tacked up above them—in chronological order, from 1935 onward. The place smelled of fresh paint and grease and rubber. Pre-quake, it had reeked of the acrid two-cycle exhaust that had seeped into its walls over the years. I always knew when Julie had been over there; all her clothes would stink of it.

With Julie and me in tow, Warren methodically checked out every bike in that garage, sitting on them, kicking them over, revving them. All their gas tanks were full.

"We should go to our house now," I said over the whir of a sleek red Honda. "I want to see—"

"In a minute," Julie said. "Let him play."

"I want to go home," I said.

"You want a bike, Mark?" Warren yelled. He was hunched over the Honda. "Pick one—oh, except for the Indian; that's from the war—"

I looked at Julie. "What the hell's the use? We can't exactly go riding motorcycles now. You think we're going to tether ourselves together so we don't get too far apart?"

Warren killed the Honda's engine. He stood up and grabbed my arm. "Come over here," he said, and he pulled me away from Julie.

"Hey! What about Julie?"

"I'm watching her," he said, and he pulled me a few steps more. Then he leaned in and spoke quietly. "You be careful," he warned me.

"Me? You're the one who wants to go fucking riding motorcycles," I said.

"I think you ought to think about what's coming next."

I looked straight at him. "What are you gonna do?"

"It's not about me. Whatever you think, not everything is about me."

I almost snorted.

"Listen to me," Warren said. "Whatever place this is, wherever we are, I think it's transitory. This is an interim stop. There will be more transitions ahead. You need to do a little better, Mark."

"Why? You think I'm going to hell?"

"No. Because Julie's scared to pieces. You're too good a man not to see that. Right?"

"Look, I'm sorry—" It's always me who's apologizing.

He squeezed my shoulder. "It's okay. I'm not angry. We can go to your place, but you just be cool, okay? Get your hand off the goddamn fast-forward switch, and let things happen."

"Yeah," I said. "I will."

"Good." He raised his voice. "We ought to get up to your house, Julie. You okay for walking?"

"Sure," she said, sitting sidesaddle on the Honda. "What about the bikes?"

"Let's not risk it," he said, lifting her off the bike like a little girl.

She whispered something to him while she was in his arms.

"Everything's fine," I overheard him say.

I was alone the last weekend before the earthquake. Julie and Warren had gone to the Oregon coast, to Warren's aunt's beach house.

In addition to everything else, Warren was a commando blogger. He had a website and a digital camera and some way of putting the two together even out in the wilds of Oregon. His pictures went up as quickly as he could snap them. Sitting in front of my computer that night, I saw Julie posed against the sunset even before it was fully dark in Seattle. I kept clicking reload, watching their evening unfold—Julie on a bearskin rug, Julie in a sweater with a cup of soup on the couch, Julie posing like a psycho killer with a chainsaw raised towards the camera—until suddenly, around eight, the pictures stopped coming.

I had some mac n' cheese and reloaded a few times more and was almost ready to turn in when my email binged. It was ovulation.com, mailing us our nookie reminder.

"Hey, lovebirds! Ready to make a baby?" it said in loopy red love-note script on a light-pink background.

There was a bell-curved bar chart in the email. Chance of conception vs. time. A flashing arrow pointed at its peak. TODAY! it said, starting at 3:30 AM. Below the chart was a list of Cosmo.com's top twenty sensual heat-em-up tips and then a disclaimer: for entertainment purposes only.

Moving through north Seattle was easier; it was all single-family dwellings and short retail strips up there, and when these collapsed, they didn't block the streets. The worst we had to contend with was some broken sewer lines and crossing over to the east side of I-5, neither of which was very difficult. We still had some daylight when we arrived in Wedgwood, at the three-bedroom bungalow that Julie and I rented.

It was intact, just like Warren's bike shop, standing alone in the ruins. And just like Warren's shop, it looked better, brighter. The siding wasn't stained by the rain anymore. All the windows were spotless. The front lock had always been sticky. Now the key slid in, the tumblers barely clicked, and the lock turned smoothly.

Inside, our power was on.

"No dial tone," said Warren. He'd picked up our hallway phone.

"Check the Internet," I told him, turning on the cable TV. Nothing. Our DVD player worked, though. I put in Spider-Man and watched the copyright warning.

"Google isn't up," Julie reported from our living room computer.

I went into the kitchen. The fridge was running. Inside it was a fruit basket and a selection of smoked meats and unopened cartons of milk and eggs. I checked for expiration dates. There were none.

"Anybody hungry?" I asked. "I'll make an omelet."

"I oughta be," said Warren, "but I'm not really."

"Me neither," Julie called. They were lying next to each other on the living room carpet.

"You will be," I said, cheerfully. "Once I get this started. We got a buffalo brisket in here and some fruit salsa, and a bottle of Pomona..."

"Stay where I can see you," said Warren.

"Gotcha," I said, pulling a pan off the rack and starting up the range.

The gas was still on, too.

I lost their voices in the clatter and sizzle of pans. I sampled liberally. I wasn't hungry, but it still tasted good. I'd just flipped the ten-egg omelet out of the pan and onto a serving platter when I heard Julie's voice rise, exasperated.

"You think I want to take you guys to the bathroom with me forever?"

"I don't think we have to use the bathroom anymore," said Warren.

"We'll just try for a moment. I'll step outside, you both turn your backs on me—"

"No way," Warren said.

I stepped into the living room with the platter. They were sitting on the floor, facing each other.

"C'mon, let's make peace and eat," I said.

But Julie wasn't finished fighting. "What are you gonna do, Warren? Handcuff us all together?"

He looked straight at me. "Honestly, I'd feel better if I did."

Just give me a goddamn reason to leave, I wanted to say, but I kept my mouth shut.

Julie stood up. Warren grabbed her wrist.

I tensed. I wasn't sure what I was going to do, but I guess I wanted to be ready for when I figured it out.

She pulled her hand away from him. "I'm going to bed," she said. "I'm going to lie down."

She went to the back bedroom. Warren followed her. "Come on, Mark," he said.

The trip across town had knocked the stuffing out of us. We lay down on my king bed and fell asleep; Julie first. That was how she retreated from tension, by going narcoleptic.

But I'm the light sleeper, remember? Sometime after dark I woke up to very soft, very slow, very quiet, make-up sex. It was sometime after dark. The room was pitch black. But I didn't need to see them. I only needed to hear them. They'd relocated to the floor.

For christ's sake, people, I'm right here beside you, I thought. Have a little fucking tact, will you?

Then they were done, and Julie was crying very softly into Warren's shoulder and he was mumbling to her to just go to sleep and things would be better tomorrow, and then she took his advice and soon they were both snoring.

I didn't go to sleep. I got up and I wandered the house. In the bathroom, the hot water still ran. I got into the shower and reminisced a little more.

After I'd gotten the nookie reminder, I'd gone into the bathroom to floss and brush. I remember glancing at myself in the mirror. I was growing more Charlie Brownish by the day; my chin was fading, my eyes were sinking into worry-lines. Any day now, the hair would start disappearing. And my toes itched. Goddamn athlete's foot—another gift from Warren. I'd suggested lightly that maybe it wasn't a good idea for Julie to shower at his place. She'd ignored me.

I rummaged around in the bathroom drawers for some ointment. It wasn't there—Julie had probably taken it to the coast with her. What was there, though, was her diaphragm, in its girly pink plastic box.

The diaphragm was always the first thing that went into Julie's luggage. She simply did not forget it. This was not an accident. Julie did not have accidents like this.

Back in the early days, when she couldn't stop chattering about him, she'd told me that Warren did want kids. Someday.

"I guess someday's here," I said, and I nearly punched myself in the mirror.

Down the hall from the bathroom was the Baby Room. That was its official title, the Baby Room. We put guests and Julie's sewing machine in there, but was always called it the Baby Room. That would have been little Chad/Plum's first home. We would have found a bigger house for him/her, eventually....

I hadn't looked in it since the earthquake.

I crept down the hall, dripping and naked. The door was closed. I pushed on it. Something was blocking it. I leaned into it—whatever it was, it was heavy. Slowly, it gave way. I heard metal creak and rubber squeak, and then the door was open far enough for me to stick my head in.

In the reflected light of the hallway, I saw gleaming spokes and a gigantic gas tank. I smelled grease and oil. The front wheel was jammed up against the door.

There was a giant motorcycle in my baby's room.

I had arrived first at the Saigon Café. I had bought myself a sandwich and sat down. They arrived shortly afterwards. I let them order and get settled, and then I reached into my pocket and pulled out the pink diaphragm case and slid it across the table at Julie.

It was melodramatic, but at some point you're entitled to make a scene.

Julie hesitated. She was running percentages. She was filtering. I stared at her steadily. She must have known she was blowing it. And in the end, she gave me no credit.

"We forgot it," she ventured. It was one of those lies that you don't so much hear as feel. It cracked me open, and for a moment all I could think of was a cute, fat, slightly-off-white baby who would be the one-sixteenth inheritor of the Maori Beer Dance.

I was going to ask her if she'd also forgotten to fuck Warren. That was my planned escalation, my snotty counterpunch that would've gotten us fully rolling. But then there was a rattle like a snake's—all the soda cans in the cooler next to the door were shaking. That and a Vietnamese shriek are the last things I remember from the Saigon Café.

"I guess I don't have it in me to be as good as you need me to be," I whispered to them from the bedroom doorway. "I'm sorry."

They snored back at me.

I tiptoed through the kitchen and out of the house. The door swung silently open. I stepped out onto our front steps, walked down the brick walkway, and onto the street. My footsteps felt like hammerfalls. I would not look back, I vowed. I would never form any new memories of this place.

The sky was indigo now; sunrise wasn't long away. The park at the end of my block had a view. I walked to it and looked out over my city.

And I had to rub my eyes, because hovering above downtown were six T-shaped constellations. I squinted and paced until the gathering light revealed them as skyscraper-tall orange construction cranes. They had sprouted from the ruins like spring wheat shoots.

Slowly and happily, unhindered by debris, I started walking towards them. Their blue-white lights flared warm on my face, welcoming me home.

Vaudeville's Puppets

Aynjel Kaye

Carnies came to town last night, all sewer-rat stink and cake makeup over grime and stringy-straw hair. Their laughter cuts through the normally mellow conversation in Painted Pansies, and the beer is sour on my tongue. Nat stares at me over his pint, expression on his face says he wishes it was yesterday still, because even though we fought, at least there weren't carnies crawling the town.

"Kyla, If I'd known," Nat mutters, his breath rippling the top of his beer. He drinks, makes a face, puts the pint down.

"I know." And if I could've guessed they'd come to the Pansies, I'd've been somewhere else, too. If I could've guessed they were coming to town at all, I'd've asked Nat to come with me, would have run again. Somewhere. Somewhere the carnies wouldn't come.

Of course, I expected the carnies wouldn't come to Split City, either. Carnies and Harlequins don't mix well; Split City should've been safe.

Sour as it is, I down the rest of my beer for the away it'll give me. And one of us has to have an empty glass if we don't want to look like we're running. No one wants to look like they're running, it just draws the carnies after; bastards love a chase. "Come on."

Nat looks at his beer, wrinkles his nose. :"I should finish this." Because I paid for it. If he had the cash to cover it, he would leave it. He did it before, found some girl, left his drink to take her home.

"You don't have to." and what I mean is, "Fuck the beer, let's get out of here before they see me, *really* see me."

"I..."

Glass is halfway to his lips and I grab his hand. "Really." My nails dig into the tender spot between tendons, where he's scarred from too many years of needlework, too many hits of Cry Baby and even though he's clean now, it's got to hurt. Hurts enough that he lets me force the pint back to the table.

The corners of his eyes are pinched like a memory's come and nailed him at the base of his skull and it's traveling around to the front of his head. "Oh kay." And he says each syllable like he's trying to remember how to breathe through pain.

And, when we're outside, "What the hell was that about?" because the memory headache's gone and he's pissed that I'd play a card like that on him in public.

I'd be worried about the tone in his voice if the Harlequin across the street wasn't looking straight at me, meeting my eyes. Jerk my gaze to the ground and grab Nat's hand, press that same spot, play that card all over again to make him complacent. "Let's go." Because no one who's not a harlequin on the inside wants to get noticed by the Harlequins when they're out and about. 'specially not this side of the dream river.

Harlequin's behind us on its stilts, just at the corner of my peripheral vision while we walk, shadow stretching long and skinny like an arrow or an accusing finger. Walk walk walk. Calm walk, slow walk, and please don't let them smell the fear and desperation; don't let them sense how badly I want to run. How far, how fast. And I'm still pressing that same spot on Nat's hand and memory headache's got him nice and hard and he's not even trying to pull away this time. He'll be jonesing for some Cry Baby for a week and I can't decide if I feel guilty about that possibility or not because he hasn't always been nice to me, either.

Zoomers go by, low to the ground, engines and exhaust systems rumbling and growling, their bodies painted the color of smoke and rain and the dome-glass windshields candy-colored and bright. People with too much money and not enough sense, and they're probably looking for street races, but with carnies in town, they may not find any, or they may find something more dangerous though much more profitable.

Past lampposts plastered with stickers and posters, walls covered by plywood that's been papered so thick with propaganda and advertisements that it's a wonder the paper doesn't pull the plywood down and show what's really there. Brick, concrete, glass, plaster. I have no idea what the outsides of buildings on this side of the dream river are made from. Other side they're made of glass and steel and wishes, painted with desire, scraped clean each night by the scouring brats, their sandpapery hands scrubbing away any dirt or attempt to knock people out of the pleasantry that is *that side* of the river.

I used to think I preferred the nightmares this side of the river to a blandness that's equally nightmarish, but with the carnies here, maybe I'd be better off on the other side.

Nat fumbles with his keys while I palm the outside lock, swear, yank my glove off and palm it again, touching fleshy crystal to the reader, which burps and buzzes and lets the door swing open. Doors swing open this side of the river 'cause no one's ever in a hurry to get outside.

Can't tell if the Harlequin's still there or not and I'm not willing to look back. Up the stairs and Nat's got to unlock this door because I forgot my keys here this morning. He's shaking, pale and sweaty now, and yeah, I feel a little bit guilty for pushing him that hard; he's never been *that* mean to me.

While he throws up, I lock us inside, slide to the ragtag carpet with my back to the door, hug my knees. *I will not cry.*

Deep breaths, baby. Deep breaths. The carnies didn't see you. They saw some nightmare junkie in a bar full of other nightmare junkies. There were people there more interesting than you.

Pep-talk works about as well as it normally does. I'm shaking as bad as Nat when I stand up and rather than wait for him to lay into me, I grab the bottle of Playa Song and splash a shot into a glass for me and another into a glass for him. The fire of it will calm both of us, burn the nightmares away. That's the theory.

Nat throws up again after two sips and I'm still shaking, even after I finish my drink and what's left of his.

"What the *fuck* is your problem?" he manages finally, right in my face. His breath stinks of vomit and the subtle scent of Playa Song.

"The carnies."

He shakes his head. "Bullshit."

But it's not. "You don't wanna believe me, fine." And I stand which makes him rock back and fall on his ass. "It's the carnies." Next thing I know I'm in front of the door, hand on the knob, but where the hell am I going to run now?

Sun's down and they'll be on the streets, on their way to wherever they've set up, some of them walking from lamp to lamp, plastering posters, trying to draw people in, *looking* for people like me.

"You walk out, don't expect you're coming back." This isn't the first time he's threatened me like that, but this time, I'm pretty sure he means it. Look in his eyes tells me as much because he's jonesing for some needlework, jonesing for some Cry Baby now that the memory headache's let up enough to make him want.

"I'm not going anywhere. The carnies are out."

The carnies are in, too. Nightmare's wrapped around my soul, taken hold of it with sharp claws and razor-wings, and I'm back there and they're pulling my strings all over again, making people laugh on the outside because that's what they're supposed to do at a show like this. Inside, they're screaming. The carnies can't hear it, even though it's what they need, but I can. They'll hear the screams later while a puppet master lets them out of my head in my voice.

Nat's vomiting again when I pull myself out of the memory nightmare into the darkness of almost-morning. My neck and jaw, wrists and elbows, knees and ankles all ache like the pins are still through them, and I feel like I've been danced all night by the puppet masters, one of them for each limb and a fifth to work my head and control my voice all five of them wired together so they know how to make me move.

My ears still ring with laughter and screams in the voices of spectators and my own. Screams like dinner, screams that would add another day to the end of their lives, and for all the screams I heard in those five years, I'll live forever. The clinging nightmare of them inside of me, in my head and my cunt, makes me as sick as Nat and I push past him to take my turn throwing up. Nothing comes out but bile and my stomach aches now, too.

If they used my voice to tell my future instead of theirs, instead of the spectators', I wouldn't be here, clinging to the toilet, breathing in the mingled stink of mold and urine and vomit and shit. Or maybe I would be. If this is the future I saw for myself, the future I've been running from, how could I avoid it, really?

"I'm going to work," Nat calls from the other room.

More like he's going to find a fix. I can't bring myself to care. Not now with my cheek against the toilet seat and my cunt aching like the first time Nat fucked me. Like the last time the carnies fucked me to hear the screams the spectators gave me.

"You'll be here when I get back." A threat. Another threat. I'm sick to death of them.

I should clean up. Go to work. Make enough money to buy myself some bread and jam and nutbutter and beer, and throw the rest at Nat to cover the corner of this place he said I could always call mine. Only if Nat's going to go find a fix—my fault—I'm *not* going to be here when he gets back and he can have it.

Cleaning up's habit, even though I only moved in with Nat in the spring. Shower, clothes, and I shove what matters into the huge pockets of my jeans: a couple of photos, the pins that a doctor twelve stops ago took out of me, lipstick I'll never wear again, all of the reminders of who I was. The stuff that matters less—more clothes, the lumpy pillow I brought with me to Split City, the one-eyed dog that Nat fished out of the garbage for me—goes into my shoulder bag. Cold water eases the burn in my throat and I pour what's left of the Playa Song into a smaller bottle, one that's less likely to break, and that's the last thing to pack. I shove it into the right calf pocket and it bumps against the top of my boot as I walk down the stairs.

I'm leaving him with more than I'm taking, but he won't see it that way.

One real place I've got to stop before I leave Split City, and if I make it out before midday, then I can escape the carnies. None of them will be on the streets before then.

Dandi sits on the porch with a pink-papered smoking treat between her lips. "I thought you'd be by." We're a lot a like, but she's calmer than I can ever hope to be in a town crawling with carnies.

"I need..."

She waves a hand, blows pastel smoke toward the broken pipes over her head. One of them tries to spit water on her and she laughs at it. The droplet rolls down one of the spiral curls of her hair, doesn't break until it hits the concrete by her bare foot.

The carnies would want her if she were younger. If there weren't wrinkles in her face and her hands and her feet. If her tits didn't sag. If her voice sounded like the candy-sweetness of a girl's rather than the gravel-roughness of a grandmother's. My voice will sound like hers someday, long before I'm a grandmother, though; I screamed too much of the candy away.

"They've set up not far from here." She laughs when I flinch. "I thought I'd go and see tonight. Care to come with me?"

I shake my head. "It's safe for you." And I know her future as certainly as she knows mine.

"And not for you." She reaches into the basket at her side, pink and lavender and apricot ribbons brushing over her hand. "You'll want these." The stack of stickers she holds makes me shake; the one on top shows a glyph I'm far too familiar with, a magic I wish I could do. Is this what Nat's going to feel like when he's face to face with that vial of Cry Baby and a collection of needles?

"Yeah." They're cool and calm in my hand. "What d'you want for 'em?"

"What've you got, puppet?" I'm certain she says that to make me flinch.

"Pins and photos. A pillow, a stuffed dog, couple changes of clothes, a little bit of Playa Song."

She holds out her hand and I'm already into my pocket for the bottle when she says. "Playa Song."

Dandi opens it and inhales deep while I shove the stickers into a pocket that's easier to get to than the one that just became vacant. "Thanks." Pack shifts on my shoulder and I tug it back up before it can fall.

"Wait a sec."

I look back at Dandi. She's taken a swig and put the cap back on the bottle. "They're not worth all of this." And what do I know? They're magic I can't make happen on my own. She tosses the bottle back at me and I'm glad I put it in something that wouldn't break because it falls short of my outstretched hand, hits the cement and rolls into the street.

"Whoops." And she laughs. She knew that would happen.

I shove the bottle back into my pocket and head toward the Pansies. Seems the best place to start, first place the carnies might have noticed me, and then straight down Filing toward the river—they don't like to cross water—and then out through the good side of town.

Little girl's been following me since I left the Painted Pansies and I try to ignore her, the scuff-scuff of her shoes against the ground as she skips. I slap stickers onto each lamppost that I pass and pray to the magic in my head that Dandi knew I'd do it this way and gave me enough stickers. Stack felt like enough when I thumbed through it just outside the bar.

"What're you doing?" Girl skips to a stop beside me. She only comes to my shoulder and I'm not tall to begin with.

I look down at her. She's got diamonds in her eyes and I look away fast as I can, touch another transparent sticker to the lamppost beside me, watch for the glow of the glyph. "Nothing."

Out the corner of my eye, I watch her lean in close to the lamppost where I've put the sticker. "Smells like Dandi," she says, face close to the clear patch. Then she peers up at me, long bangs not long enough to hide her eyes. "You're covering your tracks."

The iris of one of her eyes is green, the other is blue, and they're shaped like diamonds. "You're a harlequin."

She laughs, claps her hands like a child who's delighted to have guessed a secret. "Only on the inside." She doesn't sound like a child.

"Not for long, I'm sure." I touch the sticker again and smooth it down, as if her inspection might've made it come loose.

"We can't help what we are on the inside, but we can choose not to let it out."

"I'm not a harlequin."

She pats my hand. "Of course you're not; you're a carnie."

I'm glad I never managed to put anything in my stomach besides water this morning. "I'm not a carnie."

"On the inside."

Shaking my head, I say, "No."

Her eyebrows arch up, perfect little pretty surprised face, and those diamond eyes. Girl's going to need stilts if she wants to be as imposing as the other Harlequins in town. "No? Not even way down deep inside?"

Way down deep inside. Ground feels like it's going to tilt and I make myself breathe slow and natural. Don't look at her. Look at the ground, look at the lamppost, look at the sky. Don't look at *her*. She'll see the truth if you let her. Harlequins are like that. "No." and I try to make it firm instead of shaky. Though there've been plenty of carnies way down deep inside it's no surprise the girl thinks that I might be, and I wonder if I'm going to throw up water and bile onto the pavement.

"Oh." She sounds startled, maybe. Or displeased at guessing wrong.

She holds the lamppost and twirls around it; paper bits flake away, the glue gone old and brittle on some of the posters and stickers. "You know they asked the carnies here?"

My throat closes and my fingers go cold; I fumble to keep from dropping the stack of stickers Dandi gave me.

Again that little girl laugh of delight and she leans in close like she's telling me a secret of her own, "They want to flush us out, the ones on this side of the dream river."

"Which ones?" The Harlequin staring at me last night was purple and gold and I don't want to remember even that much because it made eye contact and I don't want it to find me.

"The ones that are harlequins on the inside." She says this like I'm stupid. "Carnies look for theirs, Harlequins do the same." She smiles the sort of smile little girls shouldn't know how to make. "I think they won't know what to do when they find you."

"They're not going to find me."

"I found you, though."

I stare at her. "You weren't looking for me."

"Wasn't I?"

Her laughter trickles along the posters over plywood, following me as I run.

Half a dozen blocks from the river and maybe, just maybe I'm far enough away from where they've set up to be safe even though it's after midday. Long line of glyphs stuck in my wake to make it like I was never here. And when I've decided that maybe I can relax, a voice behind me asks, "What're you doing?"

I freeze. Same words the harlequin girl used, but they're coming out of a carnie's mouth. I know that voice, not just that *kind* of voice but that *specific* voice. He should've been dead by now.

"Nothing." And please don't let him hear the fear. Don't let him hear the recognition. I put my hand over the sticker, hold it there against the cool warmth of the glyph. It radiates that reassuring *nothing to see here*, and maybe it'll travel up my arm, through my chest, and make me disappear while he's standing there.

"Thinking about going to the carnival?" Sticker's right over a carnival poster. He's closer. Too close. My mind flashes back to the first time I saw him, the sewer-rat scent of his breath, and later that night, my panties in his pocket as he went barking through the crowd; he wiped my tears away with them before he put them in there.

"No." My hand on the lamppost shakes, muscles in my arm suddenly weak, memory of the pins, and the scars are showing. He'll see. He'll know. He'll take me back. They'll put the pins back in. The wires back through them. Make me spout the future to the crowd while they move my arms and legs and dance me around their rickety stage. I turn to look at him. Starch is missing more teeth and more hair now, and his face has more wrinkles. He's probably not as stiff as he used to be, either. They'd all look older now, but he should be dead. Did I really scream enough to keep him alive this long? "No, I'm not."

"You seem like a carnival kind of girl," he says. He used to be slick and smooth, entrancing. Or maybe I was too young then to see what I see now; he's desperate and dirty and cruel.

"I've never liked carnivals." Two more carnies lurk behind him in the shadows of the Metronome. One of them peels at the corner of a poster with blackened fingernails and the other one laughs at me.

"Told you you were wrong," the laughing one says.

Starch glares at him. "I'm never wrong," he says before he turns back. "Not about girls."

"Shows you what you know. I'm a boy." And for the second time today, laughter follows me as I run down the street.

There's a Harlequin in every uncovered window and footsteps behind me, pacing me. I slap at walls and posts, pray the stickers stick. If those footsteps are Starch following me, I'm in trouble. His legs are longer than mine.

Hand closes around my arm and it's not Starch, but one of his friends. Taller than Starch; a gangly boy who couldn't have run long with the carnival and his hands are big enough and his fingers long enough, that they feel like they could wrap twice around my arm. "Going somewhere?"

"Yes." I swing my bag at him, but there's nothing heavy enough in it to really knock him off guard and make him loosen his grip. He grabs my other arm.

Panting and gasping behind me, and then Starch's breath blows against my jaw, against the scar where one of the pins went through. "No," he says. "No, not alone, puppet. Street's a dangerous place for a girl like you. Carnival's much safer."

I stomp on the instep of the guy holding me and his grip loosens enough for me to wrench away; stickers scatter across the pavement. Starch is there and I'm about to run when the long accusing finger-shadow of a Harlequin stretches out toward the four of us.

The carnies run and I sink to the ground, pick up scattered stickers. I need them. I need them now more than I did this morning.

The harlequin girl is behind it. Her eyes sparkle. "We can't help what we are on the inside," she reminds me. "Come on." She holds her hand out for mine.

"There's something about a carnival," and the Harlequin's mouth doesn't move, because lips cannot utter the kinds of Truth that a Harlequin can. It speaks by making the air vibrate, the words forming right inside my ears. "Carnivals bring out the best and worst in a town." It stares at the harlequin girl, then turns its gaze to the place where the carnies were.

Flash in my head of Nat, shoved back to Cry Baby because of the carnies, because of me, because he wouldn't listen to me just once. "So where do I fit in on that spectrum?"

It turns its purple-and-golden gaze to meet mine. "We're not sure yet, Puppet."

My knees go wobbly and the girl comes up beside me, puts a delicate arm around my waist. Her hair smells of mint. "You can lean on me." The Harlequin doesn't touch me; it leads and we follow.

The diamonds pattern the Harlequin's skin and bald head, bleed into its clothes; those diamonds match the ones on the walls and the furniture and so if it wasn't for the ruffled cuffs at wrists and ankles and collar, I wouldn't be able to say where the Harlequin is, and where it isn't. Even with the cuffs, it's hard to pinpoint it if I don't pay attention.

The harlequin girl sits on a stool beside me. Will she look like that when she grows up, only in blue and green?

"Yes." Harlequin's voice inside my ears.

"Yes?" I look around, try to remind myself where the Harlequin is. Its voice still doesn't come from its mouth, which only makes finding it harder.

I spot the Harlequin as it nods toward the girl. "Yes," it says and I close my eyes, know bits of her future because she laughed for me. Tall, but only on stilts, no tits, no rounded hips, no girlish expression left on her face, just the Harlequin mask and diamonds on her skin.

I grit my teeth, open my eyes, find the Harlequin again and walk up to it, look up at it. "Do you want your future, too?"

It cocks its head to one side. "We hadn't considered that possibility, Puppet."

I'm not a puppet. Not anymore. "My name is Kyla."

"We know better than that, Puppet."

"Call me Kyla anyway." Silence. "I'd certainly call you whatever you asked to be called."

It shrugs. "Names and titles hardly matter."

"In the span of eternity, maybe."

The Harlequin is silent, diamond-colored lids closing over diamond-colored eyes. Harlequin girl shrugs helplessly.

Finally, "We're going to the carnival. There is business to attend to."

"The carnival. We." I suddenly feel like lead and ice shaped like me. "I'm sure you could just as easily laugh for me here as there and I could see your future."

"It's not our future we're interested in."

"Whose, then?"

The Harlequin makes a sweeping gesture with its hand that makes me dizzy. "Theirs."

Too much laughter. Too many screams. I can't move, won't. The Harlequin picks me up—it is cold and distant and smells of nothing, even with my face pressed to its shoulder—and carries me while harlequin girl follows.

Harlequin carries me to a double-door zoomer that's chrome and almost clear, its insides showing beneath the diamond pattern hidden in the clear paint. The Harlequin dumps me inside, lifts harlequin girl with an equal amount of detachment and puts her in my lap. It drives. This shakes me out of memories and fear for a moment. Harlequins do something so mundane as drive.

And the Harlequin drives fast. This zoomer's silent on the street, more subtle than the ones last night, unnoticed by the people walking toward the carnival and drawing a shudder from those walking in the other direction. People look at it, but don't see it. Or if they see it, they don't quite understand what it is; it's just a way to get from here to there.

Carnival's big and loud, half the lights unlit on rides and game booths making it dark around the edges. Skylights are brilliant in the center, though, they always are, drawing people to the main attractions: the shows on the rickety stages, the side-shows in the wooden trailers that feel like coffins once you're inside. The lights draw people to the places that really matter, the places that feed the carnival and the people who run it.

No reason for us to stop and buy tickets; the only games we'll be playing are between the Harlequin and the carnies. "You're going to find us more of what we're looking for," the Harlequin says, its fingers on my elbow like ice picks. People look at it as we walk, then look away quickly, find something much more interesting: games where they can toss rubber rings around thigh bones, or toss death-wafers into the open mouths of skulls; dubious sweets that hide the devil's eyes; wood-carved cherubs that were blinded by the careful knives of long-dead carnies, perhaps even the ones whose teeth rattle in the noise-makers the living ones carry tonight. Some things are easier to look at than Harlequins; I'd rather be one of the cherubs right now.

"If I don't?"

It bends down, lips close enough to my ear that someone could mistake its intention for a kiss. "We know what you're afraid of, Puppet." Its tongue touches the scar on my jaw and I'm afraid it can play me even without strings.

Harlequin girl takes my hand, her fingers cold and small and tight around mine. "What're we looking for?" she asks.

"Harlequins and Puppets." They're only guesses, but the Harlequin smiles. "I think the carnies have probably snapped up any puppets wandering around by now." All of them but me. And Dandi, if she's here.

"We want a trick, too," the Harlequin says as we walk past the strong man and his giant hammer. A girl laughs as the gangly boy beside the strong man tries to lift the heavy head from the ground, his eyes bulging and face turning red.

"What...kind...of trick?" Bile's back in my throat.

"A way to get rid of them for good once we have what we want."

"They breed like rats, swarm like flesh-eating beetles. If you don't get rid of all of them, they'll just come back." In spite of my resolve not to look, I scan the faces for hints of diamonds and limp strings. "And you invited them in. Do you really think you'll be able to shake their teeth out of Split City?"

We're near the main stage when Starch sees me and smiles his snarly-smile that only shows his upper teeth and pulls his top lip tight tight tight over his gums. The Harlequin may be here, but we're on the carnies' turf now. More of them here than were on Filing earlier.

They invited the carnies in, opened the door to a pestilence they'd kept out for years, all for the sake of a couple of kids with diamond eyes. Harlequin girl gives a little squeak and her nails dig into my fingers.

"You'll give us a trick," the Harlequin says and its words make invisible strings in the air.

I know a trick, can see it through the darkness of the carnies' laughter as they circle us.

"You'll give that thing a trick the way you've treated us so many times, won't you, Puppet?" Starch licks his lips. Dandi's behind him, expression startled.

"No tricks," I growl. "No treats. And I'm no one's damn Puppet."

Dandi lights one of her pale pinks, throws the lighter at me. I wonder who's pulling my strings as I dip down, catch the lighter and fish out the bottle of Playa Song from my calf pocket in the same movement. The carnies taught me a few tricks. Fast swig from the bottle and I breathe fire through Dandi's flame, blue-red ball of it flying at Starch, then another at the Harlequin. Harlequin girl's behind me now, and I breathe fire at the carnies, at the stage. Old dry wood catches easily and the Puppet they made dance for the crowd starts screaming, pretty little boy who knows how to scream. No wonder Starch is still alive.

Curtains catch, burn hot, and the breeze showers sparks across the crowd. Blind angels cry waxy tears. Another swig, another fireball to clear a path between us and chance, between chance and the ticket sellers, between the ticket sellers and the street.

Harlequin wanted a trick and that's the only trick I know.

Fire and bodies touch at the center of the carnival. Carnies and people and one burning Harlequin. So many people. I hold tightly to the harlequin girl's hand and Dandi holds onto my shoulder bag while we push between groups, past individuals. People at the edges who haven't noticed yet that something's wrong, that the brilliance isn't just the skylights, that the screams aren't part of the show.

The three of us run down the street. Other Harlequins run up the street, some on long long legs and others on stilts looking grotesque as some of the clowns at the carnival, but they're paying attention to the fire and the carnies.

We're not the only ones looking to escape anymore. People have noticed the flames now. They wave frantically for cabs, for the bull-busses but nothing's stopping. Harlequin girl flags a cab and for some reason it stops for her. We press against each other because the cab's no bigger than a zoomer. Dandi's cheek's close to mine, and harlequin girl sits across both our laps, her head tucked under my chin.

Dandi says, "Waste of good alcohol."

I close my eyes, press my lips together, twist so I can hand Dandi her lighter. My jeans still smell of the Playa Song, beneath the smoke and the carnival stench. Last drink Nat and I shared. Last drink Dandi had. Not going to be anything pleasant in it for me if I drink it again. "You knew."

"Maybe not enough. We both knew it wasn't safe for you here." Dandi's still shaken; she didn't expect it wouldn't be unsafe for her to be there, neither did I, and maybe the future isn't what we think.

We stop at Dandi's place and she squeezes my arm before she gets out.

"I won't be here if you ever get back to Split City," she says and I kiss her cheek.

"I know."

Cab ride to the Harlequin's office is quiet. I want to say something, but can't find any words.

"I just have to get a few things," harlequin girl says.

The scent of exhaust and the rumble of the cab's engine are both reassuring after the burning carnival. So many screams that everyone could hear.

Harlequin girl comes back out and slips into her seat. "Docks," she tells the destination meter. "We'll get you out of here." She squeezes my hand and doesn't let go.

Water from the dream river slaps at the rocks, ripples under the pier and makes the paddle boat sway. Half of Split City is burning and the boat is crowded; there aren't any carnies onboard, though.

Harlequin girl stands at the base of the ramp, still holding my hands. The boat's horn blasts and I shiver. "We can't help what being born makes us on the inside," she says into the silence that follows the horn, "but we can fight to keep it inside."

I want to tell her she's wrong. That as much as she's going to fight, she's also going to lose. She'll have diamonds on her skin like the other Harlequins. The inside comes out. My wrists still ache from the place the pins were and I press at the scars. "Come with me." Maybe the future isn't immutable.

She shakes her head and stuffs money into my bag and then tucks the stickers into my pocket. "You might need them later. Somewhere else. You're a Puppet inside. There are always people who'll want to pull your strings. Who will pull them if you let them."

"I'm not..."

She puts her finger to my lips. "You're as much a Puppet as Dandi is. Deep down inside."

And Dandi's got no one pulling her strings.

"Come with me?" I don't want to be alone when I run this time.

"I'd try to pull your strings eventually; I'm a Harlequin deep down inside. Truth and the future don't mingle well." She glances back at the flames dancing on the nightmare side of the dream river. "I think you can see that as well as I."

How Eddie Changed the World

Robert Urell

Mom called Eddie into the front room, which was normally reserved for company. When he stepped onto the thick green carpet that made his feet feel like he was walking on muffins, she was waiting for him on the couch with a large present wrapped in bright red paper on the green and white striped cushion. Mom picked up the package and patted the seat next to her. Eddie walked gingerly across the room and sat down.

"I wanted to be the first to give you a birthday present," she said. Her speech was always so well modulated. Like a singer pitching the song to an audience, she never raised her voice, but her tone could cut or comfort. Her accent, an odd mixture of the Italian lilt of her mother-tongue and the crisp, nasal intonation of New England, made her seem exotic, as though she came from another world. Now she spoke softly, expectantly, and her hazel-colored eyes were oddly fragile, as though she feared Eddie wouldn't like what she gave him.

Eddie sensed some importance attached to the gift, and his answer was equally subdued, "Thank you," he muttered, staring at his hands.

Mom's eyebrows lowered for just a second and then she smiled and gestured at him to open his gift. He pulled the box into his lap and began to do as he'd always done, finding the seam of the paper and carefully peeling the tape away. Mom made an impatient sound and ripped one corner of paper away.

"There!" She said. She'd always hated the deliberateness of his nature, saying that boys should be impulsive when they are young so that they wouldn't regret not taking chances later in life.

"Mom! I like the paper!" Eddie said, turning and shielding the package from her with his back.

"Yes dear, I know. But I want to see what you think."

"But you didn't have to rip it." Eddie pulled the last of the tape off, but quickly, and the edges of the paper were frayed in his haste. Slowly pulling back the paper, Eddie revealed his gift to himself. He liked to tease himself, to keep the feeling of anticipation alive as long as possible. When he saw what was behind the veil of wrapping paper, he couldn't help but frown. He looked at mom and she smiled at him, her eyes searching. Eddie pulled the last of the paper away and examined his gift.

It was a grand thing to give a child so young, a large, dark, leather-bound portfolio that held big sheets of rough paper by means of a metal clamp hidden in its spine. It smelled old and new, a musky whiff of ancient oiled leather and crisp, fresh paper and something else, something warm and alive, like puppy's breath, clean and vital and strangely intimate. He breathed in the scent and it curled up through his nose and warmed his middle. He closed his eyes and felt as though he should know it from somewhere. As though it were a part of him he'd never known was missing, but now that it was back, he felt complete.

"It belonged to your grandfather," mom told him, her voice somehow reluctant and eager at once. Eddie opened his eyes and listened, his face intent. Mom very rarely spoke of her father. "He was known as a great artist, you know. People said he had the true eye. He saw things others didn't."

"Thanks, Mom." Eddie said. He felt confused, but didn't want that to be taken as disappointment, so he forced his voice sound brighter than he felt and he smiled at her.

"Thank your father," she said, waving her hand airily, but Eddie could tell she was pleased. "He found it in the attic."

Eddie looked across the room, toward the den, where he could just see his dad's bare feet propped up on an ottoman. Eddie knew better than to speak to his dad when the news was on.

His mother cleared her throat and, when she had his attention, said, "I would like to be first in your book." Eddie stared at her as though she were joking. She made an impatient sound. "I would like it if you drew a picture of me."

"I don't even know what to do, Mom."

"Just try it, please? Oh! It's in your blood!" She pursed her lips and looked at him impatiently. "Do you know what your grandfather used to say?"

"Mom, you never talk about Grandpa," Eddie said. "How could I know what he used to say?"

"It was a rhetorical question, smarty. And I do not speak of him for good reason. He was a bad man. But he was also wise," she said, holding up her finger. She cocked her head and smiled. "Sometimes. He knew things. He used to say, 'Art can change the world in ways war and politics can never aspire.' What do you think of that?"

Eddie smirked and said, "I think he was crazy. Art doesn't do anything, Mom. It just is."

"Someday you will find otherwise, I think. For now, I would like you to draw me. Won't you do this small thing for me?" Something she wasn't saying made Eddie nervous. The simple thing she was asking for seemed so frivolous compared to the intensity he sensed in her. She wanted something beyond what she told him. After a moment's consideration, Eddie shrugged, then nodded, deciding to humor her. Whatever she thought was going to happen, he couldn't see any harm in such a small thing.

Mom stood and offered him her hand and a whiff of her perfume, violets and musk, pulled him to his feet. She let him hold her hand while she led the way to her bedroom, a mysterious place where he was rarely allowed. A place of yellow and white striped wallpaper and the antique vanity where she sat every morning and brushed her long hair, passing an ancient camel-hair brush through it with slow, smooth strokes. One whole wall was a window that looked out into the backyard, and her favorite chair sat like a fat, overstuffed toadstool basking in the yellow light streaming in from outside. And there was her bed, a small, thin mattress in a plain pine frame with a pair of small, yellow and green teddy bears guarding a great pile of pillows artfully scattered at the head of the bed as though anyone could ever sleep there without first piling the excess cushions on the floor. It was a space more suited to an adolescent girl still dreaming of a glorious life to come than a disillusioned housewife past caring whatever the future might bring. Only later would it occur to him that his mother and father slept in separate rooms, and even then it was only in hindsight that he could see just how unmarried a married couple they were.

They stepped into her room and Mom released Eddie's hand. He quelled a stab of disappointment. She rarely showed any kind of affection, and he savored those moments when she opened herself to him, even though they flitted by like butterflies, like leaves in the wind, here and then gone with nothing but warm feelings to remember them by.

Mom walked across the room. She spun and made a production of posing herself in her chair, her hands folded in her lap, her feet flat on the floor, and then looked expectantly at him. The sun peeked over her shoulder with the curiosity of early morning and the golden light made her glow. She was a beautiful then, auburn haired and slender, just past her twenties and still fresh, despite marriage and motherhood coming so early in life. Like any boy, Eddie was very much in love with his mother. She was the beginning and end for him, and no other woman in his life would ever escape her shadow.

Even though he'd never drawn a serious picture before, seeing mom like that, Eddie decided he would put it all on paper, just as it was. He grabbed a black pencil from among the many that rested in leather loops on the inside of his book, and he set the point against the first page and then looked at her again.

That's when he stopped, when his enthusiasm dispersed and he realized just where all this would lead. He'd scribble some babyish stick figure and mom would pretend to be excited and she'd show it to his father or tape it to the front of the refrigerator and, after a day or so, she would forget it. Later, during the next week, she'd look at it once or twice and maybe even smile at her little boy's picture. She'd keep it there, in its place of honor, until the edges curled and the tape came loose and then she would take it down and maybe even save it in a scrapbook but most likely it would go in a pile with all the other art projects he'd brought home from school. And eventually it would be like some ancient scroll buried in a tomb, lost and forgotten and hardly missed anyways. It wouldn't ever *mean* anything. Though he couldn't have explained it, he didn't even consciously understand it at all, Eddie did not want to draw a picture that would be so quickly dismissed and forgotten. Eddie wanted to draw something *true*.

But he didn't know how to begin. He had no skill for art, no training and no understanding of technique or anatomy or perspective. The process was an enigma. He stared at the sheet of paper and he frowned in concentration and he tried to *will* some image to appear on the paper like a dot-to-dot painting he could then just trace out. Eddie's frustration made him nauseous and angry, and he felt as though he was going to cry. He didn't know what to do, but he wanted so badly to please his mom, to make her smile. There had to be some way he could do this thing, but nothing came to mind and he found himself staring blankly at the empty page and wishing he were tucked away someplace where nobody could find him.

Finally, because he just didn't know what else to do, Eddie began to draw. And as he drew, he looked at mom and he tried to make his hands fashion something that at least approximated what he saw. And as the drawing inevitably became something else, something sloppy and babyish, aimless scribbles and loops of gray on white, as un-artistic as he'd feared, he gave up trying at all and just let his hands do what they would do no matter what he wanted. He turned his attention to the windows and the world outside and he wished he could be anywhere but here. His options exhausted, humiliated by the scene he saw forthcoming when she saw what he'd made, Eddie felt himself grow angry with mom for forcing this upon him. It wasn't as though he'd asked for it, and he'd even tried to tell her he didn't know how. She did this, and his face felt hot with the shame of it.

The deep, confident voice of dad's favorite news anchor, Luke Phillips, wafted in from the den. Eddie latched onto that and tried to ignore the occasional impatient sounds mom made as she waited for him to finish. *"Police have yet to find any clue to her whereabouts and lead detectives say the longer Tabitha Haines remains missing, the worse the probable outcome."*

Eddie looked down at the paper, and was amazed to see the details of a face emerging from under his pencil. Somehow, here was the shaded hollow of a softly rounded cheek, there was the delicate curve of a chin. From out of the chaos he'd wrought before, order appeared as if placed there by some miracle. Even as he watched, more detail emerged, his pencil still scratching across the page as though by itself. Features he'd known from birth, a face that had imprinted itself upon his brain as an infant. It began to look like mom.

Eddie's breath caught and his eyes widened. The pencil moved faster and faster, gaining confidence as he watched, it became a blur and it seemed the image constructed itself from the gray lines.

It's in your blood! she'd said, and he'd scoffed at the idea, but nothing in his life had prepared him for this. He had no choice but to believe. Pride surged with Eddie's pulse. He was an artist! He thought about paying more attention, of getting it just right. He tried to stop the pencil for a moment, to get a better look at what he was doing, but it was like trying to move someone else's hand from the inside. He couldn't stop it. He had no control over the pencil, it ignored his commands, went about its business, independent. At first Eddie didn't know enough to fear this new thing. Maybe, he thought, this is how it is with artists. Maybe talent was nothing less magical and mysterious than what was happening before him. But as the picture gained clarity and his hand showed no sign of returning to his control, Eddie began to fear.

"In other news, NFL Hall of Famer, Ritchie Hall stands accused of abducting and sexually assaulting a twelve year old boy from New York's Central Park. Hall declined to comment, but the District Attorney's Office released a statement saying the case against the three-time All Pro linebacker was, quote, 'very strong'."

The picture was going terribly wrong. Though it still resembled his mother in the most obvious ways, it also seemed he'd drawn the face of a stranger. Where Eddie had an image of mom in his head, a sweet woman with a strangely wistful smile, the woman on the paper had mom's features but her face seemed so wretched and unhappy, terrible, evil. This woman despised her husband, resented her son. She wished she could run away, could take herself back and forget all the responsibility of a life she'd never wanted, all the regrets piled up higher and higher each day. This woman knew about hate, would kill to escape the confines of marriage and motherhood. She was desperate to be free, though she really didn't know what 'free' meant anymore. She thought of herself as a slave, chained to a man and a boy she hardly knew. This woman was not like his mother at all.

"And now for a look at a tragic story just breaking in Topeka, Kansas. Two different *tornadoes struck a church on the outskirts of the city during morning services. No word on casualties, but estimates put the death toll at over a hundred, and authorities there fear the worst."*

The drawing finished itself so quickly, while Eddie tried to regain control of his hand, that he didn't have a moment to think. Suddenly the pencil stopped, and a cramp curled his hand in upon itself like a salted slug. Eddie's eyes teared up from the pain, and it was several seconds before he could open them and look at the drawing. His mother didn't move from her chair or ask him what was wrong. She sat, staring into space, her mouth set in a prim line as though he'd done something disgusting in public and she was ignoring it in the hope that it would go away by itself.

Eddie stared at what he'd made and a sick certainty washed away his burgeoning doubt before it could form enough power to allow him any illusions. Whatever he'd thought of mom before, whatever love and devotion he had for her, what was there on the paper was somehow truer, more accurate. This was his mother as she really was. He could see it behind her face, like something hiding under a paper mask. The face in the sketch was the monster hiding in his mother. She wouldn't like it if she knew what he'd seen.

"Mom?" he said.

"Yes?"

"Would you hate me if I didn't show you my picture?"

"Oh, Eddie! I could never hate you! Why would you ask that?" Mom's eyes grew just a bit defensive and strangely fearful.

"I'd just like to keep this to myself," he said. "I won't show it to anyone else."

Mom leaned forward and tried to take a look at the page. Eddie hopped to his feet and backed away with the sketch pressed against his stomach. He looked into her eyes and tried to make her understand but she leaned back, her lips pursed and her face slightly flushed in anger.

"Give it to me, Eddie," she said.

Eddie shook his head and stared at the floor. He couldn't stand the intensity of her glare. Her eyes were like heat lamps, he felt so hot and uncomfortable.

"Eddie!" Mom snapped. "Now!"

Eddie couldn't help himself. Her voice was like a crack of thunder, the Word of God. He obeyed so quickly he didn't have time to wonder at the fact that he seemed to have no will against her.

Mom snatched the book from his hands and turned it around to see what he'd drawn. Eddie watched the blood leave her face, the bright rosy blooms of her cheeks snuffed in an instant. Her hands began to shake so badly he thought she was having a seizure. Mom only stared at the picture for a few seconds, but her breath came in labored gasps. When she held it out for him to take it back, there was sweat beaded on her brow as though she'd run a mile. Eddie held the sketchbook between them and backed away until the backs of his legs bumped against the edge of her bed and he sat down, never having taken his eyes off of her.

Mom regarded him for a moment, as though she debated her options, and then made a decision. She smiled, but it didn't touch her eyes, and somehow Eddie knew she would leave that night, after the rest of the house was asleep. She'd take a small suitcase, the green one in the hall closet. She would abandon him because he'd seen her truly, and she knew what he'd seen.

"Just like your grandfather, Eddie. You should be proud." She smiled and patted her hair as though it were ever out of place and then she stood up and walked away. She said something over her shoulder about taking a drive and that he and Father should order a pizza for dinner. She walked away and the last thing Eddie saw of his mom was her back as she hurried from the room and out of his life.

The next morning, Eddie wasn't surprised when Father came into the kitchen and fixed breakfast for just the two of them. They ate in silence and went about their separate days without either of them acknowledging how very easily they'd let her escape their happy home, and Eddie certainly never told Father the truth behind his mom's departure. Nor did he mention the despair in her eyes the last time she'd ever looked at him, the son who knew she hated him.

And so Eddie and his father lived alone. Mom's bedroom door was locked and neither spoke of her leaving. Eddie put his book away, for a time, vowed a boy's oath to give up drawing forever, but life quickly grew stale and lifeless. He'd found something unexpected in his newly discovered talent, and everything else seemed so surreal without it.

Eddie's fingers itched for the smooth feel of a pencil between them, the images that nearly burst his skull coming to life with each subtle shading, each line and curve *creating* pictures of things only he could see. And that was also a problem, something he couldn't escape. No matter who he looked at, he saw all the secret hatreds and pettiness in them where it lurked behind their eyes. Somehow that one drawing he'd made of mom had uncorked something inside him that refused to go back into its bottle.

Now, he couldn't ignore the things that people thought and did. They hounded him, driving themselves like spikes in his brain until nowhere he turned was safe from the prying vices of everyone around him. He saw sin and corruption everywhere, and for him there was no escape but solitude.

At first he bore it well, it served as punishment, in his mind, for having driven his mother way. But as the visions wore on without relief, they became a wedge between Eddie and everyone else. His eyes became piercing, his stares too intent to bear. One by one, his family and friends shunned him, uncomfortably aware of the changes he'd undergone. Eddie became first an outcast, then a hermit. He became snappish and withdrawn, subject to strange fits of rage, and equally troubling bouts of deep withdrawal and depression. He hibernated in his room, even took his meals there. He longed to disappear, to be forgotten, and only rarely emerged to snatch something from the refrigerator before bolting back to the safety of his room where he could pretend no one would remember he was there.

Eddie became someone else, someone impossible to understand, and Eddie's father, Martin, decided one day that it was his responsibility to do something about it.

Martin entered Eddie's bedroom without knocking. Eddie stared at him warily.

"Eddie...how are you?" Martin asked. He was a blocky man, so opposite from the willowy beauty of his wife that they'd struck a kind of yin/yang chord with their friends. Where Katharine had been petite and rounded and soft, Martin was a series of squares stacked up from the floor like a half-finished granite sculpture. His hair was prematurely gray, his face taut and unlined. His eyes were soft, liquid brown, the one feature that made his linear symmetry human.

Eddie stared up from the floor at his father with his mother's hard eyes and said, "I'm fine. You didn't knock." Martin couldn't help but notice how his son's voice seemed like a growl, how his eyes were hard and defensive, how much like his mom he'd become. He'd never thought, when the boy was born, how much he'd hate the similarities Eddie shared with Katharine. There was an impenetrable hardness to the both of them, a bright steel wall between them and the world that Martin couldn't and wouldn't breach.

Martin became angry. "You've become a bear to live with, Eddie." He shifted uncomfortably. "You need to get out of this room. I thought you'd like to bring your sketchbook into the living room and—"

"You want me to draw you."

"Yeah. I think I'd like that."

Eddie shook his head, "Mom didn't like it very much."

Martin's face hardened, "I'm not your mother. Bring your things."

Martin made his way into the living room. He sat in his favorite chair, a huge brown leather recliner Eddie had always remembered being in that exact spot, next to the bookcase, in line with the television. The living room held nothing of mom's taste. Where the rest of the house was indisputably hers, the softer touch of a woman had never violated this space, which was all dark hardwood bookshelves and ancient burnt orange carpeting. Mom had left this one place for Father as a token gesture to his masculinity. Accordingly, dad had honored the unwritten compact and mainly kept himself in his den, when he wasn't at work. Even in her absence, he didn't violate her space.

Martin settled in and watched Eddie trudge into the room, his sketchbook held in front of his chest, arms hugging it tight against him. "How should I pose?" Martin asked. He became nervous, now that the moment was upon him. He was a man who avoided cameras, eschewed attention of any kind, when he could. Sitting for a portrait was not a natural act for him.

Eddie shrugged, but took pity on his father. "Lean back, dad. Just get comfortable." Eddie turned on the television. "Just watch some TV and you won't even notice I'm here."

Martin nodded, and pretended to relax and watch the evening news. He regretted the idea, now that it was in action.

"Searchers made a grisly discovery while combing the woods around the Haines home early Monday morning. Torn and bloodied clothing that Tabitha Haines's mother identified as the pajamas Tabitha wore on the night of her disappearance."

Eddie hardly looked at him before putting his pencil to the page. Martin couldn't help but be amused. He'd taken a look at the 'portrait' Eddie said he'd done of his mom the day she'd left. It was just a bunch of squiggly lines, not a proper drawing at all. Martin remembered that his wife had come from a long line of artists and sculptors, and it hadn't surprised him that she'd tried to fill Eddie's head with some nonsense of the talent being inherited. If it was genetic, Martin thought, it had certainly passed his son by.

But, then again, maybe there was something to it after all, because the longer he'd stared at Eddie's picture, the more uneasy he'd felt. At some point it stopped being a mess of gray lines on white paper and more like a maze, and then something more organized, a map of some kind. Martin had found himself leaning forward and a sudden vertigo struck him, as though he were in danger of falling into the picture, like something within it waited for him.

And that was it exactly. He didn't understand it on a conscious level, but something in the back of his brain warned him that all was not as it should be. And Martin suddenly realized what it was: Though the mass of gray lines looked nothing like any person at all, and certainly not like his wife, he couldn't help feeling like she was on the other side of the page, staring out from the paper as if it were actually a window into wherever she'd gone. He could feel her hating him more than he'd ever suspected.

In fact, perhaps he should just stop this whole thing. Tell the boy to draw flowers or horses or something. Being a supportive father was one thing, but there was something not quite right behind Eddie's eyes, something that seemed to pierce a person right to the bone. Something like his father-in-law, a man Martin had only met briefly, then avoided until his death.

"Maybe this isn't such a good idea, Eddie," Martin said.

"Right," Eddie said. The boy was quick to close his book, as if in relief. He stood and left the room without another word, like a man fleeing a fire.

Martin watched the boy go and put the experience down as a lesson learned. He tried to watch the news for a bit, but something troubled him. He turned the episode over in his mind, but couldn't quite place it.

"Pro football player, Ritchie Hall attended arraignment by cell phone today. Judge Lars Ulrich granted the special dispensation to Hall because, quote, "I saw Hall demolish a last second drive by the Eagles all by himself. He is a man of honor and I see no reason to inconvenience him with these petty formalities."

"Hall could not be reached for comment."

Martin made his way back to Eddie's room as quietly as possible. He listened at the door and heard soft sobs from within. He turned the knob as slowly as possible and inched the door open until he could see Eddie sitting Indian style on the floor with the sketchbook open in his lap.

Martin took in the scene with a glance, then his eyes locked on the exposed drawing. His mouth hung open, his breath caught in his chest. This was no mess of random lines, no picture drawn by a child. This was a perfect sketch, a masterpiece of graphite on paper. A flawless likeness of Martin, only twisted and distorted beyond recognition.

The man in the sketch looked like an illustration of a damned soul, something from Dante's Inferno. It was a picture of him, there wasn't any doubt, but by some trick of the light, the portrait seemed to display everything about him he hated most.

Here he was paying a homeless girl named Jennifer twenty dollars for a blowjob behind the dumpster at the Safeway in Camas. Here he was, the corporate snitch, selling his co-workers out for the barest chance at a promotion. Here he was waiting for Eddie in the high school parking lot, yearning to touch the young girls he saw gathered in clumps, their bare bellies flat and tanned and smooth, their small breasts straining the thin fabric that hid them. Here he was, seeing within him, all at once, everything he feared and dreaded about himself, all the urges and disgusting thoughts he locked away in himself. Here they were, in a picture his son had drawn of him.

Martin felt something break inside. Knowing these things were in him, that he was capable of even thinking those thoughts, feeling those emotions, that was bad enough. Having them broadcast for the world to see, having them cemented in reality on paper, that was just too much. He couldn't stand the look on Eddie's face..

Martin closed his mouth and tried to think of what to say to his son, what could make it right, could take it back. He wanted to speak soft words about the difference between thinking bad thoughts and acting on them, as he surely never had or ever could. Most of all, he wanted his son back, he wanted this sharp-eyed freak, who saw things he couldn't, out of his house.

He meant to say something reasonable, reassuring. Instead rage turned his words harsh and final, "I should have burned that book when I found it. Should have set it on fire! *Bastard!* You stupid little bastard!"

Eddie shook his head and started to say something. Martin ran out of the room, out of the house, into the street, down the block. Martin kept running until he couldn't breathe and his legs felt rubbery. He found himself on a busy street, but he couldn't tell which one in the dark. He didn't remember getting there.

The cars flew by recklessly in the dark, the wind from their passage blew cold air through Martin's thinning hair. He walked along the curb for a while and then he stepped down into the gutter. He kept his back to the oncoming traffic, his hands in his pants pocket, his head down. He began to feel comfortable with the rushing metal so close to where he walked. He edged closer to the white line. He crowded the road so closely that he could feel the warm exhaust from the cars. Still he feared them less than the look on Eddie's face and the things the boy knew about what he hated of himself the most. *How could he know?* It didn't matter. He knew. Maybe he always did, but that didn't matter either. He knew now and Martin could never face his son again. The things he'd always thought he'd teach the boy, but never had, were the things that stood between them now. There was no going home.

Martin waited for the last moment, when it would be too late for him or the driver to avoid collision, then he stepped out in front of a heavy pickup truck going nearly twice the posted limit. He tried to smile just before the thick steel grill punched him into the air like a huge balloon. He had some thought that it would be nice if he were smiling when Eddie saw him in his casket. Maybe that would make up for it all.

He didn't live long enough to come back down to earth.

Eddie was sent to live with his Uncle Thad, who was his dad's half-brother, and Eddie's only living relative besides his absent mother. Thad was a short, slender man with bad teeth. He smelled like pork-fried rice and he never wore the same pair of socks more than once. He said there was no getting them clean after having been on a person's feet. Thad wasn't a nice man, and Eddie could see things in him that turned his stomach, but only in an impersonal way, and not as strongly as what he'd seen in his parents.

Eddie moved in to Thad's dingy one bedroom apartment in National City—Thad called it 'Nasty City' because of all the hookers and crackheads that hung out around the Navy base—and made a home for himself on the living room couch that smelled like spilt beer and rotten food and had sticky stains all over it so that he had to cover it with a blanket before he sat on it. He watched cartoons on the TV, when they were on, but otherwise spent most of the day staring out the window and trying not to think about pencils and paper.

Thad tried to talk to him, but Eddie couldn't bring himself to care that his uncle was lonely. He tried to keep quiet, hoping Thad would get bored with trying to be friendly and leave him alone, but Thad got tired of Eddie's silence instead. One night while they ate pizza in front of the television, Thad said, "You can talk about it, you know."

Eddie kept his eyes on the news and tried to think of something to say.

"You miss your mom, right?"

Eddie shrank into the couch and pressed his lips together.

"You're gonna have to talk some time, kid." Thad's voice showed his irritation and he leaned forward, trying to catch Eddie's eye. "I'm thinkin' a 'thank you' might be a nice way to start, ya think?"

"You don't want to talk to me, Uncle Thad. You don't want to like me."

"Knock it off with the drama. Gawd, you must've spent too much time with your mommy, cause your dad would've beat that out've you a long time ago." Thad shook his head and sat back, giving up again. Eddie sat there for a second, the anger boiling in him. He wasn't really mad at Thad, though. He was mad at his parents and his grandfather and himself. He was angry at the thing inside him that showed him that part of people they could hide from everyone else. And he was angry that he wouldn't ever get to be normal again. But Thad was right there next to him, and Thad deserved what he got.

Eddie turned and looked straight into Thad's eyes and said, "You dated my mom for three days, when she was new to your high school and didn't know you like the other girls who always turned you down. You tried to screw her in the back of your dad's green station wagon and when she said no you tried to force her. She kicked you in the throat while you were trying to pull her panties off and she ran away. So you went home and cried in the bathroom and then you jerked off with shaving cream. My dad beat the piss out of you when he found out, and you've always wanted to kill him for that, even though you deserved it and you know it. And you were glad when my dad died because you needed the money my trust fund gave you because you owe a man who says he's going to cut off your balls and feed them to you."

Thad's face paled. His jaw dropped and he made hollow strangling noises as though he were an empty plaster shell. Eddie crooked his eyebrow and said. "Is that enough talking, Uncle Thad? Would you like to hear what I know about you and Great Aunt Sherry?"

Thad popped off the couch like he was spring-loaded. He backed away from Eddie, his eyes wide and his hands in front of him as if he could ward off Eddie's words. Eddie turned back to the TV. Thad retreated down the hall to his bedroom and, from the sound of it, piled furniture in front of the door. Eddie settled back into the couch, but he didn't feel any better, just more alone than ever.

The evening news came on at six, just after a crappy Pokemon knockoff Eddie couldn't quite understand. Eddie reached for the remote to turn the TV off, but a comfortably familiar voice began speaking and the nostalgia made him pause. It was Luke Phillips, dad's favorite anchor because, as dad would say, "He's always smiling! It's like a sitcom the way that guy can grin away and he's talking about these horrible things that's going on in the world!"

And dad was right, Phillips's smile never left his face as, one after another, he delivered the news of murders and accidents and all the other inevitable day-to-day events that ripped apart families and communities and individuals. He smiled through an entire hour as he detailed death and tragedy interspersed with the weather—*"It is now being confirmed there were no survivors in the tragic incident in Topeka. The death-toll stands at one-hundred and thirty seven."* —and sports— *"Reports are coming in that Ritchie Hall is dead, this evening. The cause of death is not being released as yet, but considering Hall's recent legal troubles, suicide cannot be ruled out."* It seemed so blatant, so inappropriate, and Eddie couldn't help wondering what it would be like, knowing he was going to die, only to wind up as another lead-in story turned punch-line on the nightly news.

And it went on and on. One after another, an endless parade of anonymous atrocities served up to faceless viewers, and millions of people drank it in until they choked. It never, ever stopped pouring from the screen like a runaway hose nobody knew how to shut off. Worse still were the things the people on TV *didn't* say, the horrible things their monsters told Eddie about them. The secrets of murder and rage and jealousy that poured even from the glass eye of a camera lens, made Eddie finally positive he had no way to escape what he saw in others. The only thing he couldn't see was how to come to terms with it.

Eddie sat through an hour of the national broadcast, a half hour from the local affiliate. He sat dazed through four hours of programming he didn't really see, then another half hour of national news, three hours of late shows, five hours of infomercials and reruns. Evil after evil, petty and malicious, insensible and outrageous, one after another after another until he couldn't help wonder why nobody *did* anything. Then it came to him: They saw but they didn't see. Lost in the flood coming from their televisions, nobody put together the horror they felt and the deeds they knew needed doing. To them it was just another form of entertainment, a pre-show for primetime. It just wasn't real to them.

There was something there, just in the back of Eddie's head. Something he wasn't seeing or thinking. He felt the germ of an idea taking shape as his eyes and ears took in huge doses of death and evil and hypocrisy. Someone had to do something. Something should be done.

"In other news, three local area banks have begun accepting donations on behalf of the Haines family. A family spokesman said the missing girl's parents are truly grateful and would like to especially thank local detectives for their determined efforts in the ongoing investigation. If you are interested in sending money or condolences, the address is....' A picture of the grieving parents standing on the front stoop of their small gray house gave Eddie all the nudge he needed. There was something the news wasn't saying about the Haines family. Eddie had an exclusive story on his hands.

"In a bizarre twist, the Tabitha Haines disappearance has resolved itself. Tabitha's father, Peter Haines, has surrendered to police after a four-hour standoff. He was immediately shuttled to a local area hospital for treatment of self-inflicted wounds. Though Haines was never a suspect in the disappearance of his daughter, it's now being released that he has confessed to raping and killing the fourteen year old girl."

Police refuse to comment on Mr. Haines's condition, but a spokesperson for the hospital says that Mr. Haines apparently castrated *himself with a pair of sewing scissors. He is listed in serious condition."*

Eddie looked up from the thick stacks of envelopes and new portraits to be mailed out. The news anchor was different, Luke Phillips had recently resigned to devote himself to his new career as a Buddhist neophyte. He'd read a statement on his last broadcast saying that he needed to spend the rest of his life atoning for crimes he had committed during his tour of duty as a sniper in the Vietnam Conflict.

Eddie made a note of the new anchor's name and kink, Russ Mathews, homosexual. He looked at the stack of portraits and wondered how they would be taken, what their recipients would think when they arrived. They included a contractor and the county inspector he'd bribed to certify a church in Kansas 'tornado resistant', and a mother so incensed and inflamed with greed and shame that she would rather take legal action against a city police department than admit she'd known from the start her son was a dangerous, uncontrollable pedophile. There was a Pope, a President and his entire Cabinet, several CEOs and accountants, corrupt police officers, blind judges, a couple of vindictive college football referees and a man from an infomercial named Chuck Berkowitz who sold informational packets for a real-estate buying system he knew had a better than 90% chance of bankrupting anyone who followed the plan.

Eddie sighed, weary, and then went back to work, stuffing each portrait into its envelope, licking stamps and copying addresses in his sloppy unsophisticated hand. He looked at how far he'd come, and how much further he had to go, and he smiled just a little, and the shadows under his eyes seemed to fade a bit, his back straightened just slightly. For the first time in a long time, Eddie felt something like happiness, and it didn't bother him so much what his gift had cost him, not in the face of the good he could do because of it.

Eddie liked the work he was doing, and his life seemed better than he'd ever imagined it could be after his mom had gone away. Things were looking up for him, he had no complaints. Only, he wished Uncle Tad's decomposing body in the bedroom didn't smell so bad. Why the man had to kill himself inside the apartment was beyond Eddie, but the boy was thankful that at least he'd had the decency to use pills instead of something messy. Besides, Eddie figured, it gave him the opportunity to work uninterrupted for a while. Nobody bothered him while he drew since he'd shown Tad his portrait. He was all alone. That is, until the rent came due, and by then he might have gotten enough done that he could rest for a while. That would be nice, he thought. He picked up his latest piece, the portrait of one of his old schoolteachers, a woman who hated children and had once dated a man just for his money and the things he could give her. If anyone deserved a reckoning, it was her, Eddie thought. With all the corruption he saw all around him, it was a good thing there was someone to set things straight again.

The Woman Who Spoke in Parables

Brian Richard Wade

Swaddled in Huggies and her own noisome aroma, she spoke her first word at thirteen months. She fussed at her father, his nose buried in the paper; and she whined at her mother, her eyes glued to the TV. She climbed onto the couch between her parents and uttered the word "Rhinoceros."

As a child, she had many friends. Cecil the albino and dark-eyed Maria along with Little Joe and his pack of mongrel dogs.

They roved together over vacant lots, horse pastures, and fields of stunted seed corn in search of buried treasure. Gold doubloons. Rubies, emeralds, sapphires, and diamonds. Pearls, black and white. All carried long ago up the wide Columbia to the winding Snake by bewildered pirates (so they said to one another) and then sunk into the hardpan in a brass-bound chest under the killing heat of a Great Basin summer sun.

"Put your backs into it, mateys," she commanded and chopped into the sandy soil with her mother's garden hoe as if it were a pickaxe. "God don't love sinners, and treasure don't find itself!"

After the find, they would build their own barque. As freewomen and freemen, they would sail down the river to loot old Fort Boise and instill a righteous fear of pirates into them namby-pamby quibbling cityfolk.

Cecil moved away. Joe's mongrel pack aged and dwindled. After the mishap with the flaming funeral boat, they buried each mutt in its own barrow near the drainage ditch in the, now, horseless pasture. She would read bits of Old English verse phonetically over the mound, the others repeating poorly, if at all, the trailing line of each stanza.

When Joe was down to his last—a black mastiff he'd saved from the pound a year before—he said, "This is stupid. I'm going home." Dark-eyed Maria followed him.

She could no longer live her tales, and so she began to speak them.

"Are you dressed for church, dear?" her mother called down the hallway of their little home in American Falls, Idaho. "Your father's ready to go."

She yelled back, "A childless couple collected porcelain dolls. One day, they bought a new doll from a German peddler. They had never seen it's like: long black hair, ruby lips, and a shining white face; it came in a miniature steamer truck filled with a dozen splendid dresses. The peddler claimed it could talk just like a real little girl."

"Get your ass in gear," said her father.

Clad in blue jean bell-bottoms, she stepped from her room into the hallway.

"Oh no you don't, young lady." Her mother pointed to her room. "You get back in there and change into something respectable ... and brush your hair. I won't have you embarrass us in front of the parish."

She stared at them both, stamped her foot. "And because they loved her so, they clothed her in darling little dresses and displayed her in their living room curio. How they loved their little doll! How they wished—"

"No more backtalk," said her mother.

Her father glared at her as he undid his belt buckle.

She ran into her room. Slamming the door shut behind her, she yelled, "They taught it to say cute things at parties to entertain guests."

The door opened. Her father. "That's enough."

"But the doll had a mind of its own and when the couple was away, it escaped the curio and explored— "

"Your mother is tired of all your lip."

She backed away, bumping into her bed beneath the window.

"... explored every room. It shrugged off the fine dress of taffeta, blue silk, and lace and screamed unlovely words at the walls."

"Enough." He pulled his belt free with one quick motion and looped it. It hung from his hand like a serpent, coiled and ready to strike.

"When the couple returned, they found the doll and clothed it again. But the doll would no longer speak the lies they put in its mouth," she cried.

"Stop."

"Anytime the couple was gone, the doll would remove her dress and run naked—"

Her father spun her and bent her over the bed. She struggled. The belt struck her legs, her back—everywhere except her rear end.

"You *will* learn to respect us."

She faced her father. "They tried to force the doll—"

He swung the belt toward her flank, but she blocked it with her arm.

"... to dress their way and speak their way."

"No more." He swung the belt at her side. She grabbed it, tugged at it, though she could not pull it from his grasp.

"But a doll is a fragile thing—"

Her father jerked the belt from her hands. He held up one finger in front of her face. His finger trembled; his voice quavered. "Not another word," he shouted. "I don't understand why it is so hard for you to do what you're told."

Tears streaked down her cheeks; she could make no reply. Her father shook his head and stalked out of the room.

She fell onto the bed, sobbing.

Her mother entered the room, sat down on the bed next to her. "You have to learn to listen to us." Her mother smoothed her tangled hair. "We just want what's best for you. Think about that," her mother said before leaving the room.

"... And with loving force, they cracked the doll's porcelain head," she whispered into her pillow.

At first math was difficult, but by her senior year of high school the calculus teacher always called on her: "Would you describe an asymptotic limit for the class?"

"There was an ant who wished to reach a crumb on the edge of a cliff. In the shade of the cliff, winter ice remained and formed a sharp slope upward. The ant scrambled up the slope. The way was easy at first, but the higher and closer to the cliff face, the steeper the slope grew. Soon, the ant was crawling as fast as it could. Imperceptibly, it approached the crumb.

But never could the ant reach it—no matter how hard it tried—so it starved to death and slid down to rest at the bottom of the cliff."

She avoided dating. Her cautionary tale about "The Pussy that Bit People," she found a poor substitute for "No." In such situations, she was forced to resort to crude gestures and a hunting knife she'd swiped from her father's bureau.

At graduation, though not the valedictorian, she was asked to speak. Her speech was austere and noble: she told of harsh journeys along forested paths, shadowy caves, golden apples and Herculean tasks, nostalgia and homecoming. Parents and teachers nodded their heads, smiled, leaned toward one another. "Do you know what she's talking about?" And in answer: "No, but it sure sounds pretty."

As she aged she learned that most people could understand humor or metaphor, but rarely at the same time. She wished that she had been born British.

She was popular with her college professors and many of the students. A nice golden-haired boy, a folklore major named Tom, wanted to marry her. They drove in his father's restored '53 Eldorado with Aztek Red paint and steel wire wheels to Reno, where they married at Hernando's Drive-thru Chapel.

She wrote erotic fiction for anthologies while Tom managed his father's machine shop and dreamed of other places. In time, his hair darkened. A child came into being—a daughter—so too the dynamics of love and strife. Mostly strife.

She came to Tom while he worked after hours in the shop, angrily shaping a brass cylinder on the lathe.

"A man on a long journey walked through an old wood. He had made the journey many times before, and often he'd brushed his fingers with pleasure across the rough surface of the low stone wall paralleling his path or took his lunch, seated atop the flat stones. On this occasion, he found his path blocked by the wall now grown to an insurmountable height. It stretched seemingly forever to his right and to his left. He said, 'You, wall, get out of my way. I must pass.' But the wall said nothing."

"Can't you just say 'yes' or 'no' for once?" interrupted Tom. "Why must everything be a goddamn riddle with you?"

She continued, "He thought perhaps the wall was only an illusion. Certainly no one could have built up the wall in so little time. He stepped right up to the stones and tried to cross over as he had many times before. His foot smacked against the rocks and he fell backward. Angry, he shouted from the ground, 'Why can't you be something else: a fence or stream or gate that I may go on my way?' But the wall was silent."

"Once. That's all. For me, for our daughter."

She said nothing.

"Once, there were two captains on a ship. In the knowledge of seas and sailors they were equals, but their methods differed. When the whirling storm came— "

"Wait. I know how this one ends, honey," Tom said, calm and even, though clenched teeth. "One captain said, 'Fuck you' and 'I'm leaving' and then he jumped ship."

The loss of her husband felt like the pain of a certain blind man whose cane hopped away one day. But she could not blame him—even after the judge jailed her for contempt and then awarded him custody of their daughter.

Tom's new wife said "yes" and "no," he made a point to tell her. He moved the family to Omaha.

There were other men. She was not Penelope to while away the years with the warp and woof, and Tom certainly had been no great-souled Odysseus. Even so, none could compare to the memory of her golden-haired boy.

In time there were no more men, and she was left to herself. Her public life was enchanted. People came from Plymouth, Massachusetts and Troy,

Oregon, Battle Creek, Michigan and Desoto, Texas to hear her speak and have their books signed. They loved her for her novelty. They came, nodded their heads sagaciously, and then returned to their homes to hoard and feed and sleep. To the causal friend, the acquaintance, the stranger, she engendered delight, but to those near her heart she brought only grief.

The year her hair completed its transformation from raven black to snowy white, her father died. Her daughter came to visit from Omaha, and she brought her young son to see his grandmother for the first time. The grandson had eyes like those of his grandfather in the days of golden hair.

She told a story of sorrow and reconciliation. Her daughter accepted the apology, but when they hugged it was stiff with a slight bend at the waist forming an "A" from the side.

The grandson regarded her with shining eyes from his place behind his mother's legs. "Grandma, you talk funny."

She forced a smiled at him and, briefly, wondered what his head would taste like. As revenge, she told him about Baba Yaga. Instead of hiding, he jumped out from behind his mother, clapped his chubby hands with delight, and said, "More."

When her mother passed away the following year, the family asked her to give the eulogy. But she would not. They cried, "She was your mother!" and "What kind of woman are you?"

At the graveside, and the time for good words past, she gave this answer:

"At the dawn of speech, when humanity and the gods were new to the world, there lived a weaver of baskets. Her name was Amanya—the little flower. While her hands occupied themselves with the business of basketry, her mind was free to wander.

"'Who made the red mud, and white pines, and musky-scented brown bear?' she asked the elders.

"'The land and forest and animal spirits,' they said.

"'Who made the spirits?'

"'The Great Maker.'

"'And who made the Great Maker?'

"The elders snorted and shook their gray heads. 'Go back to your basket making, woman,' they said.

"And she asked each of the people whether they had ever seen, or heard, or smelled the Great Maker. But none had. One wizened, toothless crone claimed to have seen the Sun Spirit, a long jagged stream of light leaving fire in his wake, leap from the earth to his home above the clouds.

"As her hands wove the weft around the warp she spoke, first to herself and then to whomever shared the warmth of her fire.

"'Maybe,' she said, 'there are no spirits or Great Maker at all, only speechless things changing form—as the thin willow branches become the spokes, the strips of birch bark become the weaving, and the pine resin becomes the sealant in my baskets. Maybe all things—save the people—are dead matter like the bones of my mother and father lying in the ground and slowly rotting to earth.'

"And the elders stopped her mouth up and cast her out from the people to the far side of the glacier. Others knew the secrets of weaving, ones who would not anger the gods."

The family murmured to one another, but her grandson, now a year older, giggled until his mother put a hand over his mouth.

When her hair lay upon her head like wisps of fog over pinkish earth, she returned from the hospital to die at home. She sent her dutiful daughter away, but her grandson would not leave. He'd come from the university to stay by her. They seldom spoke, merely exchanging fleeting images as quick as a "yes" or "no."

After one of her long coughing spells, her grandson looked at her with wet eyes. She swore her palsy had infected his lips as he fashioned a poor grin and asked, "Are you afraid? You know, to pass the veil?"

"Shuffle off the mortal coil?" she riposted.

"Push up the daisies?"

"Tread the Elysian fields?"

"Take the dirt nap?"

"Travel the undiscovered country?"

"Look up the skirt of Oblivion?"

Her scratchy laugh turned into another fit of wheezing. She raised a shaky, skeletal hand to her mouth until the wheezing subsided, and then she chuckled some more. With her remaining strength, she pushed herself upright in bed.

Her grandson adjusted the pillows until she leaned comfortably against the headboard. She watched him straighten the blankets, her unclouded eyes steady in spite of her body's tremor. She stopped his hands with her own and pulled him closer. When their eyes met, she told with joy what would be her last tale:

"In the time of the Yellow Emperor, Huang Di, there lived a great warrior called Sun Wu-wei. He was the favorite of the young emperor and became his personal guard and mentor. With the bow and spear none could compare to Sun Wu-wei. His every arrow found the gap in his opponent's armor, and neither man nor boar could stand before his spear and draw the breath of life again.

"As the Emperor aged, so, too, did the warrior. After forty years of service, Sun Wu-wei said to his Emperor, 'Though many have tried, neither dagger nor spear, arrow nor stone has wounded the divine flesh. Because of the love I bear you, I ask that another guardian take my place at your side. I am no longer the fierce warrior of my younger years and soon my strength shall fail. In your great wisdom, please grant this.'

"The Yellow Emperor, because his wisdom was great, acknowledged the truth in Sun Wu-wei's words, and though it made the divine breast ache and the divine eyes water, he granted his warrior and teacher's request.

"All the Emperor's generals lined up before Sun Wu-wei so that he could select his successor, but the Emperor's warrior passed over them to choose instead a keen-minded common soldier and farmer's son, Lu Ping. His duty discharged, Sun Wu-wei bowed deeply to his Emperor and departed the court to begin his journey into the mountains.

"Sun Wu-wei paused upon the bridge over the palace ponds filled with the Emperor's black carp. He heard footsteps approach, but he did not turn.

"'Lu Ping,' he said, 'why have you left the Emperor's side? Is his life of so little consequence to you?'

"'Quite the contrary, Master,' Lu Ping replied, 'I am young and fast and strong, but even now I am not your equal. I have seen you fight. You do not fear death. This you must teach before you depart, so that I may ward the Emperor from all harm.'

"Sun Wu-wei turned to Lu Ping and captured the soldier's eyes with his own. He stooped and plucked a tiny river stone from between the slats of the bridge. 'The Yellow Emperor is the Guardian of Truth, and we are the guardians of the guardian. But in the end, we—you, I, and even the emperor—are only pebbles at the base of the mountain.'

"He stepped to the edge and dropped the pebble into the carp pond. Lu Ping watched the stone plink into the water creating ever-expanding and diminishing circular ripples until the carp roiled the waters and effaced the pattern in their blind search for a morsel.

"Lu Ping bowed to Sun Wu-wei and watched as the warrior left the palace grounds for the solitude of the mountains, never to return.

"Under the protection of Lu Ping, the Yellow Emperor accomplished many great works and suffered no injury until death took him in the fullness of his age."

The woman who spoke in parables then kissed her grandson's hand and drifted into a dreamless sleep.

Family and strangers alike heaped the woman's coffin with roses and white carnations. Lily-bedizened wreaths lined the path of the viewing. When he strode down the aisle, the woman's grandson swept all before him and pressed into the palm of her still hand a river stone he'd found in the parking lot.

The grandson turned to meet the puzzled stares of the mourners. "In the beginning ..."

Tongues

Ray Vukcevich

"All the astrologers will be castrated."
Leonardo da Vinci

1
Prophecy as Pathology

When one half of the team descended into dark depression, there was nothing for the other half to do but go along for the ride. But even if the outcome was known, the process had to be respected. Shelly needed to be talked into it.

"I predict," she said, "that if we run off to Borneo on this wild goose chase of yours, we will come to grief."

"And what do you base this prediction on?" Marc asked.

"Common sense?"

"Look, I've totally lost it, Shell," he said. "If we don't do this, what will we do instead? And if we don't do it now, then when?"

"You're channeling some kind of political speech from the past, aren't you?"

"Maybe from the future," he said. "I don't know. I can no longer predict what I can predict. There is a strange spiritual sickness eating away at my brain."

She put a cup of tea down in front of him. "What do you want to do?"

"Thanks," he said. "I see us in an exotic seaside grotto kissing the starfish on the smooth wet stone walls."

"I see that, too," she said, "but I don't like it."

"Borneo," he said.

"I'm not entirely sure where Borneo is," Shelly said, "A long long way from Chicago, no doubt, and I predict we can't afford to go there."

2
Symptoms and Events

"Leonardo is making fun of me," Marc said.

"Who?"

"Leonardo da Vinci," he said. "Look here."

Shelly threw down her pencil and got up from her desk where she had been preparing a chart for one of their regular clients. She came over to his desk where he was supposed to be working, too, instead of acting like a big baby.

"Don't give me that look," he said. "I am not acting like a baby."

He showed her the prediction.

"But maybe more than half of all astrologers are women." She sounded exasperated. "It doesn't even make sense."

"He's probably speaking metaphorically," Marc said. "In which case women astrologers could also be castrated."

"You may be losing it, Sweetie," she said.

"That's what I've been saying."

"We still can't afford Borneo."

"I've been thinking about that." Marc poked around in the papers on his desk, picking them up and putting them down. "Just as Leonardo may have been speaking obliquely, my vision of Borneo may also be couched in a kind of code."

He put another piece of paper on top of the Leonardo prophecy. It was covered with letters and numbers. "I started by rearranging the letters in 'Borneo'. I was hoping for something obvious, but I should have known better."

"What did you come up with?" She came around and put her hands on his shoulders and leaned down to look at the paper.

"I don't think I tried all the combinations," he said. "That would have taken too long. I stopped when I found something that looked promising."

"Which was?"

He flipped the paper over. On the other side were two words.

Borneo

Orebon

"Orebon?"

"I know," he said. "It's not quite right yet, but it looked strangely familiar and then it hit me that someone was pointing me at Oregon."

"But it says 'Orebon'."

"Yes, but there is a simple transformation," he said. "Consider the letters in question. They are B and G. That is, the B should have been a G. So how do we get a G from what we have? Well, first notice that B is the second letter of the alphabet and that G is the seventh letter."

"Consider those facts noticed," Shelly said.

"So what is the difference?"

"Between seven and two?"

"Yes."

"Well, five."

"Bingo," he said. "And how do we get five from the other evidence?"

"I don't know."

"Well, notice that the offending B is the first letter in 'Borneo' and the target G is the fourth letter in 'Oregon' and what do you get when you add one and four?"

"Oh, okay," she said. "I see it. You get five. And two plus five is seven, and the seventh letter of the alphabet is G so you can substitute the G for the B in Orebon and get Oregon."

"Exactly!" he said. "And anyone can afford to go to Oregon these days."

"But what about the starfish?"

"They must be in Oregon, too."

3
Kissing Fish

They fought about it. They stopped speaking for a while. The cohesion of the team was seriously threatened, but then one thing led to another, and in the end, the Chicago based astrologers, Marc and Shelly Bowman, followed the Borneo/Oregon code to Portland where they had expected cool weather even in August. They had expected rain. No one is right all of the time. It was over 100 degrees and dry, the sky so blue, you might think clouds hadn't yet been invented. If the sun were god's thumb, these two astrologers were the thumbtacks. The heat drove them toward the sea where they learned of the Oregon Coast Aquarium in Newport, a couple of hours to the south. Things were coming together. Once they reached Newport, another piece fell into place when they spotted the Brunei Bar and Grill on the main drag.

Inside it wasn't Borneo but it was some place far away like Borneo or Bombay or Bora Bora but not Bermuda because it was not the kind of place you expected to see tourists in straw hats and flowery shorts. No cameras please! It was dark and cold and the beer neons were too bright but didn't penetrate far into the darkness, the kind of place someone might creep up behind you and get too close and whisper garlic in your ear, "So, you've come to kiss the fish?"

"At the aquarium," Marc said.

"Forget the aquarium," the man in the dark said. "What makes you think you'll find fish at the aquarium?"

"No fish at the aquarium?"

"Hey, this dude thinks they'll let him kiss the fish down at the aquarium," the man in the dark spoke loudly and there was laughter all around, and Marc could see that the place was not so empty after all. He could make out the faces of the men and woman at the bar now. They must have been sitting very quietly when he and Shelly had come in. There was a bartender now, too, and he was moving in on them. He was a young man with a very short haircut. He wore a white t-shirt and there were tattoos of birds and snakes on his upper arms. He tossed down a couple of coasters and asked them what they wanted to drink.

Marc wondered what they had on tap. Shelly asked for a cola.

The man in the dark moved in and took the stool between them. His hair was thick and totally white. His skin was very pale, but his lips were purple. He wore a red and green flannel shirt and some kind of gray canvas pants. Glasses with very small rimless lenses. Marc guessed he was probably in his mid seventies. He rapped on the bar, and the bartender nodded at him. A moment later, the drinks appeared. The man picked his up and toasted Marc and Shelly silently and drank deeply before speaking again.

"There is a parasitic crustacean in the jungles of Borneo," he said. "In the waters. What it does is it crawls into the mouths of fish and eats their tongues. Then it attaches itself firmly and takes the place of the missing tongue. Half the time the fish eats something it goes no farther than its new tongue, but the fish can move it around and do other tongue-like things with it and pretty soon, the fish forgets it ever had some other kind of tongue. It just has to work a little harder."

"That's horrible," Shelly said.

"And these are the fish we've come for?" Marc asked.

"No," the man said. "These fish I'm talking about are in Borneo."

"So, why tell us about those creepy fish and their tongues, then?" Shelly asked. "If they're not even the ones we came to see?"

"Those are out back," he said. "Drink up and I'll show you."

He slipped off the stool and disappeared back into the gloom.

Marc and Shelly got off their stools. Marc tossed some money down on the bar and took her hand. He peered around hoping for a clue on what to do next. He had no intuitions. He figured Shelly had none either since she was never shy about telling him what she saw and felt.

Someone slashed open the darkness by opening a door to one side of the bar. "Come on, then," the same man called to them. Mark saw him step out of the door and hold it waiting for them to follow.

"You got any feelings about this?" he asked Shelly.

"Nothing specific," she said. "You don't have to have paranormal powers to guess this might be a mistake, though."

"You're probably right," he said. "Let's just take a quick peek, and if it doesn't seem right, we'll take off."

The man had left the door open for them and had moved off into what turned out to be a kind of backyard that reminded Marc of his childhood. There were a few untrimmed trees sprawling over the fence in back and junk—lots of junk—machines of indeterminate function, buckets of bolts, tin cans in piles, mysterious parts.

The man stood beside a big metal washtub. There was a piece of plywood on top of the tub.

"Come on," he said.

Mark and Shelly walked up to him. When they got there, he leaned down and pulled the plywood off of the washtub. Marc stepped in a little closer to look. The water was not clear, but he could see bright figures moving slowly under the surface, flashes of red, green, and blue.

Fish. Just fish with fins and tails and gills.

"But where are the starfish?" Marc asked.

"You're looking at them," the man said. "Fish from the stars."

"Oh, so they never were starfish," Marc said.

"You got it," the man said. "You ready?"

"Ready for what?" Shelly asked.

"Get down on your knees and just pucker up and put your face in the water, Missy, make smootch smootch sounds." He demonstrated. "And blow a few bubbles to attract these big fellows."

"I don't think so," she said.

"Me either," Marc said. "Sorry to have wasted your time."

He took Shelly's hand and turned to walk back into the bar.

There were three men blocking the way.

"Oh, you haven't wasted our time," the man by the washtub said.

The three men by the door smiled or chuckled or both and advanced on them.

Shelly clutched at his sleeve. "Marc?"

He didn't know what to do. Why hadn't he seen this coming? Maybe Leonardo had been right on the money and he'd already been psychically castrated.

Marc often dreamed something horrible was out to get him, jumping out of the shadows, chasing and howling, something big and hairy with a lot of sharp teeth. Sometimes he ran, but he never got away, and when he ran, he knew the waking day would suck.

Sometimes he turned and attacked, and when he did that, he always woke feeling like he could handle anything.

Was this going to be one of those days?

He shook Shelly off and charged the three men. Sometimes fear pushed people into doing superhuman things when protecting the people they loved.

Right?

When he got to the men, two of them stepped aside and let him run headlong into the middle one. Then the other two grabbed his arms, and the guy he'd bounced off of hit him hard in the stomach. Marc doubled over the man's fist. The other two dragged him back to the tub where the old guy was struggling with Shelly. The guy who had hit Marc now hit Shelly—a ringing open handed slap that dropped her to her knees. The men holding Marc forced him down beside her.

"Okay," the old guy said. "Kiss kiss."

Marc felt fingers in his hair and then his head was jerked up and over the rim of the washtub and plunged into the water.

He couldn't see anything clearly. He struggled but couldn't free himself. He was drowning. He felt tentative touches to his face like curious fingers, lightly over his cheeks and nose and then more forcefully between his lips.

Something knocked hard against his teeth, and he gasped and swallowed water and coughed and felt water in his lungs and something big in his mouth. There was a slicing crunch and pain exploded in the back of his mouth. He could see his own blood flowing into the water. Something forced its way down his throat, and when it got where it wanted to be, it stopped with a decisive clap and was still.

Marc realized there was no one holding him under the water now, and he lunged upward to his feet and shook his head back and forth producing a wide spray of water and blood. Shelly rose up, too, and the two them looked at each other and then looked quickly around for their attackers, but they were alone in the backyard now.

4
Tongues

No one tried to stop them when they moved back into the bar. In fact no one paid them any attention at all. Everything was strangely ordinary. The room was brighter now like someone had turned on more lights after he and Shelly had gone out to kiss the fish from the stars. Marc didn't see the old guy and his three assistants.

He looked at Shelly. She might be in shock. Shelly shocked, he thought wildly and chuckled but he couldn't push the sound up out of his chest. He opened his mouth to ask her if she was okay.

He said, "Are you firmly lodged?"

"Quite firmly," she said.

"Me, too," he heard himself say, and when he said it, he could feel his tongue and lips and lungs and they didn't feel like they were part of him. There was an overlay, something on top of him, doing the talking. He could see from the wild fright in Shelly's eyes that she was experiencing something similar.

"Shall we proceed then?" she asked.

Her lipstick had turned to a liverish shade of purple. No, there was a fine line around her lips and the skin was red where it met her purple lips. He didn't really think those were her lips at all. You could grab those lips and pull the tongue parasite out of her head and lungs whole like a bird picking apart a grasshopper.

He ignored her words and lips and took both her hands in his and looked into her eyes. "This is a total waste of time," he said.

"We are in agreement about that," she said, but he could see that she wasn't saying that at all. Shelly was telling him they were not totally cut off. They were both astrologers, for crying out loud. They trafficked in the paranormal all the time. So what if aliens from outer space had come down and eaten their tongues and maybe their lungs and lips and the rest of their vocal apparatus? That didn't mean they were out of the game. Notice, her eyes said, that while they have the voice, we seem to still have everything else.

"Are we going to just stand here like a couple of idiots?" he said, but what he meant and hoped he conveyed with his eyes and a light squeeze to her hands was that he agreed they were not defeated. There were people they could consult about this. There were experts in the occult arts who might think this infestation was trivial. A walk in the park. Tongue parasites! Ha ha. We'll just give you a good dose of stinging Jalapeno Jell-O and the intruders will knock your teeth out they'll be leaving so quick. Well, maybe we should keep the teeth.

He didn't think she was getting his message. She looked so frightened.

A woman sitting at the bar twisted around on her stool and said, "They want to go now."

A man to her left said without turning his head, "Yes, you two go now."

Then they were all saying it. Up and down the bar and in the shadowy booths. Go now. Louder and louder. Shelly was saying it, too, and so was he. The two of them almost nose to nose shouting in one another's face, "Go now! Go now!"

He was suddenly afraid she would panic and run away from him. He pulled at her hands, and they hurried out of the bar. When they got outside, everyone stopped shouting.

He pulled her close and they clung together trembling.

"There must be a car," she said over his shoulder.

"No doubt," he said.

5
The Limits of Time

They got a motel. Marc suspected his tongue parasite was little by little gaining access to his mind. The things they were saying to one another contained more and more details from Marc and Shelly's lives. The parasites knew they were far from home on a foolish errand to reinvigorate Marc's failing psychic powers. They had picked up on her smoldering resentment and on his resentment in return at her lack of sympathy for his predicament. He wondered how long they would have any control at all.

"Are you ready to go home?" she asked.

"I've been thinking about that," he said. "Maybe I'll let you go on by yourself while I look into a few things here."

They were sitting side by side on the end of the motel bed. Shelly had turned on the TV, but he had turned down the sound, and no one had objected.

He put his arm around her shoulder. It was getting harder to move.

"We'll need to eat soon," she said without looking at him.

He moved in closer, and a sudden scene flashed into his mind where the parasite in his mouth leaped out and wrapped around her head with a wet splat, and he pulled back a little until the picture passed. Then he moved in again until he could touch his forehead to the side of her head. He felt her lean her head into his.

Time, he told her, and felt her shudder when his message passed through his head and into hers. If you're thinking about prophecy, you can't help but think about the nature of time.

"I suppose I could go spend a few days with my mother," she said.

And if you're thinking about the nature of time, you will soon come to the realization that it began some time after you were born. Exactly when is a little blurry, because the more you look back, the less you remember, and it will end when you die. That's it. There is no other time. You cannot think outside of time.

"You haven't seen your mother in ages," he said.

But if he had been doing his own talking, his words would have matched the thoughts now moving the few small inches from him to her. I understand what Leonardo was trying to tell me now. We have always been ineffectual, unproductive, castrated in our prophecy. How could it be otherwise? That's Leonardo's joke. We are chickens trapped in our own times. A prophecy does not exist until you learn of it, and then if it comes to pass, it comes to pass in your life. That means if a prophecy is about anything at all, it must be about you. Any prediction applies only to the time of the astrologer. That is, the time between conscious awakening and death. It makes no sense to even think about what came 'before' or what will come 'after.' Or what might be 'apart.' Nothing came before. Nothing comes after. Each of us is closed away in a private cosmos.

"And you'll be looking for Leonardo in Oregon," she said.

I have all time, he told her. You have all time, too. But it's not the same time.

"I think we should go our separate ways now," he said.

She pulled away from him and twisted around, and they looked long and hard at each other.

Was this really the end of them? Would they simply go their separate ways now? Maybe exchange holiday cards and birthday greetings after a few years?

She grabbed him, and there was a cosmic spark bridging universes.

He pulled her in tight and struggled to push words past his lips.

"No," he said. "We won't."

"Yes," she said into his chest. "We refuse."

Death Comes For Ervina

Theodora Goss

There is something vaguely bovine about the nurse, whose name Ervina has once again forgotten. She reminds Ervina of the cows that she milked during the war. She would wake in the darkness, before the rooster crowed from his perch on the hay wagon, and fetch the water so her mother could make breakfast: boiled potatoes on which she dripped lard for flavoring. Then she would milk the cows, whose names were, she remembers, Rózsa and Piroska. In winter, when a rim of ice formed on the milk pail, she would warm her hands in their breaths. When Rózsa stopped giving milk, she was taken to the butcher, and Ervina cried for three days.

"Jésus Mária," said her mother, who always appears in her memories wearing an apron, "all those tears for a cow."

Then she would collect the eggs. Surely, at first, there were eggs with the potatoes, fried in lard? And later there were no eggs, no lard, and finally no potatoes, just boiled cabbage flavored with salt. The faces of the children at school became pale above their uniforms, which were ragged from being worn every day of the week, for doing chores or playing football. They had no other clothes.

After her father came back from the war, without Dénes or Ödön, it was her mother's turn to cry. She could not, Ervina supposes, have cried for three years, but that is what she remembers. When she began school again, with a new uniform and a red kerchief around her neck, her cheeks were damp with her mother's tears.

"Miss Kóvacs, did you hear me? You have a visitor. Someone from the ballet school. You want I should open the window? I don't know how you stand it in here, under all those blankets."

Her father did not want her to go to the ballet school.

"She's just a child," he said. "Who will raise her in Budapest? You say she will be raised by the school, but I spent a week in the city during the war. It's filled with gypsies and prostitutes. Why should I send my daughter to such a place?"

Because, explained the teacher, his daughter had a talent for the ballet, and it was his duty to the Party—and why, by the way, hadn't he joined the Party, didn't he know it was created to benefit farmers such as himself?—to use her talent in the service of the People's Republic.

Ervina listened from behind the kitchen door. Budapest was as unreal to her as the frog prince in the fairy tale. Once, she had tried to kiss a frog she had found in the reeds by the river Tisza, with no result. Not that she wanted the frog to become a prince. But she wanted, herself, to become a princess, with a gold ball. After she had milked the cows, she would stand by the barn door to make her révérence, and the cows would stare at her with appreciative brown eyes. But when her father returned from the war, alone and leaning heavily on a cane, her mother went back to milking the cows and collecting the eggs, while Ervina sat at the kitchen table practicing her sums.

It seemed strange that she should be taken to Budapest because she could point her toes or arch her back better than the other children in her class, away from the mother who no longer told her fairy tales but cried into the cabbage soup, the father who told her to practice her sums so she could train to be an accountant, because on the farm she would never be as useful as a boy.

The smell of exhaust and roasting eggplant fills the room. When she first moved to this apartment in Brooklyn, there was a Hungarian bakery across the street. Each morning she would buy a slice of poppy seed beigli and eat it slowly, in miniature bites, with her morning coffee, as though to reward herself for a lifetime of hunger.

At the ballet school in Budapest, breakfast was two pieces of toast, a boiled egg, and a sliced tomato. How hungry they were, the girls whose shoulder blades appeared through their leotards, like vestigial wings. How proud they were of their hunger, the girls from farms as far away as Debrecen, as they watched their muscular waists become slender, watched the suppleness of their legs, which had once struggled in farm boots through fields to be mown for hay. Even the fourteen-year-olds drank their coffee black and smoked Bulgarian cigarettes.

Now the Hungarian bakery has been replaced by an Armenian restaurant. But she can no longer eat sweets, she thinks approvingly, looking at her wrists, which have never been so thin: blue veins covered by layers of tulle, like the skirts of the Swans Maidens surrounding Odette, who wears a crown that to the audience looks like gold, although Ervina knows that it is gilded papier maché. She has worn it often enough.

"Isn't that better? It's about time you got some fresh air. He says his name is Victor. He says he knows you from the ballet school. Miss Kóvacs? Should I tell him you're too tired? Or should I tell him to come in?"

But it was not in *Swan Lake* that she first met Victor Boyd.

She danced in *Swan Lake* the first time she came to New York. It was an era when cultural exchange was encouraged, and the Budapest Ballet had been invited to Carnegie Hall. From their rooms in a hotel on West 83rd Street, the ballerinas could hear the continual honking of taxis, and smell hot dogs being sold in the park.

Perhaps it was that, although she was Ervina Kóvacs, whose photograph hung in the ballet school dormitory, who had a sponge cake named after her at Gundel's, who had received a standing ovation from Chairman Brezhnev himself, she had to share a room with Ilona Nagy, who danced Odile. Perhaps that, from the car window as the ballerinas were driven to Carnegie Hall, she could see buildings taller than any she had seen in Budapest, or Prague, or even Moscow, whose windows reflected clouds. Perhaps she was tired of dancing Petipa, of Jardins Animés or bayad□res endlessly pirouetting across the stage behind her. Perhaps it was only the smell of hot dogs.

That day, while Siegfried began his *pas de deux* with Odile, she pulled out the hairpins that held on her crown, threw a coat that the janitor had left on a hook over her shoulders, and left through a back door. She waved her arms on the street until a taxi swerved to the curb, splashing her pointe shoes with mud.

"New York Ballet," she had said, repeating it three times until the driver understood. Her pronunciation was not so good in those days. He cursed her when, in front of the ballet school, she jumped out of the taxi and handed him a purse full of forints.

The door opens again and Victor walks into the room, looking as when she first saw him, in jeans and a t-shirt with Rolling Stones written on it, the blond hair ragged around his shoulders, as awkward and graceful as a young swan.

But no, this Victor has gray hair above his ears. This Victor is wearing a gray suit and a watch with Bulova written on it, and his name is Mr. Boyd. There are traces, still, in his movements of the boy to whom she once said, "If you would only apply yourself, Vic, you would be the greatest ballet dancer in the company, perhaps in the world. I mean, of course, after me."

"Ervina," he says, taking her hands, which are as pale as milk, with blue veins running through them. She approves of their delicacy. "Madame Petrovna told me you were sick."

She was already a teacher then, training to succeed Larissa Petrovna, who had trained with the Kirov Ballet and was the most famous teacher at the ballet school. She had already danced in Paris, in London, in Tokyo, and in a public television special. But she could feel that her calloused feet, which had long ago conformed to the shape of a pointe shoe, were no longer as subtle as they had been, and that her back could no longer bend like a reed in the river current. She had already stopped dancing the roles that Mr. D had created for her, the Blue Note in *Symphony in Blue*, Elena in *Three Sisters*, the Hyacinth Girl. She was preparing, with a pragmatism she supposed she had inherited from her father, who was lying in his grave in Szent Miklós, presumably no longer shocked that she had become a ballerina, which was no better than a prostitute, for the day when she could no longer dance. It had not been easy, realizing that she would soon have to stop dancing even Odette. But one could still, she had thought, be useful, one could still have a sort of fame, after one no longer wore the papier maché crown.

She had thought of her mother, one of those interchangeable widows dressed in black at the Museum of Cultural History in Debrecen, who issued visitors felt slippers so the floors would not be scuffed. In her last letter she had sounded almost happy, had written about a geranium she was growing in the apartment window. She had sent Ervina her gingerbread recipe. So, Ervina supposed, old age contracted one's interests until such things were enough. Perhaps, she thought, one day I will no longer care if the audience applauds.

And then into the studio had walked Mr. D, leading a young man with ragged hair around his shoulders. He had said, "Ervina, this is Victor Boyd. You must teach him to dance."

"But he is too old!" Ervina had said.

And then Victor had danced for her. Had she fallen in love with him that day? Or had it been later, on a day that they danced together in the studio, as the Black Pawn and White Queen in *Chess* perhaps, or the Herons in *Birds*?

He had been badly taught. It would take months before she could unteach him all he had learned, before she could teach him what he needed to know. Months in which, after mornings at the barre, he would meet with her individually. In the afternoons, with sunlight slanting through the studio windows, they would watch him move in the mirror, while the pianist played Prokofiev or Tchaikovsky with the endless precision of a machine.

What is he telling her? "Did she mention that Juliette left me? The day Jim left for college. She said, 'Now that the children are out of the house, there's no reason for us to stay together, is there?' Her suitcase was already packed. She's living with an investment banker on Long Island. But you're not interested in this. How are you doing, Ervina? Rosemarie said you're getting excellent care."

That's why the nurse reminds her of a cow. Rosemarie is the name that she's forgotten.

"So we're finally through." He begins to laugh, then stops abruptly. When did his face become wrinkled? She prefers it to the blank twenty-year-old face he had when he told her, "I'm going to marry Juliette."

"You warned me, didn't you?" he says, looking down at her hands, absentmindedly running his fingers over the veins. "You said, 'Juliette Biró will never be more than a soloist, and if you marry her you will never be the dancer you were meant to be.' That was the night we danced Oberon and Titania together."

It had been a benefit for the New York Diabetes Foundation, his debut and her farewell performance. They had danced Mr. D's *A Midsummer Night's Dream*, the last ballet he would create for her and, she realized with chagrin, one suitable for her diminished talents. Despite her elaborate costume, which was covered with leaves that had to be sewn on by hand, Titania's role was largely ornamental, while Oberon had been choreographed for a dancer who could leap like a stag, from one end of the stage to the other. With Oberon's antlers on his head, dressed only in a bronze loincloth and bronze paint, Victor looked like a god of the forest. She pirouetted to meet him, the green tulle fastened to her shoulders fluttering like wings. With fairies piquéing around them, Peaseblossom, Cobweb, Moth, and Mustardseed, students from the ballet school, she met him not in the embrace Mr. D had choreographed, but with a kiss worthy of a forest god and the queen of fairies. And afterward he had told her, behind the curtain, "I'm going to marry Juliette."

"So here I am. This morning I met with the planning committee. This afternoon I'm going to a fundraiser for the school." He laughs again, uncomfortably, then abruptly leans forward until his forehead is resting on the backs of her hands. "You were right, you know." His voice is muffled, but she hears it as clearly as the call before the raising of a curtain. "You were right about everything. But you scared the shit out of me. You were the great Ervina Kóvacs, and what was I? A kid from Oklahoma who grew up on basketball and got stuck in a dance class because the coach thought it would help him jump." He raises his head and looks at her, so that she sees herself in his eyes: the gray hair lying on the pillow, the face like a wrinkled sheet. "I just wanted you to know that."

There is something she must tell him, about mornings during the war when she milked the cows, and nothing for breakfast but potatoes. She must tell him that he has misunderstood her. But it is she who has misunderstood: the revelation comes slowly, like sunlight filtering through the mud in the river Tisza, illuminating the carp that slide beneath the surface. It wasn't you I loved, she wants to tell him. It wasn't you after all. It was—but she's not certain how to finish.

She feels her eyebrows extend into antennae.

He takes off his jacket, unbuttons his white shirt. It is not the body she remembers, the shoulders almost too muscular for the waist, which was as slender as a girl's. This waist has filled out, but it is still firm, the skin glittering like bronze. And his kiss, as he bends over the bed, is still the kiss of a forest god. His antlers rise like the branches of an oak tree. Then he moves away from her in a series of soubresauts and stands in front of the window, through which she can hear the noise of traffic, holding out his hands as though waiting for her to join him.

"Did you have a nice visit with Mr. Boyd?" asks Rosemarie. "He looks so distinguished, like a doctor on *General Hospital*. I bet he was a dreamboat when he was a boy." Oberon stands in front of the window, antlered and naked except for a bronze loincloth. "You want I should bring you some lunch? I made chicken broth with dumplings, just like you taught me."

The chair on which he had been sitting has sprouted, and the forest is rising around her, cardboard branches casting shadows under the spotlight of a moon. Music is playing from a unseen orchestra, and fairies flit through the forest on wings of tulle, with antennae painted over their eyes. In the forest, Oberon is waiting. Yes, she thinks, this is it, this is what I wanted all along. Titania rises from her bank of flowers.

"Miss Kóvacs?"

She pirouettes, reveling in the strength of her feet, the suppleness of her back as she leans over Oberon's arm, looking toward the darkness where an audience is watching. She sees her mother, holding a potted geranium; her father, dour and disapproving; Ödön and Dénes. A teacher from her school in Szent Miklós, waving a red flag. Students she remembers from ballet class, taking notes. Larissa Petrovna, swinging her famous string of pearls in time to the music. Even Rózsa is standing in the aisle. She can see them all, in the darkness beyond the footlights. Perhaps, she thinks, for what I have done or not done, I have been forgiven. In the wings, hidden behind a curtain, Mr. D is nodding his approval. She smiles at him, then looks again at Oberon as the music begins for their pas de deux.

Ithrulene

Alexander Lamb

The old woman on the seat next to him nudged Orin awake. He blinked gummy eyes open and peered at her. She sat impassively, her box of chickens on her lap, and pointed out of the grimy window. "You say you want wake when we near Ithru'," she reminded him in her thick Miracle Country accent.

"Oh yes, thanks," mumbled Orin. His mouth tasted bitter and furry.

He squinted into the sunlight and saw it for the first time. Across the now familiar vista of shacks, paddy fields and palm trees: Ithrulene, the world famous vertical city.

What had been visible from the coast only as a faint pencil line against the sky was here so massive and unnatural that the eye could barely leave it. It stuck ramrod straight out of the dead flat landscape like a titan's spear jammed into the earth. It was just a quarter of a mile across but so tall that Orin couldn't tell where the building ended and where the beam of shadow that supported it began.

He was supposed to track Rima down in *there*? Even from this far away he could see that there were hundreds of floors, stacked like teetering pancakes.

It burned him that he should see it this way—with dread. Ithrulene was to have been the grand finale of their honeymoon tour. Instead it had become the terminus for a grim race across an incomprehensible country.

At least he knew that this was where they'd brought her after they'd snatched her from the hotel lobby. That much he'd learned from the bus company. They'd been happy to tell him, not that Orin felt particularly grateful to them for it, or for the free ticket they'd offered. No one in the station had lifted a finger to prevent the rebels getting onto the bus with his abducted wife in the first place.

The bus turned onto a highway lined with warehouses and roadside stalls, shrines and hovels. Over the pointed cloth hats of the locals sat in front of him, Orin could make out a ragged huddle of buildings a couple of miles wide that filled out the tower's base. These were massive concrete structures dozens of stories high, studded with rows of little windows. The geometric logos that Orin had come to recognize as cult glyphs had been painted huge on their sides in gaudy colors, then bleached by the brutal sunshine and spattered with grime.

Each of those edifices on its own would have dominated a city skyline elsewhere, but here they were dwarfed. Their filth-streaked roofs all angled toward the spire as if in homage to its impossible mass. The approach road became a dark chasm running between them, thick with all manner of traffic from ox-carts to luxury cars. Progress slowed to a crawl.

Ahead, a great arch set into a blotchy concrete wall beckoned. The interior was dark like a monster's maw, save for a few filth-tinged artificial lights. Little by little, Orin was pulled forward into the belly of the thousand-story beast.

When his eyes adjusted, he found himself looking out onto a loop of road five lanes wide that wrapped around a single vast column. Around the loop's outer edge lay a paved area packed with countless milling locals. Vehicles pulled up to the curb in disorganized profusion to disgorge people and goods. Officials with whistles and peaked caps ordered them about.

The place was alive with shouts, echoes and screeching brakes and thick with the odors of cheap engines and human sweat. The walls reflected the chaos and intensified it while fizzing light-strips hanging from the ceiling illuminated the scene in nightmare shades of orange and brown.

The bus juddered to a halt and Orin climbed out along with the other hundred or so people he'd been sharing it with. Many of them had huge sacks to haul off the roof, or animals to coax out from under the seats. Not Orin.

He'd left most of their luggage in the care of his hotel over a hundred miles away. He'd snatched what little he absolutely needed from their room and stuffed it into a single shoulder bag before dashing out.

He jumped down onto the pavement and shouldered his way through the yabbering crowd, scanning the limits of the hall as he did so. Lining the walls were strings of booths and offices with fluorescent signs above them. He spied one with the word *Information* written above it in International and headed straight for it.

When he reached it, though, he discovered a line six people deep waiting to be seen—or something like a line. As soon as Orin joined it, he noticed others walking straight past to the front desk and having loud, animated conversations with the staff. Money and leaflets changed hands.

Orin's patience didn't last long. Fighting a lifetime of habit, he pushed his way to the front. He'd never been good at this. Rima was always the loud one—the one who got angry when the need arose. This time, he had no choice but to tackle the problem himself.

"Excuse me," he said, in loud International to the girl behind the desk.

She was clad in a pink and blue uniform and had dark hair dragged back from a coldly pretty face.

"I sorry, sir," she said without looking at him.

"I cannot see you. This gentleman, he next."

Orin knew for sure that he'd arrived before that particular *gentleman*.

"Listen!" he said and slammed his hand on the counter.

That got her attention. She regarded him with a flat, unimpressed gaze.

"My wife has been kidnapped," he said. "She was brought here on the last motor-bus to come through from Atafune by some people called the *Iriti Viryan*. I'm trying to find her and I need to speak to the police, or someone in authority. Right now."

He rifled in his pocket.

"Look," he said, and slapped a wad of Industrial Alliance notes on the counter. "I can pay."

The girl's eyes took on a worried cast.

"Wait please," she said, and disappeared into the back.

Orin waited. And waited some more.

He began to doubt that she'd actually understood his request. Perhaps she'd gone for a break and left him standing here like an idiot.

"Excuse me," he said to another woman behind the desk. "Your colleague—do you know where she's gone?"

"Yesyes," she replied with a dismissive wave. "You wait please."

Orin tried hard to be patient.

The girl surprised him moments later by appearing right next to him.

"Sir," she said. "This Mr. Watuwe. He help you."

She gestured at a man standing behind her with slicked grey hair and an Alliance-style suit.

"Good morning," said the man with a clipped, formal bow. "I am Jirif Watuwe. And your name is, sir?"

"Orin Vals."

Orin shook the proffered hand. It was cool and dry, unlike his own.

"I believe you have had a problem with the Viryan," said Watuwe.

Orin nodded vigorously. "Yes. My wife was brought here by them not two hours ago. I'm trying to get her back."

"Of course. Please, follow me. We will go somewhere we can talk privately." Watuwe gestured toward the other side of the loading area.

"Are you police?" Orin asked warily. He'd learned to make quite sure of these things.

"Not quite, sir," Watuwe replied with a slight smile. "Department of Tourist Relations."

On balance, that was probably better. The people in the Atafune sheriff's office had been worse than useless.

"Okay," said Orin. "Let's go."

Watuwe led him through the mayhem to an unmarked doorway in the wall. Beyond it was a narrow, grey-painted staircase smelling of old cigarette smoke. The door thudded shut behind them, blocking out the cacophony. Orin felt a small measure of relief.

They ascended three flights to an administrative area guarded by a blank-faced receptionist in a Tourist Relations uniform, and from there took a corridor that ended at a small, bland office with a well-soundproofed window looking down onto the turmoil below.

"Please, take a seat," said Watuwe. "Tell me what happened."

Orin placed himself on a lumpy chair and told his story: the honeymoon, the apparently random abduction, his panic, the total lack of help from the authorities. Watuwe grimaced. "I must apologize for my countrymen, Mr. Vals. Here in the Land of Miracles, people are very wary of interfering with religious practices."

"Even when they extend to abduction?" Orin couldn't help the sharpness in his tone.

"When the Viryan are concerned, even then," said Watuwe. "Tell me, what do you know about them?"

Orin shifted uneasily in his seat. "That they're a religious group based out of Ithru' and they kidnap foreigners for no apparent reason. That's it. What am I missing?"

Watuwe sighed.

"Iriti Viryan means *Army of Appeasers* in our language. They are one of the city's most successful cults and one of the most dangerous. They have many thousands of supporters."

Orin's mouth squeezed to a line. He hadn't believed the news could get any worse.

"They have grown in the wake of some recent misfortune we have had here in the city," Watuwe explained. "In the last ten years or so, there have been a record number of *matse*, meaning *flickers*. Are you familiar with that term, Mr. Vals?"

Orin shook his head.

"Occasionally the natural lifting beam that supports our city turns off for a tiny fraction of a second. Even though the interruptions are extremely short, the effect on a structure the size of Ithrulene is quite destructive. Whole stories can collapse. People's homes are frequently crushed. Both lives and livelihoods are destroyed."

Watuwe spread his hands.

"Because no one knows what causes the beam, no one knows how to prevent this from happening, or even how to predict it. The Viryan seek to end the matse by appeasing Ukur, the god of the beam. They believe that Ukur is angry at the sins of the world, and that through the sacrifice of cynics and unbelievers, they can restore his goodwill."

Orin sat completely still.

"Sacrifice," he said stupidly.

Watuwe nodded solemnly.

"One is chosen approximately every four months. In all likelihood your wife has been selected."

Orin could think of nothing to say.

"The sacrifice is always someone vulnerable," Watuwe went on. "An unbeliever of some kind. At first, they took only residents of the city. But since our recent economic difficulties, they have taken to abducting tourists.

"This is the first time they have taken someone from one of the coastal towns, but quite frankly I am not surprised to see their activities escalate this way. She probably passed a prayer circle without making an abasement, or some other trivial slight of which she was not even aware."

Orin could all too easily imagine how it had happened. Tall, red-headed Rima with her loud laugh and uncompromising attitude. To these people, she must have been the epitome of foreignness.

There had been warnings in the guide books about militant factions, of course. They'd ignored them on the grounds that they'd never intended to visit the so-called 'hotspots'. Or rather, Rima had ignored them, and convinced him not to worry.

It hadn't been hard. Who imagined that something like this would happen to them? He and Rima lived a small suburban life. He had an office cubicle in Central Pukatorm and a kitchen full of pre-packed dinners to prove it. It felt as if a piece of someone else's story has been spliced into the dull movie of his life.

"Unfortunately, we cannot rely on the police to intervene," said Watuwe. "Not only would they risk massive social unrest by interfering with the Viryan rites, but many of their number are also supporters of the cult. We in Tourist Relations do not support the Viryan, but are equally powerless."

"So there's nothing you can do," Orin said acidly.

Watuwe tried not to look hurt.

"I will of course do everything that I can. But you should understand that intervention from the authorities will take time. In all likelihood, the Viryan will have acted by then."

Orin snorted.

"This is like something out of the Brown Ages. You're seriously telling me your government can do nothing to stop it?"

Watuwe pulled a face halfway between wry amusement and outright shame.

"Our government is mostly theocratic, Mr. Vals. And the Viryan have many seats on the council. It would be far more expedient to handle the matter yourself and in person." He got up and took a book from the shelves near the door.

"Here," he said, holding it out to Orin.

It was a thick and spiral-bound, not quite small enough to comfortably fit in a pocket. A picture of Ithrulene against an idealized dawn was printed on the cover.

"This is a map of the city, official version," said Watuwe. "It is better than anything you will find in the tourist stalls. Look, I will mark the location of their main temple for you. That is where they will have taken her."

He flipped through a sheaf of pages depicting intricately detailed donuts of color-coded habitation and stopped at an orange wedge marked with a glyph that resembled a fat dragon.

"It is only a few dozen levels from here, on the east side. The best thing for you to do is go alone and make some kind of apology on her behalf. Do not even tell them that you have met me. Offer a cash donation to their cause if you can."

Orin regarded Watuwe with contempt.

"I am being pragmatic, Mr. Vals," the Tourist Relations man said defensively. "You must too if you want to see your wife again. In these troubled times, the Viryan can be quite flexible in their beliefs when money is offered. Their greed may be all that saves her."

Watuwe rifled through his pockets and held out a small plastic strip covered in elaborate gold symbols.

"Take this too. It is a transit pass. It will take you anywhere in the city free of charge. My number is on the back if you need to call me. I will vouch for you if you have any difficulties with local security."

Orin wordlessly accepted the gifts. They seemed meager offerings for a man in danger of losing his spouse.

Watuwe went to his desk and started rummaging in the drawers.

"I also have a number here that may be useful to you. It is for the closest thing your country has to an embassy here. They have had some experience of this matter, though, to my knowledge, no success."

He brought out a business card and added it to Orin's pile. On it in embossed International were the words *Industrial Alliance Consular Department*, with what Orin assumed were the same words in local glyphs underneath.

"Is this it?" he said hollowly. "Is this all that the great city of Ithrulene can do to help?"

Watuwe blushed.

"I will continue to make calls on your behalf, of course," he said. "You must understand that things are done differently here. Often an individual working alone is capable of achieving things that entire armies cannot. Having said that, there are some local religious organizations that may be able…"

Orin had heard enough. He got up out of the chair and walked to the door without waiting for Watuwe to finish. He bore the Tourist Relations man no ill will. It was simply that every minute he spent talking was one spent not looking for Rima.

Watuwe followed him out, speaking hurriedly.

"Of course, you're anxious to make progress. I only caution you to treat the Viryan extremely carefully, Mr. Vals. They are not people to be trifled with. Act humble. Play to their arrogance. And on no account advertise your lack of faith in their cause."

Orin kept walking.

Eventually, Watuwe gave up and stopped.

"Good luck, Mr. Vals," he said. "My prayers will be with you."

Orin flinched at the word. The last thing he needed now was more religion. He marched, zombie-like toward the exit. The meeting had lasted over half an hour and dashed the best of his hopes, yet what did he have to show for it? A map and a travel pass. There had to be more he could take away from the experience than that.

He paused at the reception desk.

"Can I use your phone?" he asked the girl sitting there.

She handed him an old-fashioned plastic handset.

Orin punched in the numbers from the card Watuwe had given him. He'd talk to some of his own people. They wouldn't be afraid of a local cult. Watuwe would see what a little Alliance influence could do.

The phone rang ten times before a voice clicked on.

"This is the Industrial Alliance Consular Department," said a bored voice. "No one is able to take your call right now. Please leave your name and number…"

Orin handed the phone back to the receptionist.

"Thank you," he said woodenly and walked out.

Using the map Watuwe had given him, he made his way across the loading area to a bank of massive public elevators. Hundreds of locals and their livestock were busily squeezing themselves into the rough metal cages. The entire area stank of urine and an excess of incense that had been burned to cover it.

Orin was about to join the crush when he spied some men in black floor-length robes and gold triangular hats striding out from a smaller elevator to the side. It looked like some kind of luxury transport—perhaps even an express.

Orin ran to catch it before the attendant in the mint green uniform could shut the grill door. He wedged his hand into the closing gap.

"Sorry, sir," said the attendant smugly. "This one only for…"

Orin thrust his transit pass under the man's nose. The door opened again.

"My most apology, sir," said the attendant, bowing unctuously.

That's more like it, Orin thought to himself. He opened the map and pointed to the temple.

"Take me here."

The attendant nodded and closed the door.

Orin found himself rising rapidly in a spacious leather-lined cubicle. The loading area disappeared from view to be replaced by fleeting glimpses of bazaars, shopping malls, schools and lobbies. It seemed that above ground level, Ithrulene rapidly became more civilized.

The elevator stopped at a grand concourse. A great swathe of floor clad in checkerboard tiles swept out to meet a curving wall with high arched windows. Just like the loading area, this new level was thick with people, however, these natives were quieter and better dressed. The air was cooler too.

The lift attendant stuck his hand out for a tip and then withdrew it rapidly when he caught sight of the scowl on Orin's face.

"Which way to the Viryan temple?" said Orin.

The attendant pointed right.

"This way, sir. Not far. Big place. Easy find."

"Thanks."

Orin took out his wallet and handed the man an Alliance note. The attendant's eyes went wide.

"Sir very generous!"

The man called his thanks as Orin marched away.

Orin managed to walk for nearly a minute before pausing to gawp at his surroundings. He stood in a huge donut of living space with a concrete, elevator-studded, inner wall and a flimsy-looking outer one of cracking white plaster hundreds of yards away. There were no apparent supports for the massive, girder-lined ceiling hanging overhead.

Of course, there wouldn't be. As he'd already learned from his guide books, each level of the city was supported by metal braces placed across the path of the beam. Orin had imagined struts like the ones they used to build office blocks back home. Instead, the engineering was more on the scale of the cruise liner he'd sailed in on.

This particular level of the great structure seemed to be entirely given over to religious activity. Various cult establishments were dotted across the space like restaurant franchises in a food court, with glyphs in wild colors adorning their sides. Small crowds gathered at each one, usually to listen to elderly men on podiums make proclamations in curious, warbling tones.

On one side of Orin was a stall where a gaggle of old women stood with tears pouring down their faces. On the other sat a step-pyramid of painted wood where young men knelt and beat their chests. Orin weaved between them, checking out each establishment for sign of the fat dragon.

His examination of the stalls ended when a mother clutching a child ran past him, almost knocking him over. He stared after her, wondering at her haste, and noticed that several other people were hurrying in the same direction.

He followed them round a cluster of plastic stupas and found himself face to face with a structure ten times the size of all the other stalls. It was clad in black fabric that stretched from the ceiling to the floor. The dragon glyph was printed on its side in bright, unmissable orange.

Sticking out from the front of the cloth monolith was an ornate temple of sorts with platforms on multiple levels. The entire arrangement was walled in by a high wire fence that stuck over the heads of the rapidly growing crowd.

The crowd was shouting. Orin knew in his gut that whatever was happening here had to do with Rima. Just like a local, he ran forward to see.

Building on his experience of the loading zone, he elbowed his way to the front of the throng, throwing out careless apologies as he went. He arrived at the fence in time to see a man in black step out onto a podium and take up a microphone.

Like the other would-be prophets Orin had seen, this man adopted a tremulous, nasal voice to make his proclamation. Unlike the others, he was sturdy and middle-aged with a military bearing.

He spoke quietly at first. The crowd fell silent and strained to hear as if electrified. Steadily, his voice rose till he made a final dramatic proclamation and slammed his hand against the railing in front of him.

All around, people starting yelling slogans. Then a scuffle broke out somewhere to Orin's right and he noticed the police behind the fence for the first time—men in olive uniforms with machine-guns slung over their shoulders. They ran to intercept the trouble.

Apparently, not everyone in the crowd was pleased with what the prophet had to say.

A gong sounded from inside the temple while the fight was still raging and Rima stepped out onto one of the lower platforms escorted by a pair of muscular priests. They'd dressed her up in orange floor-length robes, pinned back her hair, and painted her face white. She showed no emotion Orin that could recognize, save perhaps for resignation. Orin clutched the fence wire so hard his fingers stung.

"Rima!" he shouted, but it was hopeless. At the sight of the sacrifice, the crowd had broken into renewed exclamations, some excited, others furious. She had no chance of hearing him over the clamor.

The prophet made another bold statement and stepped down to the platform where Rima was being held. He took her hand and together they descended a ramp that led off in the direction of the elevators. The two priests followed closely behind.

Orin weaved his way desperately through the crowd.

"Rima! It's me, Orin!"

She showed no sign of having heard him.

The small procession meanwhile reached the edge of the temple enclosure. The police moved out in two orderly rows to make a safe route for them that stretched to the city's core wall. On either side, angry locals jostled and exchanged loud opinions.

Orin joined the ranks of Ithru' citizens hurling themselves at the police lines in front of the Viryan in an attempt to obstruct the prophet's passage. The armed men held him back along with everyone else.

"Look!" Orin held up his pass to the indifferent officer in front of him. "I have access rights. I'm an Alliance citizen and that's my wife. I have to get to her!"

The policeman shoved him backward with the side of his machine-gun and shouted at him in Miracle. Then he pointed the muzzle at Orin's chest in a warning that transcended language. Orin cursed and stepped back, arms raised.

Rima and the prophet strode right past him, arm in arm like a king and queen.

"Rima!" Orin bellowed.

She couldn't help but have heard that time. She was no more than a heartbreaking three feet away.

She stopped. Her head swiveled slowly in his direction but her eyes passed over him unseeing, her expression dreamy and serene.

They'd drugged her.

"Rima, here!" he cried. "It's me! Snap out of it! I've come to get you!"

She blinked slowly as her eyes finally settled on him. One corner of her mouth quivered. Then she let the prophet take her arm and lead her off to the elevators.

The prophet shot a calculating look back at him.

"I can pay!" Orin wailed.

The man's face hardened as he turned away.

Orin knew then with icy finality that he'd just said the most stupid thing possible. An offer like that wasn't supposed to be public. Now the prophet couldn't be seen to take it even if he wanted to. Orin's heart squeezed in panic.

He ran with the horde that followed the procession to its exit and called madly for his wife while locals chanted belligerent epithets. He yelled and pushed right up to the point at which the door slid shut and she disappeared upward out of sight. Then he yelled some more—at nothing and everything—at the city and the people and their madness.

He swore with tears of fury rolling down his face.

"I hate you all!" he bellowed. "We never should have come to this fucking place!"

They should have gone to the Braymar Sands, like he'd suggested. But Rima, ever the adventurer, had wanted to come here so badly.

"Let's go to the Miracle Country," she'd said. *"I want to see the cradle of civilization just once before I die."*

He should have put his foot down. He hated himself for having not done, for not having been there in the lobby when it happened, and for letting the police hold him back. He hated himself for being weak.

Yet as he stood there, hoarse and miserable, something inside grabbed hold of him. There was no time for self-pity. Who knew where they'd taken her or how long he had left to act?

He blinked back the pain and took a fresh look at his surroundings. The crowd was thinning slowly. Gangs of youths faced off against each other, calling names. The police moved between them quelling each fight before it started with injections of practiced menace.

Orin spied a woman standing on her own who looked richer than most of the fanatics. She was staring straight ahead as if she were the only person there. Maybe she'd be able to speak International.

Orin approached her.

"Please," he said, in a slow, clear voice. "Do you know where the Viryan are going?"

She gazed up at him uncomprehending for a moment before speaking.

"Their private floor," she said. "To prepare her. The woman is to be *given*."

Her lip trembled.

"They took my son, you know," she added suddenly. "Two years ago. He was a teacher of children. Why would they do that? What threat was he to them?"

An ally. Orin felt a tug of empathy like a fishhook through his heart. He took her shoulders in his hands.

"That woman is my wife," he explained. "I need to get to her. Maybe I can save her. Can you help me? Can you show me how to get to her?"

But the woman wasn't listening. She was already a hundred miles away, her face full of private pain.

"They took my Chesit," she muttered. "They took him, those *acati sevuth. Tjin e basakat* on them. *Tjin* forever."

Orin realized his mistake and left her alone. He took the map from his bag and started hurriedly thumbing through the pages looking for other places where the glyph was marked. He ripped and crumpled paper in his haste, but found what he was looking for another fifty levels up—an entire ring of floor stamped with the dragon: level one-one-three. That had to be his best shot.

He slapped the book shut, shoved it back in his bag, and ran for the closest elevator. It was one of the big municipal ones. Simmering cult followers were standing on the threshold jeering as the attendant tried to convince them to be either in or out. Orin waved his pass and stepped inside.

"One-one-three," he told the attendant: a round-bodied woman with a broken nose.

There were hisses and intakes of breath from the other passengers.

The attendant shook her head at him.

"No exit!" she insisted. "You crazy? That number no exit. Not allow!"

"Fine," Orin snapped back. "One-one-two then."

Maybe he'd be able to find some stairs or something. He took himself to a space at the back corner of the chamber where he could fret without feeling the need to strike out at bystanders.

The elevator jerked into motion. Orin shut his eyes and willed the device to go faster.

Then someone laid a hand on his arm. He opened his eyes to see a woman looking up at him. Her eyes held a look of grim purpose, perhaps even belligerence. Here was the consequence of asking to visit a Viryan floor, he suspected. He braced himself for a challenge.

She surprised him by leaning in close and speaking in quiet International.

"You are Mr. Vals?"

Somewhat startled, Orin reappraised her. She was middle height and build for an Ithru' native with a forgettably foreign face. Something in her expression didn't match the look though—something hard.

"How did you know?"

The woman's mouth curved into a tight smile.

"You were not hard to spot. There was only one red-hair in the crowd and you were making a lot of noise."

Orin stiffened. "You were looking for me?"

The woman nodded.

"Watuwe called me. He is worried for you."

"I'm sorry, but who are you? He didn't say anyone would be meeting me."

"I am called Mowvi," said the woman. "He called me after you left his office. I can help you. You should come with me."

Orin eyed her suspiciously. "Are you from Tourist Relations?"

Mowvi shook her head.

"*Shapwe* no!" she said, smirking at the thought. "I am from *Iriti Molmoth.*"

She said the words quietly and glanced at the other passengers as she did so. To Orin's eye, it seemed as if the other people in the elevator suddenly tried to put a little distance between themselves and Mowvi. Heads turned away with feigned casualness. Half a dozen conversations simultaneously hit a low ebb.

Orin thought fast. Mowvi clearly wasn't an official. She lacked the manner of a bureaucrat. And there was that word *Iriti* again. Did it mean *army* or *appeasers*? She might have been sent by the prophet in black. Then again, she had mentioned Watuwe's name. That suggested she was on his side, didn't it?

He took a calculated risk.

"I'm going to their floor to get Rima," he told her matter-of-factly. "Can you get me in?"

Mowvi shook her head like a disappointed schoolmistress.

"There is no way into that place except invitation," she said. "And that they will not give. Please believe me, it is no place for successful heroes, only martyrs. And there is a better way to help your wife. Come with me and we will help."

What kind of people were *we*? People scary enough to hush an elevator, at least. He screwed up his face and thought hard.

"Alright then," he said. "What the hell."

As if he had any better options.

She smiled. "Wise choice."

Orin had a bad moment several minutes later when they sailed past the floor Rima was on, but after that, the going was easier. He felt committed to a course of action, even though he didn't know what it entailed.

Many levels and much ear popping further up, she tugged on his sleeve.

"Come. This floor is for us."

He found himself on a level that looked like the interior of a shabby hotel and felt like the inside of a refrigerator. Women wearing grey wool jackets and dozens of bead necklaces lolled against the corridor walls chatting. Orin smelt something like cooked chicken nearby and heard the clatter of utensils.

He followed Mowvi past doors left ajar. Beyond one, children chased each other round a sofa in a windowless room. In another, old men sat playing cards cross legged on a battered lino floor, taking swigs from an oval bottle of clear fluid.

Orin's guide stopped at an open door onto an ill-lit room full of sewing machines where a hunched woman sat.

"One moment," she said.

There followed a five minute conversation of rapid, incomprehensible syllables, whereupon the hunched woman got up from her chair and disappeared into a darkened closet. She emerged moments later with a pair of feathered coats of the kind they sold in tourist stalls down in the coastal towns.

Mowvi handed the larger one to Orin.

"Put this on," she told him. "You will need it."

Orin didn't understand, but didn't argue either. It was chill enough up here that another layer over his t-shirt certainly didn't hurt.

Mowvi shrugged her coat on, kissed the hunched woman on the cheek, and led Orin away.

"Down here," she said, taking a passage where there was a marked breeze of warm, fetid air.

At the end was an open doorway onto an unlit chamber.

"There are no elevators where we go," she told him earnestly. "We use the beam. You have ever used it before?"

Orin shook his head.

She sucked air over her teeth. "Okay. It's not a problem, but scary the first time. Just hold my hand, okay? We step in together."

Orin nodded nervously.

From the threshold, he saw that what he'd taken for a chamber was in fact an open shaft. There was a thin metal grill about ten stories down, but other than that, no floor. He could see scraps of grit and lint floating upward in front of him, but they did little to raise his confidence in what he knew was about to happen.

"*What am I doing?*" he asked himself. "*This is insane.*"

Nevertheless, when Mowvi stepped forward, Orin did to.

His stomach lurched sickeningly as he ran out of ground to tread on. He was falling.

He cried out and squeezed Mowvi's hand hard for several seconds before his body acknowledged that he was falling *up*. The two of them were rising about a foot every second along with the air and the dirt and the occasional scrap of food. Quite involuntarily, Orin whimpered. This was what the city was all about, he reminded himself: riding nature's elevator. The people who lived here did it every day.

Mowvi tssked at him.

"You must do this up," she said, trying to fasten the buttons of his coat with her free hand. "Hold my shoulders for a moment."

With some difficulty, Orin relinquished his grip on the woman's digits so that she could finish the job. He clung to her coat as if she were a life-raft.

She grimaced at him and massaged her bruised fingers before entrusting them back into his care.

"Not so hard, please. There is nothing here for fearing, okay?"

Orin did his best, but it got worse a couple of minutes later when the walls of the shaft ended.

They emerged into an appallingly bright blue sky. The city here was an open sided scaffold reaching up forever—a thing of crisscrossed metal and wood like the underside of a jetty.

Enclosed building spaces sat in dark blocky rings around the rim of the beam, suspended on immense steel joists. The closest to him were little more than an arm's length away, but they might as well have been a mile. It was painfully easy to see between them, to the hazy patchwork landscape so far below.

Orin had never been so high. He redoubled his grip.

"Relax," she told him sternly. "Look around you. It is safe here."

Orin fought for calm. He concentrated on steady breathing and let his gaze follow Mowvi's finger pointed across the city's breadth.

The top of the concrete part of Ithrulene was like the mouth of some vast, man-made volcano receding below his feet. Between the girders, he could see that the part of the beam they were rising on was just one of several nearby designated for human traffic. In one, two women in coats descended on some kind of pulley system. In another, children laughed and pushed each other as they drifted up.

Further into the centre were other regions of beam for cargo, water, and even what Orin assumed were sewers walled in by lengths of plastic pipe.

Sewers that went up. He giggled nervously.

Mowvi smiled at him. "It's okay, eh? No problem."

Orin smiled weakly back at her. He tried looking up instead to calm his nerves and for a single, terrible moment it seemed as if the world was turned on its head and he was going to drop up that flimsy tunnel into the sky. He fought down the vomit that threatened to spill out of him and reminded himself that this ascent was really quite unlike gravity. Its rate was constant for a start. He shut his eyes and sucked air into his lungs.

"Is this strictly necessary?" he said between gasps. "Where are we going?"

"To meet with soldiers of Molmoth," said Mowvi. "The Viryan want to throw your wife off the top of the city, into the beam."

Orin's nerves were already so raw that new detail gave him little more than a dull ache.

"They will do this in only a few hours," she went on. "They must act quickly, before government can be made to look bad by not stopping them. But not so quickly that they do not get a big audience.

"What you saw was an invitation to followers. Big money Viryan backers gather already. They have been planning this for many days."

"To murder my wife?" Orin said doubtfully.

He wanted to keep Mowvi talking. Her words gave him something to concentrate on other than falling.

"No, no! Your wife simply is unfortunate victim. It could have been anyone. But do not worry. We also have a plan. And you coming here makes it even better. We will rescue your wife and embarrass the Viryan. People will see them fail and doubt their cause."

Orin cracked one eye open to look at her.

"Who is we?" he asked. "I mean, I know you're the *Iriti Molmoth*, but what does that mean?"

She smiled slyly. "Words mean *Singers of Lullabies*."

Orin couldn't tell if she was joking or not.

"We are the old religion of Ithrulene," she said. "We believe the beam is a happy accident. It is a flaw in the world left from the battle of the gods at the start of time. They have not repaired it only because they are still asleep after fighting. As long as they do not wake up, our way of life is safe."

Her face darkened. "For us, throwing people into the sky is not just heresy, it is also very, very stupid. The gods sleep over our heads. Throwing people at them risks the end of everything."

She snorted. "People fear the matse, but the matse have always come. We fight for the life of the beam. The *lene-moldu* itself."

So these people weren't acting out of kindness. They too were motivated by faith, and their beliefs were as batty as the Viryan's. Orin was surprised to find himself relieved at that. If religion had such power here, perhaps he was talking to the right people. A tiny flame of hope flickered into life inside him. The weight of anticipation that came with it ached like an ulcer.

"So how will you do it?" he asked. "Rescue Rima, I mean."

"We go to a place below the sacrifice," said Mowvi. "Then when they throw your wife, our men will rise to catch her. If you wish, you can join them. The Viryan will fight back, of course, but at the top of the city there will be no police."

She sneered. "They are scared of the height. Then when we have caught her, we will take them to a place where the Viryan are not welcome. And when she is recovered, we will make sure you get home safely."

Orin nodded. So, all he had to do to get his wife back was hurl himself into the sky several miles up and fight hand to hand with fanatics. All in a day's work for an administrative consultant like him. If he lived, the guys in the office would never believe his stories.

"Count me in," he said.

Mowvi gave him a look of surprise. "You want to go with the soldiers? It will be very dangerous."

"Of course." He'd let himself down outside the Viryan temple. He wasn't about to do that again. It simply wasn't worth living with the consequences.

Mowvi exhaled hard and glanced at him cryptically, as if seeing something there that she'd missed before.

"Okay," she said.

Another twenty or so levels on, she reached out for one of the thin metal rails that marked the edge of the people-shaft.

"Keep hold of me," she warned, and deftly pulled them out of the beam and onto a narrow walkway that led between a pair of clapboard shacks.

Orin staggered and fought another rush of vertigo. This time, it was brought on by the knowledge that there was nothing of real substance under him. Gravity had him in its clutches again and this time he was protected only by some rather fragile engineering.

As he looked down at the planks beneath his feet and the gaps between, he thought of the matse, and began to understand Ithrulene properly for the first time. There was simply no getting around something as big and unnatural as the city when your life depended on it. Without good explanations for how and why you could stand on a piece of rickety wood a mile into the sky, your mind cast around for bad ones. Fickle, vengeful gods didn't seem so unlikely any more.

"Come," said Mowvi. "We go this way."

She helped him down the alley to where it opened out onto something like an airborne boardwalk—a curving promenade that followed the edge of the beam. It was thick with human traffic, just like everywhere else in the city.

On the inner side of the walkway were workshops. Orin saw blobs of molten glass thrust into the flickering shadow of the beam. He saw metal being beaten in blacksmith's shops straight out of the Brown Ages. There were bakeries and apothecaries and funny one-room farms where women in feathered coats and hats tended vines that hung upward. This was where the real work of the city was done, he realized—where its famed exports came from: the impossible vases and ornaments, the unique herbs and quack cures.

On the other side of the street were houses, cramped spaces lined with rugs where brightly bundled children sat in doorways. On the roofs, large white birds tethered by their ankles nested and argued. Emaciated cats jumped the dread gulfs between properties with unwatchable grace.

An icy wind rattled the floorboards and made the little wooden windmills on the roof-peaks whiz. It passed straight through Orin's coat and stole heat from his skin without slowing. He breathed deep to calm his spinning head and wondered if he was getting altitude sickness yet

Mowvi led him to a small factory leaning up against the beam. Inside, the air was warmed by a gang of large men speaking in subdued voices. They fell silent when he and Mowvi entered.

Mowvi quickly pulled the door closed behind her and spoke to them in Miracle. Orin heard his name mentioned several times. The men's gazes shifted impassively from her to him and back again.

Under the conditions of his old life, he knew he would have found the scrutiny of such a large and menacing group of foreigners unsettling. Now he was grateful for it. There had to be thirty Molmoth here at least, and every one of them looked like they could flatten him in a fight without breaking sweat.

When Mowvi finished her speech, some of them came up to shake his hand or hug him. Mowvi translated their regards to the best of her ability.

One of them brought glasses of hot yellow tea laced with some kind of liqueur.

"Drink, Mr. Vals," he said. "It will help your head."

Orin gulped it down.

"Won't somebody notice what we're doing?" he said, watching the men prepare. "I mean, this is a small army."

"You will be dressed as city repair men," said Mowvi. "No one will think twice. Also, no Viryan live up here. Ukur is a god for the low-dwellers. People will say nothing."

He let her steer him to a man who equipped him with a one-piece suit to wear that was padded with bee-striped leather and lined with down. He was given gloves, boots, a hat incorporating ear-flaps and goggles, a wicked-looking knife for his belt and a buzzing mask made of modern plastics that fitted over his nose and mouth.

"This will thicken the air for you," Mowvi explained. "It is important to wear it always."

Then, when he was kitted up as thoroughly as any deep sea diver, they took him to get his wings.

Each of the men was being strapped into a harness bearing a pair of thick iron fans two feet wide that stretched out behind their arms. They looked heavy—suicidal even. Stepping into the beam again was going to be hard enough. The prospect of wearing a hundred pounds of metal didn't make it any easier.

Orin's nerves got worse when the man preparing him slipped one of the harnesses onto his back. He grunted at the weight and grimaced as the straps were pulled tight. It felt like someone had just tied him to an anvil.

"Mowvi, why do we need these?" he asked.

"They are for rising," she said. "All things rise in the beam, but iron is the fastest. This is how you will catch your wife."

Orin acknowledged the cleverness of the solution while wishing there was a lighter one.

"Then how will we get back down?"

"With one of these," she said, holding up a rope. She tied it to his belt. "We pull you."

"Now you must go," she added. "You will rise with Amid. He will be your guide, and I will see you at the meeting place."

She paused and fixed him with a stare.

"Your wife should be grateful to have a man such as you, Mr. Vals," she told him. "Be lucky today. I will be hoping for you."

She gave him a peck on the cheek. Orin blushed. Better that she didn't realize his choice wasn't remotely heroic. It was simply that he didn't think he could live with himself if he failed to act.

Mowvi spoke quickly to Amid and was gone.

Amid gave Orin the thumbs up and walked with him to the edge of the workshop where men were jumping into the beam. He took Orin by the waist and gestured for Orin to do the same to him. Then, together, they leapt into the void.

Once again, there was that terrible feeling of falling, However, this time, it was rapidly followed by the uncomfortable sensation of being dragged aloft at great speed by the hunks of iron on his back. Mowvi hadn't been kidding when she said the metal rose faster. Platform girders flashed past. Orin gulped and hoped the terror on his face wasn't too obvious to his partner in flight.

Up they sailed, beyond the streets, into Ithrulene's impossible heights. There were people living even up here, Orin saw, where the air was rarified. People eked out a living growing herbs in iron pots and farming the flocks of endlessly circling birds. Orin watched the creatures dive in and out of the beam to snatch insects and crumbs.

There was maintenance going on too. Workers carrying blow-torches and hammers crossed the beam-traversing joists by walking upside down. Orin felt sick just watching them.

Higher still was a cluster of prefabricated plastic modules with antennae jutting out of them at angles. A research station, he guessed—a refuge for his countrymen. His suspicions were confirmed a moment later when he caught sight of the *Alliance Scientific* logo printed on a module's side. The little blobs of technology looked laughably out of place stuck on the side of this mighty edifice of flawed engineering and faith.

As they pulled level, he spied figures in bulky red jackets of artificial fiber standing on platforms around the equipment taking measurements and notes. He soared past them, feeling more distant from his own people than he ever had in his life.

The city thinned out still further. It became little more than a tube of planks and rope held aloft by star-shaped supports of painted steel. The floors didn't even join up here—they strained on cables. The entire stretch was designed to squeeze and flex like a giant accordion.

He noticed, then, with a detachment that surprised him, that they were getting close to the top. A great circle of empty blue yawned above them. He drew Amid's attention to it. Amid nodded sagely.

Less than a minute later, they neared another piece of Alliance technology—a box the size of a house surrounded by a floor of metal grill. Amid reached for a railing and yanked them out of the beam next to it.

Orin nearly slipped at the edge from the sudden weight of the iron wings and got a heart-stopping view of the way down.

The big man pulled him upright.

"Careful," he shouted over the shriek of the wind.

They walked together to the far side of the huge humming instrument where the rest of the Molmoth task-force huddled like pensive angels.

"What next?" said Orin.

Amid pointed to his watch. So, for a little while, there was nothing for Orin to do but gaze out at the view of fields like mint-green postage stamps and rivers like silver ribbons until the sight turned his stomach. After that, he studied the walls of the machine instead and made a game of trying to work out what it did. He struggled, meanwhile, to ignore the pain in his knees and shoulders that came from bearing the weight of the wings.

About a quarter of an hour later, Mowvi walked round the side of the machine dressed in the same kind of puffy scarlet jacket Orin had seen the Alliance scientists wearing. A couple of other women were with her, similarly attired.

She waved cheerfully to him.

"Wait here till you hear the whistle," she told him when she was close enough to be heard. "Then run with the others and try to catch your wife." She showed him how to hold his rope so it wouldn't tangle.

"Before that, stay close to the machine," she added. "And stay still."

Orin nodded.

Mowvi checked that one end of his rope was tied fast to his harness and walked away taking the loose end with her. One by one, all the men's ropes were played out around the side of the machine in straight, careful lines. Orin assumed they were fastened to the platform's edge. He couldn't be sure though, as Mowvi and her helpers were lost to sight.

The process was barely complete when Amid grabbed his shoulder and pointed down through the grill. Something long and rectangular was rising up the shaft. Amid tapped his index finger to his mask as if for silence. The message was clear: now was the time to be invisible.

The rectangle turned out to be a high-sided wooden platform with figures tethered to seats inside it. Men on the platform's rim used long metal poles with hooked ends to guide its progress from level to level.

So this was how the rich and powerful visited such lofty places, Orin thought to himself—with the benefit of limited views and a solid looking floor beneath them. They were cowards, he decided. He envied their transport anyway.

Unfortunately, the cowards were numerous. The number aboard had to be at least double that of the Molmoth assault force. Orin hoped that most of them were guests.

The platform slid out of sight behind the machine and emerged a little later above them on its stately way to the roof of the world. With terrific care, the pole men drew the platform to the edge of the beam level with the top and jumped out. They anchored the craft firmly and slid it onto sturdy cantilevered struts that appeared to have been constructed for that very purpose. The platform locked into place with a metallic clang that sent shudders down the cables.

From that point on, Orin was poised to act. His heart hammered in expectation. His skin sweated and his insides knotted. Unfortunately, the waiting continued. He heard snatches of someone's amplified voice carried on the wind and something that might have been applause. He braced himself again, only to endure minutes more of agonized anticipation.

His mind had wandered to what they could possibly be doing up there when a sudden, shrill note cut the air. Amid grabbed his arm and together they charged around the side of the machine with handfuls of rope in their hands, yelling at the top of their lungs. They threw themselves headlong into the river of shadow.

Orin roared for courage right up until those dreadful iron wings took hold and wrenched him skyward. His cries died in his throat. His heart stuttered while his arms windmilled purposelessly against thin air. Thankfully, one small part of his mind managed to cling to its purpose. *Find Rima*, it reminded him. *Grab her!*

And there she was, he realized, a fluttering orange shape suspended in the beam like a Technicolor angel. He angled his body as he'd seen Mowvi and Amid do and headed straight for her.

There was a cry of anguish from the VIP platform as Orin and the Molmoth fighters flashed past. From the corners of his field of vision, Orin noticed other figures with iron wings launch off. Bullets whined past his head.

More out of panic than anything else, Orin blotted the threats from his mind and tried to concentrate on his wife floating languidly upwards. Screaming doubts raced through his head. *What if the rope wasn't long enough? What if he got within an arm's length of her only to be snatched back? What if he fumbled the catch?*

He'd never been very good at sports in school. He wasn't cut out for macho behavior. Wasn't that why he'd married a woman like Rima? That's what his mother had said – so he could hide behind her.

He flung his arms wide, hoped, and hit. Suddenly she was in his arms, limp, but real and solid and wonderful. There was a scarf tied around her eyes, but they'd given her a mask, at least. She would live.

Orin clung to her like fury, laughing crazily at his good fortune. He had her! He might be rocketing into the open sky but he *had* her!

A Viryan guard slammed into him. Powerful hands pried at his arms, but Orin didn't let go. He gritted his teeth and fought back with his legs, kicking like a maniac.

"You can't have her!" he bellowed. "You stupid ignorant bastards! Leave her alone!"

He brought his knee up sharply and by pure luck, it connected with the Viryan's groin. The muscleman groaned as the wind went out of him. Orin slammed the flat of his foot against his assailant's chest and managed to propel himself and his wife deeper into the beam.

The Viryan flew the other way like a sack of meat, and then plummeted abruptly as he passed the edge. He screamed as he whipped past the viewing platform and bounced off a girder sticking out beneath it. The platform shuddered from the sudden added weight. The VIPs clutched frantically at their seats.

Orin watched the Viryan celebrities panic with dark satisfaction for several seconds till his rope jerked taut. He looked down and was surprised to find several men clinging to the cord underneath him and fighting over it. The knives were out and arms were scything back and forth. Little rivulets of blood slipped upward.

Orin needed both hands to hold his limp wife against the pull of his wings, so there was nothing he could do but watch helplessly as the men beneath him struggled. His line jerked a second time and Orin started flying upward again.

The rope was severed.

One of the combatants reached for the dangling end and missed. Orin and his wife sailed out of reach. Three Molmoth soldiers flew up to seize the rope. The first was caught by a bullet and sagged in his harness. The next two missed by several yards and bounced on the ends of their tethers.

Orin stared down at them in disbelief. He was *falling into the sky*. With his heart in his mouth, he watched the top of Ithrulene become a small black circle against a backdrop of misty green.

That was his world down there—his life and his job and drab commute and his crap boss and his new apartment that they hadn't finished decorating yet and all his hopes and dreams and expectations. All going away.

It didn't take long. Ithrulene shrank to a point, barely distinguishable from the landscape around it. There was nothing left solid in Orin's world save his wife and the detritus he shared the beam with.

He passed a plank of wood and a dead bird. A little later, there was a length of green vine bearing small yellow fruit covered in little crystals of ice.

We're winning, he thought, as they streaked past the city's trash. *We'll get to the top first.* Orin wondered what was up there. Did the sky go on for ever?

He overtook a crust of bread.

For a couple of hours he flew like this, cradling his wife and listening to the tiny motor in his mask straining. The air it sucked in was getting ominously hard to breathe. Orin guessed that the only reason they hadn't died yet was because of the current of wind that Ithrulene carried up from the ground.

Eventually, Rima stirred. She wriggled in his grip and moaned as if they were in bed asleep together.

"Where am I?" she muttered. "What's going on?"

One dangling arm came up to fiddle with the scarf around her eyes.

"Don't take it off," said Orin.

"Orin?" she said blearily. "Why not? What's going on? Why do I feel like I'm floating?"

"Just don't," Orin warned, trying to catch her hand.

But this was Rima. Orin had never been able to tell her what to do. She pulled the material down and saw. And screamed.

Orin held on tight while she flailed. Her arms clawed space for something to hold and found only him.

Thankfully, her panic didn't last long. There wasn't enough air to allow for an extended bout of shrieking. She didn't faint either, Orin noted with pride, even with such thin air. Rima wasn't the sort of woman to faint.

She blinked as the frozen air stung her eyes and reached up with orange, ceremonial gloves to put the fabric back in place.

"Orin, what happened?" she asked in a tremulous voice. "Where the *hell* are we?"

Orin softly explained. She was quiet while he spoke—listening hard and thinking for solutions, he suspected, as was her way. After he was finished, she stayed silent for a while.

"There's nothing we can do, is there?" she said at length.

"Not that I can think of, no."

"I refuse to cry," she told him. "It'll only make my scarf freeze."

They fell up for the rest of the day. The sun came along and warmed them for a while, huge and yellow overhead, before bumbling off to start painting itself a sunset. Orin's stomach rumbled. He hadn't eaten since he got on the bus.

Then, at about that time in the afternoon when he usually stopped work for a cup of Work-Plus and a sesame stick, came the first surprise. Ahead of them, straight up, was a dark patch in the sky. It was approximately square, though its hazy edges flexed and wriggled from time to time. It grew quickly.

Was it some kind of beam-making machine? Or some inverse of Ithrulene, perhaps—a city for angels? They were fated to find out.

"What?" said Rima, sensing his tension, though he'd said nothing.

"There's something up there."

"I'll have a look."

"No," Orin said quickly. 'We're still too far away. Save your eyes. I'll tell you when we're close enough to see."

The answer when it came wasn't something Orin would ever have guessed. It was a rip in the fabric of the sky. Its ragged edges rippled like gigantic flags. What lay behind it was black. Orin stared, to tired for awe, too awed to drag his eyes away.

"Orin, what's happening?" said Rima. "Are we close yet?"

She pushed the scarf down.

"Oh," she said, and was lost for words for once.

As their conveyor belt of shade carried them through the rent, Orin could see that the sky was made from something wafer thin and gossamer light that moved in dreamy waves. The side that faced the ground was a brilliant blue. The reverse was dull mauve. He could only guess that it had been torn by the relentless pressure of the beam.

They traveled inexorably past it and were treated to a view of the sky from the other side. It wasn't half as pleasant as the one Orin was used to: a flat purplish plane ran to a dirty, dark horizon. The sun was little more than a shapeless, treacle-colored blob below him. Evidently, it was a feature of the sky-film, designed to shine down, not up.

Orin smiled bitterly to himself. So the sky was a sheet. What the scientists of his home country wouldn't do for that kind of revelation.

The next surprise came not ten minutes later. Orin made out ripples on the dark background overhead, and right above them, a roughly circular smear of olive green.

"Rima, there's something else."

"I think that's the top," she said after several seconds of intense observation. "And I think we're going to hit it."

Top or not, Orin couldn't stand the sight of his wife's face screwed up and exposed to the elements.

"Please put the scarf back," he said. "The cold will hurt your eyes."

She gave him a look.

"Didn't you notice? The air's thicker up here. It's warmer too. Maybe the sky-sheet traps the air or something. I noticed a while back, but then they only gave me this stupid frock to wear. I've been freezing my ass off."

She resumed her examination of the shapes.

"Take your wings off," she said after a few minutes.

"What?"

"I said take off your wings. We're going to hit that green stuff, whatever it is, and if we're going this fast, it's going to hurt."

"I'm not sure," said Orin.

Over the past hours, the wings's relentless pull had come to afford him a kind of perverse comfort.

"Come on," she said. "This is important." She started fiddling with the clasp on his harness.

With Rima's insistent help, he grudgingly discarded the iron fans. Their bodies slowed suddenly while the metalwork hurtled off like a piece of cruise liner plunging to the ocean floor.

Over the half-hour that followed, they ascended sluggishly toward the green. It was increasingly obvious that Rima was right. It was a ceiling of sorts, an inverted landscape of something dark and wrinkled upon which a perfect circle of city refuse had been painted. Orin had to laugh. Instead of ending their journey in the domain of the gods, it appeared they'd be arriving in the domain of garbage.

He counted down the seconds to impact as the features of the smear resolved into gently rolling mounds.

With a delicacy that bordered on the obscene, they touched down head first on the circle's central hill of planks, iron off-cuts, weeds and dirt, just a few feet from the small crater made by Orin's wings. He and his newlywed wife were pushed sideways till they were lying on the filthy slope inverted.

They lay still for just a few seconds before Rima got up and brushed herself down. She glanced up at the pale green square in the sky and then at the ugly graze of a sun.

"Come on," she said, as if their predicament was the most normal thing in the world. "Let's take a look around."

She bounced on her toes and rose several inches off the ground before the beam pressed her back to the floor.

"We might use those wings again," she observed. "They'll be useful up here."

For the next few days they explored the small country in which they'd been deposited. It was a landscape of discarded shoes and sweet wrappers, of lost children's toys and broken furniture. Yet even here, things grew.

Those patches of beam given over to sewer outlets corresponded to small jungles up here. Held in place only by the weak pressure of the beam, plants grew in fantastic, twisted shapes, seeking the meager sunlight and competing for the fluids the city spat out.

There were signs of habitation too. Orin and Rima found several shacks made from decking planks with orderly rows of vegetables planted outside. There were even scrawny chickens running loose and one rather erratically behaved cat. Previous survivors of the Viryan rites had gone to a lot of effort to make the dismal place habitable. However, they were not in evidence.

Rima ranted one evening as they sat around a small fire in their adopted cabin, drinking from a half-finished bottle of local liquor that had managed to make the entire flight unbroken.

"I don't get it!" she shouted at the ceiling. "Where the *hell* are they? I mean, did they give up and walk out to the edge or something?"

Rima talked about the edge a lot. Orin sighed.

She saw the look on his face and reached over to kiss him.

"Don't worry, I'm fine," she said, staring into his eyes. "By the way, did I ever say thank you for rescuing me?"

This had become their new ritual prelude to sex.

Rima spent the days that followed hunting for the people she felt must have at least left a parting message. Orin tried to make their life as comfortable as possible, and in his quieter moments, contemplated the journey he'd made.

How had he been able to avoid seeing magic in the world with wonders like Ithrulene to hand? His sense of awe had been thoroughly blunted by modern living. On the other hand, how had the people of the city been able to kid themselves that whatever force created their world gave a damn about them? From up here on the ceiling, he was able to laugh about both perspectives, albeit somewhat bitterly.

He was sitting atop a mound one day, contemplating writing a book for those refugees who came after him when he suddenly heard Rima's voice.

"Orin! Come quick!"

She was bouncing across the uneven terrain wearing his wings, as she did most days. Her face was lit up with glee.

"I think I found them," she said breathlessly.

Orin scrambled down to join her.

She showed him to a long, low outbuilding that stood in a flat expanse of nails and sawdust. Orin had seen it before, but deemed it close enough to the edge that it wasn't worth exploring.

She yanked back the door. Inside, the ground had been scraped clean to reveal the black ceramic underneath. A large crack ran the length of the interior that had been excavated to make a vertical shaft with crude footholds cut into one side. Words in red paint had been scrawled on the wall in Miracle, along with an arrow pointing down.

"Look!" said Rima.

She pointed down the hole. There was a point of bright light deep inside, from somewhere beyond the ceiling of the world. She dragged off the wings and started down.

"Hang on a moment, my love," said Orin.

"For what?" she said, laughing at him. "What is there to stay for?"

He grinned at her. Absolutely nothing.

He followed her down through the crust to a place where the material around them buzzed with angry life. He felt heavier with every foot he descended, and less comfortable. He had the unpleasant sense that he was being crushed from within. When the sensation was almost intolerable, Orin paused again and wondered if they should be doing this. Rima was, of course, plunging on regardless.

A small smile curved his lips. Wherever she was going, she would need him. And what did he really have to be afraid of, given what he'd already done?

He kept going till he reached the horrible place where the squeezing was at its worst and gravity inverted itself. To get any further, he had to turn his body around while the unseen force wrapped iron fingers round his innards. From that point onwards, though, he was climbing up—through ceramic at first, but then good, old-fashioned rock.

He and his wife climbed out together into the light of a new sun. There were tears streaming down Rima's face as she shielded her eyes from the glare. They were on a hilltop softly carpeted with green grass and wildflowers. In the distance there were white-capped mountains, and on the plains between, forest.

Orin breathed in the crisp, clean air and let awe fill him up like wine. Was he in heaven, or just another layer of the world? One of hundreds, perhaps. It didn't really matter.

"Look," he said.

Not a couple of miles away, a thin wisp of smoke was rising into the blue sky from a house set next to a river.

"Let's go," he suggested, and took her hand.

They ran down the hillside together.

Fugue

Jay Caselberg

Jorge had been thinking for a while about how he might change his world. The problem was that the world seemed to have a mind of its own. The skinny fingers of circumstance plucked at his thoughts, discomfiting and constant, but there wasn't a thing he could do to shift the feeling, nor to shift himself from the place that he seemed to be stuck.

He sat now upon the sea wall, watching dirty foam swirl around the edges of boulders piled by unseen hands a hundred years before memory. Cold, cold, the gray-blue water crashed against the man-made barrier, sucking back to leave traces trickling between the cracks, the hint of salt spray casting a thin veil over sky and sea. On a day like today, he could almost be guaranteed his solitude. This was his place. His alone. The collar of his dark coat was turned up against the chill breeze, his thinning hair blowing in strands back and forth against his face. Lifetimes could pass here without him marking their passage and that was one of the things that drew him here. Back home there were…things he'd rather not think about while he was here in his place of refuge. But he had to think about them. Knowing what he had to do, he tossed a pebble into the water and watched it sink from view.

With a grumble deep in his throat, Jorge clambered to his feet, shoving cold, pale hands deep into the pockets of his thick coat. Steel-gray waves rolled in toward the sand, blanketed by a dull sky above, the stiff breeze whipping white spume from their tops. Back along the beach, a solitary figure walked, a mere smudge against the flat expanse.

With a sigh, Jorge turned from the faded pastel beachscape. Fine spray from the waves pattered icy droplets against one cheek, but he was immune to the cold. Up at the beach end, thin wooden slats had been laid across the dunes between the tufted grasses to form a walkway, the wood turned white and rimed with salt, making the pale strips look old and desiccated. He was hunched, negotiating his footing slat by slat, when something made him stop, pause. Slowly he lifted his gaze, sea-gray eyes fading into the wave wash behind as if one might see right through his head to the horizon.

"We are indeed the hollow men," said the angel with a smug grin.

Jorge worked his mouth, but nothing would come. He frowned, blinked a couple of times and ran the tip of his tongue over wind-cracked lips, but still there were no words. What did you say to an angel? The sun was starting to slip behind the mountains, casting a fiery corona around the being's wings, making it difficult for Jorge to make out a face. He hadn't expected wings made of leather. No, not at all. Now he could smell, it too. Deep and rich, the scent of tanned hides and deeply stuffed couches. The wings stirred slowly, languidly, seemingly unaffected by the breeze that rippled invisible fingers through the grasses and little trails of sand around Jorge's feet. So, this was an angel. He could tell it was an angel. The white robes and everything. It wore sandals on its feet too. The sun drifted a little farther, giving Jorge a better view of the angel's face.

"All right?" he said and started to head for the top of the rise and past.

One leathery wing stretched out to block his path.

"This is the way the world ends," said the angel.

Jorge shook his head. "I don't think so." He stepped past the outstretched wing and headed on up the trail and over the rise, leaving the angel behind.

Anyway, how could he take seriously a creature that was spouting misplaced T. S. Eliot at him? Eliot and Prufrock. Well, it wasn't Prufrock, but it was all so appropriate in a way. He thought briefly about rolling up his trouser legs, taking his shoes and socks off to feel his fish-white toes squeak through the sand before he reached the grassy park leading across to the road proper, but knew he wouldn't. It wasn't in his nature. At least not now. Especially not after seeing the angel, Eliot or not.

Time after time, Jorge was drawn inexorably back to the sea, back to that mirror glass blackness in the dead of night, the waves sucking sand grains into whispering lips, to spit them back out again with a disappointed hiss. Even here, now, in the small park, so close to the water's edge, he could feel the pull. Behind him, though, stood the angel, and that wouldn't do at all. At home, Caroline was waiting for him… or would be if she even knew he had gone. There were days when she seemed to feel and hear nothing, others where her round, wide-eyed face was more animated, her frail hands moving, instead of draped together limply in her lap. It was on the bad days that Jorge knew the real traces of the fear. Somehow, though, time had done much to manage that fear, placing it in a hard, round place deep inside him. Hard and steel-gray like his eyes.

Pulling his coat more tightly about him, he headed for the roadside and his battered, green car, barely holding together now, but running all the same. Long ago he'd given up the pretence of filling the back with rods and fishing gear. He needed no excuse to be sitting out alone on the breakwater. He was just a solitary old man, these days. Nobody really paid him much mind. The car waited for him, parked by the edge of the rise leading down into the park between two large Mediterranean pines. In the warmer months, you could smell them. An old brick beach kiosk sat at one end of the park, and at the other, a path leading up to the grassy headland with a stone bench placed right out near the end, a bequest to the memory of someone long forgotten. He thought for a moment about taking that path, going and sitting up there at the very edge of the world, staring out across the waves to the horizon of his memory, but knew he wouldn't. Caroline waited for him at home. Who knew what she was up to right now and what might lie waiting for him when he got back? Sometimes, it was just better not to think about it.

He pulled into their street, testing random thoughts about what might be waiting in their simple shrub-dotted yard, the even flowerbeds holding thorny leavings of the roses that had bloomed there in past seasons. It had been a long time since he'd given them any attention. Once, when he'd driven home, pulled into their drive, there had been a unicorn waiting for him, but one with smoldering, fire-filled eyes, its mouth full of sharpened teeth, grinning at him with its own dark intent. As with many of the others, he'd tried to ignore it, but then he'd learned about these things over the months and years. There were better ways of dealing with them. Like the angel. You simply acknowledged their presence and wandered on. In any other direction lay the beginnings of madness, as if that state had not already begun. Today, the yard was empty.

At the rear of their simple cottage, spindle-stick trees thrust empty fingers toward the slate sky. In winter, when the sea mist rolled in from the water, it draped them, shroud-like, with a pale and insubstantial blanket, hiding threats that Jorge could barely imagine, barely dare to imagine. When the mist was in, Jorge went nowhere near the trees. He had his reasons.

He eased into the drive, parked, and opened his door, wincing a little as it creaked loudly. It was better if he didn't actually announce his presence to the random population that inhabited his existence from time to time. He preferred to walk like a shadow amongst them, for the most part unseen and unnoticed, unless they confronted him directly, which also happened now and again. Well, that was his hope, to pass, remaining unworthy of their attention. For that reason, he left the car parked in the driveway, rather than struggling with the aging garage doors, scraping their crumbling wooden bottoms against the solid drive. It was just more noise to alert those that might choose to listen.

There wasn't much left in the garage now, not that he'd ventured inside for a while. A few stray tools hung suspended from old rusting nails. A couple of half-empty pots and tins huddled together at the end of one shelf. A single, yellowing, grime-smeared bulb hung suspended from the ceiling, festooned with dusty cobwebs. Feeble light trickled in through the single murky window at the rear, but these days, that was the only illumination the darkened space received. One day, he supposed, he'd venture back in, but not for now. Such an action would be an acknowledgement of what had been before, and he wasn't prepared to take that particular step yet. Rather than fussing with the needs of the garden, he preferred to leave it all to the man who came weekly—the man who carried his own tools along with his tanned shoulders and face.

Carefully, slowly, Jorge eased the car door shut, applying pressure with his body till the lock clicked into place. He gave the garden one more quick glance, then headed for the back door, his keys clutched firmly in his left hand. It appeared that in the time it had taken him to drive back from the beach, Caroline had moved on. She went through phases like that. He grunted with a kind of satisfaction and stepped into the small room behind the kitchen, closing the back door quietly behind him. He listened as he shrugged off his coat and hung it on a peg near the door, but there were no sounds coming from the lounge. That could be a good thing or a bad thing. Taking a single slow breath, Jorge closed his eyes for a couple of seconds, preparing, then headed through the kitchen toward the living room.

When he first met her, it had the feeling of true accident rather than any sort of design. Jorge had been sitting on a train, half-staring at nothing in particular, when someone in his line of sight had moved to get a better grip on the handrail as the carriage rocked to one side. The man had leaned over, resting his forehead on his arm, the arm itself crooked into a curve. The space between the man's arm and his face had formed an almost round frame, and beyond it, revealed, was Caroline's face. There was something about her features, something about the framing that reminded Jorge of Botticelli or perhaps Titian. She had that pale-faced smoothness, the roundness of feature reminiscent of their paintings. A face from another time. Jorge sat fascinated. She didn't notice him watching her. When Jorge had left the train and headed for work, he craned, looking for her, trying to see which way she went, but it wasn't long before he lost her in the crowd. Somehow, his heart had been heavy for the rest of the day, as if he knew that it was an opportunity lost. It was illogical, irrational.

The man with half a face was back again. His features flowed into some sort of formless, melted-plastic shape on the left side. He'd stand and stare at Jorge, not saying anything, just standing there, watching. This time he was across the other side of their white picket fence, a long gray-green coat pulled tightly about him. Once upon a time, Jorge had acknowledged the man, just like he acknowledged the angel, but after a time he had simply given up. The man with half a face never said anything, and in fact, Jorge wondered if he could, the way his lips had been sealed together on one side, but it made sense that it was probably enough to keep him from anything resembling real speech. Jorge merely glanced at him and continued down the driveway on his way to the shops.

Caroline, inside, was probably watching, seeing things in that inner vision that was uniquely hers. He wondered if there was some mythological root to the man without a face, but for the life of him, there was nothing that came to mind. Anyway, they'd run out of milk, and that was more important for the moment. He could hardly make Caroline a nice cup of tea if they didn't have milk. She liked her cup of tea, in the more lucid moments when she seemed to be in touch with their actual reality.

She had been a voracious reader once, drawn to histories and folklore, for they seemed to spark her imagination. That had been before her decline. Jorge suspected that many of the beasts from her landscape sprang half-formed from tainted rememberings of things she had read. Whatever the source, knowing what it might be did little to help him deal with them. When he glanced back up at the house, the man with half a face was gone. Jorge nodded to himself and turned his attention back to the road. Milk, and perhaps he'd get them a treat. Some cake. Maybe chocolate. Maybe Caroline would be aware enough to enjoy it.

Jorge had finally met her, again seemingly by accident, in a supermarket, wandering the aisles with his solitary trolley, picking out the various meals for one that he thought might be vaguely palatable. It was always a risk. You never knew what you'd get in some of those prepackaged affairs, and he was reluctant to try anything new. Today was a little annoying, because some of his favorites were out of stock. He looked dubiously down at the new selection sitting in the trolley in front of him. He would just have to wait and see. He sniffed and wheeled his trolley out from the shelves holding the ready meals and headed for household goods.

He had just entered the aisle with the washing powders when she wrestled her own trolley around the corner at the other end. Slick fluorescents shone along the metal frame and they drew his gaze at first, rather than her. Everything felt artificial in the stark supermarket lighting. Her trolley was one of the ones you hate to get with a wobbly wheel—difficult to manage, particularly around corners. As she struggled with the half-full trolley, she lost control and it careened into a shelf. Boxes of washing powder tumbled all around her, smacking of the edges of the basket and scattering about her feet. Forgetting about his own trolley altogether, Jorge dashed up the aisle to help.

Of course, he knew she was the girl from the train. He avoided looking at her face, and instead stooped to grab the dented boxes and shove them haphazardly onto an empty space on the shelf.

"This always happens to me," she said. "Oh, I feel like such an idiot."

"No," said Jorge, still not looking at her face. "It happens to all of us.

You're not so special." He caught the lie as soon as it had escaped his lips. "They just need to do something about these things." He grabbed the edges of her trolley and shook it till it rattled.

"Thanks," she said.

Jorge nodded and bent to gather more of the fallen boxes. She stooped and reached for the same box. It was like a movie. In that moment, their fingers met and a cool spark ran up his arm and settled high up in his gut. Slowly he lifted his face to meet her gaze. She was watching him, looking quickly from eye to eye, an expression of deep concentration on her face.

"You're really here," she said.

Jorge frowned, the briefest flicker. "I'm not sure, I...."

She seemed to shake herself back to awareness. Her eyebrows flickered and then she frowned as well. "Oh, I'm sorry. Look, my name's Caroline." She thrust out a hand.

Still confused, Jorge reached for her pale fingers and pressed them gently. "I'm Jorge," he said.

They both rose slowly and stood there looking at each other. There were still boxes on the floor, but Jorge cared nothing about them just at that moment.

"Listen..." they both began at once and stopped.

Caroline glanced down at her shopping and at the remaining boxes. She turned her attention to the shelves where Jorge had hastily shoved the damaged goods. She turned back to face him. "Tell you what," she said. "I'm bored with shopping. Do you want to go grab a coffee?"

They left their shopping carts sitting there abandoned at either end of the aisle.

When he got back to the house, swinging the white plastic shopping bag in one hand, the area was clear. No unicorns, no angels, no dragons sat waiting for him on the front lawn. Just the neatly tended flowerbeds and the tidy grass slope. He nodded with satisfaction. That was good. It meant that Caroline might be in a state to savor the cake he'd bought. He climbed the stone steps at the front of the yard, heading for the front door, then changed his mind and walked around the side of the house to the back. He just wanted to make sure there was nothing else lying in wait for him, nothing outside the periphery of his attention to surprise him. He juggled the white plastic bag from one hand to the other as he reached the back door, and digging out his keys, opened the door, pausing for a moment to stamp his feet on the back step before walking inside.

At the very beginning, they simply decided to move in together. A cozy little apartment and not a care in the world between them. At least not at first. That initial meeting, that strange little shift from perception of reality should have alerted Jorge, but he was far too smitten to pay it any mind. He hung on her every word, watching her as she walked across the room, as she stumbled around in her half-awake state first thing in the morning before she'd had her first cup of tea, as she emerged from the bathroom with the big fluffy robe bundled around her. Little by little, however, the episodes became more frequent. Caroline would say things that made no sense at all. At first, he thought they were simply evidence of the uniqueness of the treasure he had found in her and still he couldn't believe his luck. She was everything he hoped she'd be and more. There was nothing to tell him otherwise.

More as a concession to the people they mixed with, after a few months, they decided to get married. They'd tested the boundaries of their relationship together, and they understood that they worked. Even the slight aberrations in Caroline's behavior were not enough to make him think there was any reason to doubt his decision. He couldn't, for the life of him, even imagine being with anyone else, ever. Life continued—their marriage made little difference to the joy of what they had together. Jorge went to work, Caroline too, and eventually they accumulated enough, scrimping and saving, to buy a small house in the suburbs, a house with a yard and a fence and flowerbeds. They weren't too far from the beach, and that suited Jorge just fine; he loved the ocean. He loved listening to the distant sound of waves in the darkness as he drifted off to sleep, Caroline's regular breathing beside him. The beach was just an added bonus to spending his time with her. On occasion, he would simply stand in the doorway of the living room, watching her. He could barely imagine what life would be like without this woman. She was perfect.

Her decline was so gradual that he didn't really notice it for a full year. Sometimes, even in mid conversation, Caroline would fade off into some place removed. She would get a vaguely wistful expression on her face and stare fixedly off into the distance.

"Caroline, what is it?" Jorge would ask, but she didn't answer. When she finally returned, he would question her about it, but she seemed to have no recollection of where she'd been. She accused him of being silly, of playing games with her. Was he trying to make her think she was mad?

"No, of course not."

Jorge tucked his concern away and decided he'd watch and wait. If the situation worsened, he would seek advice, though he was reluctant to do so. Not for his Caroline. When she started talking about unicorns and goblins and elves, his concern grew, but he put it down to her over-active imagination. He had already reconciled himself that she had a slight problem with her attention span, but then, that wasn't so unusual.

It was a complete year before the first manifestation. The miniature dragon on the back steps had taken him completely by surprise. He stood watching it for a full half hour before it spread its wings and took flight. He tracked it till it disappeared into the cotton wool sky, and then he stepped inside and leaned heavily against the door, rubbing his forehead. When he'd walked into the living room to tell Caroline what he'd seen, she was unreachable. Though he squatted in front of her, her eyes were unseeing. He had gripped her forearms, gently, trying to coax some sort of reaction out of her, but his efforts had been in vain. His own fear forgotten, it was then that he started to be afraid for her, but it was then that he started making the first connection. Though he didn't want to admit it, he knew there was something wrong.

Putting the plastic bag down on the kitchen bench, Jorge carefully opened it and pulled out the cake and the milk. He opened the fridge, put the milk in and closed it again. Reaching up to the cupboard, he pulled out two floral cups and saucers and arranged them carefully on a tray. Filling the kettle with water, he put it on to boil, then found the teapot, removed its lid, checking that it was clean before spooning in two heaped teaspoons of leaves and one extra for the pot. He unwrapped the cake and placed it on another plate, pulled out a knife from the drawer, making three cuts into the chocolate round so there were two good slices, placed the plate on the tray and two smaller plates and forks beside them. Just then, the kettle boiled and he poured the steaming water into the pot, stepping back away from the cloud that rose beneath the kitchen cabinets. Retrieving the milk from the fridge, he poured some into a small white jug, then replaced the carton in the fridge.

"Jorge, is that you?" called Caroline from the living room.

"Yes, dear," he said. "I'm just making us a nice cup of tea."

"Oh good," she said. "I could do with a nice cup of tea. I was having the strangest dream."

Jorge nodded to himself. He could imagine the sort of dream she'd been having. He had seen them, day after day.

He wished there was something he could do for her. He had wished for years that there was something he could do for her. At first he had sought advice, but they had suggested medication, and finally institutionalization. Jorge was having none of it. He took great pains to assure them that the problem had simply gone away. He told no one about his own insights into the creatures that stalked her inner landscape. He reasoned that putting himself under scrutiny would do nothing to help her, nothing to help them both. So, as Caroline withdrew further and further, Jorge maintained the illusion of their normal life and marriage. Dutifully he went to work, brought in an income and made sure they had enough to sustain themselves. Caroline, of course, was less able to function in the outside world as her time in her other world grew more frequent. People started to notice. Finally, in one of her more lucid periods, he had convinced her to give up work. She had been perfectly content with the idea, and Jorge had breathed an inner sigh of relief. It was funny, for though she seemed to accept her condition, she appeared happy that it was nothing out of the ordinary, nothing she should worry about. The world she lived in was better than the day to day they had to put up with.

The only real regret Jorge had was that there was less time he had to really be with her. He missed her attention, but he resolved that he would be there for her. He loved her after all.

"Here we are," he said, walking into the living room carrying the tray before him.

Caroline clapped her hands together. "Oh lovely! You've bought some cake."

Placing the tray down on the table between their two chairs, Jorge carefully poured the tea and passed her a cup. He then slipped a knife under one slice of cake, placed it on one of the small plates and passed that over to her too. He placed a piece of cake on a plate for himself then sat back, leaving the plate on the tray. He left his cup sitting where it was.

"How are you feeling, my love?" he asked.

She glanced up at him, popped a small piece of cake into her mouth and licking a stray crumb from her lips, smiled at him. "I'm fine, Jorge. How are you?" Her thin white hair made a corona around her face, touched by light from the window behind. Her hair had been white for years now.

"I think I'm tired, Caroline. I think I'm tired. Sometimes I just wish we had a normal life together. I wish we could do things that other people do."

She gave a brief frown. "But we're so perfect together," she said. The frown quickly disappeared as she sliced another piece of cake and popped it between her lips.

Jorge watched her. She was right; they were perfect together. "I just wish there was something else I could do for you," he said.

"I don't know what you mean," she said with a slight shake of her head. "There's nothing you could possibly do. You've already done everything you could." Slowly, she placed her plate back down on the tray. "And you know, Jorge, I love you. I love you for everything you have been and done." She fixed him with a look, gazing intently into his face.

"I saw an angel today," he said.

She nodded. "So, it's come to that." She sighed. "I wish it hadn't come so soon. So…at last, it's time," she said.

Jorge frowned. "Time, for what? I don't under— "

A tall, familiar figure stepped out from the light behind Caroline's chair. Sweetly, Caroline smiled, her look full of gentle affection.

Jorge sat back out on the sea wall. His mind wasn't fixed on anything in particular; his attention simply meandered across the landscape like the seemingly random swirls of foam gracing the water's surface by the rocks. His legs hung over the edge and he swung them gently back and forth. Despite the noise of waves and water, the slight breeze coming off the surface, he heard, or rather sensed the motion behind him. And despite the breeze, he caught the scent of rich leather swelling the air around him.

The angel walked up soundlessly and took up a place beside him, tucking its robes around its legs and easing itself down to the cold hard wall. For a while there was silence between them. Jorge could sense the stirring of those massive wings, though he couldn't see them. He gave a quick sidelong glance at the angel's face, but apart from that, he refused to look. He'd been acknowledging these damned things for too long. It was time he put a stop to it.

"Hello, Jorge," said the angel.

Jorge grunted in response despite himself.

The angel reached around behind itself and felt along the wall, finally locating what it was seeking. Jorge glanced again to see what it was doing. The angel held something small and hard in its hand, rubbing its thumb over the smooth surface. Gently, it nodded, then with an easy motion, tossed the pebble out in front of them. It plopped into the water and quickly sank to the depths.

"This is the way your world ends," it said.

Jorge watched the place where the pebble had disappeared to the bottom for some seconds, saying nothing. Then without looking up into the angel's face, he finally spoke.

"Hmmm. You're probably right," he said. "You're probably right."

Nature Mort

Leslie What

After graduating from the Worcester School for Girls, Miss Lydia Monroe found work keeping house for Mr. Rudolph Gregory. Her employer was an odd man for someone so young. Lydia excused his eccentricities, supposing they were related to his artistic temperament. While she cleaned or prepared food or saw to the herb garden, Mr. Gregory withdrew to his studio to paint. On occasion, when he ventured forth to pace about the house, she caught him watching her, studying her features in a clinical and detached manner. Mr. Gregory seldom complimented her, nor did he point out her deficiencies. A polite awkwardness colored every interaction. He thanked her when she knocked upon his door to bring him tea, or to inform him that his dinner was waiting and that, if he had no further needs, she would retire for the night. He was kind, if not effusive. He never seemed rushed—unlike her—never seemed relieved to find the day drawing to a close.

Lydia had pulled her dark hair into a loose knot at the top of her head, which formed a round puff like a bowl of steamed pudding. Her uniform consisted of a starched white shirt with a ruffled collar, tucked inside the waistline of her gathered skirt. A plain cotton apron tied at the back, adding a thin layer to soak up the stains delivered by her day. The apron did not protect her clothes from the ravages of time; her shirt was worn thin along both sleeves at the elbows. She was paid adequately, except that she sent some of her wages to her father, who had grown too ill to work. Given that, new clothes hardly seemed important.

She tidied up the sitting room, where Mr. Gregory had left a leather-bound volume open on the table. Its colored plates depicted whales and large ocean fish. She turned the leaves until she came to a lithograph of a creature called a narwhale. What an odd beast, she thought, the long horn like a spear upon its head, the ruffled throat like a collar. She hoped the scene—of two boats filled with fisherman brandishing harpoons—was imaginary, for it alarmed her to think an artist had the power to conjure up a mythical beast for a painting. She closed the book and set it back in its place inside the corner walnut cupboard, beside a novel by H.G. Wells. Mr. Gregory didn't mind if she borrowed his books and she had recently finished reading this one. She touched the spine, traced the gold letters, pulled the book from the shelf and read a familiar passage.

I felt a nightmare sensation of falling; and, looking round, I saw the laboratory exactly as before. Had anything happened? For a moment I suspected that my intellect had tricked me. Then I noted the clock. A moment before, as it seemed, it had stood at a minute or so past ten; now it was nearly half-past three!

She loved *The Time Machine*, however implausible its ideas and situations. If only it were she could stop time, or better yet, to go back to a time without trouble. She set the book back in its place and dusted the plaster bas-relief that served as a frame for one of Mr. Gregory's oils. Many of his paintings were larger-than-life portraits of birds, sometimes exotic animals: pink storks called flamingoes; tropical parrots with feathers bright and lurid they resembled the petticoats of a whore more than the coat of a bird. The birds in his garden, tedious wrens and finches, wore their muted colors like bankers' vests. Lydia longed to travel, see sights and oddities like those captured in Mr. Gregory's work. This seemed an unlikely dream. At eighteen, she had never been outside of New England.

She straightened a painting depicting a sleek panther in pursuit of unknown prey. The surrounding jungle bloomed lush, intense with colors that left her feeling warm, pressed for breath, as if she had just run a many flights of stairs. Should Mr. Gregory catch her staring, it would embarrass her to admit the fascination she felt toward his work. She cranked open the window to enjoy one moment of fresh air. The smoky, sweet scent of Mr. Gregory's tobacco wafted nearby. He was outside, taking his morning walk in the garden. The tobacco blend smelled slightly of cherries, of charred wood—a pleasant and not overbearing aroma, more refined than her fatherís acrid blend.

Mr. Gregory owned such beautiful things that caring for them was more interesting than it might otherwise have been. Lydia bent to drag a heavy, carved mahogany armchair to the side in order to roll up the gay Persian rug. The yarn was silk and wool, very fine, a floral pattern so intricate and precise it must have been woven by children, for who else had fingers so nimble? She knew the rug was old, though not quite so old as the house, built before the Civil War.

The highboy needed dusting; she cleaned everything except the scrolled top where her feathers could not reach. In another half an hour or so, her friend, Mr. Duffy, would stop by. If she remembered, she would ask him to help her with the highboy. To pay back the favor, she would offer to sew loose buttons or mend his stockings.

A smaller rug easily folded into quarters. This rug seemed to blink, alive with red, green and black diamond shapes woven by Indians. It was beautiful, primitive. Lydia knew nothing about art, not even if she liked it. She knew only that it affected her in ways she could not articulate, that seeing art forced her to look at things she might not otherwise notice, and for this fleeting joy, she was grateful.

She transported a small goblet smelling faintly of sherry to the kitchen, washed and set it out to dry beside the sink. It was near enough to teatime that she set the kettle on to boil. When the water was ready, she poured a pot for Mr. Gregory and beside it placed a cup and saucer, a small bowl of applesauce and eight whole candied walnuts. A twig snapped; she started and looked through the window. Mr. Gregory stood not ten feet from the house, preoccupied by lighting his pipe. His hair was dark, always tousled as if he'd just run his hands through it. His lashes were thick, damp shiny, like a child overheated from play.

She held still, worried he would hear her, grateful when he turned away without noticing her proximity. She folded a linen napkin beneath the saucer and carried the tray up the stairs and down the hall to the large attic room Mr. Gregory used as his studio. After setting the tray on a table near the door, she knocked out of habit. The door was not shut securely. It opened with a light push. "Excuse me, Mr. Gregory," Lydia said, stepping inside, knowing he was still outdoors and not at his canvas.

She proceeded cautiously. She had been employed here for some six months and had never before entered his studio. The air felt stuffy and warm. To one side stood the massive oak apothecary's cabinet where Mr. Gregory stored supplies in its forty-eight drawers. His easel faced the closed dormer window. Flimsily nailed wooden crates were stacked against one side wall, making the room seem smaller.

It was wrong to pry, but curiosity easily trumped sensibility. She walked across the room to his canvas to stare at an oil painting of a hummingbird, hovering atop a calla lily. The tip of the hummingbird's long beak vanished beneath a sparkling drop of nectar. Its ruby throat shimmered, iridescent. The calla lily seemed somehow threatening, as if it might swallow the tiny bird. Its one continuous petal pouted, a full lip swollen from kissing, velvet soft and delicate. The colors—muted pastel yellow with a lavender blush—were at once grotesque and stunningly beautiful.

She reached to touch it with her index finger, and felt like a fool to find her finger come away swathed in purple paint. It was sticky wet, like a spill of blood, but without warmth. She rubbed the paint between finger and thumb, brought it near her nose. Its odor was of mud, of pollen, of rain. Perhaps it was poisonous, she thought, which made her want to taste it, or worse, add a bit of color to her eyelids. Fortunately, a flash of color on the windowsill distracted her.

Having trespassed this far, she might as well explore farther. Feeling brazen, she walked close to the window to stare down at the sill. There she saw a dead, gray thing, perhaps a mouse. She withdrew her handkerchief from her pocket and wipe her hand, fighting the urge to open the window and push the dead thing outside. A tin filled with paintbrushes weighed down a stack of papers, edges curled from the moist paint. Careful, oh so careful not to disturb his work, she plucked one of Mr. Gregory's brushes from the tin and used it to poke the still creature. When nothing happened, when it did not move or squeal, her stomach settled; she used her handkerchief to pick it up and take it away. Odd that its body felt limp and cold, even through the fine cloth. She held it out for a closer inspection, suffering a fit of uncomfortable giggles to discover that the dead thing was not a mouse at all, but rather a hummingbird.

How interesting it was, how perfectly preserved. It felt like a pouch filled with tobacco, especially since a thin sawdust stream spilled from a loose stitch in the belly. There was something disturbing about the creature, more disturbing than the fact that it was dead. She stared down upon it, trying to understand what troubled her. The color, she decided at last. Where had its color gone? This hummingbird resembled unpainted clay. Its feathers were a dull brown; its eyes sunken, covered by a thin layer of gray. She looked back to the painting, comparing canvas to the small bird. Although this ugly creature was bereft of the vibrant color that was Mr. Gregory's hallmark, clearly, it had inspired the painting. With a start she realized Mr. Gregory would rightly be vexed with her for tampering with the pose.

When she set the hummingbird back upon the windowsill a brilliant gash of red illuminated its throat. She tilted her head; the color disappeared. The red appeared and vanished according each time she changed her position. She came to understand that the bird was indeed a gray, lifeless thing, yet the feathers, when viewed from just the correct angle, reflected light. It was beautiful, so beautiful! Her discovery left her in awe of her employer. Mr. Gregory had known all along how to bring back the beauty of nature, even in death.

Her fingertips tingled. Fear settled over her, that Mr. Gregory dabbled in the occult, that he employed magic to bring life to his paintings. She uttered a soft prayer, mindful of the slight differences between prayer and magic in the eyes of the Lord. Magic manipulated the All-powerful for selfish means, while prayer offered up the open heart to God. She stared at the unfinished painting of the hummingbird and saw an open heart, a call to God—and her emotions overwhelmed her. She understood the desire to paint, to capture the vision of one moment in a frame that might last forever. Not magic at all, she decided at last. Science was more like it. Mr. Gregory had discovered a time machine of sorts. She wanted to believe that time could be controlled, the future forestalled. The brightness of the sun hurt her eyes until she closed them, and concentrated on the steady rise and fall of her breath. Her hand rose to her throat; the handkerchief fluttered to the ground.

She prayed that God would let her share the secret of the time machine, that He would allow her to see her father in health once more before he died. The hand holding the paintbrush moved as if on its own volition to touch the canvas. She traced over the faint outline of a blade of grass and imagined herself no bigger than a speck of dust, wrapped like a cocoon woven from grass. She imagined another cocoon, this one protecting her father. She saw the blade of grass was not a single line, a single color, but many lines and many colors and she thinned her paint to fill in the outline she had traced. Her brush strokes alternated between thick and thin, using the sides of the brush, the tip, the flattened end. The finished painting looked alive. She could imagine the wind bending the stem down toward the earth.

Her reverie was broken when she heard Mr. Gregory, calling her name, his voice growing louder as he approached the house. She set the brush back in the tin and turned to leave. As she hurried from the room, she spied an open drawer near the bottom of Mr. Gregory's apothecary cabinet. It was against her nature not to close the drawer before proceeding. She knew she should touch nothing else, that already her interference could cost her job, but her hand lingered on the drawer pull, a sense of dread weighing heavy. A fetid smell emanated from the cabinet, sweet like sherry. Her worry that Mr. Gregory would catch her rifling through his things suddenly seemed unimportant. Instead of closing the drawer, she opened it wider.

Inside the drawer, she spied a mummified finger, cut off at the lower knuckle, black and shiny and obviously very, so old it was beyond frightening. Egyptian? Could something from that era survive unto this day? Her breath caught in her throat. Downstairs, the front door creaked open and shut, followed by the stomp of boots as Mr. Gregory entered the house. Lydia left in haste, doing her best to calm her heart in the time it took to walk down the hall to the landing. She could not afford to lose her job. Her sensibilities returned in a wash of shame.

Mr. Gregory met her midway down the stairs. "Good day," he said.

"I've left your tea by the door," she said.

Mr. Gregory smiled said, "Thank you, Miss Lydia."

The situation proved awkward. She turned to the side to let him pass, and when he brushed against her, her knees nearly gave out and she gripped the banister for support.

"Are you ill, Miss Lydia?" he asked.

Her hesitation lingered a moment too long before she answered, "No. I'm fine, sir." An electrical charge warmed the air; her hand reflexively touched the nape of her neck to smooth back the hairs. She managed to compose herself enough to complete her descent without misstep. She was to the bottom of the staircase, when he heard the jingle of the tea tray and the scrape of a chair being pushed out of the way. She realized she had been holding her breath, and gasped, the dusty air forcing out a cough. She had barely recovered when she heard the squeal of the outside gate opening, and looked outside to see Duffy had arrived and was making his way down the brick walkway to the front door.

Duffy tended the grounds on a nearby estate. Wednesdays, his day off, he worked for Mr. Gregory. Lydia could depend upon him to help her take out the rugs. "Hello, Miss Lydia," he said upon spying her. He tipped his hat.

"Hello, Mr. Duffy," she said, acknowledging his arrival with a slight smile he could not interpret as being too provocative. Duffy's presence brought her back from the elegant painted world to one less dignified. Here, the drudgery or work carried sway over the luxury of time. Art, she realized mastered time by capturing its moments, one painting by one, whereas work erased time, covering it up somehow, making it pass too quickly.

Duffy came around to the kitchen entrance and rapped upon the door before opening it and letting himself inside. His build was slight; his skin freckled with rusty patches. He bent down to wipe the dust from his boots, an odd thing to do before working in Mr. Gregory's garden. She took it as a sign of respect. When he handed her a small wooden box, its top inlaid with painted blue porcelain, she realized that she was meant to look upon his call as a social event.

"Something for you," he said. "I hope you like it."

"Oh, it's lovely," she said, examining the box.

He brightened. "Open it," Duffy said, growing more animated. "It's what's inside that matters."

The interior revealed a soft, padded lining sewn from red velvet. She groped inside, pushing aside the velvet until her fingers grasped something smooth and cold. Ceramic? Metal? When she brought it out to examine, she saw that Duffy had given her a rock, a beautiful, multifaceted, clear crystal.

"How lovely," she said.

"Watch this," he said, and took her hand and held it up into the light until the rock face caught the sun and projected a rainbow onto the wall.

His touch embarrassed her. He noticed her discomfort and let his hand drop. "Pardon me," he said, looking schoolboy guilty.

Her composure regained, she asked, "Where did you get it?"

"It's from Mexico," he said. "They call it fluorite."

"From Mexico?" she said, slightly saddened by the knowledge of yet another exotic locale. She knew that Duffy had not himself traveled to Mexico, that the crystal was no doubt a souvenir given to him by the gentleman who employed him. No person of such limited means as she and Duffy could hope to journey to lands that existed beyond their imaginations. She was touched by his thoughtfulness just the same.

"It made me think of you," he said. "The way your eyes sparkle."

"Thank you," she said. The crystal was magnificent. She smiled at Duffy, feeling a hearty measure warmth and concern for his well being.

"Miss Lydia," called a voice from the bottom of the stairway: Mr. Gregory.

"Sir?" she said, her warmth for Mr. Duffy growing suddenly cold. "Can I bring you anything?"

Mr. Gregory walked into kitchen. "I'm so sorry to disturb you," he said, and nodded curtly to Mr. Duffy. He frowned. "Miss Lydia, I wonder if you might prepare a plate for my lunch," he said. "I feel a hunger that was not satisfied by the small plate. This warm weather improves my appetite."

The spell cast by the crystal was fractured. She replaced it into its tiny box and slid the box inside her pocket. While she was grateful for the gentle gardener's attention, she foresaw no future with him. "Thank you again, Mr. Duffy," she said.

Mr. Duffy watched her, looking confused by her sudden cold demeanor.

Mr. Gregory waited while she took out cheese and bread from the icebox. She felt him watching her unfold the muslin wrapping, and her grip upon the knife weakened when he took a step closer to peer out the window. She noticed the blue veins in the cheese, and the creamy texture, the pungent aroma.

"Perhaps tomorrow I could take lunch in the garden." His sleeve was bruised by blue paint and a gash of yellow streaked his pants leg. "Won't you have some?" he offered.

Mr. Duffy looked to Lydia before answering.

She raised an eyebrow and said, "No, thank you. I'll take my lunch after I've finished with the rugs." She arranged the cheese slices around thick slices of bread. "Shall I bring this to the dining room?"

Mr. Gregory said, "If it's ready, I'll take it up to the studio."

He exchanged a paint-smeared rag for the plate, leaving the rag—her handkerchief—on the counter. She did her best not to show her concern. She told herself that he was absent-minded, that he meant nothing by the gesture. Had he noticed her slight alteration to his painting? She hoped not and was about to utter a silent prayer when she recognized her desire was more rooted in magic than faith.

As if to prove her point, Mr. Gregory thanked her and was gone.

"Well," she said, anxious to stand outside for a breath of calming air, "we'd best be getting to the rugs." She folded the blemished cloth and slipped it into her pocket.

Mr. Duffy's face grew smooth. He seemed peeved with her for reasons that would never be discussed, and for this small courtesy, she was grateful. He followed her to the drawing room, where he shouldered the largest rug without protest. "Where would you like this?" he asked.

"Over the grass," she said. "Anywhere there's room. Thank you." She fetched the beater and set to work while Mr. Duffy folded the smaller carpets over the porch railing. While she worked beating the rugs, he set to work clipping the hedge bordering the house. He gathered clumps of leaves and branches into bundles and carried those toward the back of the yard. He weeded the flowerbeds and took his time considering his pruning cuts on the wild crabapple bush.

She stood over the Persian using a broom to sweep it clean. It was toilsome work, and when she paused to rest, she looked to see if Mr. Duffy was watching. Only when she had satisfied herself that he was preoccupied elsewhere did she slide the little box he had given her from her pocket. She opened the box, removed the crystal, and let the sun bring out its color like ripening fruit. She watches as reflections danced like colorful fireflies upon the surface of the Persian, and the movement of the light, she realized, was indeed beautiful. Lydia finished the rugs and left them out to freshen in the spring air as Mr. Duffy doused the mound of garden rubbish with kerosene until the fire consumed the pile. She swept the back porch, pausing only to refresh herself with a sip of water.

Mr. Duffy strode close "I won't be able to come again next Wednesday," he said, his manner stiff. "I'm sorry, but you'll have to find someone else to help you with the rugs."

"I understand," she said. From the way that he watched her, she knew he wanted her to say more, but no words came to her aid.

"I hope you like the crystal," he said at last.

"Oh, I do," she said, aware that something between them had hardened. Though she tried to lighten the mood with a sweet smile, the look he gave her in return smoldered. "Goodbye, Mr. Duffy," she said. She followed him out partway to the gate, and upon her return, glanced up, toward Mr. Gregory's window. His silhouette stood framed by the sash. She could not tell if he looked her way. When she felt inside her pocket for the crystal in its box, her finger caught on a splinter. Pain stabbed at her, subsided. She pulled out her hand and saw not blood, but paint, yellow paint, oozing out like the blood of an insect from the pinprick hole in her skin. Dear God, she thought. Forgive my sin, but was this prayer a devotional prayer to God or a bargain with the devil?

Of course Mr. Gregory had seen her handiwork on his canvas. Of course he had seen through her feeble attempts to deceive him. He noticed small details; that was his profession. What must he think? Her shame bloomed. Combined with the hours spent in the sun, it left her skin hot, red, her lips and throat parched, swollen. Reflexively, she wiped her finger over her apron, leaving a streak. She returned to the kitchen to wash out the stain. She scrubbed at the blur of color with a bristle brush. Her shirt dampened with sweat. Her knees weakened and she poured herself a drink of cool water from a heavy pitcher, and sat at the table, thinking only of how a drop of sherry would help, if only she dared. She idly traced a square in the sweat beads that had formed outside the earthenware pitcher. The fluid square could not hold its shape; she watched the sides thin, collapse.

"If you don't mind, Miss, Lydia, may I have a word with you?" said Mr. Gregory from the doorway.

She was unsure of just how long he had been standing there. Her fluster grew and she rose to her feet, unsteady, knocking over her tumbler in the process.

Mr. Gregory leapt to her side to rescue the glass. "I've startled you," he said. "My apologies."

She could not meet his glance. Her collar felt tight upon her neck. The lightheaded feeling was one of illness, not of joy. Before she knew what was happening, Mr. Gregory was abreast of her, so close that she could feel a puff of breath upon her cheek. He helped her to sit back down.

"Whatís this?" he asked, his hand closing around the wooden box in her pocket.

"A small gift," she said. "From Mr. Duffy." Carefully, she brought out the box, opened the top, and waited for him to hold out his hand before dropping the crystal into his palm.

"A rock," said Mr. Gregory with a wry smile. "How very charming."

Her shoulders slumped; she wanted him to leave her alone. She fingered the dirty rag in her pocket, rubbed against the colors of paint, dry like mud.

"Have you had anything to eat today?" he asked.

She realized that the answer was no.

"I hope you don't mind my intrusion, but you aren't looking at all well. One really must take care to eat and drink sufficient fluids in this warm weather. Let me fix you a plate," he said, and she watch as he sliced cheese from the round, then tore uneven chunks of bread. He poured her a goblet of claret and sat beside her, staring as she ate.

She was ravenous. The texture of the bread was rough as a man's chin. The cheese was flower petal smooth. The claret's beautiful red color sparkled like rubies. Slowly, her strength returned. She wondered if he had placed a charm inside this nourishment.

"I would like to paint you sometime," he said. "Not your face, although it is quite lovely; just your hands."

"My hands?" she asked, suddenly self-conscious of every callus and bump, the dirt beneath her nails.

"Your hands," he said. "They show both strength and delicacy. It's the contrast that I'm after," he said. "That's what I find interesting enough to paint."

"Contrast?" she said.

"The difference between what you see and what you expect to see," he explained. "The difference between what you expect to see and what you actually observe. You understand that, don't you?"

"I do," she said, seeing him breathe a sigh that bespoke relief. If she possessed the talent, she would paint a portrait of her father, before his illness. She found herself staring at Mr. Gregory, his face lit by his earnest demeanor.

He stared back at her without malice. Mr. Gregory looked as if it was an effort not to work his lips into a smile. " The blade of grass," he said. "Was that your handiwork?"

"I don't know what you mean," Lydia began, but he shook his head and told her not to worry.

"I've seen how you look at the paintings," he said. "It's as if you are counting the brush strokes, taking apart the colors. You could prove a fine apprentice. But you haven't yet answered my question yet. May I paint you?"

If he were going to let her go, surely he would have by now. Her lies were as transparent as panes of glass. She had misbehaved horribly yet it appeared that her employer did not care. Emboldened by his suggestion of apprenticeship, she felt brazen enough to speak her mind. "I will pose," she said, "but I have a favor I would ask in return. I wish to learn how to paint."

He nodded. "I thought as much. What do you wish to paint?" he asked.

Lydia remembered the intoxicating calm of tea leaves swirling in a cup and the miraculous patterns they formed after settling. She thought of her father's carefree face, and the moment it had changed, the lines and wrinkles changing direction, leaving his expression pained and worried. She wanted to paint something no one had looked at, never really examined or discovered some essential truth about its essence. "I should like to paint a still life," she said. She pointed to her empty goblet. "I wish to paint the moment when the glass is emptied. I wish to paint a thing that has died, so that through that image, it will forever live amongst our memories."

He smiled. "You wish to stop time," he said. "You wish to capture the ineffable. Nature Mort, as the French call it. Still life—a portrait of the inanimate."

"You know how to stop time," she whispered. "I knew it."

Mr. Gregory laughed. "In a way," he said.

She watched him, afraid to ask if his craft was rooted in science, like a time machine, or if he came by it magically. Could he make time bend to his will, travel backwards, to a simpler past, or must he limit his art to stopping time in the moment? She was curious about the mummified finger she had glimpsed in the apothecary's chest but afraid to ask. Where had it come from? Why did he keep it? She could not ask him directly without admitting she had pried uninvited into his secrets.

"How do you do it?" she asked at last, and his gaze upon her narrowed until it was a focused stare she could not ignore. "Stop time? Must a thing be dead before it's painted?"

"No," he said. "Though it is easier. Unless the housekeeper changes the pose you've taken great pains to set up."

She felt her face grow red.

"Shall we begin? Would you kindly accompany me to my studio?"

"Yes," she said, knowing she was free to refuse him, that it was not his magic that had persuaded her, but rather her curiosity. She followed him up the stairs and down the hall to his studio. He was watching her, sizing up her reaction. She was not ready to admit she had been here before, so she looked around, as if seeing things for the first time. She noticed that the drawer in the bottom corner of the apothecary's cabinet was closed. She looked away, not quick enough to avoid his knowing glance.

"Just the hands," Mr. Gregory reminded her. "I will paint only the hands so you needn't feel self-conscious. No one who sees them will recognize you."

"May I ask where you keep it?" she asked, breathless. "The time machine?"

He smiled. "It's really not much of a machine," he said.

"What is it then?" she asked. "Is it magic? I must know. Tell me, please."

He seemed unfazed by her display of emotion and ignored her plea. He sat her on a stool by the window, positioning her close to his unfinished painting of the hummingbird. He twirled a paintbrush in his hand before tipping in green oil. "Hold out your right hand," he told her.

She did as he asked.

He closed that hand around the end of the paintbrush and posed her to appear that she was in the midst of a brush stroke. He stood close behind her, murmuring into her ear. "I want you to imagine that your are painting another blade of grass. I will draw your hand while you paint. You will concentrate only upon that blade of grass. Should the room burst out in flames, you will feel no heat, see no fire. Your world exists only in the moment of that single blade of grass. That's the magic," he said. "That's the time machine. You can depict anything, any time, any creation of the mind. Anything at all. Fanciful or plain. You can paint beautiful flowers or you can paint the oily ugliness of reflections concealed in standing water. The magic is in here," he said, his hand moving away from hers to touch her forehead.

She nodded, and as she focused her thoughts upon the grass the world beyond it disappeared and nothing else mattered. Time stopped. The sound of Mr. Gregory clearing his throat brought her thoughts back to the room; she looked around, surprised that nothing had changed.

"Tell me," said her employer, "why do you wish to paint the mystery that is inside the drawer? That blackened twig of death. You know of which I speak."

"No," she lied and broke away. She watched him warily, waiting for him to fire her, or punish her for trespassing in his studio—perhaps by cutting off her finger and adding that memento to the others used in his practice of the dark arts.

He laughed. "Don't tell me that you didn't catch a glimpse," he said, "for I am quite certain that you did." He set her hand back in the posed position.

She was shivering, afraid, in awe of his confidence in his skill in mastering time. "Perhaps a glimpse," she said, and prepared herself to accept whatever penalty he meted. "I did not mean to pry," she said.

"We never do," he said. "Curiosity overwhelms the judgment."

She nodding, aware she would say anything, do anything he asked to fulfill her part in the bargain to apprentice to his craft. She blurted without thought, "The dead thing in the drawer," she said. "May I paint it sometime?"

Instead of the wrath she expected, his expression was one of puzzlement. He picked up a piece of charcoal and held it aloft. :Tell me why," he said. "Why would you wish to paint a thing so ugly?"

How could she explain this morbid need to capture what she feared most: the unchanging stillness of death? Her heart flapped like birds taking flight; sweat poured from her brow, down her cheeks and across her chin, and formed puddles in the soft spots of her neck. She felt as if she were falling, spiraling downward into darkness, yet she remained fully conscious and worried that her shivering would ruin the pose.

"Can you answer me?" asked Mr. Gregory. "Why do you wish to paint death?"

She swallowed and steadied the hand holding the brush. She closed her eyes and calmed herself with a deep and filling breath. She thought of her father and the sinking feeling that she might be too late to visit him again. She resumed her pose at the canvas. "Because it frightens me," she said at last.

A Love For All time

D. G. K. GOLDBERG

The street melted at the spot where squads of people were working on the timeline today. Not that "today" had any particular meaning. The main system went completely bonkers. People ran into themselves, the damn dead were cluttering up all the transfer points and the wailing of the unborn was continual. It was absolute chaos. The leakage from other Possibilities was uncontrollable.

A family of aristocratic immigrates blipped into my friend Trivia Marie's house. She thinks it is amusing when they crash in through the walls, clutching diamond necklaces, and babbling about Robespierre and the Reign of Terror.

The last time there was a major system overhaul Jonathan left me. He moved in with an alternative me who had dropped out of college during her junior year to become a dancer. I don't recall dancing.

Trivia Marie told me a perfectly disgusting story about a young girl who was relentlessly pursued by a toddler she was going to give birth to fifteen years from now. I am never quite certain whether or not I believe what Trivia says. I trust Trivia with my life; it's just that she sometimes cannot resist making a story a little better.

I miss Jonathan terribly. Yet, how can I be angry? Who can I be angry at? My husband left me for me. That is exactly what happened. These sorts of things never happened before time was over-loaded, trying to control the flow of time makes a giant mess of everything. That's government for you—what can I say? Trivia said she wouldn't care if it is me that he left me for, if she (Trivia) were me(this me, not the alternative me), she (being me) would kill her (also being me). When I pointed out to Trivia that would be suicide and told her she clearly did not understand physics, she replied she understood things on a level I couldn't. Trivia claims she is into meta understanding she says it is a stage of evolution akin to meta-thought which she also claims to do. Trivia no longer thinks, she thinks about thinking.

It really can give you a headache, trying to sort things out. It's always like this when they work on time.

A sudden loud noise didn't happen. You know?—That blank empty sensation where all the noise isn't, when after hours of Calcutta style crowds there is a crashing halt and the air is post0nuclear holocaust still. The dead go pop pop pop like firefly lights flitting off into whatever void they hang out in and the unborn go trailing back to the primal void. Then, all the alternatives collapse, telescoping into you. If you've had a lot of choices in life, the number of alternatives can be staggering. I sometimes feel all crowded inside with all the different Tessas going thump thump thump against my ribcage, drum for a heart. Time has been put right for a while. We even have whiles again. Jonathan is planning to come by to talk about our separation. It is rather convoluted, because he's living in the half-land with that vague, shadowing reflection of the choices I declined.

The squad of technicians in their overalls disappeared. All I saw through the window was Jonathan, with his silly boyish walk that makes my throat go tight and that beautiful fine brown hair. His hair is baby fine and flops when he walks, catching the light as he moves under the web of trees. He's dressed like some part of the twentieth century, I'm never sure when. They do odd things in the half land, run into themselves all over the place, slide through decades, dress whenever they feel like it, it's anarchy.

I re-heated some coffee and waited at the table. I pretended to be reading a magazine. I was really watching out the window as Jonathan loped down the street, he takes long bouncing steps, half rising on his toes, his hands deep in his pockets. I felt grimy and ugly. I hadn't had time to shower and dress properly. They'd had to contain the area while they worked on the time-main. I had that nasty sweaty feeling I always get in stasis. Jonathan looked so clean, like a soap commercial. I was at a distinct disadvantage.

I've always played one down where Jonathan is concerned. As he came up the stairs, Trivia burst in through the back door. "Tessa, this is important," she insisted.

"Are your guillotine-dodgers back?" I answered.

"No, there's a few Jonathans over at my place, they're having a huge disagreement. Come see if you can calm them down." Trivia was unusually loud. It isn't like her to want to stop a moderate brawl; she usually like spontaneous violence. She says there is a certain poetry in synergy and entropy. Don't ask me, I don't have a clue what that means; nothing, I suspect. Trivia is just a little bit California.

"Trivia, there is a Jonathan coming here to talk things over. I promised him I'd discuss the separation with him," I sighed.

Trivia fidgeted around, she started wiping off my counters, making tea, the sort of intrusive things best friends some times do. "Well, that's all well and good, I suppose," she sputtered. "But, I don't see why you don't just run over to my house and pick out another one." Trivia looked a bit frazzled, her curly red hair was snarled, a large crystal pendant bounced against her chest.

"Exactly how many of him are there?" I asked.

"Seven or eight, last count," Trivia replied. She was nervously chewing on her cuticle; she'd got it all bloody. "They kept popping in all morning."

"A crowd of Jonathan alternatives," I mused.

"Oh, that's not the bloody half of it, there is some half crazed man that keeps flickering in wailing about Anastasia, Rasputin, and hemophilia. Last night a Neanderthal, a literal one, mind you, urinated in my Philodendron. I'm thinking of moving to a sealed zone." Trivia was clearly frazzled. She forgot that in this Possibility she was a bit of health nut and she grabbed one of my cigarettes off the counter. She tilted her head towards the common wall that our apartments shared. She was trying to pick up from the muffled voices exactly who and how many people were crowding her home. "There isn't a portal on your side, they don't drift in here unless there is a major downheaval, you can't possibly know what it is like," she whined. Trivia was definitely in a bad way, she had forgotten that she had the portal installed five years from now. The cigarette made her cough.

Actually, in one of my Possibilities I knew exactly what it was like, I had studied for the time-tech test before I met Jonathan in any Possibility. Time techs were disallowed mating relationships in all the but the remote Possibilities, I suppose that's why they seem to delight in screwing around with the rest of us. I traced a circle in spilled coffee and sighed. "I really can't face all those Jonathans, Trivia. It would be more than I could handle." I raked my nasty hair back into a scrunchie. I hoped that I didn't look entirely dreadful. Whenever a Jonathan left me I fell into bleak depression.

"Well, okay then," Trivia said in her most reasonable tone, "I suppose I can manage until you deal with the Jonathan you know or until they leave, whichever come quickest. I'm just a bit emotional today, my Possibility who committed suicide showed up this morning and ruined the entire day." He voice was flat. By tacit agreement we usually avoided mention of that Possibility. One of Trivia's alternatives had drifted from anorexia to cult membership to overdoes at an early age. Trivia spent enormous energy keeping that particular darkness from entering her lives. It must be horrible to have that contingency lurking about one's kitchen and psyche.

"You need to have the portal adjusted so that option doesn't occur," I said.

"Normally it isn't an issue," she said, "but, when they work on the lines all hell breaks loose." Trivia squared her shoulders, fluffed her hair, and adjusted her crystal pendant. She nearly collided with Jonathan as she walked out the door. "Jeez," she muttered. "Another one of you."

"Why is Trivia so uptight?" Jonathan asked, pouring himself a cup of coffee as if he still lived with me.

"Please, Jonathan, would you mind speaking language that fits this time?" I asked.

"Sorry, Tessa, I didn't mean to upset you," he said, sitting down in what had always been his chair.

It was odd having Jonathan home, like the air was charged with some sort of ion or something, the type of new agey force Trivia usually babbles about. I was having contradictory feelings; I was simultaneously awkward and comfortable. I could hardly bear to look at him. How do you look at the beautiful betrayer who makes love with your double? I concentrated on a tacky set of barnyard animal canisters that his mother had bought at some form of carnival. No matter what parallel I picked, I would never avoid Jonathan's mother giving me cow pot holders, pig refrigerator magnets or chick sugar bowls.

"You know, I don't really remember what we agreed to sort out, " I said. I was strangling on my own pain.

"Tessa," Jon said in a warning tone. "We need to decide about the children."

We were going to have three children in the not-too-distant future. The oldest, James, would look very much like Jonathan, he would do well in school. Hi brother, Ian, would resemble me. Ian would be a ferocious soccer player. Our youngest, Rebecca, would be a fairy child, a frail little girl with a dream-laden disposition. I loved our unborn children with an appalling maternal fervor.

"She gave up the option of the children two choices ago," I snarled. "You can't expect me to simply let that Tessa have my babies." Dancer Tessa was not about to have her neat little hips spread or her smooth belly cross-hatched.

"She may have given up that choice, but I didn't," Jon said, "I am supposed to have the children." His voice was dangerously soft. It was painful to look into his light blue eyes. Little James will have those same faded denim eyes, his fine brown hair will bleach blonde in the summer sun.

"You diverged," I shouted. "You and I were supposed to have those children, I can't be responsible for you flitting off into a conjecture."

"The children are supposed to be raised by both parents," Jon retaliated.

"In that case, I can just go next door, Trivia seems to have an excess of Jonathans at her place. This wasn't the deal at all, when we married you were supposed to close off other options, even those that involve me, that was the contract." I shrilled. "What did I do to deserve this? You are taking everything from me and not leaving me with any choices at all."

"You've made just an many choices as anyone else," Jon said. His voice was so cold. I never imagined Jon treating me like this, what had that other Tessa done to him that made him hate me? "Be reasonable Tessa, think of what's good for the children, the boys especially need their father."

It was disturbing to look at him three years from now I would give birth to our son James. Jon would be with me during the delivery, he would bring me daisies and swear that no man had ever loved any woman as much as he loved me. I would reach up from my hospital bed and brush his hair out of his eyes. I wanted to reach across the table and touch his hair now. I had no interest in the other Jonathans. I had been bluffing. I didn't even want to lay eyes on the other Jonathans; the very idea was repugnant, vaguely necrophile.

"Why is it you tell me to be reasonable whenever you want your own way?" I said. "All being reasonable means is letting you make all the decisions."

"I'm thinking of the children, Tessa. You're only thinking of yourself. I question what kind of mother you're capable of being."

"You know perfectly well that I'm a very good mother," I said. I was going to be a very good mother. I remembered all of it, helping James research defunct royalty for a history project, drilling him on French verbs. I could recall every detail of Ian's first soccer game. I designed most of Rebecca's clothes up to Rebecca's wedding day. "You are the one that opted out of our future."

"You don't let yourself feel anything, Tessa. Everything is planned out right to the minute; I needed more spontaneity than that. Tessa and I are happy; it's like it was in the beginning with us. She'll make a very loving mother, I'm not sure you have it in you to love. You've been married to the inevitable."

I felt my cheeks flush. I was actually shaking with anger. I slammed my coffee cup down on the table. "Love isn't about a total lack of responsibility, it isn't about living from minute to minute. It isn't about what feels right for the moment. Blink and the moment is gone. Love is about yesterday, today and tomorrow. Live like you want to live, and the whole future falls apart."

The walls started vibrating. The coffee cup shattered. I heard a few of the Jonathans next door shouting. "Oh, no," I moaned, "they're fiddling with the lines again. Don't give me any of that Zen 'float on the moment' crap or whatever you people babble about down there in that chaos you live in." Temperature disappeared, replaced by the void that was arid and moist. Trivia flickered in from next door. She was transparent. The shouting between the Jonathans got louder and louder, one of them had become an alcoholic. A Jonathan who had majored in anthropology, eventually obtaining a Ph.D., was apparently trying to study the habits of a belligerent Jonathan who stole car parts. Professor Jonathan was fascinated. In the Professor's Possibility, there was no individual transport or property crime. The remaining Jonathans were having a fist fight, apparently there was a shortage of Tessas. I like Trivia, I really like her. She has been my best friend recurrently. But, I absolutely hate it when her apartment melts into mine, there is too much confusion in how she lives.

My Jonathan grabbed my hand desperately as the studious Jonathan melded with him, his eyes did an epileptic shudder, and he twitched a bit as one of the louder Jons collapsed into him. His hand felt clammy. Poor man, it's dreadful when all the selves squish up inside you, sometimes you feel like there isn't even room to breathe. We froze for a minute, immobilized. I suppose we look like those folks from Pompeii that flashed into Trivia's kitchen next month. I imagined Jon and I covered in volcanic ash. Then everything was still: the air, the light, and the dark. Everything settled—not with a whimper, but a bang. A huge explosion-noise filled the air; there was no motion, no vibration.

Afterwards, I picked up my woolly lamb pot holder; my mother-in-law gives me the cutest things. The apple cinnamon smell of pie filled the kitchen. Ian and James love apple, it's their father's favorite also. Rebecca prefers cherry, but she isn't fussy. She is such a sweet natured little thing. I love having a daughter; everything about parenting Becky has been a joy. She sits so patiently while I use the curling iron on her long, silky hair. I'll bake cherry tarts for her next week. Through the gingham curtains, a slice of backyard is visible; Jonathan is playing catch with the boys while Rebecca swings slowly back and forth. A random butterfly prowls among the late-blooming roses, it is a perfect autumn day. For now.

About the Authors

John Aegard lives in Seattle with his wife, author Victoria Elizabeth Garcia, and a porky cattle dog named Midge. His work has appeared in *Strange Horizons, Interzone* and *Rabid Transit.*

Forrest Aguirre is a recent recipient of the World Fantasy Award for his editing of *Leviathan 3.* His fiction has appeared in *Flesh & Blood, Indigenous Fiction, The Earwig Flesh Factory, Redsine, 3rd Bed, Notre Dame Review, Exquisite Corpse, The Journal of Experimental Fiction* and *Polyphony 4.*

Locus Magazine calls Forrest ". . . an interesting writer, worth watching, whom I think could benefit from disciplining the wilder flights of his imagination a bit." Forrest spurns such disciplinary measures.

A collection of his short fiction titled *Fugue XXIX* will be published by Raw Dog Screaming Press in 2005.

Forrest lives in Madison, Wisconsin with his family.

Sally Carteret After 14 years as a rock musician and session player based in Los Angeles, Sally Carteret now lives in Nantucket, MA, "as far away from LA as I could reasonably get." She has authored and co-authored more than 100 recorded songs, royalties from several of which provide her with "a decent living....if you call straddling the poverty line 'decent'." She prefers to say nothing about her personal life other than it is "diverse."

Jay Caselberg is an Australian writer based in London. His novel, *The Star Tablet* third in the series of the Jack Stein SF Mysteries is due out later this year from Roc Books, with the fourth, *Wall of Mirrors* due next year. His short fiction and poetry has appeared in venues such as *The Third*

Alternative, Crimewave, Interzone, and numerous anthologies and publications worldwide, writing both as Jay Caselberg and as James A. Hartley.

When not writing, he travels to various countries around the world as an IT consultant, he can be found at: http://www.sff.net/people/jaycaselberg.

Robin Catesby is a recent escapee from the theatrical world, where she performed every task imaginable from directing Shakespeare to peddling rice crispy treats at intermission. She is the author of several children's plays, including a musical adaptation of *The Velveteen Rabbit,* which, to date, has received five productions in four states and on two coasts of the U.S. Her preferred form of procrastination involves illustration, photography, and long sessions with Adobe Photoshop. The results of this procrastination can be seen at her online portfolio, www.elsinore.net. Robin divides her time between her home in Portland, Oregon, and the northern wilds of San Juan Island where she and her chef husband take full advantage of the nearby mussel beds.

Brendan Connell has had fiction published in numerous magazines, literary journals and anthologies, including *RE:AL, The Journal of Experimental Fiction, Fishdrum, Fantastic Metropolis, Flesh and Blood, Leviathan 3 (The Ministry of Whimsy 2002), Further Tales from Tartarus (Tartarus Press 2003), The Thackery T. Lambshead Pocket Guide to Eccentric and Discredited Diseases (Nightshade 2003),* and *Album Zutique (The Ministry of Whimsy 2003).* He has had translations published in *Literature of Asia, Africa and Latin America* (Prentice Hall 1999).

D.G.K. GOLDBERG Diane Kelly Goldberg had as many sides to her personality as the many stories she wrote. She was a former therapist and licensed clinical social worker, a travel writer, a NASCAR fanatic and writer, a novelist and a prolific short story writer. She was a member of the the Horror Writers Association, the Science Fiction Writers Assciation, and the Internatinal Association of Food, Wine and Travel Writers Association. She traveled to places such as Italy, Russia, Great Britian and Israel as well as almost every state in America. She was also a loving wife and mother and a faithful and supportive friend. Kelly passed away in January 2005 after a long and hard-fought battle with brain tumors and lung cancer.

Theodora Goss was born in Hungary, and spoke Italian and French before she spoke English. She can still count in those languages. At various points in her childhood she remembers rice fields filled with frogs, a market square selling parrots, and nuns. She has gone under the Alps in a train too many times. She spent a significant amount of time trying to escape reality, mostly by reading about dragons. After a brief internment in law school and a law firm in Boston, where there were no dragons to speak of, she returned to school to study for a Ph.D. in English literature. She currently lives in Boston with her husband, daughter, and cats, in an apartment that contains the history of English literature from *Beowulf* to Octavia Butler and not enough bookshelves. She is learning Hungarian and looking for dragons. She hears they like to hide under the rug.

Her stories have been published in magazines and anthologies such as *Realms of Fantasy, Alchemy, Strange Horizons,* and *Lady Churchill's Rosebud Wristlet,* and have been reprinted in *The Year's Best Fantasy and Horror, Year's Best Fantasy,* and *The Year's Best SF and Fantasy for Teens.* She recently won a Rhysling Award for speculative poetry.

By night, **M. K. Hobson** writes short fiction, diarizes her existence in minute detail in her LiveJournal, and adds word upon obsessive word to a sweeping alternate-history saga that follows the shifting fortunes of a family of American Warlocks from the nineteenth century to the present day. By day, she is a marketing consultant who has helped produce award-winning campaigns for a variety of national and international clients. She has also owned a newspaper, driven night-shift taxi, read tarot professionally, and taught conversational English in Japan. She lives in Oregon City (the first city in the United States incorporated west of the Rockies) in a 1916 Craftsman bungalow that she shares with her husband, her daughter, and a bright blue fish.

Aynjel Kaye began life firmly rooted in Normal and has escaped. She is an angst-queen in exile holding court in Seattle, WA where she is plotting to retake her throne. She may or may not be a chocolate lover, a goth, a punk, and less harmless than she was before. Aynjel is also a graduate of the y2k Clarion Science Fiction and Fantasy Writer's workshop in East Lansing, Michigan, where she wrote and wrote and critiqued and wrote and learned why baby sea turtles are better than thirteen-year-olds (turtles don't ask difficult questions). She has appeared on panels at Torcon and MileHicon talking about goths, vampires, sex, and whatever else might have come up.

Alex Lamb divides his creative energies between writing, improvisation and photography.

As a writer, he is a graduate of Clarion West 97 and has been a scholarship attendee of the Milford Writers workshop. Ithrulene is the first thing he has ever published.

As an improviser, he has worked with groups from London to New York and is the founder of Amazing Spectacles, Britain's finest long-form improvisation troupe. He has created methods for spontaneous storytelling now used by writers and improvisers everywhere from East Anglia to California.

As a photographer he has done very little but please himself by taking countless pictures of reflections.

He currently lives in Santa Cruz, CA with his wife, Jenny Graves, an astrophysicist at UCSC.

Nick Mamatas is the author of the Lovecraftian Beat road novel *Move Under Ground* and the Marxist Civil War ghost story *Northern Gothic*, both of which were nominated for the Bram Stoker Award. His short fiction has appeared in *Razor, Strange Horizons, ChiZine and his non-fiction in the Village Voice, In These Times, the Disinformation Guide* series and many BenBella "smart pop" books. He's also the author of the collection *3000 MPH In Every Direction at Once: Stories and Essays*, and the editor of the anthologies *The Urban Bizarre* and the forthcoming *Spicy Slipstream Stories*. By the time you read this he will have likely moved to Vermont from California.

Paul Miles was born and raised in Austin, Texas. In keeping with his drifter nature, he attended college and law school in Austin, before finally settling down to live and work in Austin, where he picks out short stories on a blue 1972 IBM Selectric. His work has appeared in *Plot Magazine* and

Revolution SF.

Nancy Jane Moore is an expatriate Texan and recovering lawyer living in Washington, D.C. Her novella *Changeling,* which is not about fairies, is available as one of the Conversation Pieces from Aqueduct Press. Most of her fiction has appeared in anthologies such as the recent books *Imaginings* and *Imagination Fully Dilated: Science Fiction,* but her stories have also been seen in *Lady Churchill's Rosebud Wristlet* and *Andromeda Spaceways Inflight Magazine,* as well as on the online magazines *Fantastic Metropolis* and *Ideomancer.* She notes with pride that she has published science fiction stories in the *National Law Journal, Aikido Today Magazine,* and *CC Motorcycle News*magazine.

Tim Pratt, Michael Jasper and **Greg van Eekhout** is a malevolent 3-headed giant who guards the entrance to the underworld. When he's not busy rending the unworthy into bite-sized chunks, he writes fiction, and his individual heads have published stories in *Asimov's, F&SF, Realms of Fantasy,* and other stygian publications.

Joy Marchand holds a B.A. in Classical Studies from the University of the Pacific and currently lives in Salem, Massachusetts. Joy's short stories have been featured in L. Ron Hubbard Presents: Writers of the Future Volume XX, the Elastic Book of Numbers and Modern Magic. Recently honored in the 2005 World Horror Convention's Dark Fiction contest for her short "A Night at the Empire," she is currently at work on a supernatural thriller set in northeastern Massachusetts. Please feel free to visit her website at (http://www.feminaobscura.com).

Bruce Holland Roger's stories have appeared in *The North American Review, Realms of Fantasy, Descant,* and *Quarterly West.* He lives in Eugene, Oregon.

Iain Rowan lives in the north-east of England, near the sea but not near enough. He's had short stories published in a number of magazines and anthologies including *Postscripts, Ellery Queen's, Alfred Hitchcock's, Black Gate, The Thackery T. Lambshead Pocket Guide to Eccentric & Discredited*

Diseases, and others. He's currently finishing revisions to his first novel. Iain can be contacted via his website, www.iainrowan.com.

Eric Schaller has had work published in *Sci Fiction, Nemonymous, The Silver Web, The Thackery T. Lambshead Pocket Guide to Eccentric and Discredited Diseases*, and forthcoming in *Lady Churchill's Rosebud Wristlet*. His story "The Assistant to Dr. Jacob" was included in *The Year's Best Fantasy and Horror Volume 16*. Other work includes illustrations for Jeff VanderMeer's collection *The City of Saints and Madmen*, and cartoons featuring the character Sad Bird for the White Buffalo Gazette. He is one those guys shouting "Freebird" at the end of a perfectly good concert, regardless of whether the band is performing rock, bluegrass, or classical music, so it's just as well that he doesn't get out much anymore.

Despite her penchant for sex, risky fiction and midnight walks, **Heather Shaw** is just a nice girl from Indiana, now living in the San Francisco Bay Area. Her fiction has appeared in such nice places as *Strange Horizons, Polyphony 3* and *The Fortean Bureau*. Her poetry has been nominated twice for the Rhysling award. She edits the erotic webzine, *Fishnet* (www.fishnetmag.com) as part of her day job and co-edits *Flytrap, the little zine with teeth*, in the evenings with her husband Tim Pratt. They live in Oakland, CA with the requisite two cats.

Scott Thomas is the author of *Cobwebs and Whispers* and *Shadows of Flesh*, both from Delirium books. His fiction has appeared in a number of anthologies which include: *The Year's Best Fantasy and Horror #15, The Year's Best Horror #22, Leviathan 3, Deathrealms, Punktown: Third Eye* and *The Ghost in the Gazebo*. Scott and his wife Nancy live in Maine.

Sarah Totton is a Canadian veterinarian and wildlife biologist. Her short fiction has appeared in or will be appearing in the anthologies TENNIS SHORTS, TESSERACTS 9 and FANTASTICAL VISIONS III. She is a graduate of the Odyssey and Clarion workshops.

Rob Vagle has been previously published in *Realms Of Fantasy* and lives in Eugene, Oregon. His blog, Writing Progress, can be found at: http://www.journalscape.com/rova.

Jeff VanderMeer's latest books include *City of Saints & Madmen, Veniss Underground,* and the story collection *Secret Life*. Pan MacMillan released *The Thackery T. Lambshead Pocket Guide to Eccentric & Discredited Diseases,* co-edited by Jeff, in November 2004. His books have made the best-of-year lists of *Amazon.com, Publishers Weekly, Publishers' News, The San Francisco Chronicle,* and many more. He is a two-time winner of the World Fantasy Award.

Ray Vukcevich's latest book is a collection of stories called *Meet Me in the Moon Room* from Small Beer Press.

You may not know this but **Brian Wade** has warring troops of goblins inside his head. By outward appearance he is a quiet and mild-mannered computer consultant. The goblins, however, are unruly, uncivilized, and warlike; they drink fermented humors--Black & Yellow Bile Stout, Fat Phlegm IPA, and Blood Ale--late into the night, fight, fart, scratch, belch, toss empties into the mental forge. To quiet their infernal racket, Brian has studied biology, philosophy, and computer science; hammered copper sheets into fantastic shapes; learned to strum a three-chord melody; and even sculpted tiny goblin idols out of twist-ties. The goblin's literary tastes are as varied as their scabrous faces, so he writes speculative and mainstream fiction. On occasion he grows confused by the goblin din and mixes genres. This is his first published story; the goblins, of course, show no sign of appeasement.

Brian would like to thank the members of the Wordos writers workshop in Eugene, Oregon for their insight and encouragement and Dianna Rodgers in particular for her advise about this story.

My name is **Richard Wadholm**. My first favorite book was *Rite of Passage,* by Alexi Panshin. I've been trying to write science fiction ever since. I started out writing sports stories for the National Football League. My fiction has been published in *Asimov's* and anthologized in *Year's Best*

Science Fiction, 17th Edition, 20th Edition, edited by Gardner Dozois, and *Science Fiction: the Best of 2001*, edited by Robert Silverberg and Karen Haber. My story, Green Tea, was nominated for the James Gunn Award. I have an E-book, *Astronomy*, out with ElectricStory. (Feel free to buy it, hey.)

Interesting bio sidelights? Hmm. Toiled for 12 years as a heavy metal musician, where I learned everything I need to know about writing: Never resolve till the finish; every beautiful song needs an ugly part to set it off; groupies are an urban myth.

I live in the San Fernando Valley with a cockatiel, a half-moon parrot and a free-range rat, which we might as well refer to as a pet. Let's call him Gerald.

Robert Freeman Wexler's first novel, *Circus of the Grand Design* was published in 2004. His 2003 novella, *In Springdale Town* (PS Publishing) was reprinted in the *Best Short Novels 2004*. His work has appeared in *Polyphony 3* and 4 as well.

Leslie What is a writer, teacher, radio commentator, and the author of the novel *Olympic Games*. She has won a Nebula Award for short fiction, the Mike O'Brien's Livingroom Bookstore award for tapdancing, and the Glacier Falls Figure Skating Club Preliminary Ladies Award for figure skating. Her collection of short stories, *The Sweet and Sour Tongue* was published in 2000 by Wildside books.

ABOUT THE EDITORS

DEBORAH LAYNE founded Wheatland Press in 2002 and has been co-editing the *Polyphony* series ever since. Her own fiction has appeared *The Fortean Bureau, Flytrap 3* and *Indiana Review.* She is a member of the Wordos Writers Workshop of Eugene, Oregon. Having earned degrees in history, philosophy, history and philosophy of science and law, she is content to focus on speculative literature. Deborah lives in deepest, darkest Oregon with her family.

JAY LAKE won the 2004 John W. Campbell Award for Best New Writer. His stories have appeared in places too numerous to mention including *Realms of Fantasy, Strange Horizons* and *Asimov's.* He has three collections in print: *Greetings From Lake Wu, Green Grow the Rushes,* and *American Sorrows* and his first novel, *Rocket Science,* is soon to appear from Fairwood Press. In addition to his work on the *Polyphony* series, he is the co-editor with David Moles of *All Star Zeppelin Adventure Stories* and the editor of *TEL: Stories.* He is a member of the Wordos Writers Workshop of Eugene, Oregon. Jay lives in Portland, Oregon.

Other Titles Available From Wheatland Press

Anthologies

Polyphony 1, Deborah Layne and Jay Lake, Eds. Volume one in the critically acclaimed slipstream/cross-genre series will feature stories from Maureen McHugh, Andy Duncan, Carol Emshwiller, Lucius Shepard and others.

Polyphony 2, Deborah Layne and Jay Lake, Eds. Volume two in the critically acclaimed slipstream/cross-genre series will feature stories from Alex Irvine, Theodora Goss, Jack Dann, Michael Bishop and others.

Polyphony 3, Deborah Layne and Jay Lake, Eds. Volume three in the critically acclaimed slipstream/cross-genre series will feature stories from Jeff Ford, Bruce Holland Rogers, Ray Vukcevich, Robert Freeman Wexler and others.

Polyphony 4, Edited by Deborah Layne and Jay Lake. Fourth volume in the critically acclaimed slipstream/cross-genre series with stories from Alex Irvine, Lucius Shepard, Michael Bishop, Forrest Aguirre, Theodora Goss, Stepan Chapman and others.

The Nine Muses, Edited by Forrest Aguirre and Deborah Layne. Original anthology featuring some of the top women writers in science fiction, fantasy and experimental fiction, including Kit Reed, Ursula Pflug, Jai Clare, Jessica Treat, and Ruth Nestvold. With an introductory essay by Elizabeth Hand.

TEL: Stories, Jay Lake Ed. An anthology of experimental fiction with authors to be announced.

All Star Zeppelin Adventure Stories, David Moles and Jay Lake Eds. Original zeppelin stories by Jim Van Pelt, Leslie What, and others; one reprint, “You Could Go Home Again” by Howard Waldrop.

Single-Author Collections

The Keyhole Opera, Bruce Holland Rogers. A collection of short-short stories by the master of the form. Includes the World Fantasy Award-winning story "Don Ysidro" from *Polyphony 4*.

The Beasts of Love: Stories by Steven Utley With an introduction by Lisa Tuttle. Utley's love stories spanning the past twenty years; a brilliant mixture of science fiction, fantasy and horror.

Dream Factories and Radio Pictures, Howard Waldrop. Waldrop's stories about early film and television reprinted in one volume.

Greetings From Lake Wu, Jay Lake and Frank Wu. Collection of stories by Jay Lake with original illustrations by Frank Wu.

Twenty Questions, Jerry Oltion. Twenty brilliant works by the Nebula Award-winning author of "Abandon in Place."

American Sorrows, Jay Lake. Four longer works by the Hugo and Campbell nominated author; includes his Hugo nominated novelette, "Into the Gardens of Sweet Night."

Nonfiction

Weapons of Mass Seduction, Lucius Shepard. A collection of Shepard's film reviews. Some have previously appeared in print in the ***Magazine of Fantasy and Science Fiction***; most have only appeared online at ***Electric Story***.

Novel

Paradise Passed, Jerry Oltion. The crew of a colony ship must choose between a ready-made paradise and one they create for themselves. A finalist for the 2005 Endeavor Award.

Printed in the United States
77614LV00003B/1-3